The
Good Old Boys

Also by Elmer Kelton

THE DAY THE COWBOYS QUIT
THE TIME IT NEVER RAINED

The Good Old Boys

ELMER KELTON

DOUBLEDAY & COMPANY, INC.   GARDEN CITY, NEW YORK   1978

Library of Congress Cataloging in Publication Data

Kelton, Elmer.
The good old boys.

I. Title.
PZ4.K314Go   [PS3561.E3975]   813'.5'4
ISBN: 0-385-13315-4
Library of Congress Catalog Card Number 77–78880

This book is gratefully dedicated to:

Jim Long	Son Guin
Wes Reynolds	Raymond Glasscock
Elliott Moore	Bill Lucas
Carroll and John D. Holleyman	Manerd Gayler
John Patterson	Chuck Olson
George Teague	Brown Fisher
Tommy Cameren	P. O. "Slim" Vines

and the other old-time Jigger Y cowboys of fond memory. Their boots have tracked all through these pages.

The
Good Old Boys

I

For the last five or six days Hewey Calloway had realized he needed a bath. Now, in the final miles of a long horseback trip, it was a necessity no longer to be denied. By nightfall he would be eating hot biscuits and brown gravy at his brother's table. Sister-in-law Eve Calloway was not inclined to generosity regarding the social graces.

Ahead of him the red wooden tower of an Eclipse windmill stood almost astraddle the wagon road which meandered casually among the gentle hills and skirted respectfully around the scattered stands of low-growing mesquite trees. The leaves were still the fresh pale green of early spring. Tall above those trees, the mill's white-painted cypress fan turned slowly in the warm west wind which had stuck Hewey's old blue shirt to his skin much of the morning. A vagrant white puff of cumulus cloud drifted over him, yielding a few minutes of pleasant shade before the sun broke free again in the full heat of early May.

The more he thought about it the more he began to look forward to that cool bath, but he didn't want to push Biscuit into a trot. The brown horse was favoring his right forefoot a little. If it got any worse Hewey would have to walk and lead him.

Hell of a note, going lame the last day out. But better here than where they had started the trip three weeks ago in the melting snows of New Mexico high country.

He had known this region for years, and the sight of the red and white windmill confused him a little. Those colors were the trademark of the Two C Land and Cattle Company, old C. C.

Tarpley's outfit. Hewey would take a paralyzed oath that the place just ahead belonged to a four-section bachelor homesteader, a former cowboy who had always been glad to provide Hewey a meal or two and let him roll out his blankets on a hard and civilized wooden floor instead of the soft and uncivilized ground.

The red towers and white fans scattered from here halfway to Midland were sign to a traveler that he was crossing Two Cs land, and welcome to it so long as he shut all the wire gates behind him and didn't run the cattle. He was welcome to camp a night anywhere but never two nights in the same place unless he had a broken wheel. One night was traveling; two nights was squatting.

Gradually Hewey realized he had been right about the homesteader. He recognized the layout of the place, the fallow field, some faded, rotting stalks where last year's hegari crop had grown, and last year's cane. By now a good farmer should have plowed it up and started planting anew. The crude shed stood where Hewey remembered it, but the little frame house was gone. Nothing remained but stubby cedar posts that had been its foundation, and a weather-bleached four-by-four privy thirty feet from what had been the back door, a short run on a cold wet night. Somebody had dismantled the house for the lumber, more than likely. By the windmill's color, that somebody had to be C. C. Tarpley.

Old C.C.'s still spreading out, Hewey thought idly, begrudging him nothing, curious as to why he hadn't taken the privy too. It looked lonesome standing there by itself.

C.C.'s water would be as wet as anybody's. Hewey looked up at the Two Cs brand painted in red on the mill's white tail, which automatically held the fan into the west wind to keep the maximum driving force on its angled wooden fins. The slow turning activated a sucker-rod which clanked and shuddered down the center of a pipe reaching deep into the ground. Each stroke of the rod brought up cool water from the dark depths of the earth, rhythmic gushes pumping it into a big dirt tank which long hours of man and mule sweat had scooped from the ground.

Hewey swung his right leg across Biscuit's rump, holding the leg high to clear the rolled blankets and the "war bag" of miscellaneous cowboy accumulations tied behind the high cantle. Over that cantle was stretched a dried rattlesnake skin, supposed by many to ward off rheumatism, which became a mark of the trade for cowboys who survived the other hazards long enough to acquire it. Some said it also helped prevent hemorrhoids, another ailment common to the horseback profession.

Hewey doubted that, because he had them.

He stretched himself and stamped his feet to stimulate the blood and to steady his saddle-cramped legs. He unbuckled the girth, slid the saddle from Biscuit's back, then led the horse down to the water's edge to let him drink. Not until Biscuit had taken his fill did Hewey tie him to one of the tower legs and prepare to get a drink of water himself. He laid down astraddle the heavy pipe which extended from windmill to tank. He pushed carefully out to the end of it. The pipe was pleasantly cool. He held on with both legs and his left hand, cupping his right hand just under the mouth of the pipe. He drank thirstily from the hand as the water pumped out in time to the mill's even strokes.

It was good water, carrying only a faint suggestion of the gyp common to much of West Texas. Water was a thing to be cherished in dry country. A man prized a good sweet well the way he prized a fine horse. Hewey finally took some of the water up his nostrils and choked. He decided that was enough for a while.

He inched his way back along the pipe, misjudging where to step off and sinking his left boot into the mud. He talked to the boot the way he was accustomed to talking to his horse. "Won't hurt you none. Damn little mud you'll ever get on you in this country."

Inside a small plot which had been the homesteader's garden, green grass was coming up between last year's plowed rows and the fence. Hewey led Biscuit there and turned him loose, fastening the sagging wooden gate to keep him from straying off. He watched the horse roll in the soft dirt, taking up the sweat where the saddle and blanket had been.

Hewey was vaguely disappointed. He had counted on a noon meal from the homesteader, even if only some rewarmed red beans and hogbelly. Well, at least the horse could graze awhile. Hewey would make do with a cold biscuit and dried-out bacon brought from the Two Cs line camp where he had stayed last night with old cowpuncher friends. He might brew himself a can of coffee too, after a while. Right now he wanted to test the water in that tank.

He emptied his pockets and piled their contents on the bare tank dump. They didn't amount to much . . . a couple of silver dollars and some smaller change, a Barlow knife, a sack of Bull Durham smoking tobacco and a book of brown cigarette papers, a wallet containing his life's savings of twenty-seven dollars. He set his boots beside his treasure. On them jingled a set of scandalous "gal-leg" spurs, the shank shaped like a woman's leg, silver-mounted to show the high-heeled dancing shoe, the stocking, the garter on a plump thigh. It took a sport to wear such as that. He clutched his sweat-stained cotton socks in his hand and waded off into the tank with the rest of his clothes on.

The deepest part came up barely past his thighs. He took off his faded jeans and washed them out, then his shirt and finally his long-handled cotton underwear that once had been white. Naked except for the hat, he walked out with the wet clothing, squeezed as much water from it as he could, then hung it piece by piece to dry in the sun on the bottom brace of the windmill tower. That done, he waded back into the tank until the water was to his knees, then sat himself down shoulder-deep.

If a bath always felt this good, he thought, *I would take one every week or two.*

He sat soaking, only his head and his battered old felt hat above the water. Bye and bye half a dozen cows and their calves came ambling out from a thicket, bound for a cool drink of water and then a long, lazy afternoon shaded up beneath the mesquites, chewing cud. The cow in the lead made it all the way to the top of the earthen dump before she noticed Hewey. She stopped abruptly, her head high in surprise. Her calf spotted him at about the same time and turned to run off a little way, its tail curled in alarm. The cow stood her ground but advanced no farther. The other cows came up even with her and joined her in consternation.

Hewey spoke gently, "Don't be afraid, girls. I'd scare you a lot worse if I was to come up out of here."

The voice was not reassuring. Hewey held still, and one cow's thirst overcame her timidity. She moved cautiously to the water, lowered her head for a few quick sips, then jerked it up again to study Hewey critically, the water drops clinging to the hair under her chin. Gradually she decided he posed no threat as serious as her thirst, and she settled down to drinking her fill. The other cows, followers all, took this for a clearance and moved on to water. Hewey watched, knowing that curiosity would sooner or later lead one of the cattle to investigate his boots and his pocket possessions. When a calf warily started toward them, Hewey brought up a handful of mud from the bottom and hurled it at him. All the cattle ran. But in a few minutes they trailed down to the water again. Hewey held still. It was a cardinal principle not to disturb cattle unnecessarily, especially when they were watering. A cow had to drink plenty of water to make milk. She had to make milk to wean off a healthy calf. Motherhood—human or bovine—was a sacred thing.

Eventually the cattle trailed away to the thicket and lay down in the shade to relax away the warm afternoon and rechew the grass they had packed into their paunches all morning. Hewey began to think he ought to be fixing himself a little coffee and moving on, but the water felt good. He sat lazily watching a hawk make slow circles above the thicket, screaming a vain protest at the cattle. She probably had a nest in one of those big granddaddy mesquites. The cattle ignored her.

Too late he heard the rattle of chains and then the clopping of hoofs and the sand-slicing sound of narrow iron rims along the wagon road. A desperate thought came to him: these might be womenfolks, and they were going to catch him in this tank barefoot all the way to his chin. He weighed his chances of making a dash for his clothes without being seen. They were poor. He sat where he was, stirring the muddy bottom with his hands to make sure nobody could see through the water. The move was unnecessary; there had never been a day when this tank was that clear.

Up to the windmill trotted two matched dappled gray horses pulling a buggy. Two men sat on the spring seat. Hewey's attention went to a gaunt old man with sagging shoulders and sagging mustache. Sawing on the lines to pull the horses to a stop, the old

5

man stared at Hewey with about as much surprise as the cows had shown. He reached instinctively under the seat, where he probably carried a rifle.

Finally he found a brusque voice. "Are you alive out there, or have I got a drowned man on my hands?"

Hewey grinned, relieved that there were only the men. "How's the womenfolks, C.C.?"

"Just barely tolerable. That you, Hewey Calloway?"

"It's me. I'm comin' out, C.C."

His surprise gone, the old rancher watched with a measure of tolerant humor. "Damn if you ain't a pretty sight! I don't believe I ever seen a man take a bath with his hat on."

"I sunburn easy, C.C."

Hewey waded out, following a patch of bermuda grass along the water pipe to keep his feet from getting muddy. He felt his clothes, found them mostly dry, then began putting them on over his wet skin. His body was almost white. His hands and neck and face were browned, but the rest was customarily never exposed to the sun. Even his loose collar would usually be buttoned to keep the sun out. The last thing he did was to rub the sand from his feet, then put on his socks and boots.

The other man had never spoken. Hewey decided he probably wouldn't. He was a generation and a half younger and fifty pounds heavier than C. C. Tarpley. His name was Frank Gervin. Behind his back, people referred to him by a boyhood nickname, "Fat," but the tactful and prudent never called him that to his round and ruddy face.

Hewey said, "Howdy, Fat."

Fat Gervin winced and slumped a little deeper in the buggy seat. He gave no more than a nod, a very small and tentative recognition of Hewey's existence, and then he looked away, his eyes resting in the direction of home, shade and cool water. Fat had worked as a cowboy on many West Texas ranches, usually for only a short time at each place. He tended always to be lost on drive or to be sitting his horse in the middle of the gate when other hands were trying to put cattle through. Evidently he was better as a lover than as a cowboy, for he had somehow swayed and won Tarpley's only daughter while the old man's attention had been directed to more important things. This gave him a hold on the Tarpley inheritance, provided the old man did not decide at the end to take it all with him.

Hewey gave Gervin no more of his attention. He said, "I had it in mind to fix me a little coffee. Join me, C.C.?"

It would amount to nothing more than some water boiled with coffee grounds in the bottom of a smoke-blackened can and drunk directly out of that can. Hewey didn't even have a cup. But C. C. Tarpley, biggest cattleman this side of the Pecos River, said he wouldn't mind if he did, and he climbed down. Fat didn't say anything; he kept his seat in the buggy.

C.C. didn't look like a big cattleman was supposed to. If anything, in his frayed old clothes and run-over boots he appeared as if he might have a hard time holding down a swamper's job in a saloon. His wrinkled shirt was pockmarked by tiny tobacco burns. He didn't have to dress up to impress anyone; everybody in this country knew him. If he went somewhere else on business, nobody knew him, so he didn't dress up for them either.

The two men squatted on opposite sides of an economical fire and watched while the water stubbornly refused to boil. Tarpley said, "Boys at the Tule camp told me you spent the night there. I'd decided you left this country for good."

Hewey shrugged. "I've got kin here. Walter and Eve and their boys. I got lonesome to see them."

"How long since you left here, two years?"

"One year, ten months and twenty-odd days."

"I reckon you got lots of money, Hewey."

"Money?"

"I recollect you ridin' away on old Biscuit, leadin' a packhorse with all your stuff on it, sayin' you wasn't comin' back till you was rich and famous. I ain't heard a word about you since, so I don't reckon you're famous. How rich are you?"

Hewey grinned sheepishly. "Had twenty-somethin' dollars, last time I counted."

"What come of the packhorse?"

"Sold him."

C.C. turned his head and took a long look at the brown horse. Hewey was glad it wasn't apparent that Biscuit was trying to come up lame. Tarpley said, "Well, if you ain't famous, and you ain't rich, maybe you've come home two years smarter. Ain't you about worn the itch out of your feet, Hewey? Ain't you ready to light someplace?"

Hewey looked at the coffee. "I believe it's finally about to come to a boil."

"Ain't you ever found anywhere you wanted to stay?"

"Just about every place, at first. Then directly I get to thinkin' there might be somethin' better down the road."

"But it's never there, is it?"

"It's *always* there, for a little while." Using two big sticks as a clamp, Hewey gingerly lifted the can from the fire and set it off onto the ground. "Ought to be ready to drink in a minute. You're company; you can have the first sip."

"No, you're company. This place is mine. I bought out Sam Gentry as soon as he got it proved up."

Sam Gentry. Hewey had been trying for an hour to remember the homesteader's name. Sad, how quickly a man's name got lost. It was hard to make a big-enough track that your name was long remembered.

People here would remember C. C. Tarpley for a long time, of course. He had done well for himself the last twenty-five years, since he had stretched a castoff army tent on the Pecos River in 1881 and had turned loose his thirty-three spotted cows and one droop-horned bull. If that bull hadn't made the first winter, C.C. wouldn't have survived either. But the cattle had been prolific. People used to say that on the Tarpley place even the bulls had twin calves. It was also said that C. C. Tarpley could find and put his brand on more unclaimed mavericks than any three men on the Pecos. In his prime he rode fast horses and carried an extra cinch ring tied to his saddle so he could stop and brand any animal he came across that didn't already have a claim burned on it. That sort of ambitious endeavor was occasionally fatal to other men, but C.C. was tough enough to make it stick.

Now, six years into a new century, if anyone were to gather the whole Two C herd from where it was scattered over four hundred square miles of mesquite and catclaw and greasewood country, he would probably tally out five or six thousand mother cows plus no telling how many yearlings and two-year-olds. All that in twenty-five years from thirty-three cows and a bull.

Hard work and attention to business were the key, C.C. had often preached. But he had always said he was not greedy. All he had ever wanted was that which rightfully belonged to him, and that which adjoined it.

The hard years of acquisition had not let him run to fat. He weighed no more now than when he had first come here. He rode in a buggy more than on horseback, a concession to rheumy bones, but the fire of ambition still glowed in coffee-brown eyes.

C.C. said, "I reckon Walter sent for you to help him out of his trouble?"

Hewey looked up quickly, surprised. "Trouble? I never heard about no trouble."

C.C. had the coffee can, carefully holding his fingers high up near the rim where the heat was not enough to blister. The coffee was only a minute or so past a full boil, but he drank it without flinching. He had always been a man in a hurry.

Hewey waited impatiently for an explanation, but C.C. was busy with the coffee. Hewey demanded, "What kind of trouble is he in?"

"Same as all these nester operators . . . money. He's stretched thinner than a cotton shirt in a cold norther. Come fall, I figure he'll have to fold up and quit." C.C. stared quizzically at Hewey. "You sure he didn't send for you?"

"I ain't even heard from him since I left."

C.C. shrugged. "Not much good you'd do him anyway. You won't stay lit in one place long enough to wear out a change of socks." The statement was made matter-of-factly, not in an insulting way.

"I reckon you could help him, C.C., if you was of a mind to."

"I've tried. I offered to buy him out, same as I done with Sam Gentry. Walter ain't goin' to do any good on a little greasy-sack outfit like that. He'll just starve that good woman and them kids of his to death. I told him I had his old foreman's job waitin' for him any time he wants it back. When a man's been as good a cowboy as Walter is, it ought to be a penitentiary offense for him to ever take hold of a plow handle."

9

"What did he say to the offer?"

Fat Gervin had finally climbed down from the buggy. He put into the conversation, answering for Tarpley. "Said what all them shirttail nesters say, that he'll make it all right. But he won't. Best thing that can happen to this country will be when all them nesters starve out and leave it to people that know how to run it."

Hewey didn't look up at Fat. C. C. Tarpley gave him a sharp glance back over his shoulder, a look that told him to shut the hell up. He turned his attention back to Hewey, closing Fat out of the conversation. As if Fat had said nothing, Tarpley answered Hewey's question. "He said he'll make it."

Hewey frowned at the hot coffee. "But you hope he *don't* make it?"

"I got nothin' but his best interests at heart. I like Walter Calloway; I always did. I wouldn't do a thing to hurt him."

"But you wouldn't do anything to really help him."

Tarpley's eyes narrowed. "Best help for your brother would be to get him onto a steady job where he could do some good for himself and be of use to somebody else too. I never could understand what a man wants with one of them little old starve-out places."

"You started small, once."

"That was a long time ago. There was room in this country then. Now it's gettin' so crowded up that you can't breathe, hardly. You're apt to run into somebody's house every five or six miles. Nowadays everybody wants somethin' for nothin'. That's what's behind all these homesteaders, a hope they can get somethin' for nothin'. Everybody ought to pay his own way, is how I see it."

C.C. hadn't paid anybody for the use of the land here in his beginning years. Nobody else was claiming it, at least nobody as tough as C.C. It was too far from Austin for the state authorities to come out collecting. By the time they started charging lease, C.C. had had many years of free use and was strong enough financially that he could afford to pay. Even so, he had snorted and raised hell.

Hewey said, "Lots of people—I never was one myself—want to

own somethin' even if it's small. They see honor in havin' a place they can stand on and say, 'This is mine.' "

"There's honor in bein' a Two Cs cowboy, too, if you're a good one." C.C. studied Hewey with keen brown eyes. "I've still got a place for you, too, if you're ready to settle down."

"Still payin' the same wages you used to?" C.C. had always advocated a high sense of morality among his ranch help. Too much money being a threat to that morality, he had seen to it that they were never seriously challenged.

Tarpley frowned. "Times've been a little tight. I've had to cut expenses. But I've always paid a fair wage."

Fair but not good, Hewey thought. He said nothing.

Fat Gervin took that silence as a challenge to C.C.'s generosity. He said righteously, "The man that's payin' the money is the one to say what's fair and what ain't. Trouble with the laborin' class is that it's always askin' for more than it's worth."

Fat had been born into that class, though he had labored little. He had started at the bottom and married up. He stood with his round shoulders back and his belly out, inviting Hewey to contest his studied judgment. To his disgust, Hewey ignored him. As the probable inheritor of the Tarpley power, Fat had tried diligently to copy C.C.'s gruff mannerisms, his toughness, his sureness of self. But he bore no more resemblance to the old man than the reflection in mossy water bears to the battle-scarred stallion.

C.C. turned on him irritably. "Fat, I wisht you'd take and water the horses."

Color flushed the big man's face. He turned and started to lead the horses to the tank, pulling the buggy. Tarpley said, in the same impatient tone he would use against an errant hound, "Unhook them first."

He and Hewey then hunkered in silence, passing the blackened can back and forth, offering none of it to Gervin. A stranger, if told one of them had six thousand cattle and the other had twenty-seven dollars, would have had a hard time deciding which was which. More than likely he would simply have doubted the statement. They were alike in as many ways as they were different. They had come from the same sun-warmed Texas soil. Though they had taken different forks on many roads, their roots gave them a kinship of sorts. They had a respect and a regard for each other that transcended the vast differences in their individual codes, their personal goals and their financial status.

C. C. Tarpley had been orphaned at an early age and cast out on his own in a world where orphans scratched or starved. A few years ago, in an uncharacteristic surge of emotion, he had contributed four hundred dollars toward the building of an orphans' home in Fort Worth. The word had spread and earned him a reputation as a philanthropist among those who did not know him well. Hewey Calloway, who had never owned more of the world's goods than he could tie on a horse, gave freely of whatever he had when he had it. Last fall he had given up a well-earned spree in town before it had fairly begun and contributed his only thirty dollars to a collection for a newly widowed nester woman and her four children. No one ever knew of it except Hewey and a half dozen other cowboys who had volunteered in like manner from their own pinched pockets. Reckoned on a percentage basis, Hewey was by far a more liberal philanthropist than C. C. Tarpley.

C.C. said, "You tell Walter I'd sure like to have him back. I miss him over at the ranch. God, Hewey, you've got no idea how hard it is anymore to find decent help. Just the other day I had to go all the way to Sweetwater to get me two good cowboys."

Remembering what C.C. paid, Hewey was not impressed. But he said a noncommittal, "Well, I'll swun," which C.C. could take for sympathy if he wanted to.

C.C. continued, "I miss that little woman of his too. When Eve was cookin' for the hands I used to like to go by there every so often and debauch myself on her cobbler pie. My wife never could cook worth doodly squat."

On the Two Cs Eve had been expected to cook for the regular bachelor cowboys, plus any extra help, plus any company that happened along. She wasn't paid for it; it was simply part of the honor of being the foreman's wife. That was one reason she had clung so tenaciously to the little homestead, poor as it was. She probably worked as hard or harder there than ever before. But she cooked for her own family and nobody else.

C.C.'s eyes narrowed. "You got an ugly mark across your jaw, Hewey. Fresh, too. Where'd it come from?"

Instinctively Hewey brought his fingers up. The place burned beneath his touch. He didn't look C.C. in the eye. "Horse," he said.

C.C. grunted. "How old are you, Hewey?"

Hewey had to figure; he hadn't thought about it in a while. "Thirty-eight. Thirty-eight the fourteenth day of last February."

Tarpley mused. "You sure ain't no valentine. I'll bet by now you're beginnin' to feel the arthritis settin' in. About time for the gray hair to start takin' over too. And all you've got is a brown horse past his prime, an old saddle and maybe twenty dollars. Ain't much to show for them many years, is it?"

Hewey thought before he answered. "I've left a lot of tracks and seen a lot of country. I've worked down to the border of Old Mexico. Been to Cuba for Uncle Sam. I've worked cows from the San Saba River plumb up to Wyoming and Montana. I even went north once into Canada and seen the glaciers. You ever seen a glacier, C.C.?"

The old man just stared at him. He probably didn't know what a glacier was. "What's it ever got for you?" he demanded. "Them places are too far from here to ever amount to anything. The man who gets ahead is the one who stays put and tends to business, not the one always fidgetin' around to go, like a horse in an antbed. You've seen all of that country, but how much of it do you own?"

Hewey pondered the question. "In a way, I own it all."

Old Tarpley didn't understand that. Hewey had found a long time ago that most people never did.

After C.C. and Fat had gone, Hewey squatted to finish the coffee. The wound on his jaw still burned where he had touched it, and he couldn't help touching it again. He had lied to C.C., because this was something else C.C. wouldn't have understood.

He would have to keep on lying about it, for he would not be able to explain it to Eve, either. She was not always an understanding woman. She would not be tolerant of the truth in this case. He had never seen harm in an occasional small liberty with the facts, provided the motive was honorable. The motive in this case would be to keep Eve from raising hell and later regretting her lapse from grace. It had always been his policy to protect her from herself.

The mark on his jaw represented the only bad incident Hewey had encountered on his ride home from New Mexico. He did not consider the morning he had ridden Biscuit off into a snowdrift and had almost smothered them both. That had been a natural hazard, the kind of thing a man had to expect. What he had never been able to understand were human obstacles; they seemed so unnecessary.

He had ridden a little out of his way to pass through New Prosperity, a Panhandle railroad town, thinking he might find something there wetter than windmill water. It seemed natural enough to take a shortcut down a nice wide street where all the houses appeared to be owned by bankers and merchants because every one of them had two stories. Most were decorated by gables and bay windows, and by gingerbread and scallop trim that reminded him of a good brown-topped apple pie. The thought of having to live in one of those houses and take the responsibility for it would have scared him half to death, but they were pretty to look at. Damn few ranches and no cow camps at all had anything like that.

At a corner stood a man who hadn't missed a meal since the winter of '89. He waved his hand sharply and hollered at Hewey, "Hey, you! Come here!"

Hewey reined up in surprise and looked behind him, thinking the man might be shouting at somebody else. He had the street to himself. He sat there in the middle of it, wondering why anybody in this town could be mad at him. He had never been here before.

The man kept yelling, and Hewey kept sitting. Unlike Fat Gervin, who was big all over; this portly gentleman ran mainly to belly. When he tired of straining his voice he walked out toward Hewey, working tolerably hard at his short, choppy steps. The sun flickered off of a small badge on his black vest and called Hewey's attention to the fact that he represented the full majesty of New Prosperity law.

"Cowboy, I told you to come here!"

"I *am* here."

"What's your name?"

Hewey had heard that tone of voice a right smart in the Army, while he was in the Cuba campaign. It was one reason he had not chosen to remain in the service. "Hewey Calloway."

"This is a residential street, cowboy."

Hewey nodded. "Yes sir, and a damn nice one too."

"You're on the wrong side of the tracks."

"I was figurin' to cross over, soon as I get to them."

"Transients ain't allowed on a residential street. The only people who use this street live here or have got business here. One look tells me you ain't got no business here, Holloway."

"Calloway."

"The name don't mean anything to me. You're just another saddle tramp, and you're ridin' where you ain't supposed to."

Hewey's face turned warm. "I ain't never been no saddle tramp. I've got money in my pockets."

"How much money?"

Hewey didn't see that as anybody's business. It was impolite to ask a man how much money he had or to volunteer how much *you* had. The latter was usually either a brag or a complaint, and nobody wanted to listen to it. Money was no yardstick of a man's worth. Anyway, Hewey hated to admit how little was left to show for a cold winter's work. He inflated it. "Fifty dollars, maybe."

"Just about enough to pay a fine for trespass. You get off of this street right now, and I don't mean in a walk, cowboy. I want you to run that horse." The city marshal placed his hand on his gun butt to punctuate his order.

Hewey prided himself on tolerance, but there was a limit to all good things. He regretted the occasional necessity of giving one man authority over another because some people enjoyed that authority too much to be entrusted with it. They tended to be easily misled into a gross overappraisal of their importance. It seemed to him that when a man was too thick-headed and too low-down trifling to hold an honest job, he was usually able to find some other damn fool willing to hand him a measure of jurisdiction over the lives of his betters.

15

Hewey said, "I didn't see no sign that said to keep off."

"You see *me!*" By now the officer was swelled up like a toad at a water tank.

Hewey touched his spurs lightly to Biscuit's sides and started moving in a walk, a very slow and defiant walk. He was afraid his hatband would split in two from the pressure his anger pushed against it.

"Cowboy!"

He looked back. The officer had the pistol in his hand, pointing it at him. "I don't let nobody smart-aleck with me. You get down off of that horse or I'll shoot you off of him!"

The sight of the pistol brought a cold chill. But Hewey sat looking at the marshal a minute, the way he would look at a cull just before he cut it out of the herd. He swung his leg slowly over Biscuit's rump and touched his right foot to the ground, making it a point not to hurry his compliance. While Hewey was still off balance with his left foot in the stirrup, the officer swung the pistol barrel at his head. Hewey dodged. The barrel struck him a glancing blow along his jaw and then hit hard on his shoulder. He saw a shower of bright lights.

It was the mark of a cowardly *law* to pistol-whip a man at the outset and eliminate any resistance. The marshal never had another chance. The move startled Biscuit. The horse lunged, striking the man with his heavy foreshoulder, sending him stumbling back. Hewey swung his fist with all the force he had. The man's soft nose crushed like a cantaloupe. Hewey saw blood on his knuckles when he rubbed them and hoped it wasn't his own. The officer lay flat on his back, spread-eagled with that big stomach sticking up like a washpot turned upside down. Hewey started to go off and leave him but thought of the pistol. The marshal could easily shoot him in the back as he rode away, and he might if he could clear his eyes. Hewey picked up the pistol and shoved it in his waistband.

He rubbed his jaw and then his shoulder, both aching from the blow. He said, "You've cost this town my business. I reckon I'll save my money till I find me a friendlier burg."

He doubted the officer heard him very clearly. It didn't matter.

He made it a point to stay on the residential street and to ride in a slow walk until he passed over the tracks. He paused to pitch the pistol into a wooden water trough. He had never liked to carry one around. He kept Biscuit in a walk until he passed the last Mexican shack on the south side of town, then pushed him into a trot.

The swelling had gone down in the days that had passed, but some of the rawness remained. Hewey washed his jaw again in the dirty tank water.

Biscuit's limp became worse as the afternoon wore on. Hewey carefully looked over his right forefoot two or three times, trying to find some physical sign of the trouble. More than anything else, probably, Biscuit needed a rest. Even at Hewey's chosen leisurely pace it had been a wearisome trip down here from that cow camp where the two of them had spent the winter in the Sangre de Cristos. He knew that in most people's sight he was probably working the whole thing backward, wintering in the New Mexico snow and summering in hot western Texas. But he had always drifted as the fancy struck him, and the long winter's solitude had given him lots of time to think about his few kin. The urge to see them had grown beyond resistance.

About midafternoon he came upon a band of grazing sheep, scattered for half a mile up and down a wide draw where good moisture was bringing up the spring weeds. He was surprised to see the Two Cs paint-branded on their woolly backs. Old C.C. had always prefaced the word "sheep" with a couple or three pungent adjectives. But maybe the wool market had turned strong and the cow market had soured. To C.C., like lots of ranchers, nothing could be all bad if it paid a dividend.

Hewey hunted up the herder to *auger* a little. He was seldom in such a hurry that he wouldn't take time to visit. But the herder was a ragged, graying old Mexican who didn't seem to know three words of English. The only Spanish Hewey knew was a few cuss words, and those seemed inappropriate. Efforts at communication came largely to nought. The herder was too far from his tent camp to offer coffee, so Hewey didn't stay.

Shortly afterward he saw a wagon moving to intersect his line of travel. He could see two men on its seat. They had a considerable load of goods in its bed. One of the men tilted his head back and took a long drink from a bottle just before Hewey came up even with him.

"Hey, Alvin!" Hewey shouted. "Alvin Lawdermilk!"

The wagon driver was a young Mexican whose growth had stopped at just a little more than five feet. He brought his four young Spanish mules to a stop. A couple of them fidgeted and stomped up dust, showing they were not yet well broken to the harness. Among other livestock, Alvin Lawdermilk and his wife, Cora, raised mules. Their place had a reputation for being *Western* when raw mules were introduced to collars and hames. It was also known to get Western when Cora caught Alvin drinking. She seldom caught him.

Lawdermilk twisted his face and tried to bring Hewey into focus. Hewey heard him ask the Mexican, "Hooley, who is that?" When the Mexican answered, Lawdermilk shouted happily, "Hewey Calloway! I thought you'd wandered off the edge of the earth and fell to your doom."

Lawdermilk tried to climb out of the wagon and almost fell to his own doom. The Mexican quickly caught his arm and pulled him back to safety, somehow getting him settled squarely onto the seat and grinning apologetically at Hewey.

Hewey said, "You better stay put, Alvin. That wagon is pretty bouncy." It was standing still.

He rode up beside the left front wheel and pumped Alvin's hand. He reached across to the Mexican. "Howdy, Hooley. I'm surprised you're still puttin' up with Alvin." The Mexican's name was Julio Valdez, the *J* pronounced like an English *H*. The Anglos had corrupted it. Hooley had a reputation as a great hand at breaking mules. Though short in stature, he was quick. Hewey respected other people's proficiencies, whatever they were.

Alvin Lawdermilk's pudgy red face seemed always to be smiling, even when he was sleeping off a lost bout with a bottle. Hewey had never seen him really angry at anyone except his wife, and never in her case where she could see it. Alvin knew how to handle wild broncs, but Cora knew how to handle Alvin.

Alvin's smile was exaggerated by false teeth that were too white and too perfectly shaped, pushing his upper lip out more than was natural. He said exuberantly, "Damn, Hewey, it's good to see that ugly face of yours again, though I can't say it improves with age. Where you come from?"

"New Mexico. Spent the winter hayin' cows in the Sangre de Cristos."

"Wonder you didn't freeze your butt off."

"I did. It'll take me half the summer to thaw the ice out of my blood."

"A wee drop of kindness will build a fire for you." He handed Hewey the bottle. Hewey rubbed his hand across the mouth of it, for he knew Alvin to be a tobacco chewer. He had no objection to following somebody on a bottle, but secondhand tobacco juice took a broad mind. Alvin grinned in shared pleasure as he watched Hewey take a Texas-sized drink and wipe his wrinkled sleeve across his mouth. Alvin said, "What this old world needs is a lot more kindness."

"Truer words was never spoke." Hewey handed the bottle back, enjoying the warmth of the whisky making its slow way down to his stomach. "You ain't buyin' the cheap stuff."

"When they tote me off in that big black wagon, I want it said that I died of the best." Alvin passed the bottle to Julio, who took only a modest sip and handed it back. Somebody had to stay sober for the mules.

Hewey glanced at the goods stacked high in the wagon bed . . . flour, potatoes, Arbuckle coffee, a keg of steeples, several spools of barbed wire. Beneath the seat, where nothing could fall on it and cause grievous damage, was a new wooden case full of whisky bottles. "Looks like you went and supplied yourself for the summer."

"Only the necessaries. You'll never catch us Lawdermilks throwin' good money away on things we don't need. Waste not, want not."

Hewey knew Cora Lawdermilk. She would inspect every item as it was unloaded, and woe unto all within hearing if anything came up short, or if she found anything on the wagon which she had not ordered or approved. The case of whisky would not be there when she checked the rest of the goods. Alvin would unload it in some safe place before he reached the house. Then, as the opportunities arose, he would carry the individual bottles to secret places for ready accessibility in time of need. There was not a windmill on the Lawdermilk ranch where Alvin did not have a bottle cached to help heal some inner misery, or to cut away the taste of gyp in the water. He kept one at his milking shed, two or three in the barn and one at the corner post of the field where he raised hegari and redtop cane as feed for his horses and mules, and where he trained the young ones to work. No emergency, anywhere on the ranch, ever caught him unprepared.

Yet, with it all he was a successful rancher as success was measured in this country. A successful rancher was one who had not been broke, lately. Though Alvin did not rival C. C. Tarpley and had no such ambition, he was no shirttail nester. If the sheriff came down his road it was to electioneer, not to post a notice of foreclosure.

Hewey said, "How's my family, Alvin?"

Alvin stared at the bottle in his hand. Hewey got the quick impression that he was uncertain how to answer. Alvin said, "I see them two buttons every day, almost. They've growed like weeds."

Hewey waited until he decided that was all Alvin was going to tell him. "I had a visit with C.C. He talked like Walter is in trouble."

Alvin looked out across the pasture, framing his words with care. He looked sober, all of a sudden. "C.C. give you any details?"

"Just said there's money trouble."

"I reckon that's so."

"Is Walter fixin' to lose his place?"

Alvin didn't answer, not directly. "Hewey, I'm concerned about him. Walter labors from lantern light to lantern light. You got to tell him he's workin' too hard. Each man to his own way of dyin', but I'd hate to think mine was to be from overwork."

Hewey felt increasingly uneasy. It was Eve's doing, sure as anything. She was always pushing for better than she had. Times, just for a minute or two, Hewey would get to thinking Walter might have been better off if he had never met her. But then, he wouldn't have had those boys.

Alvin said, "A woman has got a right to a certain amount of ambition, but not to excess. A man ought to keep her under control, like I do with my Cora. I don't do nothin' on my place unless I want to."

Julio looked quickly away, studying the flight of a scissortail; its presence meant spring had come for sure.

Hewey's conscience began to stir. He should have written, should have kept the family posted so they could write and tell him if anything was wrong. It was something he had always intended to do, but writing a letter was harder work for him than breaking a bronc or digging a string of postholes. His formal schooling had stopped just shy of the last pages in McGuffey's third reader.

His rump was prickling now in his anxiety to go. "Alvin . . . Hooley . . . it was sure nice runnin' into you-all. I reckon I better be seein' about the family."

Alvin said eagerly, "You lookin' for a job, Hewey? There's a right smart more work over at our place than we've been able to get done. If you take it in mind to light someplace awhile, we'd be tickled to have you." Alvin extended the bottle again. "Better have one more. It'll make the country look greener."

Hewey shook his head. "One's enough, I reckon. Eve'll smell it on my breath. She don't hold with drinkin'."

"Neither does my Cora. Ain't nothin' like a righteous woman to drive a man to sin." Alvin reached into his shirt pocket and brought out a plug of tobacco, only a little of it bitten off. He took a pocketknife and carved a generous slice, holding it toward Hewey. "Take a chaw of this just before you get there. It'll kill the scent. Even if it don't, the sight of a little tobacco juice runnin' down the chin will keep a woman at a distance; she won't smell the whisky."

Hewey had no intention of chewing the tobacco, but he accepted it as hospitality freely offered. He also accepted one more drink from the bottle. He said, "You watch Hooley now, Alvin. Don't you let him drink too much."

The little Mexican smiled and flipped the reins. As the wagon pulled away, Alvin turned in the seat and shouted back, "Bunch of us will be over tomorrow and help Walter raise a windmill. I'll want to visit with you and hear all your yarns. Ain't many of us poor devils ever gets to travel all over the world."

The words soon became unintelligible, but Alvin kept shouting back, and Hewey kept nodding as if he understood and agreed. He watched the wagon lumber on down the trail toward the Lawdermilk place, thin gray dust drifting off and settling slowly on the grass standing shin-high and green from the spring rains. It didn't take a trail long to dry out. Hewey touched a spur gently to Biscuit's side. "Come on, old friend, we still got a ways to go."

The prickling came back as he picked up landmarks that told him he was nearing Walter's land. He stared at a small flat-topped hill with an abrupt rimrock edge running along its north face. People here called it a mountain, which in a strictly local and relative sense it might be. But Hewey had seen real mountains, so he regarded this as simply a hill. Beneath it was a dry, water-hollowed place that appeared to be a wet-weather spring, though he had never been here in a time wet enough to see it run. Indians had camped here. Many times Hewey had come with Walter's two boys to help them hunt for arrowheads. They had probably collected a bucketful. To the boys these were a treasure left from a mysterious time they had never known. Hewey had seen Indians in the Territory and up in the mountain states. To him they were not mysterious or remote; they were real.

He edged Biscuit across the old campsite and leaned low in the saddle, watching the ground. It would tickle the boys if he brought them a couple of good points. But if any arrowheads were left, the new grass was hiding them.

He came presently to a fence and reined up, surprised. He knew this was more or less the boundary of Walter's four sections, but the last time he had been here Walter hadn't yet accumulated the money or the credit to put a fence around it and keep C.C.'s cows from helping themselves to the grass, crowding Walter's own little herd. The fence had only three strands of barbed wire, still shiny from the factory, not yet dulled or rusted from standing exposed to winter blizzard and summer sun. Three strands were the mark of a nester, poor as a whippoorwill. A real rancher like C.C. would put up four wires. Anything less was unprofessional and farmer-looking.

Cedar posts were best for fencing; they lasted longer. They cost money, though, and had to be freighted in by wagon from the hill country south and east of here. Mesquite posts would not stand as long, but a man could chop them himself, close to home. They cost him only his time and sweat. These posts were all mesquite. Hewey knew how Walter had spent the winter.

He started down the fence, looking for a gate or a drop-gap.

Until recent years this gently rolling rangeland had been a haven for massive herds of buffalo driven south each fall and winter by the chill winds howling across the high and open plains. They could find shelter here in the scattered stands of mesquite which fringed the wide draws and wet-weather creeks, and on the lee sides of the little bluffs and breaks which marked the southernmost fringe of the great caprock. As recently as thirty years ago the plains Indians had roamed here, following the buffalo, hunting the deer but settling sometimes for rabbits and rattlesnakes when times were lean.

Much of this land was unsuited to cultivation, and the man who sank a plowpoint into the sod would have ample cause to regret it. Yet there were wide deep-soil flats which could be farmed if a man had patience enough, and faith. The average rainfall was less than twenty inches a year, and the actual amount in a given year could be far, far less than that. The ranchers, already here, made it a point to tell every prospective land seeker about those worst years if they could find a way to reach him in time. The town promoters and boomers told him only of the best years, those infrequent periods when rains were generous and corn made heads bigger around than a man's fist, kernels as big as cats' eyes.

Given any chance, this virgin land usually made big crops the first time or two, using up nutrients stored by the grass roots for thousands of years. Few people had farmed here long enough yet to know how poorly the land might yield when it became tired of bearing crops Nature had not intended.

Because of its shortcomings, this region had been among the last to draw the farmers and small settlers. It was among the last large stretches of state-owned land that Texas had taken out of grass lease and had thrown open for homesteads of up to four sections—twenty-five hundred acres—per claimant, to be lived on and proved up in three years. Texas was more generous in its homestead programs than the federal government had been in other western states, possibly because its legislators lived nearer to the land involved and realized its limitations. They knew a man could starve to death in a year on a hundred and sixty acres. On four sections it took longer.

Hewey found a wire gate half a mile from the point where he had struck the fence. He dismounted and led Biscuit through, flinching as he touched the sharp barbs. Though it belonged to his brother, the fence stirred a latent resentment in his free-roaming spirit. This great open land had given him a kinship of sorts to the nomadic Indian. He could remember when a horseman might ride two or three hundred miles and never encounter a barbed-wire fence. Now he was lucky to travel twenty without having to look for a gate or to pull steeples out of the posts and push down the wires to cross over.

He recognized the fence as a necessity for the small settler's survival, but it was not a thing he could accept without regret at the passing of a freer and more open time. A fence—any way you looked at it—was an obstacle. It shut you out or it shut you in.

He rode down a familiar wagon road, his heartbeat quickening. He had been here when Walter had taken up this little piece of land. Though Hewey had no liking for a plow, he had helped Walter break out his first field and build the small, ugly-plain frame house that would meet the legal requirements of the state and the shelter requirements of a wife and two sons. Walter had wanted a few cattle; that was the cowboy in him. Hewey had gone east to San Angelo and had bought him thirty cows of the upgraded type, the red body and white face of the Hereford blood showing stronger than the stubborn lean base of Longhorn. Three of the cows had calves on the trail; by the time they had reached here Walter owned more cattle than he had paid for. That had pleased Eve. She had an instinct for acquisition.

Walter had tried at the time to persuade Hewey to take up a homestead for himself. The temptation had been strong—for a couple of days. But Hewey contended that land ownership worked two ways. A man might own the land, but the land also owned *him*. Anyway, he had told himself, the state of Texas held all the best cards. It was betting a man a piddling parcel of land against three good years of his life, and the odds were against the man. Hewey had no wish to be tied to one place so small that a horse would hardly break a sweat loping across it in trade for his freedom of the whole West from the Rio Grande to the Canadian border.

All Walter owned was this one little piece of land. Hewey owned it all.

He came presently to the edge of the field and noted that it stretched farther than he remembered. Walter had added to it gradually until it took up just about all the deep soil that promised an affinity to the plow, and also some that didn't. It was farmer nature, Hewey thought, to overreach oneself.

Walter had not been a farmer by inclination. Necessity had forced him to it, necessity and a woman. In his growing years Walter had been much like Hewey, a cowboy at heart, unfettered of spirit, ready to ride anywhere he had not already been, ready to try anything he had not already tried. Motherless, they had roamed with their restless father through the years of their boyhood while the elder Calloway sought in vain for an ideal land that existed only in his mind. When Hewey was fifteen and Walter barely fourteen, they had buried their father on a grassy Kansas upland above a river where he had waited with other "boomers" for the anticipated opening of the Indian lands across the deadline in Oklahoma. This was to have been the last great bonanza. But two underage boys were not eligible to try their luck in the big land run, so they had moved on. They had worked steers for Texas cattlemen leasing grass from the Osages and the Cherokees, then moved back across Red River into the land of their beginnings, searching vainly for roots hopelessly lost during their wandering years. The place of their birth had been taken up by strangers. Whatever kin they might have had was gone, scattered like tumbleweeds in a long winter wind. So they went drifting as their father had drifted, never knowing truly what they searched for, or how they would recognize it if they found it.

Walter, at least, had been able to compromise. When he married Eve, the daughter of a poor San Saba County farmer, he had tried awhile to continue the foot-loose ways of former years. But Eve had a strong instinct for the nest. She had pressured Walter to light in one place, old C. C. Tarpley's ranch. She had seen to it that Walter stuck to one job while Hewey was working at a dozen. She had made Walter smoke little, drink nothing, wear boots twice resoled and clothes that had patches on the patches. She had seen to it that Walter saved every possible dollar, while Hewey was spending his much easier than they had come.

When parts of this land were finally taken from the grass-lease ranchers like C.C. and thrown open for claiming, Eve's time of fulfillment had arrived. Walter was at the head of the pushing, shoving, shouting line of men scuffling at the front door of the county courthouse. Hewey had hunkered with his back to the white picket fence on the courthouse square, ready to go to his brother's aid if any of the toughs and the hungry and the desperate tried to throw him out of his place in the line. But Hewey had not the slightest inclination to join that line himself. He found something offensive and dehumanizing in the system, something that robbed a man of pride and dignity, pitting friends against each other, bringing ugliness and greed and violence rising to the top like sour cream on spoiled milk.

Many of the men who homesteaded these places were cowboys for the big outfits and tacitly agreed that when they had finished living out their claims they would sell them to the ranches they worked for. C. C. Tarpley had expected all along that he would get Walter's parcel and put it back into his original holdings for perhaps the price of a good horse and a new R. T. Frazier saddle. But he had reckoned without Eve. Anything she once acquired, all hell would not prize from her grip.

Across the field Hewey could see two teams, each pulling a walking plow. It was too far to recognize the plowmen, but one would almost certainly be Walter. The other was probably one of his boys unless Walter had become flush enough to hire help. Hewey doubted that. Hiring help was wasteful if you could do the job yourself, Eve always said. Eve always said a lot.

Hewey rode down the field fence until he came to the corner gate. He found it open, marked by fresh tracks of the teams moving in and out. This early in the season the field held nothing for the cows to get into and ruin. Hewey rode up the turnrows a way, then dismounted, squatted on his gal-leg spurs and rolled himself a cigarette while he waited. He had no intention of riding or walking across that newly plowed, violated ground.

He watched a black dog following behind one of the plows, waiting to catch a rabbit or chase after a ground squirrel if one was scared up. As the plow neared, the dog trotted around it and hurried out in front, barking a challenge at Hewey.

Hewey had time to finish his cigarette before the plow hand began to shout at him. "Uncle Hewey! Uncle Hewey!"

A young boy reached the turnrow and reined the team to a stop; the two gray mules had no objection. He tipped the plow over on one side and ran across the plowed earth, the dog beside him, barking. When the boy reached the grass he shouted joyously and threw his arms around Hewey, hugging him with a surprising strength. Hewey danced, swinging the lad off his feet. Biscuit took a couple of steps backward, startled at the exuberance. The black dog kept barking, afraid Hewey was hurting the boy, but it took no other action.

"I'll swun, Cotton," Hewey exclaimed, "you've growed a foot."

"I'm not Cotton. I'm Tommy."

Hewey held the boy away at arm's length and took a long look. "You *are* Tommy. Boy howdy, you've growed *two* feet. They been feedin' you Tarpley beef?"

"You just been gone a long time."

"I didn't realize how long."

"We missed you, Uncle Hewey. Have you come home to stay?"

Hewey had no honest answer. "Maybe awhile. We'll see." A thought struck him. "How come you're not in school?"

"This is Saturday."

"Saturday?" Hewey blinked, trying to calculate. "Funny, I thought it was Wednesday." He stared at Tommy, and the boy stared back at him until the two broke out laughing again for no good reason either could have named.

Tommy said, "We got us a fishin' hole now, Uncle Hewey. I'll take you there. We'll catch us a perch."

Hewey nodded, still not able to accept how much the boy had grown. "If you're this big, how big is Cotton?"

"About grown. He's comin' on sixteen, you know."

Sixteen. Hewey knew it, yet he could not quite accept it, either. It didn't seem possible that so many years had drifted by so quickly. "You're almost a man yourself, Tommy. Couple more years . . . Which one of you is the best cowboy, you or Cotton? Tell me the truth now."

"I am. All Cotton wants to do is build things and tinker around with tools and wrenches all the time."

Hewey kept grinning. "I was thinkin' maybe when school is out I might take you two buttons with me and find us a cowboyin' job for the summer out west of the Pecos. Good chance for you-all to see a little country."

Tommy's blue eyes flashed in quick pleasure. But his smile faded as he thought about it. "Mama and Daddy will need us. We've got more land to take care of now."

Hewey didn't know whether to be glad for them or to sympathize. "How'd that happen?"

"Grat French finished provin' up his four sections that adjoined us. Mr. C.C. tried to buy the place, but Mr. French was peeved at him and didn't want him to have it. He offered it to Daddy and Mama instead. They took out a mortgage on everything we own. Except maybe my dog."

Hewey let a slow dry whistle pass between his teeth. "I'll bet old C.C. busted a gut."

"No, it was him and his bank that loaned us the money. Mama says he wanted the French land and ours too, and he figured this way he would wind up gettin' them both. She says we're goin' to fool old Mr. C.C." Tommy frowned. "But I don't know. Last year we come up shy on the crops, and the cattle market was kind of poor on our yearlin's."

Hewey saw worry in Tommy's eyes. It wasn't right, he thought, for a fourteen-year-old boy to carry a burden like this. "Well, it's just a piece of land," he said, trying to make the best of it. "There's land everywhere, most of it better than this."

"But this is *our* land. This is home."

He stared at the boy, looking at those features that marked him as a Calloway. But Tommy was Eve's son, too, and that was a side of him Hewey would never fully understand.

Land. It was a pleasant thing to ride across but a demanding thing to own. So now Walter and Eve owned eight sections of it and stood a considerable chance of losing it all. Maybe in the long run it was just as well. It would probably cost eighty years of hard labor, first for them, then for their kids and eventually for their grandchildren. Chances were that in the end none would ever feel any richer than Hewey had felt all his life.

But it bothered him, thinking that after all their planning and all their work it might fall into the open hands of C. C. Tarpley like a ripe peach falls from the tree to be grabbed up by an orchard boar. Other land-hungry men had used more direct methods; they had burned out fields and barns, run off homesteaders' cattle, even killed. C.C.'s brand of avarice ran in a subtler vein, infinitely more patient.

Hewey frowned, watching his brother working this way across the field with his plow, a mismatched horse team laboring to break new rows in the damp and grudging earth. He pondered darkly on how a man is brought down from being a hawk in flight to a slave in chains.

This was a long way from the Osage.

II

The first thing to strike Hewey about his younger brother was that Walter was wearing bib overalls. In olden times he had rather have ridden stark naked down a cow-town street at high noon than be seen in overalls. The second thing to strike him was that Walter looked like the older brother, not the younger.

He was a little slow setting the plow over. He gave Hewey a tentative and apologetic wave as he paused a moment, stretching his stiffened arms and rubbing his right shoulder. But he grinned with his whole face. Hewey forgot about the plowed ground and walked out hurriedly to meet him. They shook hands, but that wasn't enough, so they threw their arms around each other. Happy tears ran unashamed down Walter's dusty cheeks, leaving little tracks of mud across what looked like weathered leather.

"The prodigal son," Walter exulted, "finally come home. And there's not a fatted calf on the place."

"I'd settle for a wing from a drouthy quail."

"You may have to." Walter stepped back for a good long look at Hewey, from his face to his thorn-scarred boots. "I'd about decided you'd finally found a bronc you couldn't ride or a cow you oughtn't to've roped. Thought they'd buried you someplace without us knowin' it. You had three years of schoolin'. Didn't you learn to write?"

"Not to where you could read it."

Walter's overalls were old and thready, both knees patched with newer material that stood out darker than the faded blue. His old hat was shapeless, the brim flat, showing none of the flair that had been a trademark of the Calloway brothers in their wilder years.

30

The hat now was strictly for business, to keep the sun from his face; the flatter the brim the better it did that job.

Even in a winter bachelor camp where nothing could see him except three horses and a bunch of hungry cattle, Hewey had taken care about the shape of his hat. He watched his shadow sometimes as he rode. Even the shadow had style.

The two brothers, over the first flush of joy, stood back at arm's length and regarded each other critically, neither altogether pleased by what he saw.

Walter accused, "You ain't been eatin' regular."

"I never did. But I'll bet I look better than *you* do. You been drivin' yourself, ain't you?"

"Hard work never killed anybody."

"Neither did hard liquor, taken in moderation. But I've seen men that could get drunk on work and business, same as on whisky. You sure you ain't turned into one of those?"

Walter passed the question without an answer. He demanded, "What's that mark along your jaw?"

Hewey lied, "Got pawed by a bronc. Only grazed me, kind of."

"Don't you think you've come to an age where you ought to stop messin' with them bad horses? They'll kill you one of these days."

"Age? I ain't but thirty-six."

"Thirty-eight, and in some danger of never seein' thirty-nine. Don't try to hooraw me, Hewey. I got a memory for dates and figures."

Tommy watched them nervously, unsure if he should stay or quietly return to his plow. He couldn't tell whether his father and uncle were in jest or really quarreling.

Hewey wasn't sure either. There had always been a fine line between the two, and he had never been able to discern just when they crossed it. He looked at the worried boy. "Better slack up, Walter. Tommy'll think that brothers argue all their lives. That don't give him and Cotton much to look forward to."

Walter broke into a long grin that lifted ten years from his face. He said to Tommy, "We ain't arguin', son. You ought to remember; this is the way me and your Uncle Hewey always carried on. We don't mean nothin' by it."

Hewey wasn't sure about that, but he nodded agreement. "We

never used to fight, your daddy and me. We never disagreed in our whole lives, did we, Walter?"

Walter glanced at Biscuit, then turned back to Hewey. "You said you're hungry. You ride on down to the house and get Eve to fix you somethin' to eat. Me and Tommy, we'll be in about dark."

The sun was still two hours high. "Dark?"

"We need to finish gettin' this field broken and planted. A spell of wet weather has throwed us late."

"Two hours won't make that much difference in a whole year's crop. You could quit early, just this once."

Walter appeared tempted. "Two hours wasted is two hours gone forever."

Two hours. Hewey could remember one time he and Walter had camped for two *days* outside a coyote den hoping to get a shot at a calf-killing bitch as she came out. When she finally did, they both missed her.

Walter repeated, "You go on in, Hewey. Eve'll be tickled to see you."

Like a case of the measles, Hewey thought. He remembered that she had usually been far more tickled to see him leave than to see him arrive. He said, "Where's Cotton?"

"Over on the French place puttin' a windmill together."

Hewey was incredulous. "You let that little boy climb a windmill, all by himself? What if he falls?"

"That *little boy* is damn near grown. Anyway, he's puttin' it together on the ground. A few neighbors are comin' over tomorrow to eat fried chicken with us and help us raise the mill."

Hewey loosened some. "I been itchin' to see that boy. How'll I find him?"

Walter's eyes narrowed. "It's a ways over there. Cotton'll be home directly, and you can see him without tirin' your horse out so bad."

Hewey shrugged. "Maybe I could be some help to him."

Walter shook his head knowingly. "You never used to be afraid of anything, Hewey, but you're scared to go down to the house and meet Eve all by yourself. She don't bite."

"She don't bite *you,* maybe."

"I never did understand what got wrong between you two, but

that's been a long time ago, and long forgotten about." Walter kept looking at Hewey, knowing he wasn't convinced. Finally he shrugged, giving up. "Hell, it's Saturday, and tomorrow's the Sabbath. The Lord won't condemn us for sloth just this once. We've got company to celebrate. Tommy, let's unhitch the teams."

He didn't have to say it twice. Tommy was already at his plow before his father had taken three steps. Hewey went to help Tommy. They left the plow where it stood in the newly turned earth at the end of the row, ready for a fresh start on another day. Tommy gathered up the lines and jumped easily onto the bare back of a gray mule.

Hewey smiled. "Mind if I ride the other one and lead Biscuit? He's kind of wrung out."

"Hop on."

Hewey grasped the mane and bent his knees, then sprang up, throwing his belly across the mule's broad back. That part wasn't so hard, but dragging his right leg up and over seemed to take about all the strength he had. Funny, didn't seem like it used to be so hard to mount bareback. He guessed it was just that he hadn't done it in a spell. It wasn't a thing that came up every day in his normal routine. He swung the mule around so he could gather up the bridle reins and lead Biscuit.

He watched Walter struggle to get onto one of the horses bareback. Maybe he was just tired. Plowing a half-wet field was hardly restful.

Hewey quickly discerned why Tommy had chosen the other mule. This one had a trot that would jar the innards out of a seventy-dollar pocket watch. Hewey pulled his hat down tight and made it a point not to look at his shadow.

Walter said, "You can ride this other horse if you'd rather."

Hewey had much rather, but he did not wish to back down in the sight of his nephew. "I'm doin' just fine. I ain't used to no rockin' chair." He wasn't used to a sledgehammer, either.

Three trees were beginning to reach up well beyond the roof of the plain frame house. Hewey found it hard to believe they had grown so much. He turned to Tommy and pointed. "Those can't be the chinaberries we set out that time, me and you two buttons?"

33

"It's them," Tommy said with pride. "Three of them just like we said when we did it . . . one for me and one for you and one for Cotton. You promised that when they got big enough we'd climb up to the tops of them, the three of us. They're big enough now."

"I said that?"

"You sure did. You made a promise and took the oath of a Cherokee chief."

The oath of a Cherokee chief? Hewey frowned, unable to remember. Some wild idea he had thought up on the spur of the moment, probably. He had always done that with the two boys, and with other boys he came across in his travels. If they wanted a story and he didn't have one to fit, he made one up as he went along, indulging in wild fancies that seemed to drift effortlessly to him out of the clouds, and as effortlessly return there, quickly forgotten.

He was going to have to quit that. The boys were older now and had good memories.

Tommy said, "I've climbed up in them. I want to see you clear at the top, Uncle Hewey."

Hewey shook his head. "I can't do that kind of thing anymore, button. Doctor's orders."

"Doctor's orders?"

"I ain't supposed to go up high anymore. Makes my blood get thin."

Tommy didn't accept that. "How come?"

Hewey never knew where the inspirations came from. All of a sudden the yarns would be spinning and he had no real idea what the source was, or even how they would end. "Well, it was when I was up in Colorado, up in the high country. There was a boy I met up yonder . . . same age as you, looked a whole lot like you, only his name was Timmy instead of Tommy, and he had built him a great big kite, big as a haystack. He wanted me to help him get it started. Well sir, a little breeze came up, and I taken out runnin' with it to get the kite started, and somehow I got my arm tangled up in the string, and one of them big winds come along the way they do sometimes in that country. It picked me up with the kite and sailed me way up high. Just like a bird, I was, with the prettiest view of that valley down there a thousand feet under me. I just went sailin', nice and free as you please, higher and higher up into them mountains, till I got all the way to the top. Then the breeze died down, and I floated to earth on the peak of the very highest mountain there was. I could look down in all four directions and see a hundred . . . no, two hundred miles.

"I can't describe it to you, button; I ain't got words big enough. It was the most beautiful sight ever I seen in my life, big tall pine trees and big blue lakes stretchin' off out yonder as far as an eagle could see. A little bit like it must look to God, I reckon, sittin' way up high. I sure did enjoy it. But I got to thinkin' about my little friend Bobby down there at the foot of the mountain, cryin' for his kite, maybe figurin' I had stolen it from him. So, there wasn't nothin' for me to do but start down, walkin' all the way. It was summertime, but it gets cold up in them mountains. The longer I walked the colder I got, and when I come down finally to the valley where it was warm, I was still cold. I gave Johnny his kite and then went to the doctor. He told me the chill had thinned my blood too much, and I had to get it thickened up again. You know how I done that? I done it eatin' syrup. Blackstrap molasses, the thicker the better. I reckon I must of eaten a barrel of it before my blood stiffened up to where I wasn't cold anymore. Doctor told me I couldn't afford ever to go to high places again. So that's why I can't climb trees. I reckon that's a pleasure I'll have to give up for the rest of my life."

Tommy rode along in silence, digesting all that. At length he asked, "Uncle Hewey, I don't reckon you saw God while you was way up on that mountain?"

Hewey shook his head. "No, I didn't."

Tommy nodded. "He'd of told you where He sends people who tell stories like that."

Riding in to Walter Calloway's little headquarters from its back side, Hewey couldn't see that much had changed. The barn was a box-and-strip building, not one foot larger that it had to be to house his saddles and harness, some sacked stock salt, scooped from the edge of the big Juan Cordona Lake, and the assortment of livestock medicines and liniments which gave off a smell that reached beyond the door and struck a man squarely in both nostrils before he touched the latch. On one side was a lean-to roof with a trough and a hayrack where the work stock could be fed dry during infrequent rainy weather. On the other side was another rude lean-to, walled only on the north, sheltering a forge and an anvil where Walter and the boys could do whatever blacksmithing was necessary. Most horses and mules in this country went unshod. The hoofs were simply kept trimmed so they wouldn't break or split and cause lameness.

Next to the barn stood a wooden windmill tower, topped by a twelve-foot Eclipse wheel turning in the warm afternoon breeze. Its sucker-rod clanked with a steady rhythm in the pipe. Its water flowed first into a big wooden barrel, the mouth of the pipe set high enough that a bucket could be placed under it to fill with clean drinking and cooking and washing water for the house. From the barrel the water passed through a short pipe into another frame building even smaller than the barn. Hewey looked at his brother.

"There's somethin' new. You built Eve a milkhouse?"

Walter proudly held the door open for Hewey. Hewey saw that the water from the pipe flowed into a slanted open concrete trough into which Eve had set several cloth-covered milk and cream jars to keep their contents from souring too soon. The water fresh from the ground was always cool.

Walter said, "We built the trough with just enough slope to keep the fresh water runnin' through and out the far end."

Hewey saw scratched into the cement before it had hardened "Cotton—Tommy '05."

Walter said, "It was Cotton laid it all out." The water gurgled as it eddied into another pipe which led to a big open-surface tank. There it was available to the livestock after the people had finished with it. There was no water in the family house except that which somebody carried in a bucket. The windmill supplied all the water for man and beast. Without it, or another of its kind, life could not long be sustained here. Nature had not provided it at the surface, free for the taking; it had to be worked for. That was the reason this part of Texas had been slow in settling up, the last to be claimed other than by the free-sprawling cattlemen such as

C. C. Tarpley. The real enemy here had not been Indians or the thin scattering of outlaws; it had been the lack of water. The windmill had done more for settlement than all the cavalry and all the sheriffs since the Civil War.

Hewey looked up at the family's meat supply, beef wrapped in a protective tarp to keep the flies off. It was hanging from a steel hook attached to the end of a lever. Walter reached over to a peg and untied a short length of rope. Running up through a pulley, it freed the lever so that the quarter of beef was lowered by its own weight to about shoulder level. Walter pulled on the rope. The lever moved up, raising the meat back almost to the ceiling.

"Cotton's idea too," Walter said. "He designed it to make more workin' room and still keep things easy for his mother."

Moving out, Hewey stepped to the side of the barn and ran a thumbnail along a plank, testing the peeling paint. He had helped Walter put this barn up; he hated to see it looking this way. "Needs paintin'."

"First things first. We've had other things more in need."

"I'll paint it for you if you'll fetch some red paint first time you go to town." Red paint was the cheapest; its color was dark enough that even a cheap grade would cover.

"Paint don't come cheap. Barn won't fall down if it goes another year without new paint. Eve's gone *two* years without a new dress."

Hewey frowned and said nothing. The whole barn wouldn't take but a dollar's worth, maybe two. Many a time he had put a dollar's worth of whisky down his throat between two breaths and never begrudged the money. A dollar had never meant much to him, beyond whatever pleasure it might bring to him or to somebody whose company he enjoyed. Want of money was a thing he never experienced and never understood. He had been broke often, but he had never been poor.

He had never had a wife to support, of course, or two sons, or a homestead to prove up. He guessed to Walter a dollar bill must look as big as a saddle blanket, and as scarce as July rain.

Walter had added no new corrals that Hewey could see; four sections of land wouldn't carry a great many cattle, not in this part of the country. Hewey had helped him build all the pens he needed several years ago. They had used mesquite timber, stacked horizontally between pairs of heavy posts, making a fence tight enough that a kid goat couldn't crawl through. They had cut rawhide strips to tie the pairs of posts at the top instead of buying wire. They hadn't used five dollars worth of bought materials.

They hadn't had five dollars to spend.

Tommy dipped a tin bucket into an oat bin. The oats, cut last May or June and almost a year old now, had a dry and dusty smell as he spread them along the bottom of a wooden trough. The two work horses and the mules went straight to the feed. Biscuit had stood apart from the other stock, a little superior in attitude, his custom among strangers. But when he heard their teeth grinding the oats, he turned democrat and joined them at the trough.

Hewey said, "I wouldn't want to spoil him. He don't get this style of treatment everywhere."

Walter said, "He won't get enough of it here to do him any harm. You wouldn't believe, Hewey, what a bushel of oats is worth these days."

Tommy said, "We gather up most of these down at the freighters' campground, what they spill when they feed their stock."

A freight-wagon road ran nearby, a couple of hundred yards below the house. For years freighters had made a custom of camping in a grove of wild chinaberry trees and had led their horse and mule teams up to the corrals to water them from Walter's tank. It was a point of pride with Walter not to charge them for it because the Lord had provided the water. The Lord had not provided the windmill, however, except in an indirect manner. The freighters recognized this fact and usually made it a point to waste some feed that the boys could gather up in a sack.

From somewhere appeared a droop-eared burro, its brown hair still ragged with unshed winter growth. It pushed in beside Biscuit and shoved its nose into the oats. Biscuit, nettled by the uninvited familiarity, bared his teeth and took a nip at the burro's flank. The burro wheeled, showed his backside and kicked Biscuit squarely in the stomach. His point made, he went back to the oats. Biscuit stood to one side, surprised and shamed. Finally he turned back to the trough but kept one of the work stock between him and the burro.

Hewey grimaced, sharing Biscuit's shame at the hands of an inferior. "He ain't met many burros. He's got a right smart to learn."

Tommy said, "He'll learn it if he stays around this one. The burro's Cotton's. Alvin Lawdermilk gave it to him for helpin' him work some bronc mules." Many ranchers used burros to teach young broncs to lead and obey the rope. They would simply tie the burro and the bronc together. The stubborn burro would go where he wanted to and make the bronc come along whether it suited him or not. Size and weight counted for little. The burro almost always won.

"Every boy ought to have him a dog and a burro," Hewey said. "What do you call him?"

Tommy glanced quickly at his father, then back at the animal. "Mostly just 'Burro,' or 'Hey, you!' He don't answer to a name. He just answers to feed."

Hewey watched the horses and mules and the burro eat, a thing that had always given him pleasure. He had heard few sounds in his life that he liked better than a strong set of teeth grinding at a bait of oats, unless it was a good rain beating upon a tin roof in a dry country that needed it. He noticed finally that Walter was waiting for him, holding the gate open. Hewey walked out so Walter could shut the gate behind him. Walter said, "Tommy, you can milk the cow before supper."

"It's Cotton's turn."

"Cotton's still out workin'. I let you quit early."

The argument was over; neither Walter nor Eve stood for it from the boys.

They all started walking toward the house. Hewey's skin began to prickle. He never knew what kind of reception Eve would have for him on any given day. He remembered a couple he wouldn't wish on Fat Gervin. "You better go on ahead and tell her I'm here, Walter."

"She'll know it when she sees you. Come on." Walter scraped his boots on the edge of the step at the kitchen door, in case he had set foot into something he hadn't noticed. Eve would notice it; that was certain. Tommy grinned in anticipation of his mother's happy reaction. Hewey wiped his feet with even more care than Walter had taken and rubbed the toes of his dusty boots on the backs of his legs, not removing any dust but moving it around. He wished he had taken longer in Tarpley's water tank.

He heard Eve's voice, tinged with concern. "You're home early. Somethin' wrong?"

"Nothin' wrong," Walter replied. "Everything's right."

"It's still daylight. I haven't got supper fixed yet. I didn't figure on you-all till good dark." Hewey imagined he could detect reproach, but he knew he was probably giving her the worst of it.

"We had good reason to quit. Come on in here, Hewey."

Hewey took a slow, deep breath and pulled the kitchen screen open. He stopped just inside, letting it bump against his backside as the spring pulled it shut. He held his hat in both hands and was ready to hit the screen running if need be. Shifting his weight from one foot to the other, he finally managed, "Howdy, Eve." Nothing else came out.

Eve Calloway was well into her thirties, no longer really young but not yet reconciled to pass over that one-way threshold into middle age. She was at a time in her life when with the right clothes and activated by the right mood she could still seem girl-like, years younger than her actual age. Or, if tired and irritable and taking no care for her appearance, she could look years older than she was. Hewey had seen her both ways so many times he never knew which to expect. At this moment, she seemed more inclined toward the latter.

She stared at him with wide eyes. Other than surprise, he could see no readily identifiable emotion in her face. He kept his back against the screen. Waiting vainly for a reaction, he finally blurted, "I ain't stayin' long, Eve."

Walter watched his wife, waiting for her to give his brother a joyous welcome. When she didn't, he became as nervous as Hewey. He walked to the woodbox and glanced perfunctorily inside. "Low on wood. I better chop some more before supper."

Hewey quickly volunteered, but Walter cut him off. "You stay here and visit with Eve. She's anxious to know where-all you've been." He pushed past Hewey and went out the screen door, pausing to lift a milk bucket from its rack beside the steps. Outside, he was telling Tommy to get on with the milking.

Alone, Hewey and Eve stared at each other across the width of the little kitchen, neither moving.

"Well, Hewey . . ." she said at length, and let it drop there.

"Well, Eve . . ." he replied, and didn't pick it up.

When the tension between them became too heavy for her, she turned to the Majestic iron cookstove, removed the round front lid from its place, did momentary violence to the red coals with an iron poker, then shoved in a couple of chunks of dry mesquite from the woodbox. Hewey suspected it was not a thing she especially needed to do; it was something to busy her hands. Not looking at him, she said, "You'd just as well sit down and stop blockin' the door. And you'd better pitch that hat into a corner before you twist the brim plumb off of it."

Hewey dropped his hat on the floor, took one step sideways and hunkered down campfire style, his back against the flower-papered wall. The paper helped keep the wind out; the box-and-strip siding—one-by-twelve planks and one-by-four strips nailed over the joints—did not seal.

Eve tentatively touched her fingers against the coffeepot, testing its warmth. She pulled the hand quickly away. Hewey remembered it was her habit to keep the coffee drinkably warm all day. Like most farm and ranch wives of her place and time, she had rather have faced the devil in her nightgown than to be caught smoking a cigarette or drinking whisky. But she drank more coffee than Walter did. She fetched a flat-bottomed gray enamel cup from a plain open-fronted cabinet nailed to the wall. She turned with the coffeepot in her hand. She stopped at the sight of Hewey sitting on his spurs. "You're just like every cowboy I ever saw in my life," she scolded. "If I had a dozen rockin' chairs in the room, they'd still squat on the floor. You get up here and sit at the table and try to act like company! This is a house, not a cow camp!"

Hewey was quick to do what she told him. She spilled a little of the coffee in her nervousness. Instinctively Hewey rubbed his hand through it to wipe it up, then didn't know what to do with the wet hand. He dried it on his trousers, under the table and out of sight.

Eve poured herself some coffee but didn't sit at the table with him. She stared at him from her position in front of the stove. The mesquite wood was starting to crackle a little, though Hewey imagined the sound might be coming from Eve herself.

"Look, Eve," he said finally, "I got a little homesick. The boys got to weighin' on my mind. I just felt like I had to see them. A day or two, that's all, and I'll be gone."

Her blue eyes reminded him of a diamond, cutting glass. "You're lookin' thin, Hewey. Haven't you eaten regular?"

"I'm all right. I been batchin' all winter."

"Batchin'? No wonder. There's not many men can cook fit to feed a hound dog, and you're sure not one of the few. It'll take me a month to put some flesh on you."

"I don't figure to stay that long."

Her eyes lost their cutting edge. Though he knew it was unlikely, he thought he saw the beginning of a smile start pulling at the corners of her mouth. If so, she quickly got the situation under control. "You're here, Hewey, so you'll stay." It sounded like an order.

Hewey didn't know what to say, so he kept his mouth shut.

She demanded, "Where in the world did you go, Hewey? Leavin' like that, in the middle of the night? We just got up in the mornin' and found you gone. The boys cried, both of them. Walter didn't know what to think."

"You know why I left."

"You've made me live with a bad conscience. I knew you left because of what I said to you, and I couldn't tell them."

"What you told me was true, every bit of it. I didn't have no part in what you and Walter was tryin' to do here. Only thing for me to do was to leave and not come back." He looked down at his coffee cup, lifted it partway, then set it on the table again. "I stayed away as long as I could."

She took a couple of steps toward him. "Hewey Calloway, look at me!" He did. He had been watching her ever since he had come into the house. She said, "You helped us get this place. You helped us build this house and a lot of what else is here. You've got a right to stay as long as you want to."

He blinked. "That's not how you sounded when I left here."

"I was mad."

"I ain't changed any. You'll be mad again if I stay long."

She took another step. "I know. You can be an exasperatin' man, Hewey. I'll bet there's not three things in this whole world that we agree on, you and me. But the next time I get mad, you just go off out of my sight awhile and give me a little time. You don't have to stay gone for two years."

He sipped the coffee and found it bitter; it had been heating too long. But it was coffee, and that was the staff of life around most cow camps he had ever stayed in. He looked up at her. "I'll try not to make you mad atall. I'll try to keep my mouth shut."

She shook her head, a smile breaking across her face. "I wouldn't ask that much of Nature. I would as soon ask the snow to come in July and the sun to rise in the west." She leaned across the table and reached toward him. He flinched, not knowing what to expect. She took hold of his chin and turned his head a little, looking at the wound on his jaw.

"Just got it from a bronc," he lied before she could ask him. "It's a long ways from the heart."

"One of those broncs will kill you someday. It's time you settled down to somethin' steady and admitted your age."

That was what had started the quarrel the last time, and most of the others he could remember. Eve was always lecturing him about settling down, about responsibility, respectability, always trying to change him. The way Hewey saw it, the Lord had purposely made every person different. He could not understand why so many people were determined to thwart the Lord's work by making everyone the same.

He said, "I've never let a bronc kill me yet."

"*Yet.*" She repeated the word firmly for emphasis. "Let me see your hand . . . your right hand."

He extended it uncertainly. She took it, turned it over and looked at the palm, then gave his wrist a vigorous shake. "Well, it's not broken after all."

"What made you think it was?"

"You never did write a letter. For all anybody knew you could've been dead and buried somewhere."

At last Hewey began to relax, and he felt the birth pangs of a grin. "If I ever die, you'll know it right away. The Lord'll lift a heavy weight off of your soul, and you'll know I've flown."

"*Fell* is more like it. You hungry?" She answered her own question. "Of course you're hungry. You're always hungry. Well, you'll have to put up with stew tonight. Tomorrow's Sunday. Maybe I can fill you up on chicken."

"I'll be obliged for anything. You know me . . . there ain't much I won't eat."

"That," she said, "is gospel fact."

She started to turn away from him but stopped, looked intently at him, then leaned across the table and kissed him on the cheek. "Welcome home, Hewey."

His jaw sagged. If he lived to be a hundred and six, he would never figure out his sister-in-law. She could change quicker than the wind.

Occasionally on a cold winter night when he was being honest with himself, Hewey knew that if he had been the marrying sort, and if Walter hadn't seen Eve first, he might have married her. She had been pretty then, and sweeter than a fresh-stirred batch of wild-plum jelly. She still was, now and again, when she wasn't being overly protective of home and brood. At such times, if he didn't watch himself, his old feelings about her would rise up to confuse and discomfit him.

Fortunately he always got over them the first time her eyes snapped.

Eve opened one of the big warming ovens which extended forward over the cooking surface of the iron stove, taking their heat from the chimney that ran up through them. Inside, stacked on a tin plate, was leftover cornbread. "I can fix you some cornbread and sweetmilk right now if you'd like."

He shook his head. "I'll wait and eat with the rest of you. Wouldn't want to cheat Walter and the boys. They been workin'." He began to feel more at ease. He listened to the ax chopping wood and was glad Walter hadn't let him take that quick and easy way out.

A fat old gray tomcat wandered into the kitchen from one of the tiny bedrooms, pausing to stretch himself in the doorway, then studied Hewey with a look that came near being disdain. He ambled over and examined Hewey's hat lying on the floor, smelled around Hewey's boots, found nothing of particular interest and wandered back toward the open doorway again, pausing for one long backward look which confirmed his earlier low appraisal.

"I see you've still got the same independent cat," Hewey observed.

"Nothin' changes around here. We just get a little older, is all."

Hewey looked around the little kitchen, trying to find signs of anything new since he had left here. Everything seemed the same. Any improvements the family had made had been out on the place, not in the house they lived in. The table and chairs were plain and had already been old when Walter had bought them. The black iron stove had come out of a ranch's cow camp after the state had terminated the lease and put the land up for homesteading. The pots and pans, the utensils, the cheap porcelain dishes were remnants of a well-used set Eve had brought with her into the marriage. So far as Hewey could see, the only thing new was Eve's patent-medicine calendar advertising a remedy for woman's complaint. He wondered about that; he had never seen a medicine that stopped a woman from complaining. He noted one date—he had lost track and didn't know how long ago it was—pencil-marked with a small feminine X. He wondered idly what that was for.

Eve hadn't gained a pound of weight. She worked too hard to get fat, he had always thought, ignoring the fact that he had seen other country women who worked just as hard and got to weigh two hundred pounds by middle age. She wore a plain cotton dress she had made for herself from a large bolt of blue and white tiny-checkered cloth. She had bartered for the cloth years ago, trading some eggs and old boiling hens. She had been sewing dresses off of this same bolt for six or seven years to Hewey's certain knowledge. They always looked alike, differing only in age and extent of wear.

Wind and sun had been unkind to Eve's complexion, though she wore a big slat bonnet to protect her face when she went outdoors. That faded bonnet, ribbed with long thin strips of cardboard and made from the same cloth as the dress, was hanging from a nail near the door. Despite the sun's work on her skin, Eve's features were still small and fine as they had been the day she and Walter had married.

He said, "That Tommy has growed like a weed. I thought he was Cotton when I first seen him. He looks finer than a Morgan colt."

"He's a good boy," Eve replied, stoking the burning wood and putting in another chunk of mesquite. "I don't say that just because he's mine."

Hewey looked out the window, hoping. "I can't hardly wait for Cotton to get here. How's *he* been?"

Eve didn't answer for a minute. "Fine. Just fine." When she turned he saw that her lips had tightened.

Uneasy, he demanded, "Somethin' the matter with Cotton?"

"Nothin'," she said, suddenly defensive. "He's fine." Hewey stared at her, unsatisfied, until she shrugged and sat down across the table from him, her shoulders pinched. "I don't know. There's probably nothin' wrong with Cotton; it's probably somethin' wrong with *me*. I just don't understand him anymore."

She picked up her coffee cup, but she set it down again, the coffee untouched. It was probably cold anyway. "I thought all we had to do was to raise the boys in a good Christian home and they'd turn out just like us. But Cotton has gotten away from us somehow. He's different."

Hewey frowned. "You tryin' to say he's like *me?*"

Eve stared back at him. "He does have some of your ways. He's restless and all   enough to scare me, rememberin' *you*. But he's got other ways that are his own. He's not the same as us and not the same as you either. He's *Cotton*."

"He been in trouble?"

"No, nothin' like that. He works hard, never troubles anybody but us, and he doesn't intend to do even that. He did run off once for a couple of days . . . talked the freighter Blue Hannigan into givin' him a ride to Midland . . . told him he was on an errand for us. He came back on his own. Never explained much . . . just said he wanted to go and see one of those automobiles he had read about. Said he didn't ask us because he figured we'd say *no*."

"Would you have?"

"Certainly. A boy has got no business runnin' off to a big city like Midland by himself. Must be two . . . maybe three thousand people livin' over there. No tellin' what kind of sinful goin's-on a boy might see."

Hewey agreed. "Sure is a big town, all right."

"He said you told him once you'd seen an automobile in Midland."

"I did?" Hewey frowned again, looking for criticism but unable to read the thought behind her eyes.

She said, "I blamed you at first, fillin' the boys' heads with a bunch of foolishness. That was easier than to blame myself. I likely bore down on him too hard, too many times. It's a thing I do too easy, and then I don't know how to back away." She looked intently at Hewey. "Maybe it's good you came when you did. You always had a special touch with the boys. You could always reach them in a way that I couldn't, or their daddy couldn't."

"I'll talk to him."

"It'd be better if you got *him* to talk to *you*. Cotton doesn't open up to us much anymore."

The wood-chopping stopped. Walter came to the door, carrying an armload of dried mesquite cut to stove-burning length. He glanced in before opening the screen, then stopped again for a moment just inside before proceeding to the woodbox and dropping the wood carefully so that it lay lengthwise, not in a scrambled manner. He turned and studied his wife and Hewey with a little apprehension. When he saw no quarrel between them he began to smile.

"See there, Hewey? I told you she wouldn't bite."

Eve built up the fire. She pulled a pot of stew and another of beans out onto the stove's flat top to warm for supper. The heat of the kitchen became oppressive. Hewey pushed the screen door open, walked down the steps and paused to stretch the kinks out of his arms and legs. He rolled and lighted a cigarette, his first since he had gotten here. Looking to the barn, and beyond, he saw that Tommy had turned the milk cow back into the pasture for the night. This late, she wouldn't stray far before bedding down. She would be at the gate long before milking time in the morning, bawling plaintively for her recently born calf, kept separated from her in a small pen so it wouldn't take all the milk. The work stock had also edged away into the pasture and were cropping the green spring grass they had missed all day in the field. Biscuit followed them but remained to one side, a little aloof, especially from the burro.

Hewey heard the rattle of trace chains and looked to the northwest. In the dusk he made out the shape of a wagon. The black dog heard too. He came out from under the house, gave Hewey another tentative check, for he hadn't accepted him as belonging, then went trotting to meet the wagon, his tail busy. A country dog of any intelligence knew the sound of his own people's wagons and could usually tell when a strange one was coming. The same was true for his people's horses, the ones they rode most often. A dog was usually either wagging its tail or barking while humans still strained their eyes, trying to see who was coming.

It was too small for a freight wagon, so this had to be Cotton; he was the only one still out. Hewey strolled slowly to the barn, timing his pace to get there when the wagon did. He found it difficult to believe that tall boy on the wagon seat was his nephew. Lord, what a difference two years could make! Hewey exclaimed, "I'll be damned!" Talking to oneself was a habit many a cowboy developed when he was alone a lot. The sound of a human voice was a reassurance of sorts, even one's own.

Cotton didn't see him at first; he was busy maneuvering the wagon under a brush arbor where it was kept for some protection from the elements. Hewey glanced up at the darkening but cloudless sky and saw no reason to expect any trouble from the elements tonight. Shedding the wagon was a good habit to instill in a boy, though; it taught him responsibility. If he shirked the chore when he saw no need in it, he might find it easy to shirk when the need arose.

The boy handled the two mules with firm hands, backing them carefully to put the wagon into place. They were young mules—green broncs, really—and required a lot of patience. Cotton talked to them, alternating between soft approval and sharp words of scorn that Hewey hadn't heard him use before. Twice the wagon hubbed a post, and Cotton had to move the mules forward, then back again. They worked with much twitching of long ears, much chomping at the bits. Hewey guessed they belonged to Alvin Lawdermilk, and that Cotton was training them for pay or trade. He watched with satisfaction as the wagon at last rolled into its proper place. Cotton had always had a special aptitude at anything done with the hands, whether the tool be a wrench or a pair of leather reins. From the time he had been seven or eight, he could take a little lumber, a bucket of nails, a saw and hammer and build anything he set his mind to.

Hewey would not have admitted it to the Lord Jesus, should He come and ask, but Cotton had always been his favorite of the two boys by just a thin edge. Perhaps that was natural, Cotton being the first-born, the lone recipient of a bachelor uncle's adoration and hopes for two full years before Tommy showed up. By virtue of his extra age, Cotton had been the first to try almost everything —the first to ride a horse, the first to pick up a rope, the first to fall off of the barn. By the time Tommy came along to do the same things, the new was gone.

The boys had no grandparents to spoil them, so Uncle Hewey had served that function. Riding in at intervals, doing his mischief, telling them stories that would never have stood the scrutiny of a court, playing hell with family discipline, he would then ride cheerfully away to greener pastures without having to assume any responsibility for the chaos he had wrought. He had all the privileges of a grandparent but was saddled with only half the age.

Hewey spoke as the boy hopped down. "Howdy, Cotton."

He expected Cotton to come running with open arms, as Tommy had done, and he braced himself for the jolt. He saw the surprise, the quick flash of an unguarded smile. But suddenly, unaccountably, the smile was gone. Cotton stood by the front wheel, holding the lines uncertainly. His face was sober and reserved.

"I see you finally got home."

Hewey had always found it easy to talk to the boys. It had always seemed to him that their thoughts and his ran along the same trail, possibly because they hadn't had time to grow up and he hadn't had the inclination. He stared nonplused at his nephew and could not bring up an intelligent word to say. "I'm home," he replied, like an echo. He waited in vain for Cotton to come to him.

Always before, Cotton had come running, joyously, unrestrained, with laughter and shouting and love. Now it was Hewey, finally, who went to Cotton. He was unexpectedly nervous, as ill at ease as he had been with Eve. He wanted to put his arms around Cotton and hug him as in other times. He held back, watching for some sign in the boy's eyes.

All he got was that stare, not hostile but not warm. Hewey awkwardly thrust out his hand, as he might do in meeting a stranger. "It's good to see you, button."

Cotton took his hand. His grip was strong, and hard, but it was also polite and somehow formal.

"I'd better unharness the mules, Uncle Hewey."

Hewey watched him in uncertain silence, wishing to help but not sure his help was wanted. He leaned his back against the wagon wheel. For a moment or two he felt cold, like in that lonesome shack high up in the snows of the Sangre de Cristos.

Walter came to the barn as Cotton was pouring out oats for the mules. "Daddy," Cotton said, "I didn't finish. Those mules kept runnin' away. I thought sure they'd wreck the old wagon."

Walter frowned. "I'd hoped . . . well, we can't help it now. We'll need everything to be ready for them folks when they come tomorrow afternoon. Your mother won't like it, but I reckon you'd best stay home from church and finish the job in the mornin'. You ain't so sinful that missin' church one Sunday will condemn you to the fires."

Hewey spoke up. "I'll stay and help Cotton. I don't think the Lord will miss me."

A smile tugged at Walter's mouth. "Miss you? If you showed up in church the Lord would probably wonder who in hell you are."

Cotton said, "I can handle it myself. I'd be through already, only those mules . . ."

Walter replied, "I know you could do the job alone. But let Uncle Hewey help you; it won't take you much longer. It'll give you-all a chance to visit."

Hewey nodded eagerly. "We got a lot to talk about."

Cotton said nothing, but his eyes indicated that he doubted it.

A month earlier it would have been too cold to sit in the front yard and talk in the full moon's light. But the slight nip of the May night was invigorating after the heat of the afternoon. They had carried chairs out from the kitchen and set them on the ground because there was no porch. A porch was often a luxury, added to a utilitarian frame house in this part of the country only when the family reached a modicum of financial security and the wolf no longer howled by the door. The breeze was light, barely enough to rustle the new leaves of the big chinaberry trees under which Hewey rocked the straight-legged chair, flirting with a backward fall.

Walter asked Hewey about various people they had known in years past, people he hoped Hewey might have seen. Hewey told him of those he had encountered, repeating and embellishing a little on any wild gossip he had heard. Tommy asked question after question about the towns Hewey had visited, the wild cattle he had chased, the wild horses he had ridden. Hewey's answers were patterned to fit what he thought Tommy wanted to hear. The cows ran faster and the horses pitched harder than had ever been known by most mortal men.

Eve asked him about the clothes the women were wearing in the towns, and Hewey was stumped. "They was wearin' dresses," he acknowledged. "If they hadn't been, I reckon I'd of noticed."

"But what kind of dresses? What did they look like?"

"Well, they was of all colors, and long enough to cover. That's about all I can tell you."

"What about the hats?"

"Well, all the hats I seen were on top of their heads. Had feathers, some of them. Bird feathers."

Every so often Hewey glanced at the yellow glow of lamplight in the kitchen window. Cotton sat in there by himself, reading a book at the table. Hewey kept thinking he would eventually come out in curiosity to hear the stories, but he didn't.

Walter said, "I didn't think to tell you, Hewey, but old Snort Yarnell came by last summer, hopin' to find you here."

Hewey sat the chair down abruptly, smiling as a hundred pleasant memories came flooding over him. "Old Snort! I wisht I'd seen him. How'd he look?"

"Same as ever. He gets a little older along, and that's the only change."

"Still wilder'n a peach-orchard boar, I expect. He sure is a good old boy."

Eve put in sharply, "Good for *nothin'* old boy. A tramp, a chuckline rider. I'll bet in his whole life he never did three honest days' work hand-runnin'."

"But he knows how to enjoy life. That's more than most people do. Old Grady Welch used to run with him a lot. Was Grady with him?"

Walter looked at the ground. "I don't reckon you've heard. Grady Welch is dead. Horse throwed him off and stepped on him."

The moment of happy memories passed. Sadness pressed down on Hewey. "You sure about that, Walter?"

Walter nodded. "Snort was with him when it happened, out in the Davis Mountains. He helped bury him."

Hewey shook his head. "Damn, but I hate to hear it."

Eve said, "It gets them all if they stay out there and court it long enough. That's why I wish you'd find a place and settle down, Hewey."

Hewey didn't answer. At length he asked, "Eve, you still got some coffee on the stove?"

"Yes, I'll go get you a cup."

"No, you stay where you're at. I'll fetch it."

He walked into the kitchen and stopped to look at Cotton, sitting at the plain pine table, the lamplight falling on an open book. Cotton nodded but said nothing. Hewey ventured, "I've done a right-smart of readin' myself. You get lots of time for it in a batchin' camp. Have you read *Ivanhoe* yet?"

Cotton shook his head.

Hewey said, "It's got lots of good fightin' and killin' in it. You'd enjoy it."

He received no response. He stepped closer, trying to read over Cotton's shoulder. "What's that you're so interested in?"

"The theory of internal combustion."

Hewey blinked. "What you goin' to bust?"

"Internal combustion is what makes automobiles run."

Hewey blinked again. "Do you understand that stuff?"

Cotton didn't look up from the book. "No, but I'd like to."

Hewey poured an enameled cup full of coffee. He stalled a little, hoping Cotton would volunteer to say something. But Cotton kept reading. Hewey went back outside and sat down in his chair again, rocking it faster than before.

Walter said, "I been thinkin' about old Homer Ganss, up in the Territory, and some of the wild stunts he used to pull. He was a lot like Snort and Grady . . . and you. I don't reckon you came across him by some accident?"

Hewey slowed the chair and warmed to the conversation. "Not by accident. I made it a point to go and stay with him a couple of weeks last year. Salty as he ever was; ain't changed a particle, only his hair is thinner, and he's short a couple of front teeth, and he's got a stiff leg where a horse rolled on him. Gettin' a shade fat, too. Ain't changed a bit. You'd know him a mile off." Hewey launched into a story, only modestly exaggerated, about their riding into a Territory town with a string of Homer's green-broken ponies to trade to the Indians. They had gotten into a horse-race bet and lost all the ponies but had such an uproarious celebration with the Indians that it had seemed cheap at the price.

Eve was incredulous. She had heard plenty of Hewey's stories, but this one was outrageous enough to be true. "You're tellin' us that he threw away a whole year's work, just like that, on one horse race?"

"He didn't throw it away, he *bet* it. He'll have another string of ponies to sell this year. And you ought to've seen that horse race!" He began to describe it in all its thrills and spills, adding two or three to bring them up to even measure.

Walter laughed and slapped his knee. "I swear, Hewey, that sounds just like you and old Homer. I wisht I could've been there."

"I wisht you had been too. I tell you, Walter, you're goin' to have to take yourself a vacation off of this place and go on a trip with me one of these days. It'll do you a world of good."

"I know it would, and I'm just liable to do it."

Eve cut a sharp glance at her husband, then back at Hewey. "Walter," she said firmly, "we've got a long day ahead of us. I think it's high time we all went to bed."

III

Cotton hadn't said three words since he and Hewey had hitched the half-broken mules in the first light of a cool dawn and had set out over the hill for the recently acquired French place. In the bed of the wagon rattled the carpentry and digging tools Cotton had judged he would need to complete restoration of the windmill and have everything ready for the raising. Also carried were heavy wrenches and grips, well ropes, block and tackle.

Windmilling was not a horseman's type of work.

Daylight and the fresh dampness of the May morning had brought the cattle out to graze. They were gentle, a far cry from the twistified cattle Hewey was used to. They paid only momentary attention to the creaking wagon. A calf approached in curiosity, then turned tail and ran back to its mother as a wheel dropped into a hole and made everything in the wagon bed clatter in protest.

Hewey tried to bait Cotton into conversation but had only sporadic and short-lived success. He pointed to a mottley faced cow whose horns were beginning to show rough circles at their base, an indication she was moving past what might charitably be termed middle age. "I remember that old sister. She was in the bunch I brought out for your daddy from over on the Concho."

Cotton only nodded. Hewey went on, "I remember she had a good heifer calf, kind of a roan with a white face. She still in the herd?"

Cotton made the longest speech Hewey had drawn out of him all morning. "We've still got her."

"She raise a calf every year?"

Cotton nodded.

Hewey could see he was losing ground. Cotton kept his gaze on the dim trail of wheel-crushed dry grass from last year; the new green grass was attempting to heal it over. Hewey gave up awhile and studied the open, rolling country. It wasn't the best grassland he had ever seen, by a long way, but he knew it was deceptive. Here just to the east of the Pecos River the land seemed to suffer for rain more often than not, and grass tended to be of the short varieties, not the tall, thick growth that dominated farther east in Texas or up in the Indian Nations, especially the Osage. But this was strong grass. In a hard year a cow might walk herself half to death trying to find enough to fill her belly, but what she found was well supplied with minerals and nutrients. If she never got fat, at least she stayed hardy. Back east he had seen cows starve with tall weak grass tickling their bellies.

Farming, now, was a different game of poker. They ought not to allow a plow within a hundred miles of here, he thought, unless it was passing through on a freight train with the doors sealed. He had heard it said that when a man traveled west in Texas he lost an inch of average annual rainfall for every fifty miles. If this figure was correct, he could be in the red by the time he made El Paso. It seemed to Hewey that God had already put this country to its proper use without anybody's help. Grass was what it raised best, and it ought to be left that way. But this was not a popular time to be expressing such a sentiment. In fashionable circles it was considered nonprogressive, the outmoded defense of the old-line free-range cattlemen like C. C. Tarpley who didn't want to give up private possession of land that rightfully belonged to all the citizens of Texas. Anyone who spoke such a sentiment was allying himself with the forces of monopoly and greed, the reformers shouted. He was setting himself against progress and the uplifting of the common man. He was to be shunned by all good Christian soldiers dedicated to God's work.

Hewey had already seen many of God's good common men starve off of the plow and desert the land they had broken out in His name. The dried fields would scour and blow away in the hot west wind, leaving a sore that wouldn't heal in a hundred years.

"You oughtn't to ever plow it," he said, unintentionally putting his thoughts into words.

Cotton was caught off balance, his thoughts elsewhere. "Hunh?"

"The homestead law . . . I say it's wrong to make a man plow out a field to hold his claim. He ought not to rip up land that God has already planted to grass and handed to him as a gift."

Cotton's shell seemed to crack a little. "You better not say that where Mama can hear it."

Hewey nodded. "There's a lot she don't agree with me about."

"She says leavin' good land in grass is slothful, that the Lord wants us to cultivate it and make it blossom like the rose."

Hewey grunted. "Lots of people talk about what the Lord wants. Wonder how many has ever asked Him?"

"You could've asked Him yourself if you'd gone to church with the rest of them this mornin'."

"I don't have to go to church to hunt for Him. I see Him around me every day, everywhere I look."

Cotton studied his uncle with a growing interest. "That sounds like pantheism, like the preacher is always warnin' us about."

"Is that somethin' like the Catholics?"

"Must be pretty bad, because the preacher is sure down on it."

"Only religion I ever had was the same as yours. I was ducked for a Baptist. But the water didn't soak very deep. I taken up my old and willful ways again pretty soon."

"Some churchgoin' might be good for you, then."

"I always liked God better when I found Him outdoors. He always seemed too big to fit into a little-bitty cramped-up church house."

Cotton fell silent again. Hewey changed the subject, talking about things he understood far better than religion, but he seemed unable to draw Cotton far out of that protective shell. He tried to make it appear he was watching the country, while his eyes kept cutting back to Cotton. At length he said, "We used to understand each other pretty good."

"I've got a little older, Uncle Hewey."

"So have I."

"On you it don't ever seem to make any difference."

Hewey felt a cutting edge in Cotton's voice, a reproach he could not understand. "Button, if I've said somethin' that hurt you . . ."

The boy shrugged and turned his attention back to the bronc mules. "It's been a long time. You probably forgot what you said as soon as you were done sayin' it. There's no use pokin' over dead ashes."

Hewey rubbed his left hand over a knocked-down knuckle on his right hand, relic of a bad day of bronc stomping that had netted him no more than a dollar at best. "Button, I never said a cross word to you in all your life. I've never raised my voice at you."

"And never lied to me?"

Hewey kept rubbing the hand. It didn't pain him, but somehow he wished it did, as if pain might in some way compensate for whatever hurt he had caused his nephew. "I've never lied to you. Well, never anything serious. Oh, I might've stretched the truth a time or two, tellin' you stories, but never anything to hurt you or lead you wrong. I've never meant you anything but good."

"You made me a promise once, but I expect you turned right around and forgot it. You sure as hell never kept it."

It jarred Hewey a little, hearing Cotton use a word like *hell*. Sure, Hewey used it himself, but he was thirty-six years old. Times were changing, it looked like. "I reckon I'm guilty, since you say so. But I sure don't remember any promise I never kept."

"You knew how bad I wanted to see a real automobile. You promised me you was goin' to take me someplace where they had them, and you was even goin' to fix it up to get me a ride in one. Then one mornin' I woke up and you had left."

Hewey didn't remember. "Any time I ever made you a promise, button, I intended to keep it. But sometimes things come up . . ."

"Things *always* come up with you."

He didn't see any gain in telling Cotton of the sharp scolding Eve had given him about his bad influence on the boys. So far as he knew, even Walter had never learned about that. "I didn't go to hurt you."

"You told me you had seen a bunch of automobiles in Midland. After you left and didn't take me yourself, I made up my mind to go anyway. Went over there with Blue Hannigan's wagons. There wasn't an automobile in that town, Uncle Hewey. Not one. Folks said they hardly ever saw one come through."

Hewey frowned. "I don't know why you're so dead set on seein'

58

one of them devil-cars. I've seen a many of them, and there ain't nothin' to them. They smell like a sick skunk. They cause folks so much grief that I don't see how they can hold out much longer. Soon as the last one has run off into a ditch, that'll be the end of the automobile. You ain't really missed very much."

"You're wrong, Uncle Hewey. They ain't hardly gotten started yet. Pretty soon you'll be seein' people drive a hundred or a hundred and fifty miles in a single day. Show me the horse that can do that."

"There ain't any real call for it. I never been in a place I hated so much that I had to get a hundred miles from it in one day."

"You ever ridden in an automobile?"

Hewey hadn't. Another time he might have made up a story, but he sensed that this was a time for being truthful. Anyway, his experience was too limited to feed his imagination much. The noise and the smoke had always discouraged him from getting very close to one when its motor was running. He had always been sure it was going to explode any minute.

He said, "Midland ain't that much of a town anyway. One of these days I'll take you with me and we'll make us a trip to some big place like San Angelo, or maybe even Fort Worth. I'll bet you'll see lots of automobiles there. I might even take you for a ride in one."

Cotton's eyes narrowed again. "Maybe you ought to save back your promises for Tommy. He's still young enough to believe anything."

Hewey frowned, studying his nephew. He had never noticed before how much Cotton looked like his mother.

The windmill appeared almost ready to raise. The tail section lay on the ground, as yet unattached, but the big cypress wheel was mounted to the thirty-foot wooden tower. The top was propped up off of the ground by a rough but strong sawhorse fashioned from heavy mesquite limbs. The wheel and the tail had originally been red, but many pieces had been replaced by new lumber painstakingly sawed and trimmed to fit.

Hewey said, "We ought to paint it before we raise it up."

"It's cypress. It'll stand the weather."

"But it looks bad, some painted, some raw thataway. Looks like a farmer outfit."

"That's what this is."

Hewey would never have admitted it. "A windmill stands way up there, and people can see it from a long ways off. A man ought to want to dress it up, same as he dresses himself up to go to church."

"This is a long ways from church."

"Not from mine." He looked across the horizon and pointed to a distant tower. "Even old C.C. takes pride in the looks of his windmills. You'll notice they're painted, every one."

"C. C. Tarpley's got money in the bank. In fact, he's got the bank. All we have down there is a big note comin' due early in the fall. I reckon the folks'll buy paint when they've burned the note."

Cotton jumped down and began unhitching the team so they could not spook and run off with the loaded wagon. Hewey tried to help him but found Cotton aggressively self-sufficient. He began unloading the tools from the wagon instead. He said, "I'll help you with that tail section, and we'll have this thing fixed up before you know it."

"I can get it," Cotton said. "I had figured on comin' by myself anyway." Perhaps he saw the disappointment Hewey tried not to show. "I reckon you can dig the holes for a pair of brace posts that we'll need to keep the tower from slippin' when we commence to raise it. I've already staked the places."

Digging holes had never been Hewey's favorite part of the cowboy trade, but neither was windmilling in general. He liked windmills for drinking cool water from, not for greasing or repairing. But he guessed digging holes was better than being shut out altogether. He dragged the posthole diggers from the splintered bed of the wagon. He grimaced, gripping the slick handles. It was not his habit to carry gloves. He knew he would work blisters on his hands before the morning was out.

Well, it probably wasn't any worse than forking hay to cows in the Sangre de Cristos snow. At least here he wouldn't take a chill.

The hole had been drilled by a professional windmill man, and the big steel casing extended above the level of the ground. Centered within the casing and standing a little higher was a three-inch pipe through which the strokes of the wheel high above would draw the water. A set of heavy wooden blocks or collars rested on top of the outer casing and tightly gripped the smaller inside pipe to keep it from slipping down to the bottom of the hole. The tower, when raised, would be centered above the pipe. Hewey took it for granted that Cotton hadn't overlooked a thing. It was in his nature to be thorough about mechanical devices.

The well seemed to be in a slight depression. Hewey remarked, "It would've been handier to've had it drilled on higher ground. You could've gotten better gravity flow to your tank without raisin' the pipe so high."

Cotton frowned. "Daddy let Julio Valdez witch the well. He said this is where the water was. Said it would be sweet water. So this is where Daddy had the hole drilled."

"I take it you don't believe in water witchin'."

"I've read everything I can find about science. I've never seen anything that said a man could walk around with a forked stick in his hand and tell you what's fifty feet under the ground."

"You *did* get water."

"I don't know if it's sweet."

Hewey had never read much about science. He was satisfied that the world by Aught Six had already progressed about as far as it needed to go. People had already invented just about everything that the public could afford to buy. To him, water witching was a science. He had never had the *gift* himself, but he had watched other people do it, and he had seen the end of a forked peach switch turn downward as surely as if some unseen hand had forced it.

He supposed if Cotton had read it in a book he would believe it.

Hewey kicked one of the stakes aside and vigorously attacked the ground with the diggers. After a few inches the ground seemed to counterattack. Presently he looked at the palms and saw small red spots rising. These would turn to blisters bye and bye and probably break open. "My hands never was made to fit the handles of these *idiot sticks,*" he said, motioning toward the diggers.

Cotton glanced up from a heavy bolt he was tightening. "I had figured on diggin' the holes myself. Go sit in the shade if you've a mind to."

There was no shade, unless Hewey were to get under the

wagon. Once this had been a cattle-watering place for a few years, the tank would probably become surrounded by a growth of mesquite trees, sprouting from the manure. But as of yet the nearby prairie was innocent of plants taller than a broomweed.

"I wasn't complainin', just makin' conversation." He went back to the digging and didn't stop again until he saw that Cotton needed help lifting the tail section into place. He held it firmly while Cotton bolted it. He welcomed the respite, even for a bit of heavy lifting. He studied the intricate combination of wood and machinery that made up the mill's wheel section. It was fourteen feet in diameter. "You must've had to rebuild the bigger part of this. Did you do it all by yourself?"

Cotton nodded. "It got damaged pretty bad when the wind blew the tower over. Old Armbruster didn't have it anchored good. Otherwise Daddy couldn't have bought it in the first place. There's not much to it when you know how. Just a couple of days' work with the forge and the anvil, and a saw."

Hewey couldn't have done it. He would bet Walter couldn't either. Well, everybody to his own way of getting a backache. Hewey's was horses.

By the time he finished the second hole his hands burned from two blisters that had sprouted and broken against the wooden handles. He said nothing because sympathy would not help against the fire, and he reasoned that he would get none from Cotton anyway. He glanced up toward the sun. "Don't you reckon it's time we started thinkin' about fixin' us a bite to eat?"

Several paces beyond the windmill was a shallow fire pit that Cotton had used on other days. Hewey gathered up dry mesquite that Cotton or the well driller had brought here, and some scrap pieces of kindling left over from the windmill-repairing. He placed them in the pit and built a small fire. While the wood was working its way toward a strong red glow, he poured a generous measure of ground coffee into a fire-blackened bucket and then filled the bucket nearly to the top with water out of a wooden keg in the wagon bed.

"Hell of a note," he remarked. "Got us a brand-new well and we haul drinkin' water from the house."

He stirred no response from Cotton. Hewey poked the burning

wood into shape, then set the bucket on top of it. He knew a watched pot would never boil, but he watched it anyway to be sure the burning sticks did not collapse and tip the bucket over.

Other than mumbling quietly to himself when something didn't seem to fit or a nut didn't want to take hold of a thread, Cotton had said little all morning. Hewey had started three or four times to tell him of adventures, but Cotton betrayed no interest. Several good stories were stillborn. Hewey would have to save them for Tommy, he supposed, if he could remember them.

When he thought the coffee had boiled long enough he used a forked stick to lift the bucket by its bail and set it back from the fire. From the wagon he fetched a cotton sack Eve had partially filled with cold biscuits and strips of bacon fried at breakfast.

"Chuck!" Hewey called. "It ain't much, but it'll hold till the chicken."

Cotton's hands were hopelessly greasy from handling the working parts of the mill. He rubbed all he could onto an old gunny sack while Hewey poured coffee into two bent and tarnished tin cups. Cotton's hands were still black.

Hewey shrugged. "A little honest dirt ain't goin' to ruin a man's digestion. I reckon I've eaten a ton of it, one time and another."

Cotton broke a biscuit and folded a couple of strips of bacon inside, then closed the biscuit and mashed it down. While he ate, his gaze remained fastened to the mill. Hewey could see pride in his eyes. As Cotton was finishing the first biscuit, Hewey fixed him another with three strips of bacon. "Eat it up. You've done good."

Cotton's enthusiasm got the better of his reserve. "It's goin' to work just fine, Uncle Hewey. It's goin' to be as good as a brand-new one."

"Better, I'll bet. People that work in them factories, they don't take care like the man who's goin' to use it. They just throw it together and slap it in the crate, and they know that's the last they'll see of it."

"I'd like to work in one of those factories awhile. Not makin' windmills, maybe, but makin' engines, or maybe even automobiles. Somethin' that runs and has a life of its own."

"And be cooped up inside a buildin' with all that smoke and all that noise? I couldn't stay in there for thirty minutes."

"It's what's comin', Uncle Hewey."

"I sure hope not."

"They're even talkin' about buildin' flyin' machines. Speed is what everybody wants today."

"In a horse, yes. A good old cow pony can give a man all the speed he ever needs. I've had some give me a right smart more than I wanted."

"I don't expect Mama and Daddy to understand. They're livin' in the past, and happy enough with it. But you've always been the restless one, Uncle Hewey. You've always been the one who wanted to see somethin' new and try what other people hadn't already done. I'd think you'd be excited over what's happenin' around us today."

Hewey sipped carefully on the hot coffee. "Sure, I always liked to see new country, new people. But everywhere I went I used to feel like I could deal with whatever came up. It was me against a horse, or me against a bunch of cattle, or me against another man. I knew how to take a-hold.

"But now, lots of places, it's different. I been to some big towns. I've seen them automobiles chuggin' up and down, scarin' hell out of the horses, leavin' a trail of smoke that'd choke a bay mule. I've seen a man set down at a telephone in Fort Worth, Texas, and talk to somebody way off at the Kansas City stockyards just like he was in the next room. I've seen streets so strung up with wires that you couldn't see the sky through, hardly. I don't understand it. I can't take a-hold of it. It scares me so bad I can't hardly wait to saddle up and get back into the open country where you've got to look a man in the face to talk to him."

"It ought to excite you, Uncle Hewey."

"It might excite *you,* but it scares *me.*" He nodded toward the reclining Eclipse. "That windmill there, that's as complicated a piece of machinery as ever I want to fool with."

"The world is movin' faster all the time. You either go on with it or you get left behind. You never was one to get left behind."

"Because I always looked forward to the place I was goin' to. But I don't look forward to this world *you're* talkin' about."

"I'm goin' to be a part of it. I want to help build it."

Hewey frowned. "Well, I hope you like it when you get it finished."

He hated to get to his feet. He had finally broken Cotton out of his silence. Maybe from now on things would go a little easier between them. He flung the dregs of his coffee into the greening grass and pitched his cup into the wagon bed.

Cotton stood up and looked toward home. "We'll have it ready for them pretty soon. They can come any time they take the notion."

Hewey rubbed his hands; they hurt a little. The bacon grease would probably help in the long run, but its saltiness brought the fire back. "Don't take a lot of people to raise a windmill."

"The raisin' is just an excuse for everybody to visit and enjoy themselves. First chance we've had since spring came."

Hewey walked to the prone tower and slapped a hand against one of the six-by-six legs. "What say me and you raise this mill ourselves? When they get here they won't have to do anything but party."

Cotton's mouth dropped open. "You don't mean that."

"It'd give them a dandy surprise."

"It might give *us* one. Just us two, and a pair of bronc mules . . . If the least thing went wrong we'd wreck the windmill and have all this work to do over again."

"The odds are with us."

Cotton stared at him with exasperation. There was finality in his voice, the way Hewey had often heard it from Eve. "They're right about you, Uncle Hewey."

"How's that?"

"They say you've got no more responsibility than a one-eyed jack rabbit. You won't ever grow up; you'll just grow old. If you live."

Hewey shrugged. "No harm meant. Just a notion I had, was all."

Cotton said nothing more as he worked his way around the mill, checking the bolts for tightness, fondling it as if it were a pet he had just saved from harm.

That's always the way with me, Hewey thought darkly. *Take one step forward and two backward. Almost had him there for a little bit.* He took out his frustration on the posthole diggers.

He noticed a lone rider approaching, moving in a sensible slow trot, not pushing his horse. Hewey squinted, trying to identify him. Cotton only glanced, then went back to his work, evidently satisfied that this was the vanguard of the tower-raising crew.

Hewey said, "I believe that's Wes Wheeler. He still sheriff here?"

Cotton took a fresh look. "That's him, and he is. I didn't know he was interested in raisin' windmills."

Hewey had usually been able to recognize law officers about as far as he could see them. They had an intangible manner of standing, of walking, of riding, an official presence that gave them away. Hewey instinctively always classified them as one of two types, usually on first sight: good ones and bad ones. He rarely altered his initial opinion.

Wes Wheeler was one he had always put in the *good* category. He didn't go around arbitrarily telling people what to do or trying to run their lives with the excuse that it was for their own good. He recognized that his main function was to keep the peace, and he seldom raised much hell in doing it. He never bothered a man unless he was convinced that a little bothering was going to benefit the community.

Wheeler was a big man who needed a big horse. This one was a stocky dun, still shedding off the coarse winter hair. Wheeler dismounted, keeping his horse between himself and Hewey. That struck Hewey as being a little odd; he decided it was an old habit, a holdover from rougher days when a lawman occasionally needed a shield. Wheeler had cut his eyeteeth in times like that; they had left their mark on him. Wheeler came on afoot, leading the dun horse. Hewey walked out to meet him, and they shook hands firmly.

"Good to see you, Wes."

The sheriff nodded. "Heard at church that you was back."

"Got here last evenin'. Sorry I missed church."

"Guess it won't hurt you to miss it once in a while." The sheriff spoke to Cotton, congratulating him on what appeared to be a dadjimmed good job of rebuilding the windmill. But his eyes kept shifting back to Hewey.

"Hearin' you was back got me to thinkin' about an odd letter I got in yesterday's mail. You have any trouble on the way home, Hewey?"

Hewey shook his head. "Biscuit acted like he was fixin' to come up lame, is all."

"That ain't the kind of trouble I mean. You didn't by any chance have some difficulty with a city marshal back up the way?"

Hewey blinked. "Oh, that! It wasn't no trouble, really. We just had a little difference of opinion. It was over with in a minute."

The sheriff's eyes turned sad. "I got a letter yesterday from the sheriff up there. I imagine he wrote to every sheriff in this part of the country."

Hewey shook his head. "It just happened a few days ago. And you already got a letter about it? The U.S. mails are a wonder to behold."

Wheeler said, "Seems like, by this letter, that they're lookin' for a cowboy by the name of Hugh Holloway."

Hewey mused, "That marshal never did get my name right."

"They got this Holloway charged with attempted murder."

Cotton set down his wrench and stood listening, eyes and mouth wide open.

Hewey said, "That's layin' it on mighty thick. I didn't try to murder him. I didn't even hit him, hardly, just a little tap on the nose to keep him from pistol-whippin' me again. It was a big nose; I couldn't hardly miss." He considered. "Maybe Biscuit stepped on him, too. Things was a little confused there."

The sheriff walked over to the remnants of the fire and looked in the coffee bucket. He was disappointed to find it empty.

Hewey said, "We got the makin's. We'll fix you another pot."

The sheriff shook his head. "I reckon you better tell me all about it, Hewey."

Hewey told him what little there was, about the marshal shouting at him for riding down a residential street, and about him trying to hit Hewey up beside the head with a six-shooter that must have weighed thirty-seven pounds.

Wheeler frowned. "Letter says you taken the gun away from him, and that you ought to be considered armed and dangerous."

Hewey shrugged. "If they ever clean out the water trough down there by the railroad tracks they'll find that pistol. I throwed it away the first chance I got. I always figured one way to never need a gun was to never carry one around."

The sheriff's eyes were half closed, but he was a long way from being asleep. "You sure you've told me everything, Hewey?"

Hewey nodded. "It didn't amount to nothin', hardly."

Wheeler critically studied the mark on Hewey's jaw. "He done that to you just for ridin' on the wrong street?"

"He seemed like he was a little overwrought."

Wheeler said tightly, "The man was probably descended from a long line of bachelors."

Cotton ventured closer to the two men. Incredulously he demanded, "Uncle Hewey, you mean all he asked you to do was to go over and ride on another street?"

"He didn't ask me to. He told me I *had* to. There's a difference."

"If he'd *asked* you to, would you have done it?"

"Sure. I always try to get along with people."

Cotton shook his head. "I don't understand that at all."

Hewey wasn't sure how to explain it; it seemed so natural that no explanation ought to be necessary. "I'm a free-born American. I even been to war. I'd be a taxpayer, and proud to say it, if I owned anything to pay taxes on. I've got a right to ride down any street anywhere in this country that anybody else can. Somebody tells me I got to get off, and I do it, pretty soon I won't have that right anymore."

Cotton wasn't satisfied. Hewey didn't know how to satisfy him.

Wes Wheeler saw Hewey's chagrin. He looked at Cotton. "Son, I'm a peace officer. It's my job to enforce the law. I'm not allowed to *make* the law; that's for somebody else to do. If I go to makin' it, I can make it anything I want it to be. First thing you know I'll use it to help me and my friends. I'll use it to hurt people I don't like. If that ever happens, I'm dangerous. That marshal up yonder, he was goin' beyond his rightful authority. That makes *him* dangerous. You let people like that get away with it, pretty soon they'll take you over."

Hewey couldn't tell if the message had gotten across to Cotton.

But the boy asked, "Mr. Wheeler, you goin' to turn Uncle Hewey over to them?"

The sheriff's mouth twisted. "Letter said they're huntin' for somebody named Hugh Holloway. I don't know any Hugh Holloway. It ain't my fault they got a marshal who can't remember names." He looked at Hewey. "You better hope some other sheriff don't figure out that they want Hewey Calloway, and tell them where to hunt."

"I always tried to get along good with the law."

"If you ever go north again, you might better take a broad roundance on New Prosperity. Not because you *have* to, but because you *want* to."

"I didn't lose nothin' there."

"If they ever come lookin' for you and have the name right, I don't know what I can do to help you."

"You've already helped me, Wes. I appreciate you tellin' me."

Wheeler climbed back into his saddle. Hewey said, "They're fixin' to have a big chicken supper over at the house this evenin'. I know Eve and Walter would consider you mighty welcome."

"Can't stay, Hewey. Might be a good idea if you got your visitin' done and left pretty soon yourself. Just in case."

He waved, and he was gone.

Cotton said, "Just change streets, that's all you'd of had to do. Just ride over one block."

Hewey didn't know how to explain to him that a man could lose a lot of manhood in a single block. He didn't try. "Your mother wouldn't understand about this. I hope you don't feel like you've got to tell her."

"No, she wouldn't. And I won't."

IV

Alvin Lawdermilk's buckboard arrived a couple of hundred yards ahead of the others. Alvin stood up to wave before Julio Valdez reined the team to a nervous halt. The mules, young and of Spanish lineage, were as green as the pair Cotton had been breaking. As soon as a Lawdermilk mule team had the "bronc" worn off, they were for sale. Life was too short, Alvin contended, to let it be dull.

Hewey met the vehicle, grinning. "Git down, Alvin. I'm afraid you missed dinner."

Alvin lifted a bottle from under the seat. "I *brought* dinner."

Julio waited dutifully until his boss was through with the greetings, then spoke jovially to Hewey and Cotton. He climbed down with the reins in his hand and began unhitching the team. Cotton hurried to help him with the buckles, snaps and straps. He shouted back at Lawdermilk, "When you goin' to buy you an automobile, Alvin?"

"When windmills start pumpin' gasoline. You can run a mule on grass and water, but them automobiles have got to be fed." Alvin extended the bottle toward Hewey. Hewey was tempted, but it wouldn't be seemly in front of Cotton. Besides, Tommy was coming yonder with the rest of the horsemen and wagons. "Sun's too high, Alvin. Ask me again when we've raised the mill. Maybe we can bust a bottle against the tower, to christen it, like."

"An *empty* bottle, Hewey." Alvin climbed down from the wagon, and he was rock steady. Whatever little he might have drunk on the way hadn't affected him.

Julio Valdez surveyed the standing pipe with the pride of vested interest. "The water is where I said. It is a strong well, I'll bet."

Cotton frowned. "I don't know if the water is sweet."

"It is sweet."

Alvin Lawdermilk walked around the windmill, silently surveying and approving the work. "Good job. Cotton done it, I suppose."

Hewey nodded. "A wrench and a saw don't fit the shape of my hands."

"Nothin' fits your hands but a rope and a set of reins." Alvin turned. "You interested in a job, Hewey?"

Hewey pondered a moment, looking off in the direction where the sheriff had gone. "I kind of doubt I'll be stayin' long." He saw Cotton glance questioningly at him. Hewey lied, "I'm expectin' word on a job out in the Big Bend country. Not no thirty-a-month cowpunchin' job, but a *foreman's* job."

Alvin seemed to see through him, at least partway. Hewey had never wanted a foreman's job in his life; too much responsibility went with it. "I've always got some broncs that need breakin'. That's a job that fits your hands. You can come over to my place and stay, or you can bring them over here to Walter's. Either way, you've got a job any time you want it."

"Much obliged, Alvin. I'll study on it."

Cotton's brow pinched. "Uncle Hewey, don't you think you're gettin' to an age where you ought to quit ridin' those rough broncs?"

Hewey smiled. "When a man has sittin'-down work, he'd better hang on to it."

Tommy loped up ahead of the rest and slid his pony to a reckless cowboy stop. He wore his working clothes, though he had a church-clean look about him. He also had a boy's eagerness. "Howdy, Uncle Hewey. Bet it didn't take Cotton long to finish up with you to help him."

Hewey didn't look at the posthole diggers. "We each taken the jobs that fitted us best."

Walter Calloway rode up on one of his working mules. His farmer overalls presented a picture Hewey could never quite adjust to. Walter dismounted in a businesslike manner and surveyed the prone mill with a critical eye, looking for flaws. He found none. "You done real good, son," he told Cotton. He turned to Hewey. "Thanks for helpin' him."

Hewey shrugged. "I done my best."

Storekeeper Pierson Phelps climbed carefully down from his wagon and exercised his cramped legs, then moved toward Hewey with both hands outstretched. His grin was broader than a double-tree. He was on the gray side of sixty. His heavy shoulders were bent from a lifetime of heavy lifting and carrying the weight of a mortgage, but his ample belly showed he had always taken home plenty of groceries out of stock. "I declare, Hewey Calloway, it's good to see you again. How come you haven't been to town to visit with us?"

Hewey took several steps to meet the old merchant halfway. "Didn't get in till yesterday. Besides, I didn't bring home much in the way of coin. Didn't figure my welcome would be too good."

"If payin' customers were the only people who ever came, that little town would get awfully lonesome."

For what it was worth, Pierson Phelps was the leading businessman in Upton City, not necessarily a great feat in view of the fact that there were so few. Last time Hewey had been to town he had counted eight, including the Mexican wood and water hauler.

Trailing quietly in Phelps' bulky shadow was a sallow, bacon-thin little man named Schneider. He had materialized a few years ago from some unpronounceable place down in the German-speaking Texas hill country. He was considered something of an oddity, the only person of the *Dutch* persuasion in Upton City. He was known to read Shakespeare and Goethe and Zola—the last two some kind of foreign radicals—but he was nevertheless generally considered of a bit less than average intelligence because he spoke with an accent and sometimes got his words out of the customary order. He was regarded as beneath the community's established social level, such as it was, because he ran a small saloon for Pierson Phelps. The taint somehow had never attached itself to Phelps, though he owned the place. He conducted it separately from his general store and was rarely seen to enter its door except at closing time, to count the day's receipts. By then all decent women were well inside their own doors so that they never saw him; it was the women who established local social standards. Pierson never poured the whisky. Schneider did that, so it was Schneider who bore the stigma. He had long since resigned himself to the lofty, throat-cutting stares of the womenfolk.

"That horrid little Dutchman," Eve always called him. Hewey doubted she even knew his name.

"Howdy, Dutch," Hewey greeted him. "You bring any samples?"

"It is the Sabbath," Schneider said firmly. He always sat on the back row of the church, alone, keeping his own counsel and making his own treaties with the Lord. It was whispered around town that he was actually a Lutheran, which was probably about as bad as being a Catholic. But perhaps the preacher could yet save him.

It was said of Schneider that no one was ever allowed to get drunk in his saloon if he had a family. Nor could a family man buy more than one bottle at a time if Schneider suspected he might empty them all in one place. Alvin Lawdermilk was a special case. He dealt directly with Pierson Phelps, wholesale.

In another wagon sat a homesteader whose name Hewey vaguely remembered as Neely, or maybe it was Needy. He was always coming over to borrow something. *Needy* was probably right, Hewey reflected. The farmer's son was with him, a boy about Tommy's age. Lester was his name. He *looked* like a Lester, Hewey thought. That rhymed with *nester,* appropriate all around.

A couple of C. C. Tarpley's cowboys from the South Camp rounded out the group. They followed on horseback behind the wagons. C.C. might not take it kindly if he saw them here. He probably wouldn't say anything; he would just cut their wages the next payday and plead hard times. Where possible, he favored a style of punishment that yielded a profit.

It stood to reason that some of these people had brought their womenfolks. They would be at the house with Eve, helping her fix a big supper.

Sure going to be hell on the chicken flock, feeding this bunch, Hewey thought. *There'll be an egg drouth here all summer.*

The boys' black dog trotted behind the last wagon, tongue out.

He had probably started following this unaccustomed caravan with enthusiasm, but the enthusiasm was long since gone. He slowed to a painful walk, sought the shade of the nearest wagon and flopped down, panting. A jack rabbit could have walked up and kicked him on the nose for all he cared.

The howdying and shaking didn't take long. Everybody seemed agreed that the sooner they finished the work the sooner they could start the pleasure.

Raising the tower was not difficult. Hewey was still confident that he and Cotton could have done it. In its way it was probably one of the easiest parts of the operation. Walter Calloway didn't trust the bronc mules. He borrowed Prentice Phelps' gentle team for the task. Hewey mounted Tommy's horse. He and the two Tarpley cowboys each tied an anchor rope to the tower and rode off at angles, keeping their ropes taut so the tower could not tip to one side or the other as the team raised it. A cross brace was chained between the two tower legs that rested on the ground, and it was butted against the upright posts that Hewey had placed. This would keep the tower from sliding instead of coming up. As the Phelps team pulled and the mill gained slowly in angle and height, the lift became easier. The anchormen moved with the tower, keeping their ropes tight. In only a minute or so, the two forward legs set themselves on the ground.

Cotton and Walter, using steel crowbars, inched the tower one way and the other until a plumb bob showed it was centered squarely over the well and the pipe. "That's it, Daddy," Cotton said.

The ropes were firmly staked to guard against a sudden strong wind pushing the tower over. Cotton took it upon himself to be sure the tower was level. He prized and shimmed under each leg until the plumb bob and the spirit level showed the mill was in perfect alignment with the hole. The men set in to digging anchor-post holes by each of the four legs. That took a while, and Hewey deferred to his blisters so long as there were plenty of other volunteers. When the holes were finished, Cotton tied an anchor post snugly against each tower leg with wire so it would not slip, then began drilling holes with an auger. He drove a heavy bolt through each hole as soon as he finished it. While Cotton went about drilling other holes, Hewey tightened a nut over each bolt, firmly securing the tower legs to the anchor posts.

Walter turned to Tommy. "You can fill in with dry sand now and tamp the holes real good." Dry sand, properly pounded, would grip and hold tighter and longer than cement.

Hewey noticed that the nester boy Lester was adept at making the motions but contributing little muscle to the job. He would move as if to take hold but do it slowly so somebody else was always likely to get on it ahead of him and relieve him of the necessity. He looked eager enough that he got credit for trying without ever actually breaking a sweat. He grunted a lot.

Given any decent start, he probably had a future ahead of him in politics, Hewey thought.

By contrast, Cotton did his work so smoothly that it seemed to involve little stress. People like that seldom received much credit; they never grunted enough. They could not grasp the importance of showmanship.

After a while the anchor posts were well tamped and the tower was considered solid. Hewey helped lower the cylinder and the sucker-rods down the pipe a joint at a time. In a while the top sucker-rod and the red-rod were bolted together. This was the moment of supreme test. Cotton glanced at his father. Walter nodded. Cotton released the lever that held the wheel and the tail locked together. Freed, the tail swung out at a right angle and pulled the wheel into the soft south wind. For a moment the gears groaned as the big wooden fan strained off its lethargy and slowly began to turn. The sucker-rod began to stroke up and down. Hewey took off his hat and knelt with his ear against the pipe. In a minute he could hear the water working its way higher with each stroke. Then it began gushing out the end of the flow pipe.

It was muddy at first, clearing the accumulation which had silted into the bottom since the well had been drilled. In a little while the water cleared. Everybody stood around in silence, watching it gush with each stroke of the rod. They seemed fascinated by the sight. No matter how many times they had seen it, there was always a vague feeling of a miracle beheld in this dry land.

Cotton walked to the end of the pipe, cupped his hand and cautiously took a tentative sip. He blinked, as if only half believing, then took another drink, a larger one. "It's sweet," he said in surprise.

Julio smiled.

One by one, men and boys filed by to take a swallow or two. Presently Julio was the only one who had not. The little man's teeth gleamed. "I do not have to drink the water. The witching rod has told me how it tastes."

Walter signaled for Tommy to shut off the mill. "No use wastin' the water and makin' a loblolly. We've got to take time somehow to get over here with a team and fresno and scoop out a surface tank."

Hewey heard himself volunteering before he had adequately considered the ramifications of the job. "I'll start tomorrow."

Cotton glanced worriedly at him. Hewey said, "It won't take but a few days, button."

He thought about it a little more. If a shovel or a set of posthole diggers didn't fit his hands, the heavy iron handle of a mule-drawn fresno dirt-mover was no better. He already had blisters enough. But he never considered backing out, once the commitment was made.

Greasy, muddy, the men stood around admiring the results of the afternoon's work with all the self-righteousness that comes from knowing a job has been properly attacked and competently mastered. The nester boy looked especially tired, especially self-righteous. Walter told his sons to start loading the tools into the family wagon. Lester Needy trailed along behind, picking up the lighter pieces. His father told him to be careful of his back; a growing boy shouldn't overdo.

Alvin Lawdermilk, gloriously greasy and muddy, brought a bottle from under the seat of his buckboard. Its original contents had already been considerably depleted. "Here's to a good day's work," he said and passed the bottle around. All the men drank except Schneider. Nobody in Upton City could remember ever seeing him drink anything but coffee. When the bottle had made the round, Alvin took a swig from it. A little whisky remained in the bottom. Alvin said, "Every windmill has got to have a name. Walter, name this one and we'll christen it proper."

Walter shook his head. "I hadn't even thought about it."

Alvin turned to Hewey. "Then I'll name it in honor of the prodigal brother, come home to help eat the unfatted calf. From now on, this is Hewey's Mill."

Hewey protested. "Cotton done all the work. It ought by rights to be named after him."

But nobody seemed to hear him, least of all Cotton, who frowned darkly and went on with loading up the tools. Alvin smashed the bottle against a corner post, a remnant of whisky running down the clinging shreds of cedar bark.

Alvin said, "Bet you never had anything named after you before."

Hewey wondered at Alvin's extravagance with good whisky. "Once. A horse. We never did manage to get him broke proper."

"People can see a windmill a long ways farther than they can see a horse. Every time they look at this one they'll think of you."

Hewey looked up at the rejuvenated wheel, a motley mixture of old wood and new. "I wisht it was painted, then."

Cotton fetched a shovel back out of the wagon, dug a little hole against the corner post and raked the broken glass into it, then covered it up. It would be like some nosy calf to find that glass before the sun went down. Cotton gave Hewey a quick, exasperated glance as if he counted him responsible for Alvin's exuberance.

The crew trailed out south toward the house. Alvin motioned for Hewey to come up beside him in the buckboard. Julio climbed into Cotton's wagon, which seemed to suit Cotton better than riding with his uncle. The black dog got under Cotton's wagon and trotted along just fast enough to keep himself in the moving shade.

Alvin wanted Hewey to tell him about some of the wonders he had encountered in his travels. Hewey accommodated him, looseherding the truth a little but not so much that he wouldn't get away with it. Tommy rode alongside, listening eagerly.

Behind their wagon was that of the nester. The boy Lester, rested up from his work, was playing incessantly on a jew's-harp, the only noise Hewey hated more than the clatter of a gasoline engine. The sixth time Lester cut loose on "Hello My Honey," Hewey was ready to go back and finger-thump him over his left ear. But civility ruled, and he stifled his baser nature.

As they neared the house and the tall chinaberry trees, a reddish dog came trotting out toward them, barking a challenge but looking behind him every few seconds to see if help was coming. Tommy's dog took up the challenge and moved out from under Cotton's wagon into the sunshine. Both dogs took care not to carry the contest too close to each other.

The red dog was on the small side, a fact which failed to arouse overconfidence in Tommy's.

Tommy said without enthusiasm, "He belongs to our teacher. I don't know why *she* had to come over here. We see enough of her on other days without havin' to listen to her on Sunday too."

Hewey smiled. "She's not much of a teacher, I suppose."

Tommy shrugged. "She knows a lot. But she ought to, at her age."

"She got a name?"

"Miss Renfro. Miss Spring Renfro."

"Spring? That's an odd name."

"Summer would probably fit her better. *Late* summer."

Hewey smiled. He doubted that Tommy was a dependable judge of a woman's age. If she was over twenty-five though, she probably wasn't much to look at. In this country, where men outnumbered women like the Indians had outnumbered Custer, spinsterhood was a difficult state for a woman to hang on to unless she had a face that would stop a runaway horse in mid-stride. Even the plain schoolteachers tended to get married off with only a modest effort on their part, and the pretty ones seldom made it through the first school year.

Hewey had never had much truck with schoolteachers, plain *or* pretty. They always made him nervously aware of how much he had never learned, of how slowly he read and how painstakingly he wrote, when occasion demanded that he write anything at all. He never could understand why teachers should seem so superior. He'd never seen a man teacher yet who could ride a bronc more than two good jumps.

Any schoolkid could learn to read a book, but good bronc riders were few and thin on the ground.

It took several minutes for the men to unsaddle the horses,

unhitch the teams and turn all the stock into a pen for a bait of oats. Tommy said to Lester, "Let's me and you run to the house and see if we can freeze the ice cream."

Lester displayed no enthusiasm. "Turnin' a freezer always makes my arm tired."

"But the ones who freeze it get to lick the dash. Come on."

Lester followed, but he stayed a couple of steps behind all the way to the house. Walter started toward the house at a slower pace, followed by Pierson Phelps, the Dutchman and the farmer Needy, the two Tarpley cowboys and Julio Valdez. Hewey was about to follow, but Alvin grabbed his arm. "The womenfolks can wait on us a few minutes."

He went to his buckboard, rummaged around and came up with a bottle. He glanced toward the house and evidently decided he could be seen. He stuck it inside his shirt and headed for the little shed out beside the windmill. Safely behind it, he brought the bottle back out from its hiding place. Hewey could see that the cork had never been removed.

Alvin said expansively, "I love the womenfolks, God bless them. But there are times when their talk can drive me to distraction without a little drop of kindness to smooth off the edges." He pulled the cork out and extended the bottle toward Hewey.

Hewey reasoned that he would be standing within smelling distance of Eve in a few minutes. "I believe I'll pass."

Alvin took a long swallow, paused to lick his lips and enjoy the flavor, then tipped the bottle again. "I'll swear, Hewey, that batch must of been blessed by the breath of an angel. You've got to try it." He shoved the bottle into Hewey's hand.

Hewey was sorely tempted, but he had made up his mind. He tried to push the bottle back at Alvin.

A woman's voice cut like rusty barbed wire. "*Mr.* Lawdermilk!"

Hewey knew he was in trouble even before he turned and gazed into the reproachful eyes of Cora Lawdermilk. But she wasn't there alone. Beside her stood Eve Calloway, whose own eyes were like Indian flint. Beyond Eve was a woman Hewey had never seen before, and behind them all stood a man wearing a dust-tinted black suit with frayed cuffs and a top button gone. He was Brother

Averill, the Baptist preacher who hammered at the gates of hell every Sunday morning from ten to eleven, and occasionally longer when the spirit was really upon him.

Alvin was the first to get hold of his wits. "Why, howdy, Cora. Hewey was just offerin' me a drink to celebrate his homecomin', and I was tellin' him it wouldn't be proper on the Sabbath afternoon."

Hewey would cheerfully have stomped Alvin with a pair of hobnailed boots, if he had owned any. Cora Lawdermilk swung those narrowed eyes on Hewey and skewered him with them. "*Mr. Calloway.*" It was her habit to use the word *Mister* to her husband and other close acquaintances only when she was sorely provoked. Hewey was acutely aware that he still held the guilty bottle in his unguilty hand. He tried to swing it behind him, out of sight, but this was a futile gesture. Right now that bottle seemed bigger than a horse. He would have hurled it across the fence, but that would have called more attention to it.

Eve didn't speak; she only stared at him, her face reddened beneath the cover of her big slat bonnet.

Brother Averill said, "Perhaps Brother Hewey forgot this was the Sabbath."

The third woman's face was impassive, but Hewey thought he saw laughter in her eyes, struggling to escape imprisonment.

She wouldn't think it was so damn funny if Eve was her sister-in-law, Hewey thought, resentment touching him a little. He glanced back at Alvin Lawdermilk. On that face was the innocence of a child picking wild flowers in a field, a soul untainted even by original sin.

"By George, preacher, you're right," Hewey said, "it *is* the Sabbath." He held the bottle out at arm's length and turned it upside down. Alvin's innocence turned to pain as he watched the long stream of golden elixir soak quickly into the sand. But he stood in silence and bore the sacrifice like a soldier.

Cora Lawdermilk said, "In the future, Mr. Calloway, I hope you will remember not only the Sabbath but also my husband's weakness."

"I'll sure try to."

When the bottle was empty, Hewey tossed it into the sand beside the shed.

Cora took her husband's arm and led him away.

Brother Averill said, "You have done the proper thing, Hewey."

Hewey watched the departing Alvin. "I'm sure I did, preacher."

The minister looked a moment at the stiff-shouldered Eve and spoke to the other woman. "Shall we go back to the house, Miss Renfro?"

Miss Renfro still had that laugh in her eyes, though her face never changed expression. After she turned away Hewey couldn't remember what color the eyes had been, all he had seen was the laugh in them.

Eve's hands were on her hips. This was May, but her eyes said October. "You're runnin' true to form, Hewey. Just home one day, and you've already embarrassed me in front of Brother Averill and the boys' teacher, not to mention Cora Lawdermilk."

"I expect Cora has seen a whisky bottle a time or two before."

"Not on *this* place. I trust this will be the last time such a thing ever happens."

"I never had a drop, Eve. You can smell my breath if you've a mind to."

She shook her head. "Not for a ten-dollar gold piece." She set off toward the house, trailing after the others. Hewey slumped, flexing his hands, glancing once at the bottle lying by the shed, wishing he *had* taken a drink out of it since he had endured all the blame for it anyway.

Seemed like sometimes he had two left feet.

Cotton came out of the corral. Hewey hadn't realized the boy was still out there, putting up the windmill tools. He wondered how much Cotton had heard or seen. Cotton said nothing. He walked to the shed, picked up the empty bottle and carried it to a trash barrel behind the yard fence.

There was nothing left to be said except *hell*. Hewey said that and followed after the others.

As was the custom, the men stayed outside, sitting in chairs or on the ground beneath the great rustling chinaberry trees. The women were in the house. Hewey could hear and smell the chicken frying. On the front step sat Tommy, turning the handle of a wooden ice-cream freezer. A wet burlap bag was stuffed around the top to hold in the cold and extend the useful life of the expensive salt-packed ice, thoughtfully brought from town by Pierson Phelps. The boy Lester cranked slowly on a second freezer. Tommy had to remind him two or three times not to stop because the dash would freeze up.

The boys' black dog and the teacher's red one still stalked one another with wary patience, neither allowing the other to get quite close enough for a bona fide acquaintanceship to begin. They traded a certain amount of tentative and shallow growling. They reminded Hewey of his own relationship with Eve.

He wanted to think of something else, so when Pierson Phelps began drawing him out on the details of his recent adventures, Hewey obliged. He told of working his way up through the Indian Territory, and of Homer Ganss' horse race. He told of his attempt to break into the big and easy money of show business by trying to get on as a bronc rider with the 101 Ranch Wild West Show.

"They put me on for a tryout. I'm tellin' you, boys, these broncs we've got down in this country are rockin' horses against them outlaws they gather up for that show. By the third day I had eaten so much dirt that I must of gained fifteen–twenty pounds. One of them throwed me for a belly buster that emptied all the air out of me plumb down to my toes. I drug myself up against a fence post and sat there tryin' to get some wind back into my lungs when old Zack Miller himself walked up. He says, 'If you can't handle them rough ones, then you oughtn't to've hired out.' Says, 'The main trouble with you is that you've done et too many birthday cakes.'

"I says to him, I says, 'Where I've spent most of my birthdays, there wasn't nobody around to bake me a cake.' But I reckon we was both agreed that I wasn't no show-time cowboy. It would've been easy money; I was told they paid some of them boys as much as seventy–eighty dollars a month, and they didn't have to ride but five or six broncs a day.

"I reckon I wasn't cut out for that kind of business anyway. When I do a job of work, I like to know there's somethin' real goin' to come of it. If I break a bronc, it's so somebody can use him in cow work. If I break a mule, it's so somebody can hitch him to a wagon and get some use out of him. But in them shows you just ride for an audience, and when you're through there's nothin' been built, nothin' real been gained. It's sort of like for nothin'." He added as an afterthought, "Except the money, of course."

The farmer Needy said, "You talk as if you don't think money is important." It was a concept he obviously disapproved.

"I've never met anybody, hardly, who thought he had enough of it. Not even old C. C. Tarpley. Since there's no way you can ever get enough of it anyway, I don't see where a man ought to kill himself runnin' after a hopeless cause. There's too many other things in life to pleasure you."

Brother Averill put in, "There are a great many things in this life more important than pleasure."

"If it don't pleasure you, then it ain't worth your time," Hewey demurred.

"Pleasure is for the *next* life. This life was meant to be lived in trial and suffering, to prepare us for the glory of the next."

Hewey said, "I've known a lot of folks who kept puttin' off enjoyin' themselves, figurin' they'd get around to it one of these days. Then one mornin' they woke up and found out they was old. It was too late then."

"Not if they had lived a Christian life. The real joy awaits us all in the next world."

"I don't see no harm in practicin' up for it a little while we're here."

In a little while Eve came out onto the step, where the two boys had finished freezing the ice cream, and announced that supper was ready. "You men can come on in and fill your plates. Then you can come back outside where it's cooler."

Tommy asked her about her promise that he and Lester could clean the dash, but she told him they would have to wait; she didn't want them spoiling their supper.

Eve asked Brother Averill if he would lead them in the blessing. Hewey stood up nervously, forgetting to remove his hat until he saw the other men doing it. It had always seemed to him that the Lord must be awfully busy, and it must be an imposition to Him to have to stop His work three times a day and listen to people all over the world telling Him "Thank you." Surely He knew everybody was grateful without His having to hear them say it so often.

Brother Averill launched into a lengthy blessing in which he named everybody here except Julio Valdez. Hewey didn't know if he had forgotten the Mexican, couldn't say his name or simply considered the poor soul lost on account of his race. Hewey began to feel he was going to get a crick in his neck from holding his head down so long, and he thought the prayer might run on for ten more minutes. The breeze brought a strong whiff of fried chicken which tantalized Hewey almost to the point of sin. It might have reached the preacher, too, for he suddenly brought the long prayer to a snappy conclusion. "And now, Lord, we Thy unworthy servants humbly ask Thy blessings on this food which we are a-fixin' to partake of, amen."

Walter motioned for Brother Averill to lead the way into the house, a courtesy which the minister graciously accepted. His strictures against labor on the Sabbath did not extend to the frying of chicken.

Hewey hung back. So did Julio, accustomed to being last, and Alvin Lawdermilk, who had been casting uneasy glances at Hewey ever since they had seated themselves beneath the trees. At length Alvin seemed to lose an inner battle. He came up to Hewey with his head down. "Hewey, I kind of left you hangin' on the fence out yonder while ago. I hope you won't take it ill of me."

Hewey shrugged. His momentary resentment had evaporated long ago. "Who knows? If I was a married man I might of done the same."

Alvin said, "It ain't I was afraid of her. It's just that I like a peaceful house. You come over and break some horses and mules for me awhile, Hewey. You'll find out that Cora ain't a bad woman atall. It's just that it's a little easier to lie to her than it is to explain some things. You'll learn what I mean if you ever get married."

Hewey shook his head. "I don't reckon I'll ever get married, then, because I've never told a lie in all my life."

Brother Averill returned carrying a plate loaded with chicken, red beans and biscuits. One by one the other men came out. Alvin said, "We better go in, Hewey. The womenfolks won't eat till we're all fed."

Not until Alvin and Hewey went into the house did Julio trust himself to follow, the last of the men to go. Eve was standing at the plain old wooden table forking pieces of chicken onto everybody's plate. Hewey expected her to give him a couple of necks and a back, but she gave him drumsticks. Her eyes weren't warm, exactly, but the frost was gone. Cora was too busy fussing over her husband's welfare to pay any attention to Hewey, which was just as well.

Miss Renfro stood at the bread pan. She said, "You look like a big biscuit-eater to me, Mr. Calloway. How many do you want, five or six?"

They were big biscuits. Hewey said, "Five's enough. I don't want to look like a hog."

She smiled. It was the first time he had really looked at her. She wasn't a pretty woman; he supposed many people would consider her plain, and somewhat skinny at that. But the smile was pleasant. While she wore it, in the dim light of the kitchen, she would almost pass for pretty. And he would bet she wasn't too far over thirty. Well, not forty, anyway.

He poured the coffee for himself. While he was at it he poured one for Julio too. Hewey noticed that Eve had given Julio mostly chicken wings, but he was glad to see that Miss Renfro hadn't shorted him on biscuits. Julio *did* like biscuits, especially when he had plenty of syrup to sop them in. Hewey reached up into a cabinet and brought down a bucket of molasses. "Here's the lick, Hooley. Move them biscuits over and I'll pour some on your plate."

He took one of his drumsticks and exchanged it for one of Julio's wings. "Always *was* a little partial to the wing," he said.

After everyone had eaten, Eve let Tommy and Lester carry the freezers into the house. Soon they were back, each carrying a freezer dash standing in a bowl. They seated themselves on the step and eagerly went to work spooning off the ice cream that clung to the paddles.

Down at the chinaberry grove, two sets of freight wagons had pulled up for the night. Presently the teamsters came up leading their mule teams to water them at the house windmill. Eve shouted at Walter, "You tell Blue Hannigan for them not to go fixin' anything to eat. We've got a-plenty left right here."

Walter walked out and invited the freighters to eat with the rest of the crowd, an invitation they accepted without hesitation or false show of reluctance.

Tommy was chagrined. Hewey heard him tell the nester boy, "That big one's Blue Hannigan. He eats like one of his mules. We better get all the ice cream we want before he starts, because he sure won't leave us any."

About that time Hewey's horse, Biscuit, came up to the corrals from the horse pasture where he was confined. Hewey walked out to look at him, to try to see if the lameness had improved any. Biscuit stood outside the closed gate, shut off from the feed and from the horses and mules that had put in the day at work. Hewey opened the gate and let him in. He found the troughs empty, so he poured some oats for Biscuit, confident that the horse wouldn't let the others steal any of it.

As Hewey turned toward the house, he saw the schoolteacher walking toward him. She was a tall woman and thin, her plain gray dress almost sweeping the ground. In her hand she held a coffee cup with a spoon sticking out of it. "You're about to miss the ice cream, Mr. Calloway. We ran out of bowls. I hope the cup will do."

"You didn't have to bring it all the way out here to me, but I'm much obliged."

"No trouble. I didn't want to see you miss out."

She handed him the cup. Awkwardly he wondered if courtesy didn't indicate that he ought to give her the first bite, but there was only one spoon. Most people were a little squeamish about things like that, and he figured that as a schoolteacher she surely would be.

"I sure thank you, Miss . . ." He stammered, for somehow her name had slipped away from him.

"Renfro. Spring Renfro. I am the boys' teacher."

"Thank you, Miss Renfro." He knew he shouldn't ask, but he did it anyway. "How'd you come to have a name like Spring?"

86

"I was born in April. My mother said it had been a long winter, and she was glad to see Spring."

He looked at the sparkle in her eyes and decided the name fitted her. He said, "I'm pleased to meet you. I'm Hewey Calloway."

She smiled, and again her plainness disappeared. "I want you to rest assured, Mr. Calloway, that I know where the bottle came from. I have come across many of Alvin Lawdermilk's hiding places."

The country schoolhouse stood at the Lawdermilk ranch headquarters. Other teachers had stayed at the same place in years past. Cora Lawdermilk, who had lost one child in infancy and had never been able to have another, seemed to enjoy the company. It was also good to have someone extra around to help see after her semi-invalid old mother, whose legs were slow but whose sharp tongue was swift.

"Good folks, the Lawdermilks," he said. "Good place they've got." It was an empty statement, but she flustered him a little, like schoolteachers usually did. He didn't want to say much because he knew his grammar bespoke more of the barn than of the schoolhouse.

"I hope the ice cream is good," she said.

He nodded. "Fine. Just fine." He sensed that she was giving him an opportunity to initiate a conversation, and he was doing a damn poor job of it. He asked, "You come from back east, I suppose?"

"Not very far east. Just East Texas."

"We was born in East Texas, too, me and Walter. Been a long time since we left. You was probably no more than a little girl." It struck him too late that he was making a judgment about her age, a judgment one didn't make about strange women, or even those he knew well.

She seemed to take no offense. "It has been a while since I was a little girl."

"Yes'm," he agreed.

He didn't know what else to say, and the sound of a vehicle approaching from beyond the barn saved him from the necessity of saying anything. He stepped out to the side, where he could see better. It was unusual for company to come from that direction, that of the French place, where he had spent the better part of the day helping put up the windmill. Hewey squinted. He made out that this was a buggy, drawn by a pair of grays.

Spring Renfro said, "That will be Mr. C. C. Tarpley." Her voice took on a tinge of distaste. "And I suppose the gentleman with him will be Mr. Frank Gervin."

"We all call him 'Fat,' " Hewey said. He noted her displeasure. "There's some who wouldn't call him a gentleman."

"Including myself." She started in a brisk walk back toward the house, seeming not to want to be outside when the buggy arrived. Hewey walked slower, eating the ice cream and watching her. For an old maid schoolteacher she seemed to have a right smart of judgment. The fact that she didn't like Fat Gervin was proof of that. His smooth manners around the womenfolk were reputed to have fooled some of them, awhile.

All the men were standing up by the time C. C. Tarpley brought the buggy to a stop, a testament to the respect—if not liking—which people felt for the rapacious old cowman. They hadn't stood up for Fat Gervin's sake, Hewey reflected.

Walter stepped forward and extended his hand. "Howdy, Mr. Tarpley. Git down; git down."

Back in the days when Walter had been working for him it had always been "C.C." not "Mr. Tarpley." That, Hewey decided, was the difference between simply working for a man and borrowing money from him.

"Just passin', Walter," Tarpley said. "Heard you-all was puttin' up a windmill on the French place. Came by and found you'd already finished."

"Had plenty of help," Walter said, waving his hand toward the other visitors. Hewey noted that the two Tarpley cowboys had somehow melted out of sight, probably behind the house. It wouldn't do them any good. Hewey would bet a dollar to a plugged nickle that the sharp-eyed old man had already spotted their horses in the corral. He wasn't one to miss anything.

Eve Calloway opened the screen door and moved out onto the step. "Mr. Tarpley, we've still got plenty left to eat. You and Mr. Gervin get down and come on in."

Fat Gervin looked hopefully at his father-in-law. Tarpley said, "Eve, we sure do appreciate the invitation, but we ain't hardly got the time." About then he spotted the ice-cream freezers by the step. "You still got some ice cream too?"

Eve assured him they did. Tommy's face fell; he had counted on getting to clean out the last of it.

C.C. said, "Then I reckon we'll just *take* time." His decision was clearly popular with his son-in-law, who could sometimes move with surprising swiftness for a man of his bulk. The buggy seat seemed to rise three inches on its springs when Gervin stepped down.

Hewey frowned as he watched Fat. He had never been able to trust a man who had slick hands and wore a coat in the summertime.

While C.C. and Fat were in the house, the two Tarpley cowboys quickly said their good-byes and beat a hasty retreat to the barn. They rode off in a northerly direction where they could not be seen, though the camp where they lived was in the opposite direction. They would get there; it would just take longer this way.

The crowd had fallen silent. It was odd, Hewey thought, how deadening an effect one rich old man could have on a conversation. Fat Gervin, between bites, set up a one-sided dialogue that was more lecture than conversation, all about the state of the nation's economy and the alarming growth of the national debt and such as that. Hewey surmised that he had been spending a lot of time in Tarpley's bank lately and reading banker publications. Five years ago Fat couldn't have counted a herd of cattle, much less figure up the national debt.

Tommy's worst fears materialized. Eve scraped the very last of the ice cream out for C.C. and Fat. The old rancher sat in the chair Walter had vacated for him and ate with gusto while Fat continued a long discourse on the struggle between management and labor.

C.C. said, "In my day I've seen a lot of changes come over this country, and I've been opposed to almost every one of them. But one thing I was never opposed to was ice cream. This is bully stuff, Eve, bully stuff."

"Glad you like it, Mr. Tarpley. We'd freeze some more, but

there isn't enough ice. Mr. Phelps was kind enough to bring us what he had."

C.C. looked toward the storekeeper. "I'm told there are people who are actually buyin' ice to put in their drinkin' water, Pierson. Is that true?" He didn't give the storekeeper time to answer. "A dangerous thing, gettin' people accustomed to luxury like that. One luxury leads to another, and pretty soon they'll get to thinkin' they ought to have ice water every Sunday, and maybe even durin' the week. Get people spoiled to luxury and pretty soon it's not a luxury anymore, it's a necessity. It's a terrible waste of this country's resources. There ought to be a law passed right now to stop it." He paused. "But there ought to never be any law against ice cream."

Eve picked up the bowl when Tarpley was through with it, and she waited for Gervin to finish his.

C. C. Tarpley stood up. Fat, always watching him for his cues, did likewise. Old Tarpley looked around a little, taking in the house, the barn, the fences and general improvements. "You've done a right smart with this place, Walter."

"We've done the best we could."

The old man frowned. "That windmill you put up today . . . I looked through the bank records, and I couldn't find where you had borrowed any money from us to pay for it."

"It wasn't a new mill, Mr. Tarpley."

"It still cost money, even for an old one. You got to drill the hole, and I could tell there was some new lumber and fixin's went into the mill. Just about everything you've got is mortgaged to our bank. I was just kind of curious where you got the money, Walter."

Hewey frowned at the implication.

Walter said, "My boy Cotton helped Old Man Maxey drill the well. In return for the old man's time and the use of his machinery, my boy's goin' to give him three weeks' labor when school is out. I haven't mortgaged my boy's labor."

Tarpley grunted, partially satisfied. "But there's still the mill. How'd you pay for the mill?"

"It was a damaged one that had fallen over, south of Midland. It didn't cost me much. Back when it was still too early to plant, I throwed my team and wagon in with Blue's freightin' outfit haulin' lumber from the railroad in Midland. Four loads earned me enough to buy the windmill and the lumber it taken to patch it up."

That seemed to set C.C.'s mind at ease, but it simply launched Fat Gervin on another harangue. As an understudy to the old man he was trying hard to acquire C.C.'s inborn meanness with a dollar. He said, "You know, Walter, our bank has got a mortgage on that wagon and team. What if somethin' had happened to them while you was workin' on that job? And what about the unusual wear and tear? When a man is borrowin' he owes it to the institution to take good care of his collateral and see that it ain't in no way impaired or demeaned."

Tarpley nodded in surprised silence, noting with some pleasure that his hard-taught lessons might be starting to take root.

Fat got started on how great and indispensable an institution the bank had been in the development of the nation, and how everybody owed it to his country as a patriotic duty to stand foursquare with the bank at all times.

Occasionally, when Hewey was in a mood of philosophical generosity, he would rationalize Fat's shortcomings and tell himself Fat wasn't altogether to blame. Maybe Hewey and a lot of others like him were at fault too. Cowboys could be merciless in hoorawing the misfit, the inept, the unwilling. He would tell himself that they probably drove Fat inward with their ridicule, making him sullen and mean. But Hewey's spasms of nobility usually dissipated quickly, and he would recover his standing conviction that sons of bitches are born, not made.

He had heard enough about banks in the last ten minutes to satisfy whatever curiosity might arise in him for the next three or four years. He moved away from the crowd, looking toward the barn and thinking he probably ought to go run Biscuit back into the horse pasture.

He noticed the teacher's red dog making his way from one bush, one weed, to another, pausing briefly at certain ones to raise a leg and leave his signature. The boys' black dog followed at a respectful distance, sniffing at each such imprint and endorsing it.

Hewey looked over his shoulder toward Fat. The devil began to jab sinfully but deliciously at him. Fat's back was turned, and his jaw was still operating at a hearty pace. Hewey looked toward the house to make sure none of the women were outside to witness his surrender to temptation. They wouldn't understand. No properly modest woman knew much about male bodily functions, be they animal or human.

He fished a jackknife from his pocket and walked to a tall green weed upon which the red dog's greeting still clung in amber droplets. Carefully he bent over, holding the top of the weed with his left hand while he gingerly sliced through the base, taking pains not to shake it enough to dislodge the drops. Walking as if he were stepping on eggs, he carried it up behind Fat Gervin.

Most of the men were watching Hewey in quiet fascination, but they did not give him away.

He bent and shook the weed, managing to splatter a goodly amount of the dog's scent on the lower part of Fat's left trouser leg, at about ankle level. Fat was so busy talking that he never noticed. He might have wondered why Alvin Lawdermilk so suddenly turned around and covered his face, or why the dour Dutchman, Schneider, smiled, but he never let it interfere with the point he was making that most of the progress in this country resulted from the selfless generosity of a noble bank.

That had been the extent of the prank insofar as Hewey had envisioned it. In his own quiet way he had made a statement about Fat Gervin without Fat even knowing about it.

Hewey hadn't considered the black dog. That innocent animal, which had followed Hewey's strange motions with curiosity, sniffed at Fat Gervin's trousers, found there an invitation, hoisted his leg and saluted.

First startled, then enraged, Fat let out an oath that would have blistered the ears of the womenfolk if they had been outside to hear. He fetched the black dog a savage kick that sent the bewildered animal flying. As the dog ran off howling in surprise and pain, Fat tried in vain to shake the shame from his trousers.

Alvin Lawdermilk was doubled over, slapping his knee uncontrollably and gasping for breath. Pierson Phelps had choked on his pipe. Teamster Blue Hannigan got up and walked over to the

92

house, leaning against it with his back turned, his shoulders bouncing. The Mexican laughed aloud, which added to Fat Gervin's rage.

Turning, Fat saw Hewey standing behind him, trying for Alvin Lawdermilk's saintly expression of infant innocence. Fat seemed to sense that Hewey might be in some way the author of his embarrassment. The suspicion deepened, and he clenched his fists. His eyes strained from their sockets.

Hewey blinked in bland curiosity as if he had missed the whole thing.

Old C.C. *had* missed it, his back turned. He stared now in consternation. "What's goin' on here, Fat?" He looked down. "Spilled your coffee on you again, hunh? I swear, boy, sometimes you're left-handed on both sides." He noticed then the angry way Fat was staring at Hewey, trying to confirm his suspicions. C.C. seemed to sense that it was time they left.

"Folks," he said, making no attempt to hide his puzzlement, "we enjoyed the supper and the company, but tomorrow's another workin' day. We got to be at the bank on time in the mornin'." He paused, studying his son-in-law but not fathoming the reason for Fat's anger. "Some of you folks might not've heard. I've decided to spend a lot more time with my cattle and a lot less with the bankin' end of the business. I've turned the responsibility of the bank over to Fat"—he corrected himself—"to Frank here. If you folks have business with the bank, he'll be the one you want to go and see. I'll be at the ranch." He started toward the buggy, then stopped to look back for his son-in-law. "You comin', ain't you, boy?"

Fat hadn't been a boy in twenty years, but he mumbled, "Yes sir." He tore his eyes away from Hewey and followed the old man. He tried to hold his trouser leg away from his boot while he climbed into the buggy. He never looked back as they rode away.

Alvin Lawdermilk couldn't restrain himself. He broke into another fit of hilarity, wilder than the first. Soon he was lying on the ground, beating the packed earth with his fist. His laughter was contagious. It swept the other men and continued until some of them were bent over in pain.

Hewey, laughing with them, noticed that Walter seemed not to be sharing their mirth. He was watching the buggy disappear down the winding trail toward town, his face solemn.

Cora Lawdermilk came out presently and stared at her husband. "You men! There's not an ounce of shame in a carload of you. You've been tellin' those shady stories again, I can tell. And in the presence of the minister. Shame on all of you."

Hewey had noticed that the minister had laughed as hard as any of them, except of course Alvin. If laughter could ever be fatal, there was no hope for Alvin Lawdermilk.

The minister had gained Hewey's respect.

Cora said, "Alvin, dark's comin'. Time we started for home."

The rest decided their holiday was over too. Pierson Phelps pumped Hewey's hand. "Hewey, you come by the store first time you get a chance to go to town. Drummer left me a sample of cigars he wanted me to try. I'd like to see what you think of them."

The Dutchman said, "You come in sometime, Hewey. For you I will save back a bottle of the best we have. No cost. A gift for the thing you did to that Fat Gervin." They pulled away.

Julio Valdez hitched the Lawdermilk team and brought the buckboard around. Alvin climbed into the seat and let Cora struggle up by herself. The schoolteacher called for her dog, which jumped into the back of the vehicle; it was smarter than the boys' dog. She turned to Hewey, glanced around to see that no one else would hear and said quietly, "I was looking out the window while ago, Mr. Calloway. I saw what happened to Frank Gervin."

Hewey reddened. "You wasn't meant to see that, ma'am." He floundered, trying to think of something to say. "I'm sorry. I didn't go to offend you."

"Offend me? I was tickled to death. In all my life I never saw a more befitting gesture." She gave him her slender hand. "Would you assist me, please?"

He gave her a lift up into the buckboard seat beside Cora and Alvin. Julio took his place on the back, his short legs hanging over. The dog moved up beside him and licked his hand, knowing no prejudice.

Tommy stood beside Hewey, helping him watch the Lawdermilk group disappear into the dusk.

Hewey said, "Button, you boys have got yourselves a real teacher. I'll bet you learn somethin' every day."

Soon the last of the visitors had gone. The teamsters had returned to their camp beneath the chinaberries. Eve called the boys to take the scraps down to the hog pen. Hewey took a seat in a rawhide-bottomed chair and stared at the trail where everybody had gone. He got to chuckling again, remembering Fat Gervin.

Walter seemed to read his thoughts. He pulled up another chair and sat awhile in moody silence. Finally he ventured, "Looks like to me you pleased everybody but Fat."

Hewey nodded. "Looks like. I hope he didn't hurt the boys' dog."

"I don't reckon. But he could sure hurt *us.*"

Hewey's grin faded. "How?"

"You heard C.C. say he's all but turned the bank over to him. When we bought the French place we taken out a note, puttin' up this farm for security. Big part of it is due this fall. The way the late rains delayed plantin', we could find ourselves hubbin' up against the due date before we've got the money. I might've been able to reason with old C.C. But now I'll have to talk to Fat Gervin instead."

Hewey frowned. "I didn't know nothin' about that. It was just that he was blowin' so hard . . ."

"You never was one to fret much about consequences. I just hope Fat doesn't find out for sure what happened to him here."

V

The blisters on Hewey's hands had no chance to heal. He had promised to build a surface tank to catch the water pumped by the new mill. This was a brutal, grubbing type of work he would never hire out to do for pay unless he had one foot in the grave from a terminal case of starvation, but he would do it free of charge to fulfill a promise or as a gesture to someone who had provided him bed and board.

There was no dishonor unless a man took money for it.

It was a work that demanded much from the body but little from the brain. His mind was free to soar, to drift away to other times and other places, to people he had known and people he might someday meet, to things he had done and things he intended someday to do. He trudged along behind two half-broken Lawdermilk mules and guided the hungry jaws of a big steel fresno, scooping out ancient layers of deep rich soil and moving them forty or fifty feet to dump them and form the rim of an earthen vessel that would water a growing Calloway cattle herd. The sweat flowed freely and his body sometimes ached, but it was a happy time, for in his mind he relived a thousand cheerful days he had known, unconsciously filtering out and rejecting the unpleasant. He had never allowed himself to dwell on the darker times, for to live them once had been more than enough. While the mules struggled and the sharp blade cut down to the caliche undersurface, Hewey Calloway rode broncs and danced with pretty women and caroused with traveling companions like Snort Yarnell and Grady Welch. He raced horses with Homer Ganss and the Indians. He helped Alvin Lawdermilk find a forgotten hiding place and retrieve a whisky bottle he had all but given up for lost. The reunion had been a joyous thing to see. He followed the schoolteacher's red dog and watched Fat Gervin drown in the wake of a hundred black mongrels with outsized bladders, all the bank examiners in the state of Texas unable to save him.

After the third day he lost count, because time meant little to him. Days, he was by himself because Walter was busy in the fields and the boys were in school. Nights, they would sit outside after supper and talk awhile, but everybody went to bed at dark because to do otherwise meant to burn the kerosene lamps, and kerosene cost money.

"God gave us all the light we need," Eve would say. "When it's gone He means for us to rest."

The stricture was not firmly enforced, because an allowance was made sometimes for Cotton's studying.

Nobody had told Eve about Fat Gervin and the dogs, so she was pleasant to Hewey. Once she even went into her meager reserve of dried fruit and made an apricot cobbler that she knew was a special favorite of his. Watching him come dragging into the house of an evening, sweat-crusted and weary, she would tell him there was still hope of turning him into a Christian.

Tommy kept hanging on to Hewey's words as if they were gospel, prodding him to tell stories. His gullibility was no longer unlimited, however. Sometimes Cotton listened and sometimes he didn't. When he did listen, it was with a mood more of tolerance than of enjoyment. Usually he had schoolbooks to read, or books about mechanics and electricity and things of that sort, subjects in which Hewey saw no future. Nobody ever learned to ride broncs from reading a book, and knowing what made an engine run was no help in judging cattle.

Hewey decided it would do no good for him to counsel his nephew. The boy would have to find out for himself the error of his ways.

Late one evening as Hewey was taking the harness from the mules, preparing to feed them a bait of oats, he saw a horseman approaching on the wagon road. Sheriff Wes Wheeler came quickly to mind, but Hewey soon saw that this was not the sheriff.

This was a smaller man, bent-shouldered, riding a worn-out old black horse that could not have carried the sheriff's weight. The rider came by the chinaberry grove, found no freighters and angled on up toward the house.

Hewey was standing at the front step by the time the old man got there. Walter, washing the day's dust off of his face in the outdoor washpan, dried himself on a towel and stepped out a little way to greet the visitor. The old horse eyed the towel suspiciously. Despite his age he acted as if he could pitch or run if the towel made any untoward move. There were some horses that never quite gentled down, just as there were such men.

"Howdy, Mr. Rasmussen," Walter said. "You'd just as well get down. Supper'll be ready directly."

The old man sat hunched. He appeared bone-tired, reluctant to expend even the little energy it would take to get down from the saddle. "Much obliged, Walter. You don't suppose your woman will mind?"

She probably would, Hewey thought, *but she wouldn't say anything the old man could hear. She would grit her teeth and be painfully civil.*

He remembered the old man now, though it had been some years since he had last seen him, and Boy Rasmussen had gone downhill a long way. The face was pinched and furrowed, the skin dark and dry as old leather. The blue of his eyes seemed almost faded out, so that the red which rimmed them was dominant. His chin almost touched his nose, for he carried his teeth in a leather pouch hung around his neck, the leather string covered by a once-blue silk bandanna that was faded and dirty and frayed. His hands were shriveled, splotched with liver spots.

He had a smell that made the barking black dog keep its distance.

Hewey could only wonder how many years it had been since this old drifter had been given the name "Boy."

Rasmussen painfully brought his right leg over the high cantle, dragging his foot across the black's thin rump. Hewey heard a popping sound but couldn't tell if it was from the dried leather of the ancient saddle or from the thin and rheumy knees. In a high-pitched, breaky voice the old man said, "Walter, I don't suppose there'd be any whisky about?"

Walter shook his head. "We don't keep any on the place." Hewey saw pity in his brother's eyes.

Rasmussen's disappointment was plain. "It ain't that I'm a slave to it, you understand. It's just that I got the miseries tolerable bad today. There ain't a joint in my body . . ." But there was no use belaboring the point. "I don't suppose you'd have some 'baccy? Chewin' or smokin', I wouldn't be particular."

Hewey had a half-empty sack of the makin's in his shirt pocket. "Keep it, Mr. Rasmussen." It was *Mister* out of deference to age; it made no difference how far down the ladder the old man had descended. On no account would Hewey have addressed him as *Boy*. The old man eagerly took the sack in shaking hands and laboriously rolled a cigarette, spilling tobacco around the edges of the curled brown paper. Not until he lighted it and took a lung-filling drag of the smoke did he pause to thank Hewey. He stared intently through eyes that did not see well anymore except into the past. "You'd be brother Hewey, wouldn't you? Been off roamin' the country, they tell me. It's a big old country. I seen most of it myself, once. I reckon I'd go again, but this old pony here, I don't believe he could make it anymore. Them poor old feet have carried him too many miles."

Walter spotted Tommy staring curiously at the aging cowboy. "Tommy, I wisht you'd take Mr. Rasmussen's horse down to the barn. Unsaddle him, put him in a pen where the other horses won't bedevil him. And feed him some oats, will you?"

Tommy took the patched leather reins from the old man's arthritis-cramped hands, his gaze roaming over the ragged black saddle that must date back to the trail-driving times after the big war. Hewey could read the thought behind Tommy's eyes: how many wild and glorious scenes had that old saddle been a witness to or even a participant in?

Eve stood in the door, looking in dismay at this wizened old veteran. She would feed him supper; of that there was no question. But if she could help it she would not have him in the house. She said, "It's too hot to eat in the kitchen. Wouldn't you men like to eat outside where it's cool?" She didn't give them time to argue the point. "Walter, you can fix Mr. Rasmussen a plate and take it to him."

Rasmussen stared at Eve with a shyness that bordered on fear. It was a trait of these old bachelor drifters that they never quite understood women and were always nervous in their presence. The natural urges had been so long suppressed or diverted through the commercialized and mechanical attentions of the sporting women in town that they found it difficult to communicate on any level with the "good" women they encountered along the way. They put these women on a pedestal somewhere beyond the bounds of reality and made it a point to ride a long way around whenever they could.

The old man probably knew perfectly well that Eve didn't want him in the house. But he was happy he didn't have to go in there because it would have been as much an ordeal for him as for her. He took his teeth out of the pouch and put them into his mouth, dust and all. The way he tore into the supper, and ate a second helping when Walter refilled his plate for him, told Hewey it was probably the only thing he had eaten all day. He was a chuckline rider, too old anymore to find any steady work, existing off of the kindness of others, and off of grudging charity when he found no kindness. Almost nobody in this country would turn an old man away hungry, but there were some who would make him pay a price in shame and humility.

Hewey had heard old stories about Boy Rasmussen. He had been a great cowboy in his prime, pushing herds up the trail from South Texas to the railroads in Kansas, and beyond to the Indian reservations in Wyoming and Montana. There had been a time, before the years and the bottle had robbed him of dependability, that he had bossed herds and been a man of substance and repute. But the years had not been benevolent. Whatever might once have been was gone now. All that remained was a shell, a lonely and pathetic remnant, a burned-out relic of another time so far behind him that even he must find it unreal when the ghosts went roaming through his mind, stirring the dead ashes of old campfires, speaking in voices long silent.

After supper he began talking, his narrative wandering aimlessly through some long-ago time, touching on names no one else remembered. Hewey noticed that Tommy listened intently, and even Cotton was drawn to the old man. He spoke of the agonies of that old war, and he spoke of roundups so far behind him that most of the other participants, man and beast, had long since gone back to dust. Somehow he seemed to slip away from reality then, and he was back in an earlier time. He got up from his chair, saying he had best be getting some sleep because he had to be up early in the morning to point the herd for Doan's Crossing on the Red; they had to make it to Dodge ahead of the other outfits, before the buyers could fill their early needs and lower the price.

Hewey watched him shuffle toward the barn. He looked worriedly at Walter. "They let that old man ride around by himself? It ain't safe for him."

Walter shook his head. "He'll remember where he's at when he has to. He drifts through here a couple of times a year. He's got a brother down on the border that he stays with some. He's got a sister up on the plains. He'll get there, whichever way he's goin'."

Eve came outside, holding the screen door open even after she was on the front step, so she could retreat into the house if Boy Rasmussen was still around. "Did he finally go?"

Walter told her he had gone to the barn to sleep.

"Good," she said. She turned her attention to her boys. "You'd have done better to've been studyin' your lessons instead of bein' out here listenin' to the crazy carryin'-on of a senile old man."

Tommy did not agree. "Folks say he was a wheel horse once."

"Maybe so, but he's just a *busted* wheel now. You boys can learn *one* thing from him. You can learn what happens to people who drift through life with no purpose and no direction . . . men wastin' their good years seekin' after the sinful pleasures of whisky and the flesh, playin' cards and consortin' with fallen women."

She looked directly at Hewey.

Hewey said defensively, "Eve, you've never seen me with no fallen women."

"Thank God I have been spared that sight. But I have seen you dally with whisky and cards. The rest is best left to imagination."

Tommy asked, "Mama, what is *consort?*"

She purposely didn't hear him. She kept her eyes on Hewey. "If you don't change your ways you'll wind up an old saddle bum like Boy Rasmussen."

Hewey folded his arms, a gesture of defense. "I've never been a saddle bum. A bum begs somethin' for nothin'. Sure, I've been on the chuckline now and again, but I've always worked my way. Somebody feeds me or gives me a place to sleep, I always chop some wood or top off a bronc or somethin'. I never leave anybody poorer because he taken me in."

Eve fixed him with a triumphant stare. "At your age I don't suppose Boy Rasmussen did, either." She stood as if daring him to reply. Her point made, she retreated into the house, stopping only to call out, "You boys get ready for bed."

Tommy's question was still unanswered. "Uncle Hewey, what does *consort* mean?"

Hewey studied on that, looking in vain to his brother to step in with a better answer than his own. "I'll tell you someday, when I'm old enough to know."

Walter got up and left, laughing to himself. Sitting alone, Hewey saw nothing left to do except go to bed too. He walked down to the shed where he had been rolling out his blankets at night. He decided to take them out into the open to get away from the smelly old man, but to his relief he heard the old man's snoring and found that he had spread his thin roll outside the shed, on the ground. That spared Hewey from having to do it.

He awakened in the morning to the first color in the east. Throwing off his blanket, he put on his hat, then his shirt and pants and lastly his boots. He walked to the open door of the shed and called out, "Old-timer, breakfast'll be ready directly."

But the old man was gone. Hewey stepped to the corral and looked for the poor black horse. It too was gone. Boy Rasmussen had arisen earlier than anybody and was on his way to Dodge, or to the Cheyenne reservation, or perhaps to pick up a herd in Mexico . . . whichever fancy might have crossed his fragile mind.

Hewey stared out into the empty land as the sun's first good light spread across it. Whichever way he had ridden, Boy Rasmussen was a long time gone. Hewey stood a while staring, and an odd chill touched him.

At breakfast Eve remarked that Hewey was unusually quiet. He told her he was thinking about the tank-building job; it was almost finished. But the job had not crossed his mind except at the moment he needed an excuse.

Eve said uneasily, "I wish the old man hadn't left so early."

Hewey blinked. "I didn't think you liked him."

"I don't like to think of anybody, even an old saddle bum, ridin' across this big country hungry. You sure you didn't hear him get up and leave?"

"I never heard a thing."

Walter said, "He's of that old-timey breed, about as much Indian as white. They never did believe in makin' noise about anything they did. He comes quiet and he goes quiet."

Tommy put in, "Like a ghost, sort of."

Cotton ventured, "He *is* a ghost, of a kind. The world has gone off and left him."

Hewey frowned. "He's seen his hard times, but he's seen good ones too. I don't know but what I like *his* times better than the ones you're so hell-bent on takin' us into."

Walter Calloway sat bareback on the gray plow mule atop the fresh new tank dam and smiled as he studied the large basin Hewey had dug and smoothed just below the windmill. He had taken time away from his planting to ride over and look at the job.

Hewey said, "If it don't meet with your approval you're welcome to cut my wages half in two."

"It's a good job of work, big brother. I figured it would take you twice as long."

Hewey shrugged nonchalantly. "I can do anything I put my mind to."

"And your back." Walter nodded. "You've never been lazy, Hewey. You could do anything, be anything you wanted."

"I *am* what I want to be."

"I'm sayin' you could have a place of your own. Things come easy to you when you want them. You could have a place like mine. Maybe better. All you'd have to do would be to make up your mind that's what you wanted. All you need is the wantin'." He paused hopefully. "I wish you would, while you still can."

Hewey stretched out a long strip of dirty cloth that had been a sleeve. "All I need right now is a shirt. This one is past salvation."

"You can have one of my shirts."

Hewey doubted that Walter had one to spare. "I been wantin' to go to town anyway. I promised Pierson and the Dutchman . . ."

Walter grumped, "You're awful good at changin' the subject. I was tryin' to talk serious to you about gettin' a place of your own."

"I know it, and I'm tryin' to head you off." Hewey looked up at the windmill that bore his name. "I still say it needs a coat of paint."

He hadn't been keeping track of time, but after supper that night he found on inspection of Eve's patent medicine calendar in the kitchen that the next day was Saturday. "I couldn't of timed it better. It'll be interestin' to see how much the town has grown."

Tommy laughed. "One blacksmith shop and three outhouses."

Eve turned quickly, her eyes scolding, "You don't talk thataway."

Hewey said, "Be careful, button, or pretty soon you'll be talkin' like me."

Tommy replied, "That'd be all right. Will you take me to town with you, Uncle Hewey?"

Hewey would have, but Walter said, "I need you boys at home. There's still a right smart of field work needs doin'. I'll sure be glad when school is out."

Tommy didn't argue. His parents had trained him not to. But Hewey could see the boy's disappointment. He said, "Later on, when things get caught up around here, I'll take both of you boys with me on a trip someplace."

Cotton glanced at him over his book. He said nothing except with his eyes. He went back to his reading.

Tommy's eyes brightened. "You mean that, Uncle Hewey? When? Where we goin' to go?"

"I don't know, exactly. We'll figure somethin'. Maybe we'll go out to the Davis Mountains and down into the Big Bend. Or maybe we'll get us a boat and paddle it down the Pecos River plumb to the Rio Grande."

"I never have learned how to swim."

"Neither have I. But I wasn't figurin' on fallin' out of the boat."

Walter said, "I'd sure like to go on a trip like that myself." He was not joking. Eve cut a sharp, half-fearful glance at her husband.

Hewey said, "Why don't you, then? It'd be like old times."

A warmth came into Walter's face, lighting his eyes, deepening the laugh wrinkles at the corners of his mouth. "It would; it would for a fact. If I could ever see my way clear to get away for a little while . . ." He took a last sip from his coffee cup and found it cold. He got up and pushed his chair back under the pine table. "Long day tomorrow. We better all be gettin' some sleep." He walked out the door, bound for the little house out back.

The boys got up and shuffled around a little, drinking water from the dipper, Tommy wiping his mouth on his sleeve. "Good night, Uncle Hewey. We'll talk some more about that trip."

"You bet we will," Hewey answered, looking at Cotton and finding no belief in that nephew's eyes.

When the boys were gone, Hewey saw that Eve was studying him with worried eyes. Uneasily he said, "I expect I'll go to bed too."

"No you won't. Not till I say somethin'." She looked away from him, frowning. "Hewey, I made up my mind I was goin' to stay in a good humor with you if it kills both of us. And I'm tryin' to, God knows. But I wish you wouldn't talk to Walter about goin' somewhere with you. It's bad enough talkin' foolishness to the boys that way, but *him* . . . I think it wouldn't take much to get him to go."

"It might be good for him if he did."

Her voice was brittle. "No, it wouldn't. It would just wake up a lot of old notions that it took years to put behind him. He's your brother, Hewey. He's got more of you in him than he has of me." She blinked away a hint of a tear. "He gave up a lot for me and these boys. Nobody but him and me know just how much. So I wish you would leave him alone. Please . . . leave him alone."

Most people who called it Upton City did so out of jest. They said it would have a foot and a half of snow on the Fourth of July before it ever became a city. Hewey couldn't see much change in

105

it since he had left here. He couldn't even see the three new outhouses Tommy had spoken of. The town—what there was of it —was mostly single-story frame structures strung out in a casual line along a street that appeared to owe its original routing to a meandering buffalo trail. The story had been told that a trader had been on his way to set up a small post at Horsehead Crossing on the Pecos, but his heavily laden wagon had broken an axle here. There being no nearby timber big enough to hew a new axle, he had started selling goods out of the tarp-covered wagon. The story was probably a lie, but it made good telling. Hewey had never been one to let dull facts stand in the way of a good yarn.

Almost every house had a windmill of its own. Some people said that was wasteful, but Hewey disagreed; there was wind enough for everybody.

Dominating the town was a square stone courthouse, two stories plus a tall, domed cupola. It was built in the style of a storybook castle but scaled down to fit the limited assessed valuations of a land-poor ranching county. Beside the courthouse stood the stone jail, built to a similar pattern but smaller, squattier and lacking the cupola. Nobody saw any need in having the jailhouse be as fancy as the courthouse; the society there was nothing to brag about.

The best building in town, apart from the courthouse, was the Tarpley bank. It was built of the same stone as the courthouse, quarried nearby to save as much freighting expense as possible. It was limited to a single story, not one foot wider or longer than it had to be. C. C. Tarpley stressed economy in all things, including space. The fanciest thing about it was the carving of the name and date it had been built: 1898.

Fat Gervin stood in the door, leaning lazily against the jamb. Hewey saw him first and gave him a fleeting wave, smiling as he remembered the black dog. Fat turned without reply and disappeared into the mysterious realm of ledgers and debentures and compound interest.

Hewey looked again at the name over the door's stone arch: TARPLEY BANK AND TRUST.

Damn little trust there on either side of the counter, he reflected.

A man called Hewey's name and came running out from the

front gate of the wagonyard, causing Biscuit to shy and step sideways. "Hey, Hewey Calloway! We'd given you up for dead!"

The shout drew the attention of a barber and his customer in a small shop across the street. The barber stepped onto the porch to holler at Hewey. His customer came out with the white barber's cloth still tied around his neck, lifting and falling with the breeze. Biscuit did not like that cloth at all.

Hewey didn't know who to go howdy and shake with first, so he stayed where he was, in the middle of the street. They all came out to him. In a minute others came from other stores and shops, and they clustered there on the street until big Blue Hannigan's freight wagons, two hooked in tandem, came along needing the room.

"Hewey Calloway," Hannigan called, "you're blockin' the wheels of commerce."

But the wheels of commerce stopped right there as Blue got down to join the others in a drink at the Dutchman's to celebrate Hewey Calloway and Fat Gervin and the boys' black dog. The story had gotten around.

Hewey looked back toward the bank. "You reckon Fat Gervin's heard it?"

Blue Hannigan spat a brown stream of tobacco juice at a curious pup ten feet away and made a near miss. "Bound to have by now. There's always some slack-jaw runnin' to tell everything he hears."

It seemed to Hewey for a while that the only commerce in town was probably the Dutchman's, for almost everybody he knew in Upton City seemed to drop into the little saloon to shake hands with Hewey, recall a yarn or two out of old times and demand a new one or two to take along. Many a lie was told there in the space of an hour or so, and one or two stories that Hewey felt were mostly the truth. He made a show of drinking with everybody, but in reality he drank only a little. It was a quirk of the Dutchman's character that although he sold the stuff, he had the greatest respect for his poorest customers. Gradually the well-wishers drifted back to their own business, leaving Schneider and Hewey alone in the long, narrow room. The Dutchman had said little. He said nothing now. Friendship didn't have to be proven in conversation. Hewey leaned his elbows on the dark-stained bar, staring at a row of engravings nailed to the wall beside and above the mirror. In lots of bars the pictures would be of women, sometimes barefoot all the way. In the Dutchman's bar they were of racehorses. Schneider knew what was important in this world. It was said that he had been married once.

The room seemed to darken. A big man had come up to the open door and stood in it. Hewey blinked against the sunlight that haloed the man. He recognized Sheriff Wes Wheeler.

The sheriff said, "Mornin', Hewey."

Hewey sensed that Wheeler was not there to take a drink or to visit with the Dutchman. A little of the glow went out of him. "Mornin', Wes."

The sheriff came up beside Hewey at the bar. "Hewey Calloway, if wealth could be measured in friends, you'd be a richer man than C. C. Tarpley."

Hewey could see that the sheriff's thin smile had no depth. The eyes were coldly serious. He replied, "It is, and I am."

Wheeler turned to Schneider. "Dutch, you reckon you could go outside for a smoke or somethin'? I got a little business to talk to Hewey about."

Schneider gave Hewey a worried glance. Hewey knew the Dutchman was guessing there was trouble over Fat Gervin and the dog. "Hewey," Schneider said, "if you need help I am your witness. I saw it all, and there was nothing."

"There's no trouble," Wheeler assured the Dutchman. "It's a private matter."

Schneider laid down his bar rag and walked outside. The sheriff watched until he was sure he would not be heard. "Hewey, when you make friends you do a real good job of it. But when you make an enemy you do a good job of that too." From his pocket he pulled a sheet of paper, folded many times. "You'll want to take a look at that, then burn it."

Hewey had a good idea what it was before he unfolded it. It was a fugitive notice, printed on a real press and everything. It was the first time he could remember ever seeing his name in print. Well, almost his name. Big block letters read HUGH HOLLOWAY.

A cold feeling settled in his stomach, but he tried to cover it with a surface grin. He doubted he was fooling Wheeler. "Marshal up yonder still hasn't gotten my name right."

"He will, sooner or later." Wheeler's face was deeply furrowed. "I thought you was goin' to visit a day or two and then leave."

"I been buildin' a stock tank out at that new windmill."

"You through with it yet?"

"Finished yesterday."

Wheeler stared at Hewey's glass, the only one left on the bar. It was full, and had been for half an hour. Impulsively he picked it up. "Hewey, do you mind?" The sheriff downed the drink and set the empty glass solidly back down on the bar. He seemed disappointed that the drink didn't make his task any easier.

"I ain't fixin' to tell you what to do, Hewey. You're a grown man, and then some. But if it was me, I'd get my good-byes said and travel on."

"I'd hate to go now. You know, even Eve has been in a good humor most of the time."

"Them folks up at New Prosperity ain't. At least not that marshal. I have a feelin' that if he was to come across you he'd shoot first and then ask you to surrender."

"If he wanted to, he could find me no matter where I went."

"Maybe. But he'll find you for sure if you stay around here. I don't know that there's anything I can do for you if he comes. I'd even have to help him if he had the right papers and asked me to. That would distress me, Hewey."

Hewey stared at the racehorses. He wished Wheeler hadn't drunk up all the whisky. "I never like to cause distress to my friends. But dammit, Wes, this thing has been blowed up out of all reason. There wasn't nothin' to it, hardly, just a few words and one little punch. Didn't even skin my knuckles to speak of. All I hurt was his pride."

"That's all some people have, is pride. Generally the ones who take on over it most are the ones that have got the least to be proud of. Better you'd broken his head open than to've left him lookin' foolish in his own town."

"I just don't like people tryin' to run my life for me, tellin' me what to do. I don't do that to other people, and I don't want them doin' it to me. When I go someplace it's because I want to, and when I leave it's because I want to."

"I'm not crowdin' you, Hewey. At least I'm tryin' not to."

"It ain't you, it's *them*." He felt somehow trapped. He doubled his fist and beat it against the bar.

Hopefully the sheriff asked, "That mean you're fixin' to leave?"

Hewey had hit the bar too hard. He rubbed the aching hand. "It means I'll think about it."

"All right, Hewey. I just don't want you on my conscience."

"No reason I should be. Whatever I decide, it'll be my own doin', not yours."

The sheriff nodded. "I've had my say." He reached over and touched Hewey's tattered sleeve. A faint smile compromised his solemnity. "Go or stay, if I was you I think I'd get me a new shirt."

Pierson Phelps' general mercantile was the largest store in town. It was a simple frame structure decorated by a liberal application of gingerbread trim along the top of the porch. Canned and boxed goods were stacked high on a shelf inside the window, but Phelps never moved anything out onto the porch for display. It was too much work to move it back in at night. The sign out front was a small one, the letters hardly six inches high: *Phelps General Mercantile and Sundries.* He saw no need in ostentatious advertising; everybody in town knew who he was and what he sold. He also had the post office, and that fact was noted on a separate sign even smaller than the other. Anybody who couldn't find the post office probably couldn't read a letter anyway.

The old merchant stood a little way inside the door, apron around his broad waist, dark sleeve protectors pulled way up on his thick arms. He wore a small black bow tie, which always seemed to bob up and down as he talked. "I heard you were in town an hour ago, Hewey. Thought you had forgotten me."

"Not hardly. Just taken me a little longer than I figured on to get around. I don't suppose you'd have a shirt that'd fit me? Not one of them fancy two-dollar Sunday-meetin' shirts. Somethin' even a broke cowpuncher can afford."

Pierson narrowed one eye and shut the other, studying Hewey's build. He walked behind a counter on the drygoods side, where the bolt cloth was stacked, and pulled out a drawer. He poked around in it a minute and brought out a simple white shirt with gray stripes. "Normally I get a dollar apiece for these, but seein' it's you I'll let you have it for six bits. I'll even throw in a bow tie."

"Any cheaper without the tie?"

"I've already given you my preacher rate, and you're no preacher. But I'll keep the tie and give you a sack of barber-pole candy to take home to the boys."

Hewey took the shirt, felt of the plain cotton material and decided it was too high at the price. Many a time he had worked a full, hard day for a lot less than six bits. But money was getting to where it wasn't worth anything anymore.

"Merchant takes all the best of it," he lamented. "But I reckon I'll settle for what I can get."

"It's the cost of labor that makes everything so high," Pierson sympathized. "You wouldn't believe what some people earn, workin' in factories back east. They're ridin' this country down to ruin."

That was how things had always been as far back as Hewey could remember. Price of cattle was always too low, and price of everything else was always too high. "I'm goin' to find me a corner back yonder and put this new shirt on," he said.

Pierson pointed vaguely with his sharp chin, somewhere toward the rear of the room.

The post office section was along the south wall, a little more than halfway back in the store. Hewey couldn't remember that he had ever received a letter out of it, but it was comforting to know he could if anybody ever wrote to him. He went around the back side of that section, where he wouldn't be seen from the front of the store, and he took off what was left of the ragged shirt that had known hard duty almost continuously all winter and spring. His long-handled underwear wasn't a lot better, but it had one virtue: nobody could see it. He wasn't going to buy himself a new set. Pierson would probably want an extra four bits, at least.

Money didn't mean much to Hewey, but he saw no sense in throwing it away.

He didn't realize how long it could take him to put on a shirt. He hadn't figured on the thing having so many pins. Every time he thought he had found them all, another one stuck him. He was so intent on the pins that he didn't hear the wooden floor squeak under someone's feet.

He heard a woman say, "Woops!"

By reflex he turned, the shirt in his hand. The schoolteacher stood there, eyes wide in surprise. Again by reflex, Hewey brought up the new shirt to try to hide his chest, which the long underwear was doing anyway. "Pardon me, ma'am," he managed, feeling his face burn red.

"Pardon me, Mr. Calloway." She turned her back on him.

He hurriedly pulled the shirt on. A pin he had missed was scratching his neck, but he wouldn't have taken the shirt off again for a box of them, the two-dollar kind. He quickly shoved the shirttail in and buttoned his britches. "I'm decent now," he said uneasily, feeling around the collar but unable to locate the irritating pin. He decided he had rather put up with it than make a show of the thing.

She had moved around to the other side of the post office section and was still turned away from him. "I'm sorry if I embarrassed you, Mr. Calloway. I had no idea you were there. Mr. Phelps must have stepped outside somewhere."

Hewey had wondered why Phelps hadn't headed her off. "My fault," he replied. "I ought to've gone out back to the . . ." He caught himself. One did not speak to a lady about such things as outhouses. Their existence was only privately recognized, never publicly acknowledged. They were, between the sexes, in the nature of an open secret.

She said, "I was just trying to see if I might have a letter. Mr. Phelps always puts them in that box back there."

Hewey could see so many open boxes, letters sticking out of at least half, that he had no idea which one she meant. "Show me where it's at and I'll get it for you."

"Oh no, I wouldn't want to cause you any trouble."

"No trouble atall. I can reach in there easy and get it."

"That's not the kind of trouble I mean. It's against the law for you or me to touch it so long as it's behind the postmaster's counter."

"It's your letter, ain't it?"

"Not until Mr. Phelps hands it to me himself."

With his eye Hewey roughly measured the width of the counter and the reach to the boxes behind it. For the letter it would be a very short trip. "It'll be the same letter then that it is right now. Seems to me like I'd save Pierson Phelps a little work and you a little time."

"I know the rule looks silly, but it *is* the rule."

"Looks to me like if they want people to pay attention to the rules, the rules ought to make sense."

She smiled. "You have the logic, Mr. Calloway, but Washington has the law. I am afraid I have been put in the position of the devil's advocate."

He didn't know what she meant by that, but it sounded vaguely wicked. And her a schoolteacher . . .

She asked, "Have you always been such a rebel, Mr. Calloway?"

"That war was over a good while before I was born. But my old daddy was in the Confederate Army."

Her eyes seemed to be laughing a little, but he had the feeling that she was not really laughing at him. At least, the laughter did not embarrass or anger him. She said, "I wonder how you ever got along in the Army, with all the regulations you had to obey?"

"There was times when I thought sure I was goin' to wind up in that army jailhouse, but seemed like they always found someplace they needed me worse." He stared at her thoughtfully. "How'd you know I was in the Army?"

"Tommy told me. He has told me a great deal about you, as a matter of fact. He said you were in Cuba, right there beside Teddy Roosevelt."

Hewey squirmed. "Well, I was in Cuba, all right. I wouldn't say I was all that close to the President."

"Tommy told me you were in the charge up San Juan Hill, showing Roosevelt the way."

He felt his face going red again. Where in the world had the boy ever gotten a yarn like that? "You got to watch that button, ma'am. He's inclined now and again to exaggerate."

She smiled. "He's a good boy. They're both good boys. You can be proud to have them for kin." The smile faded, and the laughter gradually went out of her eyes. She seemed to be looking past him a moment, leaving this time and this place for somewhere out of memory or out of imagination, possibly some place lost. She caught herself and looked back at him, but the glow did not return to her eyes. Whatever ghost had crossed her mind, he had taken the glow with him. She said, "I've been interested in Cuba for a long time. I'd like someday to have you tell me about your experiences there."

"They didn't really amount to much."

"They would be interesting to *me*." She looked away from him again, toward the front windows and the sunlight on the street. She said, "I don't suppose you've seen Alvin Lawdermilk?"

"Not since Sunday, out at the place."

"He has talked about you a great deal. *Everybody* talks about you a great deal."

He grimaced. "I hope you don't listen to everything they say."

"They all speak well of you." She reconsidered. "Mostly well, anyway. One gentleman down at the bank might be an exception."

"I hoped you'd forgot about that."

The smile came again. "I'll never forget it. I'll be eternally grateful to you."

He frowned. "I get the feelin' Fat Gervin done somethin' to you."

"He didn't, but he would have. His intention was clear enough."

Resentment flared in him. She *was* a handsome woman, he decided. He could understand how a man of Fat's character could get to thinking things that should never cross the mind of a married man. Momentarily those thoughts came to Hewey too. But he quickly put them aside, for this was a lady, and a gentleman did not compromise a lady, even in his mind. He had no regret for what he had done to Fat. He was sorry only that Miss Renfro had seen it.

"It was a fool stunt I done."

"Not at all. It fitted him so well." She seemed ready to turn away, but she said, "Alvin Lawdermilk has been talking about how much he would like to have you come over to his place and help him break some horses and mules."

"He told me, but I been needin' to get on down the road."

"He's short-handed. All he has is Julio Valdez, and it's too much for just the two of them. He could really use your help."

Hewey shoved his hands into his pockets. In one he felt the folded fugitive notice the sheriff had given him. "I wisht I could oblige, but I got a job waitin' for me out west . . ."

"And a job here, if you want it."

Pierson Phelps came in the front door, looking around. He spied Spring Renfro, and his round face lighted up like a barn-dance lantern on a Saturday night. "Miss Renfro! I just saw your paint horse tied outside. I hope you haven't waited long."

"Not at all. I've had a pleasant visit with Mr. Calloway. I came to see if I might have any mail. I've been expecting a letter from my sister."

"Yes, a letter came for you yesterday." Phelps stepped inside the little cubicle that was the post office and reached up into one of the boxes. Hewey grimaced. *He* could have reached it, and Miss Renfro could have read it by now.

Phelps handed her the letter. She glanced at the handwriting. "It's from her, all right."

Phelps came out from behind the counter and leaned his heavy body against it. "School's about out. I suppose you'll be leavin' us soon for the summer?"

She shook her head. "No. My sister is all the family I have anymore. She has her own home, and her own family. I'd be company for the first few days. After that I'd be a burden. Cora Lawdermilk has asked me to stay and help her see after her old mother."

Phelps smiled. "That's fine. We've gotten used to havin' you around here. We'd miss you if you left."

"And I'd miss this place." She moved to the front door. Phelps and Hewey followed her. She paused and looked out into the street. "Odd, the hold this West Texas country takes on a person. First time I saw what I had come to, I hated it. I was used to trees and tall green grass and running streams. All I saw here was open country and desert. Or so I thought. But it's grown on me. I don't know if I could ever go back to the piney woods again."

"You shouldn't ever have to. If some eligible bachelor here doesn't come along and grab you up, I'll be awful disappointed in the whole bunch of them." He glanced at Hewey.

Hewey felt his face redden once more.

She walked out to her horse, tethered at a rail. She untied him and stood a moment, looking at the sidesaddle, then glancing back at the store.

Pierson Phelps gave Hewey a push. "What're you standin' there for, cowboy? She needs a lift up."

Hewey had been thinking about it, but he had wanted to make up his *own* mind. Stiffly he stepped down from the porch and gave her a boost, careful not to touch her anywhere except the foot. Even being close to her flustered him a little.

Once she had her right leg in place over the horn, and her ankles properly covered by her long riding skirt, she thanked Hewey. "I hope you'll keep in mind what I said about Alvin Lawdermilk. He *does* need your help. And it would be nice to see a new face." She smiled and rode up the street on her paint horse.

Hewey stared after her. He had decided she wasn't really so old as he had judged the first time he saw her. He doubted she was past thirty. Not much past thirty, anyway.

Phelps said, "You could do a lot worse."

"Worse than what?"

"She's a real nice lady."

Hewey could see no argument with that. "Seems like it."

"I'll admit she's not the greatest beauty in the world."

Hewey turned and challenged him. "Show me one in Upton City who looks better."

The way the storekeeper smiled, Hewey suspected he had stepped into a trap. Phelps said, "She's got no gentleman callers, far as I've heard."

"She still ain't got one."

Phelps regarded him with amusement. Hewey was sure now about that trap. The old man said, "I believe you'd better have *two* shirts. Tell you what I'll do—I'll give you the second for just four bits. And I believe you'll be needin' that bow tie after all."

VI

Biscuit had never cared particularly for the Lawdermilk ranch. A horse, like a cat, prefers the familiar, and the Lawdermilk headquarters was always unpredictable, always a spooky menagerie. If blue-gray guinea hens were not picking and gossiping their way across the barnyard, a peafowl was spreading its feathers and screeching. A handful of undisciplined Spanish goats always had free run of the place, crawling through corral fences at will, jumping up into the horse troughs and helping themselves to feed that rightfully belonged to their betters. The noise was often distracting. Because Alvin Lawdermilk raised horses and mules to sell, there was always a certain amount of snorting and bawling and shouting, of young broncs threshing and running against ropes and trying to tear down the wooden fences to which they were secured. Worst of all, perhaps, were the numerous burros. As a well-traveled horse, supposedly more sophisticated than most, Biscuit had never conceded much merit in that inferior, intractable breed. His unfortunate encounter with Cotton's burro had only deepened his ingrained prejudice.

The feed was good, but after all other considerations were taken into account, it was a degrading place for a patrician.

Hewey had no such problem. He had always had a happy facility for adaptability into any environment where the chuck was good and the society congenial. Both conditions were met at the Lawdermilk ranch. As a result of his own natural generosity, aided by Cora's insistence, Alvin had built a free-style one-story frame house of mixed architecture that rambled over a considerable plot of ground in the general shape of an L, with a broad and breezy open gallery all the way around it. Cora had intended it for a large flock of children, which she never had. So she alternately babied Alvin and chastised him, much as she would have done to the sons who were never born to her. The two of them had long shared the big house with her aging mother, who sipped copious quantities of Prickly Ash Bitters and spent most of her waking hours talking. She could get around on a cane when she had to, but she usually preferred sitting in a wheel chair of fiendish mobility. Her treatment of Alvin was the same as Cora's only to a point: she never babied him, but she chastised him often. Alvin put up with it with the patience of one of his burros.

In recent years, lacking children but not lacking a love for them, the Lawdermilks had provided a country schoolhouse at their headquarters to accommodate the school-age youngsters who lived on neighboring ranches and farms, too far from Upton City to ride there and back every day. They also provided room and board for whatever person happened to be teaching. Except for the first one, that had always been a woman. The man teacher who had opened the school had made the unfortunate mistake of finding too many of Alvin's secret whisky caches one idle Sunday afternoon. He had done considerable damage to the schoolhouse and had left his opinion of various and sundry local citizens scrawled on the blackboard in correctly spelled but awesome English to greet his pliable young charges in his absence Monday morning. Even students who had never been able to memorize a line of Shakespeare or Keats seemed to have learned that day's lesson by heart on only a few minutes' surprised scrutiny. Now, some years later, it was often repeated verbatim on festive occasions by students and former students who still couldn't remember the opening line to the balcony scene.

Unlike some ranches where Hewey had worked, the hired help always ate in the main house with the owners, at the same table and all. That even included Julio Valdez, who on many places would have been expected to cook for himself, or at best to have filled his plate and to have retired to the gallery to eat alone while everyone else sat at the long plain table in the dining room. Julio made it a point to sit at the far end of the table, well away from

Old Lady Faversham, Alvin's sharp-eyed mother-in-law. She could remember back almost to the time of the Alamo.

Hewey always sat by Julio, not so much to demonstrate his liberalism as to keep away from the old lady too. Her opinion of foot-loose cowboys was roughly the same as her opinion of Mexicans; she lumped both in a general category of undesirables. Some days Hewey and Julio had to move over and share that category with Alvin. The old lady had never forgiven him for proving her wrong thirty years ago when she declared he could never support her daughter.

Nothing the old lady said could offset the fact that Cora Lawdermilk was a splendid cook. Hewey wouldn't have told Eve for all the money in C. C. Tarpley's bank, but Cora's biscuits were better than Eve's, and good biscuits to Hewey were at least half of the meal. Old Lady Faversham could prattle on to her mean old heart's content and say anything she pleased as long as there were plenty of biscuits on a platter within Hewey's easy reach. And there always were. He didn't have to look at her anyway, more than once or twice a meal. Mostly, when he could steal glances without her catching him, he looked at Spring Renfro. She always sat across the table from him, wearing her clean and simple teacher dresses in just the right combination of gentility and poverty to please a country school board. Times, when he looked at her, his mind began involuntarily to stray from a gentlemanly plane, and he would have to force himself to think about horses and mules.

Evenings, Hewey would sit on the gallery with Alvin and swap windies. Sometimes these set-tos took on the nature of a contest, but Hewey had a definite advantage because he had traveled a great deal more. Alvin had been tied down physically, though not in spirit, by the struggle to build a respectable ranch for himself and a comfortable if not excessive standard of living for his wife. He was a man of contrasts, a free soul trapped within a body that was tied to one piece of ground. That soul sought its release in great stacks of books, magazines and newspapers which he devoured with the appetite of a lion. He could at almost any given time name all the crowned heads of Europe, unless the urgency of the horse and mule business had made him miss reading about some overnight revolution. He could describe in some detail all the major cities of the world, though the largest he had ever seen with his own eyes was Kansas City, to which he traveled in the caboose of a cattle train. Now and again, when his soul could not be satisfied by his reading of faraway places, it sought refuge in the bottles he had stashed liberally all over the ranch. Since Hewey had been here Alvin had found little need to drink. His questing spirit found vicarious release through the stories Hewey told him.

Sometimes when Cora felt like it she would sit down in the evening at the upright piano in the parlor and play from the reams of sheet music she had accumulated over the years. Hewey had flipped through the stack and found such titles as " 'Tis Not Always Bullets That Kill," or "Do Not Tell Her I Am Bad," or "Please, Sir, Don't Ask Me Again." He could tell that Pierson Phelps always kept her supplied with the latest. Occasionally Spring Renfro would stand beside her and sing with Cora the lyrics to songs like "Is She Only a Friend After All?" and "For the Love of a True Woman's Heart."

Hewey felt himself fortunate to be exposed to so much culture.

At bedtime he would walk down near the barn to a small frame building that served double duty as a cowboy bunkhouse and a shed for storing windmill tools and the like. The walls had cracks he could almost throw a cat through, but that was something of an asset in warm summertime. He didn't intend to be here in the winter.

He shared the room with Julio. To some people this would have appeared an unseemly display of racial equality, but Hewey had a little the best of it. He slept on a steel cot, while Julio's was a less sturdy one of wood and canvas. The proprieties were met.

Sunup never caught Alvin Lawdermilk in bed, or anybody else on the place except Old Lady Faversham. While Cora fixed breakfast, Julio would milk the two Jersey cows and scatter grain for the pampered flock of Barred Plymouth Rock hens. Hewey would saddle the night horse and ride out into the small fenced trap to bring in the mounts the men would be needing for the morning's work. Alvin would be stomping around in the corrals, putting out bundle-feed and oats. He had a field of redtop cane stretching just beyond the barn. In that field he and his help would break and train those horses and mules intended for a lifetime of work to the plow or wagon. In this manner he was able to get some farm work out of Hewey without calling it by its true name. As long as the main object was to break stock, Hewey could tolerate the plow. But if the plow itself became the admitted object, he would ask for his time and move on down the road. So had many another cowboy and horsebreaker before him.

Alvin Lawdermilk was always careful in the way he named his priorities.

A rancher buying "rough-broke" horses might not think to ask, but it would have been to his interest to have done so, whether the bronc buster had been working by the day or was paid by the number of horses he rode. When Hewey was being paid by the bronc, he usually considered one ready to go after being saddled and ridden six or seven times. If he was being paid by the day—as at Alvin's place—he was more likely to put a horse through nine or ten saddlings.

His bronc-riding sessions caused Spring Renfro some difficulty. One morning he had several broncs hackamored and tied to fence posts outside the round corral in which he would ride them. From his rough observation point atop a pitching sorrel gelding he saw eighteen or twenty youngsters spill out of the little white-painted schoolhouse for morning recess. Most of the boys and some of the girls came running toward the corrals to watch the show. Several rushed heedlessly past the tied broncs. This startled the young horses, causing them to thresh against the strong hackamore ropes.

"You kids watch out for them horses," Hewey yelled. "They'll kick the whey out of you!"

He was too busy staying in the saddle to do anything more about the problem. And because the Lord watches out for kids, fools and drunks, nobody got hurt. They perched on the corral fence, watching. Hewey let the pony have his head and gave the kids the exhibition they had wanted to see. When the sorrel had finished pitching and set in to running for all it was worth around and around the corral, lathering itself with sweat, Hewey was able to pick out Tommy sitting on the fence beside the nester boy

Lester. Lester was twanging that infernal jew's-harp as if he thought the show needed musical accompaniment. Hewey looked around for Cotton as best he could, considering that he still had a double handful with the sorrel bronc. He could not pick him out of the crowd of kids sitting on the fence like blackbirds.

He'd be here if I was driving an automobile, Hewey thought, feeling a touch of resentment. But any coffeepot polisher and ribbon clerk could learn to drive an automobile. It took somebody special to fork a wiry bronc and keep one leg on each side.

The sorrel finally ran itself down, and Hewey began pulling its head first to one side, then to the other, giving the first lesson in reining. He could hear a bell ringing and in a moment of comparative quiet looked across to the schoolhouse. Spring Renfro stood on its tiny porch with the bell in her hand, calling for the youngsters to come back. A few melted away, mostly girls, but a majority of the boys clung to the fence.

"You buttons better get back over there, or she'll whip you-all and then come after me," Hewey told them.

In a little while all the chicks had returned to the nest. Miss Renfro walked to the corral by herself, having put the youngsters to studying whatever subjects were pertinent to their respective ages and grades. Hewey saw her coming just as he was about to climb aboard a stocking-legged black that had a wicked gleam in its left eye and a wicked kick in its left hind foot. Julio was earing the pony down. "Let him go, Hooley!" Hewey hollered as he jammed his right foot into the stirrup. The bronc bawled and went straight up.

Because the teacher had been so unfortunate as to miss the other show, Hewey was determined to make up by giving her a better one than he had given the kids. The dust was heavy and the action thick for two or three minutes until the black began wearing down. Hewey put on a show that he thought would have impressed Teddy Roosevelt, but it didn't seem to impress Miss Renfro. She stood outside the fence showing more of impatience than amusement. When Hewey finally dismounted she moved up against the fence and peered at him through the dust.

"Mr. Calloway, I think you and I are going to have to come to some accommodation."

"How can I accommodate you, ma'am?"

"I realize you have your job to do, but I also have mine. For the few days that school is still to be in session, could I prevail on you to find something less spectacular to do during recess?"

After that, Hewey made it a point at that time of day to be out of sight, either in a field pairing a bronc mule to a gentle one and working them to a plow, or in a far corral tying hackamored broncs to Alvin's gentle burros and turning them out to run in the open pastures. There the stubborn little creatures soon taught them the rope was to be obeyed.

At the supper table several days later, Spring Renfro thanked him. "After tomorrow," she said, "I'll not interfere with your schedule anymore. In fact, in honor of the last day of school it might be a nice present to the boys if you *did* put on a little show. I'll let the final recess be a long one."

The black bronc was still unregenerated, still a sure bet for a show even after several saddles. Hewey saved him for recess time. The entire class walked down to the round corral, including Cotton and the teacher. Despite several days of work, Hewey and Julio still had to tie up one of the black's hind feet to be able to get the saddle on him. His back was still humped as if a watermelon had been placed under the blanket. Hewey drew the cinch as tight as he could and untied the rope while Julio took a death grip on the pony's ears.

Tommy yelled from the fence, "That old horse is goin' to throw you."

Hewey said, "Boy, I ain't never been throwed in my life." He looked up at the railbirds as he gripped the saddle horn with his right hand and the heavy rein and a healthy piece of mane with the left. "I'm fixin' to show you buttons somethin' you'll never find in no joggerfy lesson." He swung up, and Julio let go, stepping quickly back out of the way. The youngsters hollered and cheered.

Either the black had saved back a few tricks or he had learned something new. His first jump set Hewey a little off balance, cracking his tailbone painfully against the sharp edge of the snakeskin-covered cantle. He kept his chin down to try to prevent getting his neck popped by the pony's fast twisting and changing

123

of direction, by the hard jarring as all four feet hit the ground at once. It was an old adage in cow country that there never was a bronc that couldn't be rode, and never was a cowboy that couldn't be throwed. Hewey realized after the third jump that he was about to bear personal witness to the latter proposition. It was no longer a question of whether, but only of how.

The *how* was an ignominious belly buster, out over the right shoulder and down to the ground with a dull thud that took most of his breath and much of his pride. He held still, partly because he didn't think the black would step on him except by accident but mostly because he was so numb he couldn't move much anyway. The youngsters' cheering had turned to laughter. Kids, Hewey thought, were bloodthirsty at heart.

Julio's first responsibility was to catch the horse, not to help Hewey to his feet. Hewey pushed up onto his hands and knees and felt around for his hat. It lay just ahead of him, well stomped by one of the black's hoofs. He got to his feet, dusted the hat on his britches leg and pulled it back down over his head.

The first thing he saw was that Cotton was walking back to the schoolhouse by himself.

Hewey's face reddened. *I let him down again.*

The smart-aleck Lester said, "You showed us what not to do. When you goin' to show us the rest?"

Hewey had in mind a little different demonstration, and it involved that jew's-harp. But this was not the time or place. "I'm just lettin' him keep a little confidence in himself. You don't want to plumb kill a horse's spirit."

Julio brought the black back and eared him down. Hewey swung into the saddle again, for it was a cardinal rule of the trade that you never let a horse throw you and get away with it; that was what created outlaws. This time he rode the black to a standstill. The pony stood heaving, the sweat running down his hide and dripping off onto the ground. Only the flesh had been exhausted; the fighting spirit was still intact. He reached around and tried to bite a chunk out of Hewey's leg. Only the heavy leather chaps saved Hewey from a nasty set of tooth marks.

He said to Julio, "If he can't throw you off he'll pull you off with his teeth, a mouthful at a time. He'll make somebody a good horse one of these days."

He found the kids still talking more of his fall than of his final victory. Sourly he remembered something he had heard one of the Miller brothers say while he had his short-lived job with the 101 Ranch Wild West Show: "Those people don't pay to see you ride; they pay in hopes of seein' you get yourself killed."

He thought it remarkable how young they became corrupted.

Spring Renfro began calling the students down off of the fence and back to the classroom. "Show is over," she said. "It's time for a little more learning before I turn you loose for the summer."

She waited at the fence, and Hewey sensed that she wanted to speak to him. Acutely aware of his disgrace, he reluctantly shuffled over there, hat in his hand. "They sure didn't get much learnin' out here," he conceded.

"Perhaps they did." She smiled. "Humility is a valuable lesson for anybody."

"Well, I *am* humiliated, that's a natural fact."

"But not too humiliated for some ice cream after a while, I hope. I'm giving the children a picnic at dinnertime, up under the trees."

"A bronc-ridin' show and then a picnic? They won't learn much today."

"If they haven't learned it by now, one last day won't make any difference. You'll be there, won't you?"

"Sure. I'll fall off of a horse any day for a dish of ice cream."

It turned out that the invitation hadn't been necessary. Cora Lawdermilk didn't serve dinner in the house anyway. Everybody ate beneath the trees with the children. Hewey sensed that Miss Renfro had given him the invitation as a special gesture, perhaps to soothe his wounded pride. He didn't know how good she might be at reading, writing and geography, but she knew a lot about human nature that hadn't all come from books. And she had learned it young, for he was convinced by now that she lacked a whole lot being thirty.

After the supper dishes had been washed and put away that night she came out onto the porch where Hewey sat with Alvin

Lawdermilk, listening to the night birds setting up a contest out beyond the town road. "May I sit down with you-all?" she asked.

Both Hewey and Alvin got up quickly and offered her their cane-bottomed chairs. She motioned for them to sit back down and dragged up another for herself. She made a few preliminary comments upon the loveliness of the night and the fullness of the moon, observations with which Hewey found no quarrel. Abruptly she said, "I want to thank you, Mr. Calloway."

He tried in vain to remember anything he had done for her, other than offer her his chair.

She said, "I know how badly you felt about being thrown off in front of all those children. But I appreciate the way you got up and went right back to the job at hand. The children don't all realize it, but they learned a valuable lesson."

"What? That a cowboy looks foolish lyin' in the dirt with all the breath knocked out of him?"

"No, that one doesn't just quit when he is faced with a reversal. One gets up and tries again until he has succeeded."

"I don't know if I'll ever succeed with that black bronc. He's pretty strong-minded."

"You'll win. You'll be a better man for having done it, and he'll be a better horse for having fought so hard."

Hewey rubbed his shoulder. He didn't think there was a joint in his body that didn't ache. "I hope I'll be a better man than I feel like right now."

"You're a better man than you know, Mr. Calloway."

Cora Lawdermilk pushed the screen door open a little and poked her head out. "Alvin, you've got some bookkeepin' work to be doin'."

Alvin blinked. "I don't remember any bookkeepin' work."

"Well, you've got some. It's waited long enough."

Alvin stood up, stoked his pipe and seemed confused for a minute while he stared at Hewey and the teacher. His confusion left him. "By George, I do remember." He walked into the house, leaving the two sitting alone.

Hewey found the teacher was studying him. He cut his gaze back to some forlorn-looking and bewildered young broncs staked out on the prairie, obscured by the deepening dusk. "Kind of hard on them. First time they've ever been tied up thataway. They've lost their freedom, and they don't know what to make of it."

"It's something most people go through too. You've never lost *your* freedom, have you, Mr. Calloway?"

"No. I've given up lots of other things at times, but that's one thing I've made it a point to keep."

"I guess you've run on to horses that never would give up, either."

"I've seen some break their necks against a fence. I've seen a few just lay down and die rather than give up to the rope and the saddle."

"You strike me as a man who might do the same thing, in your own way."

"I don't know. I've never had to face up to it."

"You've never been tempted to? Not for a home, a piece of land . . . a woman?"

"Tempted, sure. I've been tempted by a good many things. I've given in more often than I'd want to admit to a lady. But that's one temptation I've always managed to shed in time."

He saw the same fleeting sadness in her face that he had seen that day in Phelps' store. She said, "I knew somebody once, a lot like you. . . ." She looked off into the night. When her gaze came back to him, she had put on the smile again. "I hope you never change."

"I don't intend to. I'm satisfied the way everything is."

"Even though everybody seems to be trying to change you?"

"The way I live doesn't affect anybody but me."

"Eve . . . Walter . . . the boys . . . they all worry about you. What happens to you *does* affect them."

"There ain't nothin' goin' to happen to me."

"It could have today. That horse might've killed you."

"It didn't. Been a many a one tried."

"One may, someday."

"You're startin' to talk like Eve."

"I don't mean to intrude where I have no business. And I'm not trying to change you. I just want to point out that you mean something to a lot of good people, and they worry about you."

Hewey stood up. "If I tried to change, I'd be like one of them colts out yonder, staked to stumps and logs and old wagon wheels. I'd be lost and fightin' my head like them. And sooner or later I'd probably break my neck hittin' a fence. Folks have got to take me like I am or leave me alone."

Hewey was too busy during the week to visit his brother and the rest of the family. On Sundays, right after the women got home from church and served the noon meal, he would hitch a pair of mules to an old wagon and head out across the country. It was partly for pleasure, partly for work, because one of the mules was always a bronc being broken to the harness. The other, for balance, would be relatively gentle and stable. One mule could not run fast or far if the other did not choose to go.

The third Sunday he was there, Hewey had Julio help him hitch up an eye-rolling brown mule that had already seen a couple of training sessions in the cane patch but was a long way from being ready to deliver on Alvin's contract to the Texas & Pacific Railroad for working stock. He intended to match this one to a placid old gray known as Callie, but Callie came up lame. He caught out what was handy, a bay mule with a reputation for kicking when a man's attention was focused elsewhere. The bronc mule put up such a struggle that Hewey was tempted to give up the trip and spend the afternoon gleefully kicking hell out of her. By the time they finally got her harnessed and buckled into place across the tongue from the bay, the older mule was nervous too.

"I think," said Julio, "that maybe you better watch them pretty close, Hooey."

Knowing the answer, Hewey asked, "I don't suppose you'd like to ride over to Walter's with me, Hooley?"

The Mexican smiled. "This is for me a day of holy rest."

As Hewey drove by the big house, Spring Renfro called and waved her bonnet at him from the gallery. "Just a minute, Mr. Calloway. I would like to go with you."

He pulled the team to an uncertain stop, the bronc mule fidgeting in the still-unfamiliar harness, looking around for something to run from. The teacher's red dog barked from a safe distance. Hewey watched with concern as Miss Renfro came down the steps and out into the yard. If the wind should happen to pick up and flare the long skirt of that gray dress, and the mule caught the movement from the corner of her eye . . .

Alvin Lawdermilk followed Miss Renfro into the yard and to the gate in the white picket fence.

Hewey argued, "Miss Renfro, you can see this ain't no proper team for you to be ridin' behind. I mean, if anything was to go wrong . . ."

"Mr. Calloway, I have promised Eve and the boys a visit. You said the other day that no bronc has ever killed you yet. Well, you may not know it, but I am an old farm girl. I've been around mules all my life, and none of them has ever killed *me* yet. If you would be so kind as to give me a hand up . . ."

Hewey looked to Alvin for help, but Alvin just stood at the yard gate puffing his pipe and wishing them a nice afternoon. He looked around for Cora, hoping she might take up his argument. But Cora was nowhere in sight. There wasn't any use asking Old Lady Faversham. She wouldn't see any danger in the mules, but she would lecture Miss Renfro for an hour on the danger in Hewey Calloway.

Hewey didn't dare get down and relinquish control of these mules for a minute. "Ma'am," he pleaded, "I'd sure a lot rather you'd change your mind." But she wasn't going to, so he leaned down and gave her his hand. She grasped it and stepped up into the wagon. Once seated beside him she proceeded to pull the slat bonnet over her head to protect her face and her long brown hair from the sun and wind. "Ready any time you are, Mr. Calloway."

He made one more weak plea. "This sure ain't no comfortable wagon. The seat hasn't got any spring left in it, hardly."

"I am sure it will suffice. I am not a pampered woman."

He gave up, dropped his chin a little and flipped the reins gently. The older mule started off in a walk, half dragging the younger one until she caught up to the stride and began reluctantly doing her share of the pulling. Hewey felt for a moment that things were going to work out all right after all. But just as they started by Cora's henhouse, one of Old Lady Faversham's pet peafowls strolled out in front of the mules, spread its tail and screeched like a banshee.

The younger mule had been watching for a booger all along,

and its terror at the sight and sound of the peafowl was contagious. The older mule caught it too. Hewey felt his neck pop as the mules suddenly broke into a run. "Whoa!" he hollered. "Who-o-o-a!" He half stood up, sawing futilely at the reins. The wagon bounced as the front wheels struck a shallow ditch, and Hewey almost lost his balance. Miss Renfro, holding tight to the seat with her left hand, caught Hewey with her right and pulled him back. Otherwise he might have tumbled out onto the tongue.

"Thank you, ma'am," he said.

"Don't mention it. I didn't think I wanted to be sitting up here by myself."

He managed to exert some control on the older mule, enough to get it running a little to the right and thus pull the wagon into a wide circle. In a minute they were heading straight back toward the ranch house and the corrals.

"Hold on tight!" he shouted needlessly as he saw the ditch coming again. His bronc-riding instincts made him duck his chin to avoid popping his neck, and he saw Miss Renfro do likewise. All of her learning hadn't come out of books. They took the bounce in fair grace, though the ribbon came untied from Spring Renfro's bonnet, and the whole thing went sailing off behind her. Her long brown hair began to string out in the wind.

He thought they were going to run through the front yard, but the mules veered to the left and carried them on a swing around toward the rear. The right front wheel caught the corner of the picket fence and uprooted the corner post, then smashed the next twenty or so white pickets into kindling. Pieces came flying up at Hewey, causing him to throw his arm up defensively over his face.

"Whoa!" he hollered again as he saw they were going to skirt dangerously near the weather grayed, unpainted outhouse. He tried to pull the mules to the left but didn't quite manage it. The older bay mule, on the right, brushed against the outhouse in passing, and the right front wheel gave it a resounding thump that splintered wood from it and set the little structure to rocking.

Hewey heard a shriek and knew it came from Cora Lawdermilk.

Julio Valdez ran out from the barn, waving his arms. He made a run at the mules and tried to grab at the harness, but the speed wrenched his hands loose and sent him spinning. The left wheels just missed hitting him.

Next came the clothesline, three long pieces of thin cotton rope stretched between tall cedar posts and propped up at strategic points between the posts by long pieces of pine planking, notched in one end.

"Watch it," he shouted. "That line'll cut us to pieces." He grabbed Spring Renfro and forced her down in the seat, then threw himself protectively over her.

The mules swerved and missed the line.

After that they were in open country. He saw nothing to do but let them run off their fear and try not to get bounced out of the clattering wagon. He kept sawing on the lines, giving what little guidance he could to the direction they ran. The wagon bounced and groaned. The right front wheel squealed in protest, needing grease. If the mules would have co-operated, Hewey would gladly have stopped and greased it then and there, in his good shirt and all.

Jack rabbits ran, frightened by the noise and the careening wagon. Cattle scattered, tails hoisted over their rumps. Quail flushed in a flutter of wings.

Hewey had a chance for a good look at Spring Renfro, her brown hair awash in the wind, her face grayed by dust, her dress in disarray. Modesty had taken second place to survival. He expected to see terror in her eyes. Unaccountably, she was laughing.

"Ma'am," he gritted, "I wisht you'd let me in on the joke. I could stand one about now."

"No joke. I just haven't had so much fun in years."

"Fun?" He almost broke into swearing. "I didn't think they let crazy women teach kids in school."

He looked behind but could see little for the dust kicked up by the iron-rimmed wheels. He thought it probable that Alvin and Julio were back there somewhere, spurring to catch up. There had been horses in the pen that they could saddle. Maybe they could throw a rope on the mules and get them stopped.

The team seemed to be slowing. Both mules were shiny with

131

sweat, and saliva dripped in foamy flecks from their mouths. Hewey was about to decide the thing was going to turn out all right.

Then, just ahead of them loomed a washout, a place where runoff water from a steep hillside had cut a deep gash across the sloping prairie. The older mule saw it and turned abruptly, whipping the bronc mule to the right with her. It was too sharp a turn for the wagon to make. Hewey felt a hard bump as the right wheel slammed back against the wagon bed. He felt the wagon lurch upward and heard the loud crash as the coupling pole broke. He realized too late that he had let the leather lines get themselves wrapped around his hands. He felt himself jerked out of the seat just as the wagon bed flipped upward and then over. He heard a shriek from Spring Renfro.

He slammed to the ground belly-first, and much of his breath went out of him. His mouth was full of dirt. His arms felt as if they had been jerked out of the sockets. He felt himself being dragged, the grass and weeds and small brush grabbing at him, ripping at his clothes, scraping the hide off of his arms and his chest. He couldn't see for the dirt that burned his eyes like cigarette ashes blown into his face.

He had no way of telling how far he was dragged before the reins pulled loose from his arms and he stopped sliding. He blinked at the dust and sand and saw, through a painful haze, the two mules still running at full speed, the wagon's front wheels bouncing crazily behind them.

They've took to the tules, he thought, not much giving a damn at the moment. He pushed himself to his hands and knees and started looking back for the schoolteacher. Good God, she was probably lying there somewhere with her neck broken in six places!

He tried to holler, but the sand in his mouth and throat stopped the sound before it rightfully came out. All he managed was a grunt. He spat, trying to work up enough saliva to clear some of the good earth he had plowed up with his chin. He rubbed his eyes, trying to regain enough sight to tell what direction he was moving. He stumbled along, choking for breath, glancing around wildly to try to determine where Spring Renfro was.

He heard her before he saw her. She was laughing. She was sitting on the ground beside the wreckage of the wagon and laughing.

He stopped a moment, trying to get a clearer picture of her. Laughing, dammit!

She sat there with her legs apart, the wind blowing her hair, her face covered with dirt, her dress torn and littered with grass and weeds and chunks of dirt bigger than a banty egg. Her laughing slowed, then started again as Hewey neared. She sat and pointed at him and broke into a fresh seizure.

Hewey's anger rose a little at first, but her laughter was infectious. In a minute he began to smile, then to chuckle, and finally he flopped down beside her, laughing as hard as she was.

He didn't know why. It wasn't all that damn funny. But he couldn't help it. She made him feel heady and drunk, and he couldn't do anything but join her. They laughed until the tears were rolling down their cheeks. He didn't know what prompted them to do it, but they put their arms around each other and laughed some more.

They were still laughing when Alvin and Julio came loping up on horseback. Julio jumped down nimbly and came running. Alvin moved a little slower and more carefully, but he got there only a few steps behind Julio. The two men's eyes were wide with concern until they saw for themselves that nobody was hurt. Gradually the contagion took them, and they laughed with Hewey and the teacher.

They finally managed to quit, only to look at each other and start again.

When Hewey had laughed himself out and his lungs ached as badly as the rest of him, he looked up at Alvin. "I believe I have damaged your wagon."

Alvin gazed at the wagon bed, lying there upside down and sprung out of its proper alignment. God knew how far the mules had gone with the rest of it. "If you improved it any, I'll be glad to pay you the difference."

"You can take it out of my first million."

Alvin shrugged. "It's just an old trainin' wagon. I've busted up better ones. We'll patch it together and use it again." He looked at

Miss Renfro. "But we won't let any lady schoolteachers ride in it anymore." He turned to Julio. "Better go see if you can bring home the mules. They'll run themselves down directly."

Julio nodded, still looking first at Hewey, then at Miss Renfro, his face creased from one end to the other by a broad smile that showed two rows of perfect white teeth. He got on his horse and rode off in the direction where Hewey had bade good-bye to the mules.

Neither Hewey nor Miss Renfro had made any move to get up. Hewey said thoughtfully, "Alvin, ain't you had some trouble with coyotes gettin' into your chickenyard?"

Alvin stared critically at him, for the problem at hand had nothing to do with coyotes or chickens. "Happens pretty often. Why?"

"If a man was to slip out there at night and shut them peafowls out of the chickenyard, you reckon a coyote would catch them?"

Alvin grinned. "My mother-in-law would get up out of that wheel chair and throw a stompin' fit."

Hewey nodded. "The exercise would probably do her good." He pushed to his feet. His legs were shaky, but he thought they would hold up all right. He leaned down, stretching out his hands. Miss Renfro took them, and he pulled her up. She swayed. He caught her. She leaned against him a moment, and he was in no hurry for her to get her strength back.

Alvin watched them, his eyes narrowed a little in silent appraisal. "Hewey, you better let her go. I'd hate for us to lose a schoolteacher after she's only been here a year."

"She's all right now. The danger is over with."

"I don't know as I would say that."

Walking was one of the hardest tasks a cowboy ever had to do. A job that could not be done on horseback stood some chance of never being done at all. Hewey figured it was well over a mile back to the house, and he dreaded every foot of it.

If there had to be a washout, why couldn't it be closer to the barn?

Alvin motioned for Hewey to help Spring Renfro up onto his horse. It was a little awkward, for Alvin had not been farsighted enough to bring a sidesaddle. It was an uncommon thing for a woman to ride astride, especially when she wore a long skirt that by necessity slipped up far past the high tops of her buttoned shoes and exposed a limb that had rarely seen sunshine. Hewey tried not to look, but he failed in that effort, as he had failed in many things.

"You comfortable up there, Miss Renfro?" he asked.

"No, but I am probably more comfortable than the two of you."

Hewey glanced ruefully at Alvin. This, when it was over, was sure to send Alvin to one of his secret places. "We ain't goin' to die. We're only goin' to sound like it."

He had been struck more than once by the different view a man got of the range when he was down at ground level, compared to that he saw from the saddle. He had walked to camp many times after having come up second best to a strong-minded bronc. The grass never looked as green or as pretty from down here. His boots' high heels were made for digging into the ground when braced against a rope with a horse at the other end, or for keeping the foot from slipping through a stirrup. They were made to be worn out from the top down, not the sole up. His feet were hurting before he had walked the first two hundred yards. He grimaced and made up his mind not to whimper.

He must have been weaving a little, for the teacher asked with concern, "Are you all right, Mr. Calloway?"

"The Lord has seen fit to keep me alive. Maybe if I'd been a better man in my younger days He would've been merciful and struck me dead before the walk started."

"I hope you're not making light of the Lord, Mr. Calloway."

"No, ma'am. I've never felt closer to Him."

As they neared the barn Cora Lawdermilk walked hurriedly out to meet them. Her mother toddled behind on her cane. It had been Hewey's observation that Old Lady Faversham could move along pretty well when it suited her. It just didn't suit her often.

Cora made a fuss over the teacher's bedraggled look and had to feel twice for herself to be satisfied that there were no broken bones. Old Lady Faversham shook her cane at Hewey. She shrilled, "I could of told you, young lady. Go ridin' with a crazy one like that and there ain't no tellin' what kind of jackpot he'll get you into. They're a wild and uncarin' lot, them cowboys. I ought to know. I've had a daughter married to one for thirty years."

"Now, Mother," Cora said, "Alvin ain't all *that* bad."

Hewey helped Miss Renfro down. He took special care to keep his eyes away from her legs since the other two women were there to seize upon anything he did, and perhaps things he didn't do.

Spring Renfro came immediately to Hewey's defense. "It wasn't Mr. Calloway's fault. He tried to talk me out of going, but I wanted to see Eve and the boys. Under the circumstances, I thought he did a masterful job of handling the team."

Cora was unconvinced. "He could of killed you."

"But he didn't; he saved me."

Hewey nodded agreement with all she said, though he didn't really believe it all. It was *luck* that saved her, and he knew it. He had had about as much control over that wagon as a matchbox tied behind a freight train. But he took it kindly that she tried to bail him out of trouble with the womenfolks. He cautiously eyed Cora and thought perhaps she was beginning to lean his way. As for the old lady, he didn't even look at *her*.

Cora dismissed any further pleading. "Land sakes, Spring, you are a sight. We've got to get you into the house and see what we can do about you." She glanced at Hewey. "As for you, Hewey Calloway, you'd better get yourself some needle and thread and do somethin' about your modesty. Haven't you seen the rip in those britches?"

He hadn't. He blushed, thinking how Miss Renfro had seen him that way, all the long walk home. It was not a thing a modest young lady would mention. Nor, for that matter, should an old married woman.

Miss Renfro said, "I'd like to try again, Mr. Calloway, after we've both had a chance to clean up. But I think we'd better ride horses this time."

Alvin said, "I'll catch up Biscuit and the paint."

Hewey had had a bath the day before, it being Saturday, but that was of no help now. He had to do it all over again. He guessed that was all right as long as he didn't make a habit of it. It was his conviction that bathing too frequently was bad for the skin and its natural breathing apparatus. He went to the surface tank behind the barn, out of sight of the house. There he washed away the dirt and the leaves and the miscellaneous and extraneous trash which the dragging had driven beneath his underwear and into his hair. He found numerous hidden bruises and contusions as well as several thorns firmly ensconced beneath a hide that was not as tough as he sometimes liked to think. Some he could remove with the point of his pocketknife. The rest would have to find their own way out in their own good time.

As clean as tank water could make him, he pulled on a clean suit of long cotton underwear and a clean pair of ducking britches. Barefoot, he picked his way carefully through patches of sharp goathead stickers back to the shed which he counted as home. He seated himself on the edge of his steel cot and went to exploring for thorns.

A shadow fell across the open doorway. Alvin stood looking at him. "Find anything broken off?"

Hewey shook his head. "Far as I can tell, everything's here that belongs here."

Hewey's shredded shirt lay on the rough pine floor where he had dropped it. Alvin picked it up and shook his head. "I hope this wasn't your last."

"I got one more." The casualty had been one of the two he had bought from Pierson Phelps' store. It didn't seem any too hardy to have cost six bits. Fortunately, its mate was still intact.

Alvin lifted a saddle rack. That surprised Hewey, for it was the first time he had noticed it was hinged rather than nailed solidly to the rough pine boxing of the wall. Beneath the rack's single leg was a small trap door that had escaped Hewey's notice; Julio had done what little sweeping had been accomplished. From a tin box nailed beneath the door, Alvin drew out a bottle two thirds full of whisky.

"This'll heal your bruises from the inside out."

Hewey took a long drink and handed the bottle to Alvin.

Alvin said, "Never liked to watch a man drink alone. It does injury to his moral fiber." He took a long drink himself. He sat there then, the bottle in one hand and the cork in the other, as if undecided whether to bring the two together. He stared at Hewey.

"For a man with just one good shirt to his name, you're about as rich a man as I know."

Hewey frowned. "I wisht I knew how you figure that."

"You've got one treasure the rest of us can never have— freedom. Any day the notion strikes you, you can saddle old Biscuit and just ride away. You can go anyplace you want to. You don't have to ask anybody, and you don't have to lay awake worryin' that you've shirked your responsibilities, because you don't have any. There's times I envy you."

"You, with this ranch, and that good house yonder, and enough horses and mules to outfit Lee's army? You envy *me?*"

"Just at times, mind you—times when I'd give my right arm to be you. *Just* my right arm, nothin' else. I wouldn't give up this ranch, and I wouldn't give up Cora. I just let the thought run through my mind when the pressure gets heavy. I let it pleasure me a little while. Like a man, I guess, who wouldn't really dally with some woman that's not his wife, but he gets pleasure out of thinkin' about it anyway. It sort of eases the load on these old shoulders, knowin' there's somebody with that kind of freedom. I can never be like you because I couldn't bring myself to pay the price. But it makes my load lighter, knowin' you're out there someplace. It's like watchin' an eagle fly high and free. I'll never fly, but at least I can watch the eagle."

Hewey was still frowning. "What's that got to do with a tore-up shirt?"

Alvin took another snort from the bottle. He stared at the floor. "My eyesight ain't as good as it was in my prime; I been thinkin' about gettin' me some eyeglasses. But I can still see when somethin' is shoved up under my nose. I seen the way you and that schoolteacher looked at one another. Now Cora knows without me sayin' a word. I reckon her eyesight ain't too impaired by age. First thing you know, them women'll be workin' up plans for you, Hewey."

"I've always made my own plans."

"That's one thing I've admired about you. But when a bunch of women gets their heads together, you better sleep with one eye open. Pretty soon they're settin' up this thing and that thing and the other for you, and they'll make you think it was your own idea. You're caught like a coyote in a number three trap."

"I've never been trapped in my life."

"Maybe nobody's ever made a brass-plated, double-rectified effort." Alvin's eyes narrowed. "I don't have any notion of tryin' to tell you what to do. But whatever you do, be damn sure it's your own idea and not somethin' somebody has put off on you."

VII

Biscuit hadn't worked much since they had been at the Lawder-milk place, a fact which helped offset the indignities to which the menagerie-like atmosphere subjected him. He had established a rapport of sorts with Spring Renfro's paint, though he clearly considered himself the superior. It took some attention on Hewey's part to ride along side by side with the teacher. Biscuit wanted to pull ahead to the position that befitted his rank.

Spring said, "I hope you're making this trip because you want to, and not simply for me. It occurs to me that you may not be feeling well after that dragging you took."

Hewey knew he felt better now than he would feel tomorrow, after the soreness had time to work to the bone. "I been wantin' to see the boys."

"I can understand why. They idolize you."

He shrugged. "I suppose one of them does."

"Tommy has always talked about you in school. He thinks you're without doubt the greatest cowboy who ever lived."

As long as he believed his uncle's stories he would probably continue to think that way. But give him a couple more years and he might turn out like Cotton. "How about Cotton . . . does he ever say much?"

"Cotton's mind is on other things a long way from home. He's looking to far horizons."

"I thought I'd ridden to all there was, but he's lookin' past any I've ever been to. I suppose I'm too old to understand him."

"You should understand him better than anyone. People say you've always had a way of looking at the distant hills."

"But when I got there I always felt like I knew where I was."

"When Cotton reaches *his*, he'll know where he is, too. He's of another generation, Mr. Calloway. More than that, he's of another century. You can't hold him back any more than his parents can. Of all people, you should know that and understand."

"I understand him lookin' away. I wisht I understood what he's lookin' *at*."

"You don't have to. The main thing is that you understand *him*, and help him. He needs help."

"He don't act like it."

"He has gone as far as this school can take him. I've taught him all I have to give. He has to be set free now, or he'll be tied to this place or another like it all his life."

"Ain't no use talkin' about it. Eve ain't goin' to let him go."

"She should. Perhaps you can help her see that, if you will. Tommy could stay here all his life and be happy, I think. But Cotton has places to go. I hope you'll find a way to help him."

Hewey stared at her until she looked away self-consciously. "You're somethin' different yourself, Miss Renfro. Not many women around here—or menfolks either—understand how it is with a boy like Cotton, or with an old fiddlefoot like me. Most people are always tryin' to change us into what *they* are instead of lettin' us be what *we* are."

Her eyes softened with a memory. "I knew a man once. He was very much like you. He was always looking to the distant hills. When he heard of gold in the Klondike he made the big run. He didn't find any gold, but it might have ruined things for him if he had. It was the search that always interested him, not the finding. He came back without a dollar to his name. But he was rich with experience, I suppose."

She fell silent. Hewey gave her some time, then asked, "This feller . . . were you-all kin?"

"We were going to be. But he hadn't been home long before the war started in Cuba. He had to go, and I had to let him."

Hewey sensed the rest of it. "He didn't come back."

She shook her head. "A friend sent me a picture of his grave, with a little white cross on it. I carried the picture with me for a long time. I finally decided that was bad for me, so I put it away."

Hewey pondered. "Did he look anything like me?"

She looked at him a moment. "No."

He felt relieved. For a minute he had had an uncomfortable feeling she looked upon him as a substitute for someone else. Never in his life had he wanted to be anyone other than Hewey Calloway.

She said, "I guess you know now why I was interested in your having been in Cuba. Tommy has told me about you at San Juan Hill."

"The boy gets a little enthusiastic, me bein' his uncle and all. He gets his facts mixed up."

"I'd like you to tell me the facts sometime."

"It's not a thing I enjoy talkin' about."

She nodded gravely. "I can understand. But if you ever do feel like telling me, I'll always feel like listening."

The first thing he noticed was the black horse standing where the wire gate was supposed to be, providing an opening in the barbed-wire fence that separated Alvin Lawdermilk's land from Walter Calloway's. He could see that it was an old horse, standing with head down. It was saddled.

"That's Boy Rasmussen's. But where's the old man at?"

Spring's lips were tight. She pointed. "There, on the ground." Her eyes were fearful.

Hewey saw a form stretched out in the green grass. His nerves tingled with alarm. "You better stay back." He touched spurs lightly to Biscuit's sides and moved ahead in a long trot. The breeze tugged at the old man's ragged clothing, fluttering it as if he were a rag doll casually dropped by some careless child's hand. Biscuit made an uneasy rolling sound in his nose.

Even as Hewey stepped down, before he touched the old man, he sensed that Boy Rasmussen was dead.

The drifter lay on his face. Hewey hesitated a moment, then gently turned the body over. Rasmussen had not been dead long.

Against Hewey's advice, Spring rode up close. She looked down with eyes wide and anxious. "Did somebody . . . ?"

Hewey shook his head. "No." His throat was tight. Speaking was painful. "Nobody killed him. He just wore himself out."

The wire gate lay twisted on the ground where Rasmussen had dropped it. "Heart seizure, I reckon. He probably got down to open the gate but never lived to go through it."

"It's an awful thing to die all alone."

Hewey swallowed. "He'd lived alone, most of his life. I expect he'd of wanted to die travelin'."

"Where do you think he was going?"

Hewey shrugged. "Dodge City. Cheyenne. Laredo. Who knows? He probably didn't know either." Unbidden, unexpected, a tear rolled down his cheek.

Sympathetically Spring said, "He must have been an old friend of yours."

Hewey stared down at the peaceful face. "I never seen him more than two or three times. But I feel like I knew him all my life."

He knelt awhile, staring. Finally he pushed to his feet, rubbed a hand over his face as if it itched, surreptitiously running a finger across his eyes to wipe them dry, hoping Spring Renfro hadn't seen.

"Miss Renfro, you'd best go on up to Walter's house and tell him. He'll need to fetch a wagon. I'll stay here and watch that nothin' bothers the old man."

"That's the proper thing," she agreed. She rode carefully around the body, the paint horse shying a little, then she went through the gate and struck a long trot down the dim wagon road.

The old black horse stood patiently a dozen steps away, the patched old leather reins dragging on the ground. Hewey walked carefully toward the animal, talking softly to avoid boogering him. Sometimes a horse used to just one man was shy and distrustful of strangers. But the old black seemed to welcome him as a friend. Hewey put his arms around the shaggy neck and patted him and told him of his sympathy for the loss of an old companion. It wasn't the words that counted; it was the tone. The horse nuzzled him a little and thus spoke its own feelings.

Hewey uncinched the saddle and let it slip to the ground, relieving the black of its weight and the binding of the girth. He noted the Meanea, Cheyenne, signature stamped into the leather. The saddle was at least thirty years old, its cantle of the once-popular Cheyenne roll style already old-fashioned when Hewey had been a boy.

"I'd turn you loose over in Walter's pasture, old feller, but you might not find water. You better stay here awhile with me and Boy." He had no fear that the old horse would run away, so he didn't tie him. He went back and sat down cross-legged by the still figure. He studied the sleeping face, wondering where the old man was now. He wondered if he was still an old man, or if in that unseen, mysterious new life to which he had gone he was a young man again. Was he riding the range once more, perhaps taking a herd to Dodge or to the Nations?

Hewey had never spent enough time in churches to know much about conventional preachment. Though he had no doubt whatever of an afterlife—his father and other good people had assured him there was one—he had only the vaguest notion what kind of life it would be. He liked to think heaven was what each person wanted it to be. He could see no future in lying around on a fluffy white cloud and listening to somebody playing on a harp, a picture of heaven he had seen numerous times in one form or another. Even if it *was* that way, his personal preference would have run more to the fiddle.

To him, heaven ideally should have something of the familiar for each person. He would like to think there would be work to do, but only pleasant work, and no more of it at one time than a man felt like doing. There would be sunshine, but only pleasantly warm, never oppressively hot. There would be rain, but only when a man could sit in the comfort of the bunkhouse and watch it through the open door while he sipped his black coffee and smoked his Bull Durham cigarettes. He would never have to be out in it on horseback, miles from house or chuck wagon, soaked to the skin and chilled to the marrow of his bones. All would be familiar in heaven, and all would be friendly, if he could have it made up to order.

"I reckon you know by now what it's like," he said to Boy Rasmussen. "I wisht there was some way you could tell me."

He stared into the quiet, composed old face. It occurred to him that he saw none of the haunted look, none of the anxiety he had seen that night at Walter's. He saw only peace.

He thought on that awhile, and he decided the old man probably *had* told him.

After a long time he heard the rattle of trace chains. He pushed to his feet and turned to meet the wagon. Walter and Eve sat on the seat. Spring and the two boys followed on horseback. All were solemn as they pulled up. Walter stepped stiffly to the ground, took off his hat and looked at Boy Rasmussen in silence. Following his example, the boys self-consciously did likewise.

Walter looked then at Hewey. "You sure there wasn't no accident? He wasn't dragged or anything?"

"Nothin' like that. The Lord just called him, and he went home."

Eve shuddered. "Knowin' the life he led, I hate to think of the reception he's gettin'."

Hewey lifted the old hat he had used to cover the features. "Eve, just look at that face. They're treatin' him gentle."

Eve said, "He's a merciful Lord." She turned and pointed with her chin at the wagon bed. "I brought a quilt to wrap him with."

Hewey stepped up to fetch it. It was a new quilt, never used. She had spent many a quiet winter's night piecing it together on a quilting frame. Hewey took a quick glance at his sister-in-law, then looked away so she wouldn't see the tears come back into his eyes. She might have spoken harshly about Boy Rasmussen when he was living, but at his death she gave him the best she had. "This is good of you, Eve."

"He was one of God's children," she responded tightly. "It's for heaven to judge him, not me."

He spread the blanket in the wagon. Carefully he and Walter lifted Boy into the wagon bed, then folded the blanket over him.

Walter said, "We'd best take him into town. You'll need to go with me, Hewey, since you're the one who found him."

Hewey nodded. The sheriff would want to know the circumstances.

Walter turned to Cotton and Tommy. Both boys had watched with solemn eyes and had not intruded upon the occasion with talk. "You buttons see Miss Renfro back to the Lawdermilks',

145

then go on home and take care of the chores. Your mama and me, we'll spend the night in town. We'll probably put up at the wagonyard. We'll see to everything that needs to be done for the old man, and we'll be home by at least tomorrow evenin'.''

Tommy had seen little of death. He gave his uncle a cautious glance. "You reckon it hurt him much to die, Uncle Hewey? Do you reckon it scared him?"

Hewey saw that Cotton was waiting to hear the answer, though he had too much reserve to have asked the question. Hewey gave his response a long and careful study. "For a minute, maybe. We're all a little scared at somethin' new. But then, judgin' by his face, the pain was gone, and the scare too. Death comes to all of us sometime. Old Boy done a lot of ridin' the last few years, tryin' to find a place that was really home to him. Well, he's home now."

That satisfied Tommy. Cotton looked once more at the quilt-covered form in the wagon, then turned his horse away. Walter spoke to the team, and the wagon started to move. Hewey was about to fall in behind it when Spring Renfro rode up beside him. Her eyes glistened. She reached out and took his hand, holding it for a moment.

She said, "You're a good man, Hewey Calloway. Don't ever let anyone tell you otherwise."

Because Upton City and its surrounding trade territory were sparsely populated, the nearest thing the town had to an under-taker was barber Orville Mulkey. In his small back room, the shades rolled down, he looked over the body by lamplight with Sheriff Wes Wheeler to certify that there were no marks of violence, bearing friendly witness to Hewey's testimony.

"I'll touch up his hair and his beard," he said, "but it'd be a shame to shave him clean. St. Peter wouldn't recognize him."

"Just make him look as good as you can," Wheeler said. He turned to Hewey and Walter. "You're real sure you don't know the names of his kin?"

Walter said with a sense of guilt, "I don't remember that I ever taken the trouble to ask him. I just know that he's got a brother somewhere down on the Rio Grande and a sister up on the plains.

I ought to've taken more interest in him than that. I just never thought about him dyin' at my gate."

The sheriff grimaced. "Nothin' to do, then, but to bury him here. I'll write a letter to officers in that part of the country to see if they can notify any of his relations."

"Seems a shame," Walter said, "for a man to be buried so far away from all kin."

Hewey put in, "It don't matter where they're buried. They'll all find each other bye and bye."

The barber frowned. "I'm afraid I've got a practical question for the here and now. Who pays for this?"

The sheriff said, "The county will. There's nobody else to do it."

Hewey looked up quickly. "And declare him a pauper? No sir! His friends'll bury him."

Wheeler was dubious. "He didn't have any friends to speak of."

Hewey said firmly, "I'll get up a collection. We'll see how many friends an old cowboy has got."

Wes Wheeler was not the kind of man who smiled much. He came close to smiling with his eyes.

Hewey turned to the barber. "Orville, you just go ahead and fix him up. Put some good clothes on him, too. I'll see to the pay." He glanced at his brother. "You comin' with me, Walter?"

Walter nodded.

Hewey said, "I'm liable to take you to a place that Eve won't approve of."

Walter grunted. "You think I'd let you go into such a place all by yourself?"

They stepped out into the street. Hewey could see a dozen or so horses tied in the vicinity of the Dutchman's saloon. "That'll likely be as far as we need to go. I'll do the talkin'. You just back me up." They walked along the dirt street, found an opening between the tied horses and strode up onto the narrow porch. Hewey paused in the open doorway. Walter had been a step behind him, looking back as if wondering whether Eve would see. She wouldn't. She was visiting with church friends who weren't going to let her sleep in the wagonyard tonight.

Hewey rough-counted a dozen cowboys, most of them Two Cs

hands who had delivered a string of Tarpley steers to a trail outfit earlier in the day. Even C. C. Tarpley wasn't insensitive enough to send them home without giving them a chance to partake in a drop or two of kindness. Anyway, the broker they were, the harder they worked. The faces were mostly young, in their low to mid-twenties. Many a young fellow gloried in the cowboy profession a few years but eventually gave it up for something which paid better and involved less physical stress and risk. The man who stayed in it past the age of thirty was likely to remain in the cattle business one way or another the rest of his life, on its fringes if not in the middle.

Hewey stepped up to the bar where the bartender Schneider waited. He ordered a drink for himself and Walter and plunked a silver dollar on the walnut bar. He downed the drink in one long swallow, then turned to survey the cluster of cowboys playing cards and shooting billiards.

"Fellers," he spoke loudly, "I wisht you'd all stop and listen to me for a minute."

The conversations trailed down and finally stopped as the men turned to look at him. Some who knew him spoke to him. Those who didn't know him recognized that the others held him in some regard.

"Fellers," Hewey spoke gravely, "me and Walter here, we just brought an old-timey cowboy to town. He was old Boy Rasmussen. Now, some of you knowed him and some of you didn't. Whether you knowed *him* or not, you all know the breed. He was followin' the mossyhorns up the trail when most of us was still followin' our mothers around the kitchen. It was him and his kind that beat out the trails and shot at the Yankees and fought off the Indians. It was them old fellers that taken the whippin' so me and you could have the easy life we're livin' today.

"Now, I figure we owe an old man like that somethin' better than a pauper's grave. I think I know most of you fellers, and I think you'll agree with me. I got ten dollars in my pocket. It all goes in my hat to help bury old Boy in the style he's rightfully got comin' to him. Walter, how much you got?"

Caught by surprise, Walter said, "Five dollars."

"That's fifteen. We got to start someplace." He took off his hat and put his ten dollars into it. Walter put in his five. Now he couldn't afford to sleep in the wagonyard tonight, even if he wanted to. Hewey held the hat out at arm's length. "Now, how about you fellers?"

The cowboys began drifting up, dropping in whispering money if they were that flush, clinking money if they weren't. Hewey kept shaking the hat so the silver would work to the bottom and only the paper would show on top.

C. C. Tarpley and son-in-law Fat Gervin chose an inopportune time to enter the saloon. Hewey trapped them before they could reach the bar. Hewey ignored the hostility in Fat's eyes and concentrated his first attentions on C.C. He explained the reason for the collection. "Look in that hat, C.C. You don't see nothin' in there but foldin' money. As an old-time trail driver yourself, I know you'd want to contribute as good as your own cowboys have gone and done."

The gaunt old man's gray mustache wiggled as he seemed to say something, though no sound came out. He tried to cover up the fact that he was touched. Reluctantly he extracted ten dollars from a leather wallet that had long been protected from too much sunshine. He said, "Philanthropy will be my undoin'."

"A pleasant giver is a joy to the angels, C.C. When your time comes you can hire a hundred people to cry at your funeral. But old Boy needs our help."

C.C. said, "I'll get my ten dollars back in just a little while on the grub that old chuckline rider won't be eatin' anymore at my line camps." He sounded harsh, but Hewey knew even tight-twisted C. C. Tarpley had never turned a rider away unfed. There was a practical as well as a humanitarian reason for it. These drifters were occasionally a source of cheap short-term labor. Sometimes, moving casually across a country, they would come upon something amiss and report it if they were friendly. On the other side of the coin, a drifter who had been accepted and fed wouldn't set a range afire out of spite.

Hewey swung the hat over to Fat Gervin, challenging him with his eyes. With all the men watching, Fat could do no less than equal the contribution his father-in-law had made. Hewey saw how much it pained him. "You can make that up in a few days, Fat. Just raise the interest."

He carried the hat to the bar and dumped the money carefully, grabbing at a couple of coins that tried to roll away.

C.C.'s eyes narrowed. "All foldin' money, you said."

"Foldin' money is all you saw."

The collection lacked only seven dollars and some cents of being an even hundred. The Dutchman dug into his cash drawer and made up the difference.

The gesture brought thanks from Hewey. "A hundred dollars ought to send Boy off in style."

Schneider nodded. "You did well, Hewey. I think it is due you another drink."

"I'm broke."

"I am not. For you and Walter, one on the house." To Hewey's surprise, Schneider poured one for himself. It was a thing he rarely did. He raised his glass. "To Boy Rasmussen."

Hewey looked around the room. Some of these were men he had never seen before, men he probably would never see again. But not one of them was a stranger. He lifted his glass. His voice almost cracked. "To *him,* and to all other good old boys!"

The bank stayed open, but most of the few other business houses closed for a couple of hours out of respect for Boy Rasmussen's funeral. Though nobody in town had known him well, a goodly crowd followed the casket out to the burying grounds. Brother Averill, the preacher, didn't say a word about Boy's shortcomings, his failings in the sight of the Lord. He spoke only of his contributions to the civilizing of the West, of the hardships he had endured, of the new home he had found where the grass was always green and the water everlastingly sweet. When he was done, everybody filed by the open box for a last look at a link to another time that was rapidly becoming a faded memory, only occasionally revived in pale colors through meandering tales told by old men awaiting their time to go.

Finally Eve's quilt was folded over the old man's face. The lid was nailed down, and Boy Rasmussen was lowered into his final resting place, a long way from Doan's Crossing on the Red.

Eve wept.

Hewey tied Biscuit behind the wagon and rode away from the cemetery on the wagon seat beside Eve and Walter. They held their silence a long time, Eve clutching her old family Bible. At length Hewey told her, "I'm glad you was here. I'm glad there was a woman or two here to weep for him."

"I wasn't weepin' just for him. I wept a little for you, too."

"For me?"

"You'll end up just like him someday, buried by strangers in some strange place. I only hope there's somebody around who will do for you what you did for Boy Rasmussen."

"And maybe some good lady who will donate me a new quilt."

"I'm serious, Hewey. I've never told you before, but I've prayed for you sometimes. The answer to those prayers is at hand, if you'll just open your eyes and see."

"See what?"

"There's a certain fine lady who thinks a lot of you, Hewey. She sees possibilities in you, the same way I saw possibilities in Walter."

Hewey was suddenly appalled. "You tryin' to marry me off?"

"For your own good. I've been tryin' to marry you off for fifteen years. I don't want you to be lowered into your grave by strangers. I want to see family and loved ones mourn over you. That is the Christian way."

A one-eyed mule could have seen that some type of conspiracy was afoot between Eve Calloway and Cora Lawdermilk.

Hewey had two eyes.

Though the two women had been friends for years, they had done most of their visiting in church. Only occasionally had they spent time in each other's homes. Now Eve was over to the Lawdermilk place every few days. The two women were everlastingly using a hot curling iron on Spring Renfro's long hair, putting more waves in it than Hewey had seen on the troopship bound for Cuba. Afraid Hewey wouldn't notice for himself, Eve or Cora

151

were always pointing out to him how pretty Spring looked. It was embarrassing to agree out loud, but it would have been more so to have denied it. The two women were continually whipping up something new in the way of clothes for Spring to wear. Hewey wondered where the material came from, for Eve had been making her own housedresses from the same bolt of plain cloth for years. There was a great deal of talk about filling Spring's "hope chest." Hewey had a strong notion the hope was higher on the other women's part than on Spring's or on his. He sensed an uneasiness, even an embarrassment, in Spring. It was much like his own.

Times he walked in unexpectedly and caught fragments of their conversations. Once he heard Eve assuring Spring that Hewey was not lazy, that he did not shrink from honest labor when there was a need for it to be done and that all he really needed was the gentle but firm hand of a good woman to set him on the path of righteousness and industry.

"A good woman's love will make a man out of him," she said.

The old Mrs. Faversham was the only one who kept faith with the truth, as she saw that truth. "He's just another cowboy with the itch in both feet. A woman would be a lot better off with a good dog and a hot-water bottle, Spring. You've already got the dog." When Cora and Eve protested that she was wrong, she declared, "I have never understood why we women always seem to settle for less than we should have."

One Sunday afternoon, pursuant to custom, Hewey and Spring rode over to Eve's and Walter's. After the amenities had been met at the front door, Eve looked around for Tommy. She said, "Spring, the sorrel mare had a colt a couple of nights ago. I'm sure you'd like to see it. Tommy, take Miss Renfro out and show her the colt."

Spring Renfro had seen a lot of colts and wasn't all that curious, but Eve made it plain that she intended for her to see this one, too. As soon as the teacher was halfway to the barn, Eve turned to her husband. "Walter, tell him."

Walter gave his wife a sidelong glance of impatience. "Don't rush things, Eve. Hewey'll think we're puttin' pressure on him."

"We *are* puttin' pressure on him. When the iron is hot, strike it."

Walter gave her that glance again.

Hewey said, "I don't see no hot iron."

Eve demanded, "How much money have you got?"

It wasn't a subject he ever let concern him much; he hadn't added it up lately. "If it cost a hundred dollars to go to heaven, I might make it to Fort Worth."

She said, "House Barcroft has proved up his place. He'll sell it to you real cheap."

Hewey immediately began looking for boogers that he could point out. "How come he wants to get rid of it?"

"It's a good place," she said. "A person could make a good livin' there."

"House never did. He's been haulin' freight for Blue Hannigan. If the place would make him a livin', he wouldn't be skinnin' mules."

"But he's a bachelor."

"If a man can't make a livin' as a bachelor, he sure can't make one yoked in double harness."

"A man with a woman to help and encourage him could do a lot with a place like Barcroft's. He could make a garden out of the desert."

"If he was like me he'd probably make a desert out of a garden. Anyway, I don't have a woman, Eve. I was born a bachelor, and I've stayed one for these thirty-odd years."

She angered. "Sometimes I think you're stone deaf to what people are tryin' to tell you."

"Sometimes I wish I could be. But it's hard when I've got two women like you and Cora, both tryin' to make me jump over the broomstick."

"You like her, don't you?"

"Cora? Sure, she's all right."

"I'm talkin' about Spring Renfro, and you damn well know it!" When she let herself use a word of that intensity she was at the point that a man had better agree with everything she said or find some other place to pass his time.

He said, "I like lots of people. That don't mean I want to get married. Anyway, how do you know *she* does?"

"That's for you to find out. All you have to do is ask her."

"If she wanted to get married to me, she'd of let me know."

"A woman can't do that."

"Why not? She speaks English, and a damn sight better than I do."

"It just isn't done that way, at least not by decent, God-fearin' women. They let the man do all the askin'."

Hewey remembered that Eve had made it clear enough to Walter when she wanted to get married. If she hadn't exactly asked the question, she had hazed him into a corner and shut all the getaway gates. But he wouldn't point that out to her in her present state of agitation.

"Even if I was inclined to ask her, it'd be embarrassin' to ask and have her say *no*."

"I bet you she won't."

"She should. I sure ain't no prize catch."

"Why not? You're Walter's brother, and look what I managed to make out of him."

Walter turned and walked off toward the barn, saying he was going to help Spring and Tommy look at the colt.

Hewey made an excuse about going into the house and getting himself a cup of coffee. Cotton sat there reading. He only half hid a grin which showed he had been listening to all of it.

Hewey asked, "You readin' about automobiles again?"

"I think you could make good use of one yourself, Uncle Hewey. It could take you a long way from here between now and dark."

Riding home after an early supper, Hewey noticed that Spring Renfro was having nothing to say. Whatever thoughts were working behind those studious eyes, she was keeping them to herself.

He said, "I hope Eve hasn't embarrassed you as much as she's embarrassed me."

She gave him a faint smile. "She and Cora both. They're about as subtle as a sledgehammer."

He didn't know what *subtle* meant, but if it had been bad she wouldn't have said it. He observed, "Looks like we've got a problem, me and you."

"I suppose we have."

"You're a nice lady, Miss Renfro. It's pleasured me considerable, bein' around you, ridin' over here with you and all. But I don't reckon you'd want to get married, would you?"

She was suddenly flustered, caught unprepared. "Well, I don't know . . ."

"I didn't think you would. That's what I kept tellin' Eve, but she don't listen to anything she don't want to hear."

Spring turned her head away. He decided she was embarrassed by the whole uncomfortable situation; he knew *he* was. "If I was a marryin' kind of feller, you're sure the one I'd ask, Miss Renfro. If I was thataway inclined . . ." He let it go.

She was looking straight ahead, not at him. In a minute she said in a strained voice, "Thank you, Mr. Calloway. There's not anyone I'd rather have ask me, if *I* were so inclined."

His face warmed. "The last thing I'd want to do on this earth would be to cause you any more embarrassment. I figure the only way to put a stop to it is for me to leave. Alvin's got a string of horses ready to deliver over into the Concho country. I'll take them, and after I get to San Angelo—for the good of both of us—I'll just keep on ridin'."

She looked at him then. Tears glistened. "You'd leave?"

"Seems to me like it's the only way out for either one of us."

She did not reply. He took that as an indication she agreed. He stole a long look at her, riding along with her head turned away a little. He felt a sudden strong desire to put his arms around her. He knew that as a decent woman she was sure to resent it. He was glad he had self-control. A man who would give in to such a base impulse with a good woman would deserve the horsewhipping some strong and righteous citizen was likely to give him.

He said wistfully, "I almost wisht we *was* thataway inclined. We'd make a handsome-lookin' couple, me and you."

For the next two days Cora Lawdermilk saw to it that Hewey received biscuits with the bottoms thoroughly burned, and steaks with plenty of fat and gristle. Her eyes were cold as a witch's breath. She had little to say, and that little was in clipped words, punctuated by a look that would kill cotton at twenty paces.

Old Lady Faversham, on the contrary, managed a civil word for Hewey now and again. Her behavior had shown a definite improvement.

Hewey saw little of Spring except at mealtime. She always seemed to have things to do elsewhere when he was around. It was just as well, he thought. It had been a narrow escape for both of them.

He couldn't drive the horses to San Angelo by himself, and Alvin needed Julio too much to spare him for six or seven days. Hewey remembered a promise he had made to Cotton and Tommy. He asked Alvin, "If Walter can spare the boys a few days, would you pay them cowboy wages?"

Alvin didn't wheedle. "A dollar a day." Some ranchers would hire a kid for fifty to seventy-five cents and expect as much work out of him as out of a man.

Alvin had always been inclined to smile a lot, but he was smiling even more than usual the last couple of days. He put his big hand on Hewey's shoulder, then went to his secret cache beneath the saddle rack. He held up the bottle in toast. "To wise decisions. May that be the only kind we ever make!"

Hewey accepted the bottle in the spirit in which it was offered. "I hope I made the right one, Alvin. She *is* a good woman. Sometimes when I'm with her I get feelin's . . ." He could hardly bring himself to the admission. "I get feelin's I'm downright ashamed of. I get to thinkin' things a man don't think about with her kind of woman."

"You've always lived a free man, Hewey. For the sake of us who got ourselves caged, don't let anybody ever shut the gate on you."

Eve hadn't been to Cora's, nor Cora to Eve's house, so Eve hadn't found out yet that her wedding plans had gone for nought. He rode up to the Calloway house late in the evening and said he needed the two boys for a few days' wrangler service.

"I don't know," Eve said dubiously. "Walter put his plow on Blue Hannigan's freight wagon day before yesterday and went into

Midland to get some smithin' done. He won't be back till at least tomorrow."

"I came by the field. I didn't see no weeds in there that'd take over the cane patch in the week or so these boys'd be gone."

"I don't now that I can spare them. There's so many chores . . ."

"Alvin'll pay both of them full wages, a dollar a day apiece. Six days, six dollars. Two boys, twelve dollars. You could buy a whole wagonload of groceries with that kind of money."

He had found Eve's weak spot, if she had one. There were never enough dollars around here to stretch over everything that needed covering. It had always been Eve's job to do the stretching, for Walter had never been a much greater money manager than Hewey. Hewey could see her counting the money in her mind. But she was still hesitant. He didn't give her a chance to turn him down. He stepped outside and hollered for the boys. He had seen both of them working by the barn.

"Cotton, Tommy," he half shouted as they approached the house, "you-all hurry up and get your chores done so your mama won't have to worry about them. Me and you are drivin' Alvin's horses to San Angelo."

Tommy gave a whoop and turned back toward the barn in a dead run. Cotton moved up a little closer to Hewey, his hands in his pockets. He stared at his uncle with a measure of lingering doubt. "You really mean to take us this time? You ain't just loadin' us again?"

"You'll see pretty quick if I'm loadin' you or not. We go back to Alvin's tonight and leave with the horses at daylight. Now, you go do up your chores like I told you. I'll pitch in and chop some wood to be sure your mama has enough to last till your daddy gets home."

Eve stood on the front step, her right hand shading her eyes. "Hewey Calloway, I never told you those boys could go."

Hewey was not a very good poker player, but he knew when he had a royal flush. "Then I reckon it's up to you to tell them they can't."

She could see Cotton working feverishly to feed the stock while

Tommy was milking the cow. "If a horse doesn't kill you some-day, Hewey, I may just do it myself. I'd best get a little supper started so those boys don't ride on an empty stomach." She turned back into the house. Hewey flexed his reluctant hands as he walked to the woodpile, looking for the ax.

At the supper table Cotton queried cautiously, trying not to show too much interest, "You reckon we're liable to see an auto-mobile in San Angelo?"

"Things are mighty up to date in San Angelo. I'll bet you they've got half a dozen automobiles around there by now."

Eve frowned. "San Angelo's a big place. I've heard it's even wickeder than Midland. That's a long way for two little boys to go away from home."

Hewey argued, "They're not little boys. Anyway, I went up the trail when I was younger than either one of them."

"And look at you now."

It was something akin to rites of manhood for a boy to go off away from home on his first paying job. Cotton had done so be-fore, but Tommy hadn't. His mother hugged him. "You take care now, son, and come home safe."

The boys didn't need long to get their horses saddled, tie their small bedrolls behind the cantles and wave at their mother as they started up the wagon road. Tears on her cheeks, she yelled after them to turn their eyes away from the evils they might encounter in a godless city like San Angelo, Texas.

They had ridden perhaps fifty yards at Hewey's side when he drew rein. "You boys just keep on ridin'. There's one thing I neglected to tell your mother." He turned around and rode back.

Eve was watching from the front steps. She moved out into the yard. Hewey rode up just close enough for her to hear him as he hollered. "They're good boys, Eve, so don't you worry none. They're plenty big enough to find their way back by theirselves."

"By theirselves?"

"After I deliver the horses, I'm ridin' on."

"But what about the Barcroft claim? What about Spring Ren-fro?"

"Me and her, we talked it over. We decided neither one of us has got a marryin' urge. So long, Eve. See you one of these days."

158

He turned and spurred Biscuit into a stiff trot to catch up with the boys.

Eve cried, "Hewey Calloway, you come back here!"

She tried to run after him, but she was no match for Biscuit. Hewey didn't look back, and in a little bit the wind whipped her words away. It was just as well, because she was saying some things she would regret Sunday when she went to church.

Cotton looked around as Hewey came up to him and Tommy. "What was she hollerin' back there?"

"Just tellin' you boys to behave yourselves and earn your dollar!"

VIII

The weather was warm but beautiful. Rains had come at decent intervals all spring so that the grass was good. Tommy's excitement was contagious. It was a bad thing, Hewey thought, that most boys weren't turned loose on their own anymore like they used to be. Some boys these days didn't leave home until they were fifteen or sixteen. They should not be so deprived of the many wonders the world held for them.

It was always less monotonous moving a band of horses than driving a cow herd. Horses moved faster. Of all the broncs Hewey had broken in this string, he had given the most cussing to a long-tailed bay that showed by looks and temperament a goodly drop of mustang in its veins. But now that bay had established itself as the leader. Its sharp teeth and ready hoofs defended the front position when another horse moved up as if to challenge its lead. The bay seemed to know where it was going and to look forward to being the first to get there.

When Tommy wasn't singing, he was asking questions.

"How big is San Angelo?"

"Last time I heard it was five or six thousand people."

"That many? That must be near as big as Chicago. I'll bet it's a mile and a half across."

"I wouldn't be surprised."

"You reckon they got an ice-cream parlor? A real ice-cream parlor?"

"I believe I remember seein' one, but I never was in it. It was a few doors up from the Arc Light Saloon."

"You've been in the saloon though, I suppose?"

"Had to go in there to see a feller."

Cotton hadn't said much, but he had done a lot of quiet thinking. "I hope you're right about them havin' some automobiles."

"I wisht I knew what gets you buttons all so muzzy over automobiles."

Cotton smiled. "You keep sayin' they're just a passin' fad. I'd like to see one before they're all gone."

"They ain't much to see. When the new wears off and everybody goes back to sensible transportation, I'll bet the price of good horses and mules will go up by fifty or seventy-five dollars a head."

They cut across country until they struck the head of the Middle Concho. Once they made the river, all they had to do was follow, because it would ultimately lead them to town. The three Conchos—Middle, North and South—all converged at San Angelo and formed one Main Concho River. It flowed on east to contribute its clear waters to the red-muddy run of the Colorado a little way beyond the Indians' painted rocks.

It seemed to Hewey there wasn't a foot of this region that he hadn't ridden over at some time or other. Seeing it again was like meeting an old friend after a long separation. He had ridden from the Mexican border to Canada, and he was hard put to say which was his favorite part of the country. Usually it was the place where he was now, or the place he was on his way to.

He found himself singing along with Tommy, though he couldn't carry a tune in an oaken bucket. It was nice to go home, but it was good also to be out moving again, not knowing, really, where he was going once he got the horses delivered, free to make up his mind at any time and to change it just as suddenly in the middle of the road without pausing for consultation with anybody.

The horses suddenly stopped and bunched up along an unexpected fence. The barbed wire was shiny and new. The horses tentatively moved down it a little way, then up, uncertain which way they were expected to go. Tommy rode out to one side, Cotton to the other, to keep them from taking any wrong notions. When the horses had quieted and seemed disposed to graze the good grass awhile, Hewey rode down closer to the river. He found no gate, but he found a drop-gap where the barbed wire was tied to the posts with slick wire rather than fastened down securely with steeples. This was a substitute for a gate. He untied the wires from several posts and signaled to Cotton to help him push them down to ground level. This opened a pathway for the broncs to pass over. When they were all on the other side, Hewey tied the wires back in their proper places.

"Seems like it ain't been more than a year or two since I was along this very same way. There wasn't no fence here then."

"It's sure here now." Cotton looked at the big cedar posts, more permanent than the mesquite posts he was used to at home. "Looks like they mean for it to stay."

Hewey grumbled, "Every time you turn around anymore you run into a new fence. Seems like somebody is bound and determined to turn this whole world into one big barbed-wire jail."

"We came a long ways before we ran into this one."

"Used to not run into *any*. Used to ride a thousand miles and never open a gate unless it was to somebody's yard or his tater and turnip patch."

Not far ahead somewhere lay a set of old wooden corrals he remembered from years past. They were near the river and would be a good place to hold the horses while they camped for the night. Dusk was closing as he saw a pinpoint of firelight ahead. Disappointment touched him. If someone was already there and using the pens, he and the boys would have to go on a few miles farther to a ranch house he knew about. He hadn't brought hobbles or bridles and picket line because for him this was to be a one-way trip, and there was no handy way of getting them home. They would be too bulky for Cotton and Tommy to carry. Yet they were worth too much to leave or give away. Even Alvin Lawdermilk wasn't that generous.

Nearing the pens, he saw to his relief that they stood empty. The campfire was down by the river, where a man had a horse staked on a long rope to graze beneath a towering stand of big native pecan trees.

"We'll water them first," he told the boys, "then we'll pen them."

They hazed the horses down to the river and let them spread out to drink. Hewey gave them all the time they wanted. He saw the man at the fire saddle his blue roan horse and ride up to the pens to throw the gate open. It was less than a hundred yards, and it took him longer to saddle up than it would have taken to walk the distance. That told Hewey he was a cowboy, not some town dweller casually passing through.

He saw something familiar in the way the man sat on his roan as Hewey and Cotton and Tommy pushed the freshly broken broncs up to the pens. When the rider moved in to help them, Hewey knew.

"Well, I'll swun!" he exclaimed. "Snort Yarnell, you gotch-eared old mule!" Snort did have a little wilt in the upper edge of his left ear. Depending upon when he told the story, and to whom, it had been acquired either from a horse or from a saloon fight.

"Howdy, Hewey Calloway. What you doin' in God's country?"

"Tryin' to get across before God sees me."

Snort Yarnell was a legend over Texas and half of New Mexico. When people talked of great cowmen they spoke of Charles Goodnight and Shanghai Pierce. When they talked of cow-country bankers they might bring up the names of George W. Littlefield or Charles Schreiner. But when the conversation turned to bronc stompers and wild, reckless cowboys who knew not fear nor hesitation, they were likely to speak of men like Booger Red Privett and Snort Yarnell. Snort, it was often said, could ride more broncs, heel more calves and drink more whisky—separately or intermixed—than anybody who had ever trailed Longhorn cattle out of the South Texas brush. He was always the envy of other cowboys, and occasionally the dread of county sheriffs, city constables and lone bartenders who had big breakable mirrors.

Snort sported a full gold tooth in the middle of his broad grin, installed by some show-off dentist during one of Snort's rare moments of temporary prosperity. Standing next to it like a kid brother was a gold cap filling out a tooth that had been only half broken off. Snort's nose was nearly flat and a little askew, a mark of the bad moments that inevitably arose to one in the bronc-stomper trade.

He said, "Hewey, I know you don't own them horses legal, so where'd you steal them at?"

Hewey explained that he was delivering them to San Angelo for Alvin Lawdermilk.

"Now, ain't that a stroke of good luck for you? I'm headin' for Angelo myself. Goin' to slip up on the boys' blind side and win the money at the big steer ropin'."

Hewey's pulse quickened. "I never heard about no ropin'."

"Day after tomorrow. You ought to get in on it. I'm figurin' on takin' first place, naturally, but you're welcome to second prize."

Hewey shut one eye and narrowed the other. "The day I couldn't beat you with a rope was the day I was laid up with my right arm broke."

Snort turned to Cotton and Tommy. "You're Walter's boys, ain't you?" He didn't wait for the answer. "Your Uncle Hewey is a notorious liar, but in spite of all that he's the second-best cowboy in this whole neck of the woods, me bein' number one. Your old daddy was no slouch in his own time. I'd of ranked him number three before he taken himself to the plow."

The boys stood slack-jawed. They had seen Snort Yarnell before, but he was ever a wonder to them.

Hewey shut the gate on the broncs and tied it securely. He wouldn't have trusted that mustang bay not to open it. He would have liked to have brought some corn or oats for the broncs, but he had let them graze enough through the day to carry them through. "Let's stake our horses and let them at the grass," he told the boys. "Snort, what you got down yonder that *we* can graze?"

"Three cold biscuits and a can full of coffee. I was hopin' some pilgrim like you would happen along and take pity. Don't tell me you ain't got nothin'."

Hewey let his disappointment show. "Some jerked beef, which is the next thing to nothin'. Half a slab of bacon. We'll have to cook that."

"I can wait. If you need more firewood, there's aplenty down yonder. All you have to do is go fetch it."

The best that could be said for the supper was that it was filling. Hewey didn't eat much; he left most of his for the boys, because he could remember how painful hunger had been to him when he was that age. Nowadays it was no stranger to him; he took it in stride. He made up the difference with black coffee, boiled strong enough and thick enough to pass for blackstrap molasses.

Snort did the major part of the talking. Tommy hung on every word, his eyes wide and credulous. Snort didn't have to embellish much. In his case even the truth strained belief. After telling about having his leg crushed in a horse fall, he pulled up his pants leg for proof. The scarred and crooked leg was an awesome thing to behold. "Them San Antonio doctors said it had taken an infection and there wasn't nothin' I could do but let them saw it off if I wanted to live. But I told them the Good Lord had sent me into this world on two good legs and I wasn't goin' to short change Him when I turned them back in. I had some friends take me out to a little adobe house on Salado Creek. I packed this old leg in horse manure and wrapped it up tight with gunny sacks. I smelt like I was three weeks dead, and I lost most of my friends for a while. But when I left that place I left there walkin'."

Cotton said, "They've made a lot of progress. I'll bet nowadays they could do you a lot better job."

"A wore-out one-eyed horse drops better medicine on the ground behind him than most of them quack doctors have got on their shelves." Snort slapped the leg smartly. "You couldn't ask for nothin' sounder than that."

After Hewey sent the boys to their blankets, he sat up awhile with Snort. Mostly they hunched in thoughtful silence, smoking, thinking. Spring Renfro kept coming to Hewey's mind, unbidden. He tried to shut her out by dwelling on other times, other people. At length he said, "I heard you was with old Grady Welch when he got killed."

Snort's face saddened as he stared into the remnant of the fire. "I was there when he taken his last breath on this earth. I cried like a baby."

Hewey nodded, for he could understand that.

Snort said, "Every time we lose one like him, a little flavor goes out of life. There ain't many of us left."

"Horse stepped on him, Walter said."

"Big black horse, it was. Sixteen hands high, four stockin' feet. I never did trust a horse with four stockin' feet."

"Tough way to die."

Snort shrugged. "Maybe. I don't know but what it's the way old Grady would've wanted to go, though. Beats hell out of livin' till you get so old you can't ride anymore. Or gettin' bad hurt. Most ranches don't feel responsible for you if you get crippled for life, workin' for them. They'll thank you for your help, give you a little foldin' money and send you to town to fend for yourself. If you're damn lucky you might get a job cookin' for a wagon. If you're lucky but not *that* lucky you might get a job washin' out spittoons in some saloon. If you're not lucky atall you'll wind up beggin' for handouts on a street corner and tellin' everybody how great a cowpuncher you was before you fell on hard times. I've seen all three. I'd druther it'd happen to me like it happened to Grady, when my time comes."

Hewey frowned deeply, staring into the fire, remembering grand old times with Grady and Snort, and with others who had gone on. "When we get to town we'll have a drink to old Grady."

Snort looked up, struck by the appropriateness of the idea. It was, in its own way, almost a form of prayer. "We'll do that, Hewey. We'll sure as hell do that."

They delivered the horses to Nasworthy's stables across from the huge courthouse. There buyer Norton Bates waited with a couple of Mexican cowboys to pick them up. Bates rode with Hewey to the First National Bank, a block east. It was a brand-new structure with four magnificent white columns and a stone eagle perched on top.

"You wouldn't believe it," Bates said, "but they spent twenty-five thousand dollars puttin' up that buildin'."

Hewey whistled. A man could buy a good-sized ranch for that kind of money. They could have lost C.C.'s Upton City bank in a corner of this one and not found it for a week.

Bates drew a draft and arranged for the bank to mail it directly to the Upton City bank for Alvin's account. Hewey knew nothing about the handling of such big financial transactions. His twenty or twenty-five or thirty dollars a month had always been paid in cold cash.

"I owe you boys a drink," Bates said when the business was

done. "The Arc Light Saloon is down yonder a ways." He pointed south.

Hewey knew full well where the Arc Light was. "These young-uns here are a mite underage. They been wantin' to visit a real ice-cream parlor. Reckon you could point the way to one of those?"

Bates opined that ice cream was dangerous because it froze the stomach. But if the boys were bound and determined to risk their lives, he would pay for a spread. Afterward he took Hewey and Snort to the saloon, where the goods had the opposite effect, warming all the way to the toes. There Hewey found a lot of cowboys in town either to watch or to participate in the roping. By the time all the howdying and shaking was done, his arm was almost too tired to lift a rope.

The boys were waiting outside, both excited. "Uncle Hewey," Cotton exclaimed, "we've seen us an automobile."

Tommy pointed. "It's just around that corner yonder."

Hewey wasn't all that interested. He was itching to go and get his name into the pot for the roping. But he decided to smile over an automobile and act as if he liked it, though telling a lie was a mortal sin.

To him it looked like every other automobile he had ever seen in his travels, mostly just a glorified buggy with rubber tires, and without a horse. Down beneath the bed was an ugly-looking engine, leaking oil. Over the dashboard was a long shaft with a wheel on it that he knew was the mechanism for guiding the brainless contraption. All in all, he didn't see much there to detain a man for more than a minute or two.

Cotton walked around the automobile, learnedly pointing out all its features, telling what each was for and what part it played in making the monster lumber down the road and scare good horses half to death. Cotton seemed to know a lot, never to have laid eyes on one of these before.

Snort Yarnell seemed impressed by Cotton's knowledge, though he understood no more of it than Hewey did.

Cotton was leaning over the seat, pointing to some doodad and thingamajig on the dash when a tall man with a derby hat, a new suit and a waxed mustache stepped out of a nearby barber shop.

He reeked of bay rum. "Boy," he shouted, "you get your grimy hands away from that automobile!" He came striding purposefully down the plank sidewalk.

Cotton drew back as if he had been shot.

The man pointed a finger at him. "Don't you know the meaning of private property, kid? Don't you know that's an expensive piece of machinery? Be damned if I'll let some ignorant farm boy hoodoo it."

Cotton reddened.

Hewey moved between his nephew and the angry-eyed dude. "The button didn't mean no harm. And he may be a farm boy, but he's noways ignorant."

The well-dressed gent gave Hewey a hard stare that silently put him in a class no more than one notch above a yellow mongrel dog. There were a lot of people who didn't realize what a good cowboy was worth. "Every generation ought to make a *little* improvement over the one before it."

This time Cotton stepped between Hewey and the man. "Uncle Hewey, I've seen the automobile now. Let's get away from here."

Hewey had never been a fist fighter and had customarily gone well out of his way to avoid a fight when he could. In this case he was disposed toward making an exception.

Cotton caught him by the arm. "Let's go, Uncle Hewey."

Snort had put a fresh chew of tobacco in his mouth after the drink. Now he needed to spit. He deposited a brown blob on the rear tire. It began to stretch and run and drip. The dude made a strong comment about Snort's ancestry and stepped quickly to wipe away what he could with his white handkerchief. Snort said, "Hewey, we better go see about that ropin'."

Hewey nodded but looked back as he walked away. "I hope he's forced to trade that thing for a mean Missouri mule. And I hope that mule kicks him so hard it melts the wax out of his *mus*tache."

Snort tried none too subtly to change the subject. "I had a *mus*tache one time. Kept it two or three years. You remember it, Hewey? Finally got rid of it. Kept burnin' it off smokin' my cigarettes short."

After he had put up his five dollars, Hewey ran a finger down the handwritten list of entrants and glanced quickly at Snort. "They got Clay McGonagill and Joe Gardner here, the champions of the whole world. And Fred Baker and Jim Barron and Bob Mims. All the good ones, just about, except Ellison Carroll. You ever rope against these fellers before?"

"Nope. But that gives us the advantage, don't you see? They don't know what they're up against."

Hewey and Snort and the boys went to the Trimble Grocery and splurged a dollar and a half on luxuries such as cheese and crackers, sardines and canned peaches. These they carried down to the bank of the Concho River. They squatted in the dense shade of the big native pecan trees, where Hewey opened the cans by slashing a big X in the tops with his Barlow knife. They fed sumptuously. Done, Hewey rubbed his stomach. "Them bankers in Kansas City don't have it a tittle or a jot better than this."

Tommy enthusiastically agreed. "If I ever get rich, I'll do this every day."

The fairgrounds lay in a big open flat east of town. The arena was almost the size of a horse trap; Hewey guessed it at ten acres, its far end reaching all the way to the steep bank of the Main Concho on the south. At the north end was a small grandstand and the holding pens where sixty or seventy long-legged, long-horned Mexico steers pulled hay out of wooden racks as if it were free, trampling half of it underfoot. Wagons and buggies lined up along the arena fence on either side. The roping was supposed to begin at two o'clock.

Snort strayed off to visit with old friends and to bask in the glory of his reputation. Hewey rode Biscuit leisurely through the crowd, looking for people he knew, studying the ropers and their mounts. He gave special but quiet attention to big Clay McGonagill, freshly back from a triumphant tour of South America with some other noted ropers like Joe Gardner. Hewey sort of liked McGonagill's big bay horse, which had an apple branded on the shoulder, but not enough to propose a trade for Biscuit.

Once his breath came short as he saw a woman in the crowd. She looked for all the world like Spring Renfro. He couldn't imagine what Spring would be doing here. He eased Biscuit up closer and saw that he was mistaken. She didn't look like Spring at all. The woman stared at him, disturbed by his uninvited attention. Hewey turned away, perplexed by his error. He had no idea why Spring should remain so strong on his mind.

Cotton shouted, "Uncle Hewey, yonder comes that automobile."

Hewey reined Biscuit around and saw the same red vehicle, driven by the slicked-up dude. Sitting with him in the front were two young and handsome women dressed like Christmas packages. Hewey doubted that they were his sisters. The driver tooted his horn and almost caused a runaway. A man with a woman and three kids in a hack had to saw desperately on the reins to keep his team from taking the bits in their teeth and leaving there. Horses snorted and scattered as the dude pushed the automobile through the crowd to seek a place beside the arena fence.

Someone shouted, "Be slow with that noise. You'll hurt somebody."

For answer the dude tooted the horn again. One of the girls laughed.

If some husky fellow would go over there and take the curl out of that mustache, he would be the most popular man at the fairgrounds, Hewey thought. He was not seeking honors, however.

Presently Snort was back. "Hewey, how much money you got?"

As little stock as Hewey placed in money, Snort cared even less. Hewey had most of the pay from Alvin, but caution made him reply in the most general terms. "Some."

"Let me have it. I'll double or triple it for you. There's a damn fool over yonder got more money than sense. He's givin' odds."

Hewey kept his hands in his pockets. "The competition is fierce."

"Competition is like sugar sprinkled on cobbler pie. Where's your faith?"

"Faith is one thing. Charity is somethin' else."

"It's that fool yonder who's bein' charitable. Come on, let me have what you've got."

Snort Yarnell was a hard man to refuse. Against his judgment Hewey dug out most of what he had. He was careful to retain a little wad of paper in his pocket, hoping it didn't show. He had no idea how much it was, or how much he handed over. Snort disappeared again.

Cotton stared at Hewey in exasperation. "Uncle Hewey, you've ridden broncs, doctored wormy cattle, done God knows what all to earn that money."

He had that much of his mother in him and couldn't help it, Hewey thought charitably. "Easy come, easy go."

Cotton shook his head over lost causes and turned to watch Tommy, who was making a tentative and cautious acquaintanceship with some town boys of about his own age. Hewey kept an eye on the youngsters for a minute. Sometimes town boys were prone to hooraw country boys shamelessly. But there seemed no harm in these.

Hewey turned his attention to the roping. His name was two thirds of the way down the list, which gave him time to see how most of the others performed before he had to go out and give his due.

The roper who was "up" held his horse in readiness beside a narrow wooden chute into which cowboys had put a single spotted steer. Fifty feet out from the chute gate was the score line, drawn with white powdered chalk. As the gate opened, another rider chased the steer out toward the line. When the steer crossed the chalk mark, a judge dropped a red flag and gave the roper his signal to start. By this time the steer was gaining speed and distance. The roper might require sixty to a hundred yards of running room to catch up with him and make his throw.

Snort was up just before Hewey. He spurred out, swinging a loop big enough to catch a boxcar. As the loop sailed, its size diminished. When it fitted over the steer's horns there weren't more than a couple of inches to spare. But success was what counted. He spurred past the steer, flipped the rope over the animal's rump and rode off hard at an angle. The steer was jerked into a sudden hundred and eighty-degree turn that lifted it off its feet and thumped it down soundly on its side. Instantly Snort was on the ground with tie rope in his hand. He gathered and wrapped three feet while the steer was still too stunned to kick much. He threw up his hands to stop the timekeepers' watches. Snort swaggered to his roan horse and remounted, waiting to hear the time and get his rope back. The crowd cheered.

The time: thirty-eight and three fifths seconds. That put him in the lead for the first go-round.

Snort rode toward Hewey, those gold teeth shining. "You better whip up if you want to take second."

It had been a long time since Biscuit had been in a steer-roping contest. He remembered enough to be nervous. So did Hewey. The flagman stood poised at the end of the chalk score line, the flag up. The gate was opened. A paint steer with a horn span of more than three feet entered the arena in a long trot. The whip-up man put it into a good run across the line. The red flag dropped. Hewey touched spurs to Biscuit, but he didn't really need to. Biscuit remembered. He leaped out and after the steer in a dead run. Hewey had his loop built and ready. It was a big Blocker, after the style of the trail-driving Ab Blocker, but not as big as Snort's. He gave it a few swings, judged he was positioned right and flung it over the steer's horns. He jerked up the slack, sent it across the thin rump and rode away. He felt a jarring impact at the end of the rope. He caught a glimpse of four legs in the air, then a small cloud of dust. He was on the ground and running as Biscuit kept charging ahead, dragging the steer to keep it from gaining its feet. Hewey made a quick tie, threw up his hands and lost his balance. He fell backward, landing hard. He heard the dude honk his horn two or three times. Hewey got up and dusted himself off, his face warming. His embarrassment was more than offset by the far-off announcement of his time: thirty-eight seconds flat.

Grinning, he sought out Snort with his eyes. *Second, hell. That's the best time yet.*

He rode out of the arena expecting to accept the congratulations of the two boys with becoming modesty. But they hadn't seen his performance. Tommy was out past the crowd with several boys, testing his prowess with a slingshot. Another automobile had arrived, this one green. Cotton was down there on the arena fence inspecting it.

Hewey remembered the applause and reflected glumly over the fact that it always seemed easier to impress strangers than one's own family.

172

Snort said, "I hope you appreciate me lettin' you get your confidence."

Hewey would have more confidence if he still held his lead after McGonagill and Gardner had performed. As each man roped, he held his breath. They were good, but they came in just shy of his and Snort's times. McGonagill scored thirty-nine seconds, Gardner thirty-nine and two.

The second go-round started immediately. Warmed up now, many of the ropers bettered their original times. Snort went out and finished in thirty-eight one. He came back laughing. "You better draw her down fine, Hewey."

Hewey drew down fine and came back with thirty-eight flat.

The girls who sat in the red automobile cheered and clapped their hands for him as he rode by, to the annoyance of the dude. Hewey made a little show of tipping his hat to the ladies.

Again he looked around to see if the boys had witnessed his moment of triumph. Tommy was out of sight. Cotton was on his knees, studying the running gear beneath the green automobile.

Thank God for pretty women, Hewey thought wryly.

He felt the tension building in him as McGonagill roped, then Gardner. Gardner trimmed Hewey's time a little and came out fastest for the second go-round. Hewey scratched the figures in the dirt with his finger, did a little arithmetic and found to his satisfaction that he still led for the average. If he could do that well on three more steers, he might still carry away the silver watch he had seen down at the saloon.

He didn't know what he would do with it if he won it. He wasn't in the habit of carrying a pocket watch because if it ever stopped he might be three months getting the correct time to reset it. He lived by the sun.

Hewey and Snort seesawed through the next two go-rounds, not taking the best time in either but staying close enough to be in strong contention. Snort did his third steer up a little faster than Hewey, which brought him back laughing loudly enough to hurt Hewey's ears a little. Hewey topped him by almost a full second on the fourth.

The last go-round was usually the wildest in any roping. Those men who trailed would bust a buckle trying to catch up. All they had to lose was their necks, so they took long chances and fast loops. Some missed altogether, some caught just one horn. One let his horse get off stride just as he hit the end of the rope. The horse went down and rolled over him. The crowd jumped to its feet. But the cowboy got up with nothing worse than a slight limp and a shredded shirt.

Hewey was beginning to feel the pressure building on him when he saw a familiar figure striding through the crowd, and heard a familiar voice call his name. It was Walter. Hewey's chin dropped in surprise. He put the shock behind him and rode over to shake hands.

Walter said, "You're a hard man to catch up with once you hit the trail. But I heard there was a ropin', and I figured I'd find you. How you standin'?"

"Pretty good, up to now. What you doin' here? Ain't the weeds growin' up out at the place?"

"Eve didn't trust the boys to get home by theirselves, and not to get in trouble. She sent me to fetch them, and to maybe talk you into comin' back too."

"Mad, wasn't she?"

Walter rubbed his jaw. "I'm not sure *mad* is the word. But it'll do till I think of a stronger one."

"You ain't goin' to try to talk me into goin' back, are you?"

Walter thought about it. "You're of age, Hewey. You've got a right to make up your own mind and live by your own lights."

"Damn few people seem to think so."

Snort Yarnell's time came. He took a fresh chew of tobacco and rode up into place. He was the picture of supreme confidence, sitting straight and proud, shoulders reared back, gold teeth agleam.

He spurred after the steer, swung his loop and completely missed.

It was a big surprise to both Snort and his blue roan horse. The horse slowed, confident Snort had made a catch; he almost always did. By the time Snort built a second loop and finally caught his steer, he was way out of the money. But defeat rolled off of his shoulders like water from a duck. He came back grinning as broadly as if he had won. "Did you notice the shape of that loop, Hewey? I do believe it was as pretty a one as I ever throwed."

"But kind of empty, don't you think?"

Hewey sensed when he spurred out after his own steer that everything was perfect. The steer was just right. Biscuit was just right. The loop felt like prize money when it left his hand. It fitted over the horns as if it had been measured and trimmed. He laid the rope over those red and white hindquarters and rode off. The steer flipped over and flopped down as if it were trained and on his payroll. Hewey jumped down to finalize his victory . . .

. . . and tripped over his spurs.

He went down hard on his face and belly. He pushed up just in time to see the steer before Biscuit dragged it right over him. His face was pressed down into the arena, and he came up spitting dirt. His eyes burned from the sting of sand, and his ears burned from the laughter of the crowd. He got to his feet, looking around desperately for Biscuit and the steer. He saw them far down the arena, still going. Hewey spat some more dirt, hollered at Biscuit to "Haww!" and went chasing ignominiously after them. He heard the honking of an automobile horn over and over and over again. The dude was taking his revenge.

He managed to make his tie, just to keep the record straight. But he didn't hear his time and didn't much give a damn.

The dude and one of the girls laughed at him as he rode by. The other girl looked guardedly sympathetic.

Snort and Walter were waiting for him. Snort said, "You'll never get anywhere, Hewey, tryin' to put both feet into one boot."

Walter didn't say anything.

The two boys were there. They had finally watched Hewey, one time. Cotton took a cue from his father, but Tommy said, "Uncle Hewey, that was awful."

When all the times were tallied up, McGonagill finished first in the average, Gardner second.

Hewey shrugged. "Well, I reckon I got a little coffee-drinkin' money comin' to me for the first go-round, anyway. Aside from that, I'm purt near broke."

Snort said, "You-all wait for me," and disappeared into the departing crowd. In a little he was back. He counted out a considerable handful of bills to Hewey and shoved the rest of the roll into his own pocket.

Hewey's mouth dropped open. "What's that for? We lost the ropin'."

"But not the bet. You didn't think I'd bet our hard-earned

money on *us,* did you? I put it on Clay McGonagill and Joe Gardner against the field." He swung back onto his roan horse. "Let's go to town. We'll get them boys a ice cream and us somethin' stronger."

The traffic strung out in a long, dusty line of wagons, buggies, hacks and horsemen, as well as numerous bicycles and a goodly number of people afoot. From behind came the insistent honking of a horn. Hewey looked over his shoulder and saw the dude impatiently making his way through the crowd in that ugly red automobile. He wasn't having any trouble clearing the horses; they were snorting and faunching to get out of the monster's path. As the automobile came up close behind Cotton and Tommy, the dude tooted that horn again.

Tommy's horse squealed and broke into pitching. Surprised, Tommy grabbed too late for the horn, sailed up into the air and came down on his belly. Walter jumped to the ground to see about him.

The dude honked again and went around without stopping. The crowd was shouting ugly threats but doing nothing about it.

Snort and Hewey looked each other in the eyes. Hewey saw the intention in Snort's face and concurred with a nod. Both unfastened their horn strings and shook loops into their ropes. Snort shouted, "I'll rope the head of the goddamn thing, Hewey. You come in there and heel it!"

Spurring the roan horse, swinging the loop, Snort gave chase. One of the girls glanced back, saw him and gasped. The dude looked over his shoulder, recognized Snort's intention and began trying for more speed. But the wagon road was rough and bouncy.

"Damn you, cowboy, don't you dare!" he shouted as Snort came up abreast of the vehicle. The roan was rolling its eyes and snorting in fear, but Snort kept spurring. In the final analysis, the horse feared Snort more than it feared the automobile.

Snort threw that great boxcar loop and landed a catch around the dashboard, one carbide lamp and a front wheel. He jerked up the slack and took a dally around his saddle horn. "Now heel it, Hewey!"

Hewey spurred Biscuit in, cast a quick loop over one of the rear wheels and rode south. Snort rode north.

The dude shouted and shook his fist. The girls grabbed hold of the seat and screamed.

As the two cowboys hit the ends of their ropes, they jerked the automobile half around and ran it into the ditch. The dude was thrown out over the dashboard.

Snort shouted, "We got it roped, but how do we hog-tie an automobile?"

The dude was stunned only for a moment. He got to his feet, eyes blazing and looking for somebody to fight. Hewey was closest. He came running, his fists knotted. Hewey dismounted and stepped away from Biscuit. As the dude swung on him, Hewey ducked under and took a solid hold. He wrestled the man to the ground. Snort, still on horseback, pitched Hewey his tie rope. "Since we can't tie up an automobile, maybe we can tie up an automobile jockey."

Hewey got the little loop over both of the man's hands and then over one foot. He trussed him the way he had been tying steers.

In a sudden flush of showmanship he stepped back and threw up his hands in the manner the ropers used to stop the time-keepers. A goodly crowd had gathered around. Most of them clapped their hands and cheered.

Clay McGonagill rode forward and leaned down to shake Hewey's hand. "Friend, if you'd done that in the arena, *you'd* be carryin' that silver watch."

One of the girls sat big-eyed in the car, saying over and over, "My goodness." The other climbed down and untied the dude. Snort rode the blue roan over to her. "Pretty miss, I'd be much obliged if you'd throw me my strang."

Some of the crowd rescued Hewey's and Snort's ropes from the automobile. The driver rubbed his hands where the rope had burned him, and the fight was still in him. But the crowd was laughing him down. He climbed back into the automobile and sat there baking in the heat of his anger. He looked at nobody and spoke to no one.

Snort showed those gold teeth. "I do believe he's sulled on us."

Hewey looked back to be sure Tommy was all right. He was. The laughing, cheering crowd then swept him and Snort along toward town, rejoicing.

Snort declared, "I'll bet you we made history here today, Hewey, old pardner. I'll bet me and you are the first cowboys to ever head and heel an automobile!"

All the way to town they were congratulated and back-slapped by well-wishing strangers who now considered them friends. Snort looked behind him to see if the automobile was coming. It still sat in the ditch.

"I read in a paper a while back where some damn fools are a-fixin' to try to drive an automobile all the way from New York to California."

"Hope they ain't in a hurry," Hewey said.

"Hope they don't run into no ropers along the way."

Cotton and Tommy found new friends among the town boys, who wanted to show them how good the night fishing was in the Concho River. Coming out of a dry country where it was hard to find even a water dog, Walter's boys were receptive to the notion. It was just as well, because Hewey knew he would have been a poor chaperon. Boys that age needed a lot of leaving-alone, anyway.

As they started to leave with the other boys, Tommy admonished, "You watch out now, Uncle Hewey, and don't you get drunk."

"Button," Hewey assured him, "I ain't ever been drunk in my whole life."

He could have gotten roaring drunk without spending a dime, had he wanted to. Snort was well on the way. Friends and strangers kept crowding around them in the Arc Light, trying to buy drinks for the men who had roped and thrown the wild devil-car.

Walter sat at the table with Hewey and Snort, but he drank very little. He grimaced each time he lifted the glass to his lips. "Whisky must've come a long way downhill. Seems to me like it used to taste better than this."

Hewey thought perhaps a residue of something had been left in Walter's glass. He took a sip from it. "Nothin' wrong with the whisky."

"It's me, then. I've lost my taste for it. One drink is fine. The second drink ain't worth a bucket of cold pee."

"I'm sorry, little brother."

"It's just as well. If I didn't have anything in life that I liked better than whisky, then I'd really have somethin' to worry about." Restlessly he looked around him at the growing crowd, noisily bustling about the tables, clustering at the bar. He listened to the clink of glasses, the jingling of silver coin, the roaring of boisterous laughter as someone told a joke that would not have stood the daylight. His frown deepened.

Hewey asked, "What's the matter?"

"Nothin'. Just kickin' myself for the time I've wasted the last few years, worryin' about missin' all *this*."

Hewey looked at the people. "Everybody seems to be havin' a good time."

"Maybe they got nothin' better at home."

"You tryin' to lecture me? This is a poor place to be holdin' church."

"I promised I wouldn't argue with you, and I won't. But I'll have to admit that I don't understand. There was a feelin' between you and Spring Renfro. Anybody could see it. Wasn't it strong enough?"

Hewey poured himself a fresh shot of whisky, but he didn't drink it. He stared into it. This wasn't a thing he wanted to talk about, especially not here. But he supposed everybody was making so much noise that no one except Walter would hear him. "It was strong." He remembered a feeling of guilt because of its strength. "It scared me, I reckon."

"Scared you? That's not the way it's supposed to be. It's supposed to lift you up and make you happy."

Hewey turned the glass in his fingers. He looked around to see if anyone was listening. Nobody could have heard him. Walter would be lucky to. "I had feelin's about her that wasn't right and proper. She's a lady, Walter. She's got a right to decency and respect. But when I was around her I'd sometimes get to thinkin' things . . ." He turned up his hands. "I know about women; I ain't no schoolboy. I been upstairs with a many of them wheeligo

179

girls, and no blush ever touched my cheek. Spring ain't that kind of a woman, but sometimes she gave me the same feelin' I'd get from them wheeligo girls. She deserves a lot better than that."

"It's a natural feelin'. Everybody gets it. It's nothin' to be ashamed of."

"Well, I am. And if I was to marry her I'd have to face up to it. Sure, I know everybody does it. If they didn't, this old earth would get short of people in a hurry. But, Walter, I couldn't see *me* doin' it, not with *her*. How could I, the first time? How could I look her in the eye afterward and not want to crawl off under a rock and hide?"

Walter's eyes softened. A smile seemed about to break, but he restrained it. "Hewey, you're worryin' about a ladder when there ain't even a wall. Believe me, when the time comes it'll be the most natural thing in the world. There won't be any guilt. It'll be the opposite, if anything. It'll be like you went to church."

Hewey couldn't visualize any resemblance.

Walter said, "There won't be any shame in it for her, and there won't be for you either. You think there was any shame in it for me and Eve? No sir, it's a natural thing, a part of life. It's part of bein' human, for the woman as well as for the man."

He finished what was left of his drink and showed no pleasure in it. "You'll never know what I'm talkin' about till it happens to you. Then you'll wonder why you waited for thirty-eight years."

"Thirty-six," Hewey said. It *was* thirty-eight.

Walter shrugged. "Whichever, you've wasted too much time already." He pushed to his feet. "I'm goin' down by the river where me and the boys made camp. I've had about all of this wild pleasure that I can stand." He gripped Hewey's shoulder, then nodded at Snort.

Snort acknowledged the benediction with a salute of his glass, which he promptly emptied. When Walter was gone, Snort said, "You know what he's tryin' to do to you, Hewey? He's tryin' to get you to fit into the same tight little mold as everybody else. But me and you, we broke the mold that made *us*. We're free men. There ain't many of our kind left in this world."

"Walter was free once. Givin' it up don't seem to've killed him."

"Because they've changed him. They've cut him. A steer don't realize what he's missed, but he's missed it just the same. You ain't no steer, Hewey. Don't be lettin' all them people make a steer *of* you. Show them you're a bull, and damn proud of it."

Hewey poured a drink and downed it all at once. "We showed them today. We showed them we was bull enough to head and heel an automobile."

Snort poured Hewey another drink. "Damn betcha we did." He lifted his glass in toast. "Here's to the best automobile ropers that ever straddled leather."

Hewey drank to that.

Snort leaned across the table, anticipation bright in his eyes. "What do you need with a skinny old maid schoolteacher, anyway? Somebody to tie you down and put a ring in your nose, and what do you get out if it? A life sentence to hard labor is all." He pointed his thumb back over his shoulder. "I know where we can find us a couple of the prettiest gals a man ever slid under a sheet with. Not skinny, either. Plump. Somethin' you can really get ahold of. Not cold-blooded like some schoolteacher, but hot like Mexican peppers. They don't ask you where you been or where you're goin'. They don't tie no strings on you or cry when you leave. But they'll be somethin' to remember on them long nights you're layin' out alone in some cold camp. What you say we go over yonder and get us a couple of them gals? We got it comin' to us for the work we done here today."

Hewey shook his head. "I don't know, Snort. I ain't sure I'm ready."

"You got that schoolteacher on your mind. You ever see a schoolteacher erase a blackboard? One good sweep of her hand and it's all gone. Well, erase *her*. We'll find you a pretty gal down yonder, and that's the last you'll ever worry about that school-teacher."

Hewey still didn't move.

Snort said, "You don't have to really do nothin' if you ain't got the notion. Let's just go down there and look. Won't hurt nothin' to just look."

The whisky burned Hewey's stomach, and his eyes were blurry. He was not yet so drunk that he didn't realize he wouldn't stop at just looking. They always looked good, those wheeligo girls, and

181

they smelled good. When a man got close enough, they *felt* good. Once he ever went that far he wouldn't stop. He never had.

Snort was up on wobbly feet, trying to talk a couple more cowboys into taking a walk with them down West Concho Avenue. Before he could help himself, Hewey was out in the street with them. They were hustling him along in the cool night, singing an outrageous song in three keys. Hewey hoped to hell those two boys of Walter's had gone to bed by now and weren't still up prowling around where they might see him.

It was a two-story house a block or two down from the Landon Hotel. Hewey's vision was none too clear; he couldn't tell much about the place. The electric lights hurt his eyes. He had never been around the damn things enough to get used to them. San Angelo had set up a power plant in the nineties. Some people nowadays even had a light bulb hanging in their cowsheds.

A player piano was twanging away unattended over on one flower-papered wall. Hewey thought it was badly in need of a tuner's services, but maybe it was just his ears. Some couples were dancing. Among them was the dude.

They saw each other at about the same time. Snort saw him too. He made loud and public mention of the fact that this was the jelly bean whose automobile he and Hewey had brought to its knees. The dude's face reddened, and he showed some momentary disposition to fight. The girl he danced with told him the house had strict rules against violence, and they had a bouncer as big as one of the Twin Mountains to enforce the regulation. He would keep things peaceful around here if he had to kill half the cowboys in San Angelo.

Hewey saw the bouncer standing in a corner. He was tall enough that he had to duck to come through the door, and he stood two ax handles broad. Hewey could understand why the dude quickly quieted down.

It occurred to him that the girl the dude danced with was one of the two who had been with him in the automobile. She was doing a lot of whispering in the man's ear. Presently the two of them disappeared down a hallway. Hewey felt confident that when the dude came back he would be in a better humor.

A hand gently touched his shoulder, and he tried to turn his head. That proved difficult. He finally brought his eyes into focus on a pretty face he remembered seeing before. "How's the great car roper?" she asked, grinning. He thought she had the brightest-looking teeth he had ever seen. Maybe that was from the electric lights.

His tongue was thick. He thought he had a good answer, but he couldn't bring it out. He mumbled something which even he didn't understand. This was the second girl who had been with the dude, the one who had had gumption enough to get out of the automobile and untie him. The fact that the dude now had gone down the hall with the one who just sat and whimpered told him something, he thought, about the man.

"Old Foxy has had that comin' to him," she said.

"Foxy?"

"Fox is his name. Us ladies just call him Foxy. He's got a right smart of money but damn little else." She smiled again. "I don't want to talk about him. I want to talk about *you*. What's your name?"

For a minute he thought he had forgotten it. He had to try twice before he got it said.

She tried it slowly. "Hewey. My, that's a sweet name."

He never had thought of it in that light before. It occurred to him that, yes, it *was* a sweet name.

Her hand kept moving slowly along his back until her arm was around his shoulder. "I don't believe I ever knew but one other man named Hewey. That one liked to dance. I'll bet you like to dance too."

"Sure do," he said, though in reality he had always had two left feet. Shortly he was with her in the center of the parlor floor. The player piano was still off key but trying hard, as was Hewey. His feet weighed fifty pounds apiece.

She said, "What you need, cowboy, is a drink."

He vaguely remembered already having one or two, but her arms and her soft, warm body rubbing tantalizingly against him persuaded him that whatever she thought he needed, he needed. He took that drink, and soon another. She was whispering things in his ear that sounded very nice, though he never quite understood the words. That damn piano.

First thing he knew, she had her arm around his waist, and his around hers. They were stumbling up the stairs together. They were both laughing, and he was pinching her where it seemed nature had intended for her to be pinched by making it so irresistible. She led him to a door, opened it and helped him into a small room. He saw a brass bed and a bureau, and a washstand with a china bowl and a pink-flowered pitcher. The place had a strong aroma of perfume. Over the bed was an embroidered and framed motto: "God Bless Our Home." He thought the sentiment was nice.

She sat him down on the edge of the bed and put her arms around him. He turned his head to kiss her but made the mistake of looking up toward that bare, glowing light bulb. He realized he shouldn't have tilted his head so far, but he was somehow hypnotized by the blazing filament. The light seemed to start circling around and around over him like some fiery bird of prey about to swoop down and grab him. His head became heavy. He sank back onto the bed. All of a sudden the light seemed to go out, and he was falling backward, falling, falling . . .

He awoke slowly, dreaming that twelve spans of Missouri mules were running over his head, and when they finished the freight wagon behind them got him too. He became conscious of daylight through the drawn paper shade that covered a window. He found his hand, which weighed seventy-five pounds, and then his hand found his head. It came to him gradually that he was lying in a bed. He blinked. Slowly his vision began to clear. He saw dimly the outline of a woman sitting in a straight chair, slowly brushing her long hair. His first thought was that she was Spring Renfro, and he tried to understand what she would be doing in his bedroom. It came to him in a minute that he *had* no bedroom. He managed to clear his eyes a little more and see for certain that this was not Spring.

The girl continued brushing her long brown hair and watching him dispassionately. She said, "I do believe, old boy, that you'll live after all."

Hewey rubbed his head. "Damn, I hope not."

He blinked again, trying to remember where he was and how he got here. The smell of the perfume helped bring it all back. The memory slowly seeped through his brain. With the memory came shame, drawing over him like a shroud. What would Walter's boys think? What would Spring Renfro think?

They ought to pass a law to keep anybody under forty from drinking.

He hadn't intended for anything like this to happen. Only three or four days gone from Spring Renfro, and now he lay in an upstairs bedroom of a Concho Avenue parlor house.

Eve had been right in everything she had called him.

As he studied the girl with clearer eyes, he decided she looked ten years older. He rubbed his hand down his side and found that he was barefoot from heel to forelock. "What happened to my clothes?"

"You took them off," she said evenly. "You did pretty good, up to that point."

"I don't remember a thing that happened."

"There ain't nothin' to remember." She seemed to be laughing at him a little. "Quick as you laid down, you was gone to China, or someplace. You sure wasn't here."

He blinked, hope beginning to flare. "You mean I didn't . . ."

"I mean you *couldn't*. You went out faster than an electric light." Her brow knitted into a frown. "I hope you ain't figurin' to ask me for your money back. I was here all night, even if you wasn't."

Never in his life had Hewey been so glad not to get his money's worth. "Honey, you keep it. In fact, I'll be glad to give you five dollars more."

Her frown was gone. She suggested, "It's still early. I got nothin' particular to do right now."

"But *I* have. If you'll get me my underwear and my britches . . ."

He swung his feet over the side of the bed and almost fell off. She caught him and cradled his aching head against her breasts. "Honey, you're in too much of a hurry."

Reluctantly he pulled himself away. He knew if he stayed any longer he would become attached to the place and not leave until bankruptcy strained his welcome. He got his underwear on, then his hat, his britches, his shirt and finally his boots. He said, "I reckon my pardner, old Snort Yarnell, is in the house somewhere."

She nodded. "He taken a shine to Flo."

"Well, when you see him, tell him Hewey Calloway has decided to go back to school."

She didn't know what he was talking about, but Snort would understand.

She kissed him one more time and patted his cheek. "You come back, honey, anytime you take the notion."

He fumbled his way down the stairs, the girl following a few steps behind him, showing a concern that wasn't all bought and paid for. The early morning sunlight hit him like a sledgehammer when he stepped through the door. He had to cover his eyes with his hands for a minute.

She asked, "You goin' to make it, hon?"

"If I can live through the next ten minutes." He hitched up his pants, pulled down his hat, straightened his shoulders and staggered out into the street. It took him a minute to get his bearings. He looked up toward the big Landon Hotel and remembered the red-light district had always been to the west of it. The hotel itself was impeccably clean and moral, a place where preachers could stay and feel at home. But if they took a constitutional, they were usually advised to walk east, not west.

Walter and the boys should be more or less south, somewhere down on the riverbank. He headed in that direction, trying to get his feet under better control. Presently he spotted the camp. Rather, he spotted Biscuit tethered on a long stake rope, and with him Walter's and the boys' horses. A lot of other horses and other camps lay beyond. Many people had come to watch the roping but could not afford or did not choose to spend the price of a hotel room or even a little space at a wagonyard.

He heard voices and looked back. Far behind him he saw four men. At the distance and in the condition of his eyes he could not make out who they were. He knew no reason it should make a difference. Trudging down toward camp, he smelled coffee on that fire or on some other. At the moment coffee seemed vastly superior to whisky.

Tommy shouted, "Yonder comes Uncle Hewey." Walter,

hunched over the fire, turned and glanced at his brother but made no move. Tommy came running. "Where you been, Uncle Hewey? We thought you'd come down here last night and camp with us."

Hewey avoided meeting his nephew's gaze. "I ran into a friend."

"You must have friends everywhere."

"I try to."

Walter beckoned. "We found a woman who had some eggs to sell. You look like you could find a place for a few."

Hewey's stomach roiled. He wasn't sure eggs would find hospitality in there, but they stood as good a chance as anything. He was about to reply in the affirmative when a rough voice shouted:

"Yonder he is. Now get the son of a bitch!"

He turned. Three of the biggest men he had ever seen advanced down the riverbank toward him. Their eyes were purposeful and cold. Behind them, hands on his hips, stood the dude who owned the red automobile. He was disheveled, unshaven, a far cry from the handsome picture of yesterday. He, like Hewey, evidently had put in a bad night.

Hewey backed away a few steps, holding up both hands. "Fellers, I don't know what he's been tellin' you about me, but it's all lies."

He knew immediately that truth was of little interest to them. One he recognized now as the bouncer from the parlor house. He looked as if he could wrestle a bull to the ground.

"Fellers," Hewey argued, still backing, "there ain't no use in us goin' through all this. I'll gladly give up before we start."

The bouncer said, "It ain't nothin' personal, cowboy. Mr. Fox yonder, he paid us to stomp hell out of you, is all."

Hewey was almost to the edge of the river. If he backed any farther he would take a bath he had not planned on. "Tell him I've already repented of my willful ways."

"Talkin' won't fix things. He wants to see some blood spilt. You can just stand there and take it, or you can fight. To us it don't much matter one way or the other."

Fox stood well behind the three advancing men, waiting to get his money's worth. Hewey saw that argument was useless, and apology never crossed his mind. It had always been his contention that when you faced a snake you didn't waste time stomping on its rattles; you tried to smash the head. He attempted to dart around the three and get to Fox, but his heavy feet didn't dart well. The bouncer grabbed him, hauled him off of the ground and swung a fist the size and consistency of an oak stump. Hewey thought his head had exploded. He thumped down solidly on his back.

He heard Walter shout, "Boys, go for the law!" With an angry roar Walter came running, swinging a chunk of firewood. The bouncer went down with a grunt. The other two quickly turned their attention to wresting the firewood from Walter. One of them bear-hugged the wooden chunk to keep it from causing harm while the other furiously pummeled at Walter. Cotton jumped up on that man's back and tried to take a strangle hold around a thick neck that would have been counted an asset to a Durham bull.

"Boy," Walter shouted, "I told you to go for the law!"

"Tommy went," Cotton gritted, still struggling for a hold that would have any effect. The big man pitched like an outlaw horse. In a minute Cotton went sprawling. The man kicked at him but missed. Anger boiled up in Hewey and brought him to his feet. They didn't seem so heavy anymore. He made for the man who had tried to kick Cotton. The man turned to meet him and they went down rolling, wrestling. Hewey didn't have much chance to see what else was going on, but he caught a glimpse of the bouncer trying to push to his feet and dropping back on his knees. He heard Fox shouting at him to get up and get back in there.

Hewey had only a vague idea what to do; he had never been much inclined toward this type of endeavor. During most of his life he had been able to talk his way out of scrapes, or to have a horse that would outrun anybody else's. He twisted and punched and gouged where and when he could. Sometimes he was on top, sometimes on bottom. His head was reeling so much he didn't always know. But he had the drive to keep struggling.

He sensed that Walter was making a better show of himself, helped along by Cotton until finally the bouncer made it to his feet and punched Cotton in the stomach so hard that Cotton went down choking, gasping for breath. Then the bouncer and the other man together gave their full attention to Walter. In a minute they had him down. The bouncer, his head bleeding because of the lick he had taken from the firewood, angrily began stomping on Walter. Hewey bawled in rage but couldn't work loose from the fellow holding him. He heard something snap, and Walter cried out in pain.

Someone shouted from on top of the riverbank. Fox started running away. Men spilled down toward the fighters. In a minute the three hired toughs stood hunched together while a big man with a shining badge addressed them in terms that would blister a mule skinner's ears. They stood and took it like whipped pups.

Somebody lifted Hewey to his feet. When they tried to lift his brother, Walter screamed.

"His leg is broke," somebody said. "Send for a doctor."

Hewey wiped the back of his bruised and torn hand across his face, and it came away bloody. He knelt beside his brother. "Walter, do you hurt bad?"

Walter couldn't answer. He gritted his teeth and tried to keep from crying out again. Hewey almost touched Walter's leg but caught himself in time. He turned and looked back over his shoulder. "It was that biggest one done it. That bawdy-house bouncer."

The big man's anger was gone, and fear had taken its place. "You takin' us off to jail, Sheriff?"

The lawman's reply left no possible doubt of his intentions. "Plumb to the third floor. What did you do it for, Jayce?"

"For money. We come after that feller"—he nodded his chin toward Hewey—"but there wasn't no hard feelin's on our part. We was paid to teach him a lesson, is all."

"I hope everybody has learned one," the sheriff declared. "Who paid you?"

"That fancy gent, that Fox."

"If there wasn't anything personal, how come you to break this feller's leg?"

"It got personal when he hit me up beside the head with a tree stump."

The sheriff had a deputy with him. He detailed him to go hunt up the dude and deliver him to the courthouse. "I'll take these three fine gentlemen up to the jail and entertain them at county expense." He turned to Hewey. "You'll want to stay with your brother, I expect. A doctor's on the way. When you can, I wish you'd come on up to my office in the courthouse. We've got some talkin' to do."

Hewey nodded. He looked back at Walter. The two boys were with him, one kneeling on either side. Tommy cried at the sight of his father lying hurt. Cotton's nose had been bleeding, but that had stopped. A big splotch was turning blue on his left cheek. He lifted his gaze to his uncle. Hewey couldn't decide whether he saw rebuke in the boy's eyes or not. Cotton said, "This all come about because of you ropin' that automobile."

Hewey had nothing constructive to say. He only grunted.

Cotton said, "I reckon it seemed like a good idea at the time. But I remember somethin' my daddy told you. He said you never was one to think about cost, or about consequences. What do you think about *this?*"

"I wouldn't have had it happen for the world."

"But it did, and Daddy has got to live with it." Cotton grimaced, close to tears. "You're a good old boy, Uncle Hewey. But sometimes you're a danger to everybody around you."

Hewey bowed his head. He could see no argument with that. He heard Walter rasp to Cotton, "Leave your Uncle Hewey alone, son. He didn't mean nobody any harm."

"He never does."

The doctor drove up in a buggy. He examined Walter's leg and found what everybody already knew. He made up a temporary splint and directed some of the crowd in loading Walter into the bed of a wagon. They hauled him to the doctor's office. There he completed his examination, set the leg with help from somebody steadier than Hewey, and he put it into a cast.

"How long's he got to stay in that thing?" Hewey asked.

"Six weeks at the least. Eight, more likely."

Cotton protested, "Doctor, my daddy's a farmer. We've got crops to finish up, stock to be worked."

The doctor sternly shook his head. "I don't care what he is. If he tries to walk on that leg in less than two months he'll be a cripple the rest of his life."

Cotton turned to Hewey, his eyes stricken. "What're we goin' to do, Uncle Hewey?"

Hewey had no answer. At times like this it seemed he never did.

The best he could muster was a weak and meaningless, "We'll get by."

"How? You just tell me how!"

"Someway."

The courthouse was a huge Gothic stone structure like something out of a book on the terrors of the olden times when young princes were smothered to death and queens had their heads chopped off. Its cupola stood a full two stories above the three-story building itself. It made Hewey's head hurt all over again to look up at the big clock near the top. He didn't know why he looked. It made no difference what time it was.

He found the sheriff's office without trouble. He could hear the sheriff's stern voice as he entered the hallway. He walked in reluctantly, hat in his hand. The sheriff had Fox and the other three men sitting on a bench along one wall, thoroughly cowed before the majesty of the law. He looked up at Hewey. "How's your brother?"

"In a bad fix. He won't walk for a long time."

The lawman frowned. "I suppose you know you're partly responsible?"

Hewey hung his head.

The sheriff asked, "How you figurin' on gettin' him home?"

"I don't know. I reckon I'll have to borrow or hire a wagon."

"A banker in town is fixin' to leave early in the mornin' to inspect a loan out in that part of the country. He's takin' an automobile. I believe I could talk him into carryin' your brother."

Hewey considered. "You reckon that'd be faster than a wagon?"

"Anything is."

Hewey gave his consent. "If there's any expenses . . ."

The sheriff pointed his chin at Fox, who looked very little like the dude he had been yesterday. "Mr. Fox here is in a generous mood. He has already agreed that he will foot any and all expenses havin' to do with your brother's . . . accident. Otherwise he'll roost in the jailhouse till the snow flies." He looked at the other three. "Unless you have some objection, I've decided to let these men go. They all seem to have remembered that they were about to leave town anyway."

Hewey nodded. "As long as it ain't west."

The bouncer looked at his huge hands. "Don't worry, I ain't goin' west. They got some rough old boys out there."

The automobile had a broad seat in the back. With some effort they were able to prop Walter up so that he could be reasonably comfortable. Cotton was to go along and help take care of him on the trip. Hewey and Tommy would follow, bringing home the four horses.

Hewey said, "Cotton, I always promised I'd get you a ride in an automobile. I didn't mean for it to be like this."

"You can't help bein' the way you are, Uncle Hewey."

"I'm goin' to change, boy. Believe me, I'll change."

Cotton gave him a quiet gaze that told all of his doubts, then he climbed into the green automobile.

Hewey watched the machine pull away, leaving a trail of smoke that smelled to him as if it would chase the devil out of hell. Cotton never did look back. Shoulders slumped, Hewey turned to Tommy.

"Boy, we'd just as well be on our way too. We've seen about all there is of this place."

They went first by the Alvin Lawdermilk headquarters, getting there at dinnertime the second day. Hewey had talked little to Tommy on the way; his mind had dwelled much on what he would say here, and later at home. He burst through the front screen and faced a surprised group at the table. Spring Renfro looked at him in astonishment, holding her fork motionless halfway to her open mouth. As he had expected, she looked a lot better than that wheeligo girl.

"Miss Renfro," he blurted, "I've changed my mind. I'm thataway inclined. But before I ask if you are too, there's somethin' I want you to know. While I was in San Angelo I tried to consort with a lewd woman. I couldn't do it, but you got to know that I tried."

She pushed her chair back and slowly came around the table. Her initial surprise gave way to the beginnings of a smile. "It's all right, Mr. Calloway."

He held up his hands. "There's somethin' else. I wasn't *at* San

Juan Hill. I never even *seen* Teddy Roosevelt except from a long ways off. The day they went up that hill I was flat on my back with the drizzlin' dysentery."

She walked up until her thin body was against his. Smiling, she laid her fingers across his mouth and brought her left arm around him. She momentarily forgot all her schoolteacher training and lapsed into the vernacular as she leaned her head against his chest. "Hewey Calloway, I wisht you'd just hush."

IX

Hewey had rather have taken a whipping with a wet rope than face the reception he knew he would get from Eve. It would be colder than a witch's kiss. He put it off as long as he could, taking the horses to the barn, unsaddling, pouring out oats. Cotton came from the house to see his brother and his uncle. Hewey found no cheer in his nephew's face. The bruise was almost black.

"How's your daddy?"

Cotton shrugged, eyes downcast.

"How's your mother takin' it?"

Cotton took a long breath and slowly expelled it. "You'll just have to go see for yourself."

"You-all make it all the way with that stinkin' automobile, or did you have to swap for a wagon?"

"We got in before dark. Fixed three flat tires. Only had motor trouble once, and I got that cured in about half an hour."

"*You* did? How about that banker?"

"He don't know much about engines." Cotton looked up. "Uncle Hewey, he offered me a job. Said I could work for him, drivin' and takin' care of his machine."

Hewey pondered that. He couldn't think of any job he would personally like less. But Cotton had a right to his own view. "You take him up on it?"

"I can't, with all that's facin' us here now. But I wisht I could. In San Angelo I could take some more schoolin' while I worked. He told me I could."

"Maybe things'll work out, son."

Cotton looked at the ground again, a catch in his voice. "There ain't nothin' to work out around here. Not anymore." Cotton walked on down toward the barn. Tommy turned and followed him in silent understanding. They quarreled on occasion, but at a time like this they were brothers.

Hewey took a long look at the house, then started toward it. He glanced back once, wishing the boys would follow him. But they were at the barn, and there they intended to stay. He took that for a bad omen.

He thought he had prepared himself for anything, but the look in Eve's face was worse than the wildest stretch of his imagination. She met him at the front screen, blocking his entrance. In her eyes was a cold fury, almost hatred.

"Hewey Calloway, you'll not set foot in this house!"

Stung, he moved back down from the step and stared at her from the ground. He felt as if he might choke. "Eve, I'm sorry."

"Sorry! You're always sorry. But sorry doesn't fix anything. You blunder around like a bull in a china shop, you ruin other people's lives, and then you think all you have to do is say you're sorry? Well, it's not good enough.

"You hurt other people and don't even know it. You have no idea how that good woman cried after you when you left. And Walter! For years you've tried to lure him away from this place to wander around with you willy-nilly over the country. You've tried to tell him this farm wasn't good enough for him, that he ought to leave it. Well, you've finally succeeded in takin' care of that, Hewey Calloway. You've just lost us this place!"

"Eve, I didn't mean . . ."

"He's laid up here now, helpless as a child. You think those two boys and me can make enough money to pay off Fat Gervin and C. C. Tarpley? They'll come and take us this fall, lock, stock and barrel. Everything we've worked so hard for, suffered for . . . it'll be gone. And it's all your doin', Hewey. But of course you won't be here to see it. You'll be off to Timbuktu or some such of a place."

She came down the step, pointing her finger into his face. He backed away some more. She declared, "I ought to shoot you, Hewey. No jury would convict me, and I don't think even God would care. If you don't get on your horse and leave here now, I swear I'll do it!"

Words had left him. Shame brought fire to his cheeks. He couldn't even bring himself to look into those furious eyes. She had every right to take a whip to him, and maybe even a gun.

"Eve, I . . ." Hell, there wasn't any use. He backed off a few more steps, then walked toward the barn with his head down. He stopped once and turned, but she towered in front of the door like some avenging angel, her eyes ablaze.

Biscuit hadn't finished his feed, but Hewey pulled him off and left the rest of it for that burro which had no name. He bridled and saddled the horse, his lips pinched hard against his teeth.

Tommy stared with wide eyes. "What did she say?"

Cotton touched his brother's arm and shook his head. As Hewey swung into the saddle, Cotton broke his silence. "We're goin' to lose this place, Uncle Hewey."

Hewey's throat was tight. He knew if he tried to say anything he would break down like a child. He didn't want to do that here, not in front of the boys. He might later, but it would be where nobody could see him. He gave the boys a tentative wave of his hand and touched spurs to Biscuit. Reluctantly, for he was leaving good feed, Biscuit moved into a trot. Hewey headed him in the general direction of the Lawdermilk place. But he drew off a little to one side, skirting around the lower end of the field. There, green leaves rustling in the wind, was the crop of redtop cane which was Walter's hole card toward paying off what he owed the bank this year. Standing outside the fence, trying to reach across to the feed but unable to stretch their necks that far, were three of the yearling cattle also intended to pay part of the obligation.

That much, he knew, the boys and Eve could somehow handle. But it wouldn't be enough. Walter had counted on breaking horses and mules for pay to finish out the balance. Laid up the rest of the summer, he had no chance to do that. Eve was right. All Fat and C.C. had to do now was wait. A nice juicy plum was about to fall into their laps.

And Hewey Calloway was the one who had shaken the tree.

He reined up and turned in the saddle, looking back down toward the house. It wasn't much, just a box-and-strip, hot in the summer and cold in the winter. But dammit, it was home. He remembered the work he had done, helping Walter nail the thing together out of fresh green lumber. He looked at the shed and the corrals and remembered his part in building those. He regarded the chinaberry trees and let his mind go back to the day he had dug the holes to transplant them.

A lot of his own life would go when the place fell to the bank.

When! Not *if*, but *when*. It struck him that he was taking it as a foregone conclusion. And by God it wasn't! There was still time, and there was still a chance.

"Biscuit," he declared, "before C.C. adds this place to his ranch he's goin' to know he's seen him a horse race!"

He reined the brown around and touched him none too gently with the spurs. He put him into a lope that ate up the ground in a hurry. Biscuit started to turn in at the gate where the feed was, but Hewey held firm to the rein and took him right up to the front of the house. He saw the two boys at the barn look at him in surprise and climb up onto the fence to watch.

He slid Biscuit to a stop and stepped down as if he were back in the San Angelo arena. He strode up to the step and pushed through the screen door. Eve, standing at the stove, turned to look at him, first in astonishment, then in rekindling anger.

"Eve," Hewey declared, "everything you said was right. The worst of it wasn't half bad enough. But this place ain't lost yet, and by God it ain't goin' to be. You can go ahead and cuss me all you want to, but I'm stayin'. I put Walter where he is, so now I'm here to take his place. We're goin' to make that crop. We're goin' to raise the money, and we're goin' to pay the bank!"

Her face was flushed with anger, and her eyes crackled. But this time it was Eve who couldn't bring up the words to say.

Hewey pointed to the rifle on the wall. "If you're goin' to shoot me, go ahead and do it now or forget about it."

The words came to her then, mostly a repetition of what she had been saying before, though this time her voice was on the verge of breaking.

From a bedroom came Walter's voice. "Eve . . ."

She heard, but she went on with the invectives. Walter's voice was stronger this time, and commanding. "Eve, goddammit, shut up!"

That shocked her into silence.

Hewey said, "I'll sleep out in the shed. If you don't want to feed me, that's all right; I'll cook for myself, out yonder. If you don't want to look at me, that's all right too. I'll stay out of your sight as much as I can. But I'm here, Eve. And right here I'll stay!"

Tears trailed one another down her cheeks. She looked at him awhile, gazed at the floor, then raised her chin and looked at him again. She squared her shoulders, cleared her throat and wiped her eyes on her long, faded sleeve. In a quiet, half-breaking voice she said, "You'd better go unsaddle your horse and then wash up. Tell the boys, too. Supper'll be ready directly."

He slept little that night. He rolled out his blankets in the shed and lay on the floor, his eyes wide open in the darkness. In his frustration and anger he lashed out at various people in his mind: at Snort Yarnell for starting the escapade that had led to trouble; at Fox and his three hired toughs for breaking Walter's leg; at Walter himself for mixing into a fight that was not his own. He made these rounds a dozen times, but each time at the end of it he had to come back to himself and accept, for a little while, the blame upon his own shoulders. He could have said *no* to Snort and ended the whole fiasco before it started. But he had joined into it with whole heart and empty head. No matter how he rationalized it—and he tried—the ultimate fault was his own.

So was the ultimate responsibility for salvaging whatever was possible out of a deplorable situation.

He might have dozed a little, or he might not. He was smoking cigarettes and staring at the ceiling of the shed when the first light came. His stomach hurt as if a cold lump of pure lead lay in the bottom of it. His eyes were as blurry as if he had been on a three-day drunk. He got up and rolled another cigarette, which seemed only to burn his tongue. He rolled his blankets and trudged toward the house when he saw smoke rising from the chimney. Eve was in the kitchen. They exchanged a quick glance apiece, but neither had any words. It was just as well, he thought. If she had any they wouldn't be pleasant to listen to. They would be a repetition of the ones he had used against himself all night.

He poured a cup of coffee and started out the door with it.

She said in a rough voice that told him she hadn't slept either, "I'll have breakfast ready directly."

"Ain't hungry. I need to go and look things over."

He saddled Biscuit and set out on a round, surveying his problem. He found it worse than he had anticipated. The frequent rains had been good for the growth of the feed Walter and the boys had planted, but it had also been healthy for the weeds that were always trying to take over. Normally, in this region where rainfall was usually light, a farmer could raise a crop of feed without the weeds getting bad enough to cultivate, provided he planted on good clean ground. Walter had no cultivator; those cost money, and he owned nothing he could do without.

He did own some good strong hoes, and he had a couple of boys who knew how to swing them, whether they enjoyed the work or not. It was going to be a mean job to get ahead of the weeds and stay ahead. It might take a mean man to push the boys and keep their noses to the grindstone. Hewey could have been a straw boss or even a foreman on several ranch jobs if he had been willing to take it upon himself to supervise other men and get the maximum work out of them. That kind of drive had never been part of his make-up. He had always preferred to stick to cowboy wages and keep his friends.

He grimaced, surveying the start the weeds had made. The boys were likely to be calling him something stronger than *Uncle Hewey* by the time this crop was made. The thought made his stomach hurt worse.

His relationship with Eve was not true peace, not by a long way. At best it was a cold and silent truce. But at least it *was* silent, except for her accusing eyes. For the next two or three days Hewey made it a point not to look into them more than he had to. He never went into the house except to eat, and he wasn't eating much.

Alvin Lawdermilk always had horses and mules that needed

breaking. Hewey set the boys to hoeing the feed, then rode over to Alvin's and made a deal on price to bring a string of animals to the place and break them here rather than at Alvin's. The facilities were not nearly so good, but the convenience of having them here counted for a lot.

In the first days he needed someone to help him catch and hackamore and tie and saddle them. He alternated between Cotton and Tommy until he decided Tommy was somewhat better at it. Cotton's inclinations ran to the mechanical. When he was through with Tommy each morning he sent him on out to join Cotton at the field. Twice a day Hewey put the broncs through their paces. At other times he went out to help the boys or he rode among Walter's cattle looking for cases of screwworms that needed treatment.

He had a raw mule snubbed to a post and was bringing up a wagon with a tame mule hitched to it when he saw a buggy coming at a brisk pace on the road from town. The boys' black dog always barked at Hewey every time he rode up, but he didn't bark at the buggy. He trotted out to meet it, tail wagging.

Hewey knew the occupants by the way the vehicle listed badly to one side from the poorly balanced weight. They were C. C. Tarpley, whippoorwill-poor, and Fat Gervin, packing fifty extra pounds of pure hog lard. C.C. was driving; he never trusted that to Fat. He almost hubbed Hewey's wagon as he came up alongside it and stopped.

C.C. stared at Hewey in surprise. Fat didn't look at him at all.

"Howdy, Hewey," the old rancher said, his voice pleasant enough. "Thought you'd be in Mexico by now, or Canada, or some other damn place."

Hewey shook his head. "None of them, C.C. This is home."

"Maybe you're takin' a step toward reformation after all. Or maybe it's just age. Always seemed to me like age has reformed more people than religion."

"Speakin' from personal experience, C.C.?"

"I ain't reformed. I've just turned some of my romantic responsibilities over to a younger generation." He glanced at his silent, simmering son-in-law. Hewey read between the lines that the old man knew things Fat had as soon he hadn't found out.

C.C.'s gaze shifted toward the house. "Mighty sorry to hear about Walter's hard luck. How's he comin' along?"

"He ain't chasin' any rabbits."

The old man frowned. "I come out to see about that. You know I—the bank, that is—has got a lien on this here property. I was countin' on the obligation bein' met this fall. Now I can see that it won't be. I thought I better—*we* better—be gettin' a man over here to see after our interests. There's a crop out yonder we can't let ruin, and there's cattle that need carin' for, and . . ."

"It ain't your interests yet, C.C. That obligation is goin' to be met."

The old man didn't seem to hear him. He went on talking about the things that needed doing.

Hewey said again, "We'll meet that obligation."

The rancher blinked. "We? You said *we?*"

"Me. Eve. Them two boys. *Us.*"

C.C. had to suppress a smile. "Now, Hewey, me and you have known each other longer than either one of us wants to talk about. You may think right this minute that you're goin' to stick, but I know better. One mornin' you'll see a rainbow and go ridin' off after it. You can't anymore stay here than you can flap your arms and fly."

Hewey squared his shoulders. "I'm stayin', C.C."

Fat Gervin had been staring at the black dog, skewering him with an evil gaze. The black dog looked back and cheerfully wagged its tail, assuming friendship where none was offered. Fat turned to Hewey and put in an unsought opinion. "You won't stay here three weeks."

Hewey glared at him. C.C. turned and cut his son-in-law short with a hard glance that made him shrivel, if a fat man can. When men were talking, boys didn't stick their bill in. C.C. said, "You won't stay here three weeks. You'll never see a bundle of cane cut or a yearlin' delivered."

"I'll be here."

C.C.'s smile turned hard. "If you're still here this fall, I'll kiss your ass."

Hewey said, "I'd rather have Fat do it, if it's all the same to you."

Fat showed a flash of anger, then his eyes turned little and gloating. Hewey shoved his hands into his pockets to keep from doubling his fists. Tarpley was a greedy old man with narrow ways, but at least he was open and basically honest about it, after his fashion. Something about Fat Gervin reminded Hewey of a coyote, sneaking around looking for a way in when a man wasn't watching.

The old man started to flip the reins, then thought of something. "Almost forgot, Hewey. Wc get the San Angelo *Standard* at the bank every week. Thought you'd get a kick out of the article about you and Snort." He pitched Hewey the newspaper. The buggy rolled. C.C. called back, "You won't stay three weeks."

The dog trotted after the buggy, wagging its tail as if imploring them to stay. *Dumb dog,* Hewey thought, *doesn't know who his friends are.*

Resentment glowed as he watched the buggy retreat. But resentment presently took a back seat to curiosity. He unfolded the newspaper, searching. He found the story on an inside page, circled by a pencil mark.

Disappointment touched him. It was the first time he had ever read his name in a newspaper. Seeing it misspelled shook his faith.

The festive spirit engendered by the big steer-roping contest here extended a bit further than many of its jovial participants expected, with the net result that one man took home a broken leg as his prize, and a local sport spent a night as a guest in the county hotel, later enriching the public coffers at the kindly suggestion of the judge.

The set-to was initiated when two lads of the limber loop took affront at the automobile-herding activities of one J. Fox, a member of this city's sporting community. Having done none too well in the afternoon's hemp-twirling contests, these daring cowboys headed and heeled the automobile belonging to said Fox. When that gentleman complained vigorously about their prowess with the lasso, one of these knights of the range proceeded to hog-tie him in the fashion normally restricted to the beeves.

This fun-loving cowboy was, according to public record, one Hugh Colloway of Upton City, that fledgling metropolis to our west. The other was the redoubtable Snort Yarnell, late of San Antonio and any other point you might choose to name.

This was by all accounts a crowd-pleasing affair, roundly cheered, and the two lads acquired many admiring new friends by their feat. However, it did not please the said Mr. Fox, who according to officials sought redress in the form of blood. He hired three husky and fearless fellows of our nocturnal society to exact the payment.

In the course of their attentions to Mr. Colloway they bestirred the wrath of his brother, whose name we were unable to discover, with the result that he attempted the rescue of his kinsman. In the ensuing unpleasantness his leg was broken.

The authorities were sent for and calm restored. The three hired revengers have remembered urgent business in other climes. Mr. Fox spent a restful night as a guest of Sheriff J. S. McConnell and paid his compliments next morning, along with fifty dollars and costs to the court on a charge of malicious mischief. He also is said to be considering a removal of his business ventures, whatever they may be, in the very near future.

The cowboys have retired back to the range to consider adding one more event to the next steer-roping contest here, namely car-roping.

Eve came out of the house and worked her way down to the front of the barn, where Hewey had resumed his activity with the wagon and the bronc mule. She stood back out of the way, for she knew the havoc a raw mule could create. When Hewey volunteered no information she asked, "What did C.C. want?"

Hewey didn't look her in the eye. "He came to take over."

"He's a little premature, isn't he?"

Hewey thought *premature* was something having to do with babies. Eve rephrased the question.

He said, "That's the view I taken of the matter. I told him this place still belongs to the Calloway family."

"The *Walter* Calloway family," she stressed firmly.

"And it'll stay that way. I gave you my word, Eve."

She turned and walked back toward the house, her shoulders drooped. Hewey watched her, his face furrowed. She had all but given up already. If her loss of hope became contagious, he was going to have a hard time pushing the boys enough to get the job done.

But he would do it. By God, he would do it!

He turned back to the mule, which was fighting as he attempted to bring it into the traces. Gentleness had always been his way with horses and mules. But he slapped the mule alongside the head with the flat of his hand. "Settle down, damn you! You'll work whether it pleases you or not!"

West Texas was never an easy, benevolent land. For whatever it yielded up, it exacted a price. The most common price was drouth, which put to severe test the endurance of those settlers who dared accept its challenge. In the uncommon years when rain was plentiful—as it had been this year of Aught Six—the tariff was imposed in other ways. There were the weeds which sprang up and thrived, robbing the crops upon which the homesteaders' toenail hold was based. And there were the insects, which seemed to explode by the millions after a rain. In particular there was the screwworm, which brought death of a slow and agonizing kind to animals wild and domestic.

The screwworm fly thrived in warm and humid weather. It was attracted to any scrape or cut that brought warm blood to the surface. This could be a man-made wound such as a castration cut or a peeling brand. It could be accidental, from running against a rough tree or a barbed-wire fence, or horn gouges incurred in fighting. It could be natural. In newly born calves the flies attacked the bleeding navel and set death's time clock to work in the very same place where the umbilical cord had given life. The flies laid their eggs, which soon expanded into a wriggling white mass of flesh-eating screw-shaped worms that gorged themselves and drew more flies and grew in numbers until death put an end to the animal's torment.

Every cowboy carried worm medicine, usually in an old cut-off boot top tied to his saddle. In this stained and odoriferous make-shift case would be two bottles or cans, one of chloroform for killing the worms in the wound, the other of cresylic ointment to smear on afterward as a healer and fly repellent. It was a bloody, smelly, unpleasant chore and a constant one, for every day that an animal went untreated made crippling or death a greater probability.

Each morning early, Hewey went through a self-imposed quota of work with bronc mules and horses. That done, he set out a-horseback to ride over the Calloways' eight sections—eight square miles—watching for screwworm cases. If he saw a cow lying down while the others were grazing, he took that as suspicious. If he saw one retreat into the occasional mottes of heavy brush, he rode in after her, for an afflicted animal usually seeks solitude and shade. He made it a point to ride up close for a thorough look at every small calf, for these were the most vulnerable, the quickest to die in bewilderment and pain. Much more often than he would have liked, he found screwworm cases that needed doctoring. It was one of the heaviest infestation years in his experience. Every time he found one, he knew the graveling feeling that he was probably overlooking another, somewhere nearby. Moreover, when he doctored a case today that was no assurance he was through with the animal. A raw wound could reinfect swiftly despite the cresylic ointment.

It was hot, sweaty, exhausting work, for usually he had the boys assigned to the fields, and he had to do this job alone, roping the infected animals and doctoring them where he found them. It gave him an opportunity to ride some of the Lawdermilk broncs that had advanced to the point of some cow-work schooling. On the other hand, roping was difficult on a bronc because it always took time for the animal to get over its fear of the lariat. Caught in any bind, it was likely to pitch, or at least to run away, perhaps dragging a caught calf at the end of the rope. It was a dangerous job, but Hewey knew it was necessary. He would need every dollar he could earn, from Alvin or from anyone else.

Often this search for worms gave him no chance to come in at noon and eat. He had missed many a meal in his time, and he did not mourn. But some days he seemed not to have the stamina he had always taken for granted. Times he came in from a screwworm hunt and faced another working-out of broncs in the late afternoon with little energy or enthusiasm.

The fields were a critical problem. Hewey rode a sorrel bronc by the field one morning and saw the boys working close together, evidently talking, moving somewhat slowly through the cane. Hewey swung down, tied the hackamore rein to a fence post and strode purposefully through the open gate. It seemed the weeds were growing faster than the boys could get around to them.

He walked up to Tommy and grabbed the hoe out of his hands. Curtly he said, "Damn weeds are goin' to grow right up your pants leg if you don't work faster than that!" He chopped fifteen or twenty with a flare of anger he couldn't rightly explain, and he did it rapidly. "There! That's the way you chop weeds. You don't love them to death, you whack them down. And you don't take all day about it!"

Tommy stared at him in surprise and dismay. A few feet away, Cotton was chopping, but his eyes were on Hewey. "Another thing," Hewey said, "you boys been talkin' instead of workin'. Cotton, you get yourself on down yonder, *way* down yonder. I want you where you can't even holler at each other, much less talk." He pointed, and Cotton quickly moved to comply. Hewey thrust the hoe at Tommy. "Take it now, and see if you can earn your keep instead of leanin' on the hoe."

He got on the bronc, using the spurs when it seemed a little reluctant to go north the way he wanted it to. He looked back once and saw the boys bent over, working in earnest.

That night was another of his sleepless ones. Lying on his back, he listened to the night birds out in the mesquites and up in the chinaberries. He heard a coyote, or maybe it was half a dozen, setting up music somewhere toward the field. He listened to horses nosing around in empty feed troughs they had cleaned up hours earlier.

Over and over in his mind he went back through the way he had jumped on the boys. He kept seeing their surprise, their hurt faces.

That's not me, he thought miserably. *That's not the way I am.*

But he knew that if a similar situation and similar stress were to come up again, he would probably act the same.

Eventually he dropped off into fitful sleep, only to be confronted by C. C. Tarpley and Fat Gervin. He opened his eyes and found himself in a cold sweat, the faces still clear in his mind. Fully awake, he began picturing Walter and Eve and the boys leaving this place, Walter lying in the back of a wagon, helpless, the family's few belongings piled on either side of him, Eve and the boys crying. Over to one side, in that buggy, would sit Fat and C.C., watching in smug satisfaction as the plum fell off of the tree and into their laps. Walter, if lucky, would wind up working for C.C. again on patched-britches pay, and Eve would again be cooking for Two Cs cowboys and getting no pay at all.

He hammered his fist on the floor. *It's not goin' to happen! I ain't goin' to let it happen!*

But the nightmare played itself over and over in his mind. He made the rest of the night on Bull Durham cigarettes. The nightmare was still playing when he pushed to his feet and walked to the shed door to stare out into the cool, damp dawn.

That morning he rode by the mill which bore his name and heard it squeaking when he was still a hundred yards away. He growled, remembering that he had told the boys to be sure they greased it. Eclipse mills needed a greasing at least once a week. Twice was better.

He found and doctored several cases of screwworms, reluctantly turning the cattle loose because there was nothing else he could do with them, knowing half would probably have to be doctored again. By the sun, and by the gnawing of his belly, he knew it was well into afternoon when he rode by the field to see what kind of job the boys were doing against the weeds. He did not find them there.

He looked up at the sun and took another guess as to the time. Knowing boys and their hunger, he doubted they had just now gone to eat. They should have had dinner an hour or two ago and been back out here hoeing down the weeds that kept springing up anew, threatening to outgrow the feed.

His shoulders ached from the work and the loss of sleep on that hard shed floor. He was hungry yet felt no particular pleasure at the thought of stopping to eat. There just weren't enough hours in a day, and those two boys were wasting the ones they had. Resentment smoldered in him. He knew it was a childish feeling, but it persisted in spite of his efforts to put it down.

Dammit, he thought, *I can't do it all by myself.*

Approaching the barn, he heard hammering and reined the bronc toward the sound. Under the shade of the lean-to he found Cotton hammering some lumber and pieces of steel together. Tommy stood behind him, looking on.

Hewey's anger slipped out of his grasp. "Boys, them weeds out yonder are gettin' ahead of you again. You better quit this shade and go back to work."

Cotton said, "The hoes are too slow, Uncle Hewey. We're fallin' behind. What we need is a go-devil or some other kind of a cultivator."

"There ain't money for such as that."

"I'm experimentin', Uncle Hewey. I think I can take some scrap and make us somethin' that'll do the job without costin' us a dollar."

Hewey's eyes narrowed. "When you say *experiment,* what you mean is that you don't know if it'll work or not."

Cotton looked at him, catching the implied criticism. "I think it might."

"And again, it might not. But I know what *will* work, and that's elbow grease and a good sharp hoe. If you feel like you've got to experiment, do it at night when you can't see to use that hoe. Right now, you two drag your butts back out to that field and get busy!"

Reluctantly Cotton laid down the tools and the lumber and the steel sweeps he had been handling. He didn't look Hewey in the eye but started toward his horse. Tommy quickly followed his brother's action.

The pet burro tagged along after Tommy. The boy turned and walked back into the shed. He came out in a minute with a bucket partly full of oats.

Hewey demanded, "What you doin' with that feed?"

"The burro is hungry."

"Those oats are worth money. That burro ain't been workin' for his keep, so he doesn't get any oats. Save those for the *workin'* stock. Turn him out in the grass; let him hunt for his feed."

He turned away, but he heard Tommy softly calling the burro, trying to get it to come to the gate. "Here, Hewey. Come on, Hewey."

Hewey stopped and looked back. "I didn't think that burro had a name."

"He's *always* had a name," Tommy replied resentfully. "But I didn't used to think it fitted him."

Eve, tired and harried, turned from the stove as Hewey entered the house. She wiped her hands on her apron, more out of nervousness than of need. "I put some dinner on the back of the stove for you, but I don't know what it'll taste like; it's been there too long."

"It don't matter. I ain't hungry anyway."

"Hungry or not, you've got to take nourishment, or I'll have you laid out in there with Walter."

"I'll just take a biscuit and a piece of meat. I got to be gettin' after them broncs."

Eve slipped the apron from around her waist and slapped it smartly across the corner of the table. "I said you'll eat, and by God you'll eat!"

Surprised, Hewey pulled out a chair and sat down at the table. "First time I can remember you ever bein' so concerned about my welfare."

"First time I ever had to be," she replied curtly.

After he had eaten he walked into the bedroom where Walter lay with his leg propped. "How you doin', little brother?"

"Terrible. I wisht I was up takin' care of things."

"Well, you ain't, and you won't be for a while. So you just lay back and let me take care of the work and the worry." Hewey started to leave. Walter called him back. "Hewey, the boys have been a little downcast lately. You sure you're not ridin' them too hard?"

"No harder than I have to."

"They're just boys. I wisht you'd go easy on them."

"Fat and C.C. won't go easy on them. They'll throw them off of this place the same way they'll throw you and Eve off. I'll go easy on them boys when we've finished our job."

Hewey rode broncs the rest of the afternoon. After supper he went back to ride one more before dark. He took it on a good circle, tiring it mercilessly to work out any inclination toward pitching. As he returned at dusk he heard hammering again at the shed. He unsaddled the bronc and staked him where he had been before. Then he walked to the lean-to.

Cotton was again working on his contraption. Tommy was again watching interestedly from just out of his brother's way.

Hewey could feel the boys' uneasiness. He studied Cotton's

design, trying to figure out how the boy intended it to work. "You really think that contraption will cut weeds?"

"I think it will."

Hewey watched a little longer, then walked into the shed and got a kerosene lantern he had been using. He lighted it, carried it outside and hung it from a nail up under the lean-to roof.

"Then you'd better have some light. You boys'll put your eyes out tryin' to work in the dark."

Spring always rode straight-backed and proud, with the ease of a woman who has spent much of her life on a sidesaddle. Her paint horse was gentle enough, but it was no lazy pet. She demanded a standard of performance from him and got it. Riding along, Hewey was looking at her rather than at the landscape. He had seen this part of the country a hundred times. The wide flats, the low hills didn't change. But Spring seemed fresher and younger and prettier every time he saw her. Perhaps, in part, it was the contrast between her and Eve which made it so. This summer was being extremely hard on Eve.

Spring pointed. Excitement crept into her voice. "Yonder it is, the Barcroft place."

Hewey pulled his gaze away from her and turned to face forward. Somehow, what he saw did not bring a rush of excitement to him. He saw a three-strand barbed-wire fence, reasonably tight, with a wire gate where the wagon road went through. He had always suspected these treacherous wire gates were designed to keep the womenfolks at home; a lot of women couldn't open one without tearing a dress or half breaking a jaw on the discarded wooden hames invariably used as a boomer to pull the wire tight.

Two or three hundred yards beyond the gate stood—or sat, or maybe crouched—the small box-and-strip house the settler named Barcroft had built to live up to the requirements of the Texas homestead law. He had not expected it to last forever, but it had had to last at least three years to satisfy the state. From here Hewey would casually guess that it might still have another three years left, if the wind didn't get too strong.

In front of the house stood two small and lonely looking chinaberry trees. "I always liked trees," Spring said, pleased.

"I'm partial to them myself," Hewey agreed. He wished he saw some.

He got down and opened the gate, pulling it back and letting it lie loosely on the ground because there were no cattle here to get out. If any got in, they were probably welcome to the grass.

Spring said, "To begin with, it has a good stout outside fence."

Hewey swung back onto Biscuit and looked behind him. He had never decided when he went through a fence if he had the feeling of going in or going out. Something about a fence seemed always to choke him a little, to cut off the flow of air like shutting a door into a room. "At least I won't have to build one," he said.

Riding to the house, Spring spotted the small bachelor garden and talked about how easy it would be to expand it to family size. She pointed farther west. "There's a nice little field over yonder. You could expand it a little every year until it was a good-sized farm. You'd hardly even miss the grass."

Hewey nodded, making a show of agreement. From here he could almost see across the whole claim. C. C. Tarpley had horse traps bigger than this.

Spring said, "Since he's moved out already, I don't think Mr. Barcroft would mind us going inside." That was her way of inviting him to help her down from the saddle. As he did, she touched her lips softly to his cheek, catching him by surprise. "There." She smiled. "I did it to you before you could do it to me."

"I'm keepin' track. I always like to square up my accounts sooner or later."

"Anytime you want to."

The wanting boiled up in him, and he knew a wicked impulse to rush her into the house and then see just how much she was willing to abide. But as they walked through the door together and he looked at the place, the wanting ebbed out of him. It was all in one room, and not much of it, kitchen, bedroom, the whole thing. The walls had been covered with old newspapers instead of wallpaper, mainly to keep the cold air from blowing through the siding and the blowing dust from filtering in quite so badly. A small stove was the only piece of furniture; it had been left only because one leg was broken off. Ashes lay black and cold on the floor.

"It would need some brightening up," Spring admitted. The

house had dampened her spirit a little too, but only for a few minutes. Soon they were back outside again, and she was stepping off rough plans for a yard fence, a flower bed.

Hewey stood slump-shouldered and tried not to let his feelings show in his face. He looked around in silence and thought of a time he had once spent in jail.

They rode back to Walter's place together because Hewey had promised Eve he would bring Spring home for Sunday supper. The women went into the house together, talking about the Barcroft place. Hewey walked to the barn, looking around at all the improvements Walter and Eve and the boys had wrought here. He tried in his mind to transplant them to the Barcroft place to see if it could be bettered.

Before long he was back at what he enjoyed most, looking over the broncs staked out to teach them respect for the rope. He picked a sorrel which had developed considerable tolerance for the saddle. Talking softly, he walked up to the doubting bronc, holding his hand out in front of him. The horse pulled to the end of the rope, then leaned back on its haunches. Relentlessly Hewey moved his hand up the rope to the hackamore, then up the side of the horse's head and back out onto his neck. He talked gently all the while. The pony trembled a little but gradually relaxed and let up on the tension of the rope.

The tenderness Hewey had never felt free to express to a woman, he had always felt free and easy in expressing to animals, especially horses. He spoke to the bronc as if it were a child, an advanced child. "Whoa, son, see there, I ain't fixin' to hurt you. Just wantin' to love on you a little. You're a pretty one. Goin' to make somebody a damn good cow horse, if I'm any judge. Like to have you myself, only I got all I can afford."

He rubbed on the pony's neck, gradually letting his hand move down to the shoulder. The skin would ripple a little, a showing of fear. Hewey would back off, but then he would return, and when the ripple didn't show he would go farther. It occurred to him finally that in a way he was substituting the horse for Spring Renfro. He didn't know whether to laugh at himself or be ashamed.

He had been so wrapped up in the pony that he had not noticed the approach of a horseman. The man swung down from a blue roan and peered at Hewey through the corral fence.

"Well, Hewey, I see you ain't lost your touch. I don't know which you're the best at, handlin' horses or ropin' automobiles."

Hewey saw the gold tooth shine in a grin that stretched as wide as a singletree. The heaviness lifted from his shoulders. He trotted eagerly toward the fence with his right hand shoved way out. "Snort Yarnell, I wouldn't of thought about you for a dollar and a half."

"I ain't offerin'. I ain't got a dollar and a half."

They shook hands through the fence. About that time Eve came out onto the front step and hollered, "Supper!"

She saw the blue roan horse, and she saw Snort. Even at the distance, Hewey could tell that she sagged a little. She said something, and Spring Renfro came out. The women stood together, watching the two men walk up from the barn, slapping each other on the back.

Snort removed his old greasy hat and bowed slightly to the women. "Howdy, Eve. You're always a sight to my sore old eyes." He shifted his attention to Spring Renfro. "Well, I'll swun. I'll just bet you're the pretty schoolteacher that's turned Hewey's head."

Spring was too embarrassed to know what to say. She stammered something to the effect that Hewey hadn't turned his head very much.

Eve asked, "You'll have supper with us, won't you, Snort?" Her eyes were saying she hoped he wouldn't.

Snort didn't seem to read eyes very well. "I'd be much obliged."

Eve would be hospitable if it killed everybody. A little stiffly she pointed to the washstand. "You-all can wash up over there." The words were directed at both men, but they were meant especially for Snort.

Snort visited a little with Walter in the bedroom, then came out to the table. He visited very little with anybody for a while then; he was too busy eating woman's cooking. For a man who had no interest in permanent alliances, he always made top hand at the table any time he was privileged to eat in a woman's house.

213

When Snort seemed to be tapering off on his third helping of everything on the table, Hewey said, "You headin' anyplace special?"

Snort nodded, going after the cobbler pie. "On my way out to the KC outfit in the Davis Mountains. Goin' to pick up some horses and take them back to Old Man Dotson on the Middle Concho. Thought if you didn't have anything to do you'd like to go with me."

Eve spilled half a cup of coffee.

Hewey rubbed his tired shoulders. He thought of unbroken broncs and wormy cattle and weedy fields. And of the Barcroft place. Travel seemed a grand idea.

He happened to look across the table at Spring and catch the sudden concern in her eyes.

Snort said, "I'll bet you never been out to that place, have you, Hewey?"

"Not right there, no."

"You ought to see it. It's all mountains and canyons and wide pretty valleys with clear blue creeks runnin' down through them. If the Lord was to ever get heaven overstocked and start lookin' for a place to branch out, He couldn't do no better than them Davis Mountains. They're a feast to the eyes and the soul. I wisht you'd come and go with me."

Hewey remembered the times he had seen the fear in Eve's eyes when he was telling Walter about some place he had been, urging him to get away from here awhile and go somewhere with him.

Spring's eyes had that look now.

He took a long, silent sip of the coffee and tried to keep his growing disappointment from showing. "No, Snort, I got more work here than I can see around. I reckon I'll have to let you go on without me."

X

Hewey had made a round looking for screwworms and, as usual, came by the fields to see how the boys were doing in their constant battle against the weeds. The black dog came running out to bark a challenge at him. Hewey spoke back to him in kind.

To his surprise he saw a mule working in the feed, Cotton following close behind him. Hewey rode up to the turnrow, hooked a leg over the saddle horn to show the bronc he wasn't afraid of him, and waited. To pass the time he lectured the dog on fidelity and true friendship. The dog gave him a haughty look which told him to mind his own business.

In a few minutes Cotton came out to the end of the row, following the mule-drawn contraption he had designed and built. Tommy trailed behind him with a hoe, giving the *coup de grâce* to any weeds Cotton had missed or left wounded.

Hewey's mouth hung open. "Boy, does that thing really work?"

Cotton made a cautious, tentative smile. "It's no go-devil, but it cuts weeds." The evidence lay behind him, in the row he had just finished.

Hewey marveled at his nephew's ingenuity. "It ain't much for pretty. Any honest-to-God farmer was to come by here, he'd die laughin'."

Cotton said defensively, "While he's laughin', we'll be cuttin' a good clean crop of feed."

Hewey looked across the field. The cane was soon going to be ready to harvest. He dismounted and stood there a little, studying Cotton until the boy self-consciously turned away. Hewey put a

215

heavy hand on his shoulder. "Cotton, I been hard on you boys. I ain't real bright, so the chances are that I'll do it again. But if I ever fuss at you about takin' time for an invention, I want you to hit me over the head with that contraption there."

Cotton's cautious smile came back. "I hope you'll remember that."

"I probably won't. But you remind me."

"Uncle Hewey, you reckon when we get this job done and the crop all in, you might talk to Mama about me?"

"You still thinkin' about that job in San Angelo?"

"I lay awake nights, thinkin' about it."

"Your mama doesn't take much stock in what I say. You'll need to ask her yourself."

"I have."

"What did she say?"

"You can guess what she said."

The dog looked up, lifting its ears, then went trotting out on the trail that led up from the house. Hewey saw a familiar buggy, this time with a lone occupant. "Damn!" he grunted.

Cotton looked. "Fat Gervin."

"In the flesh, and there's a hell of a lot of it. You boys get on back to your weedin'."

The black dog had reached the buggy and now came trotting back alongside it, tail wagging vigorously.

"Damn dumb dog," Hewey grumbled. He remounted the bronc, holding the rein up tight. He had no intention of putting on a free show of riding skill for Fat Gervin, a man who did not know how to appreciate true ability.

Fat reined the gray buggy horses to a stop and sat looking across the waving green feed. He pointed his round little chin toward Cotton. "What kind of a rig do you call that?"

"That," Hewey said evenly, "is a bank beater. That little contraption is one of the things that's goin' to beat you, Fat. We've got that feed crop as good as made, unless you can stir up a hailstorm or somethin' pretty soon."

Fat nodded. "You've got some yearlin's to sell, too, ain't you?"

"They're as good as sold already. Walter says him and Old Man Thomas made an agreement back in the spring."

"Did he get anything written down on paper?"

Hewey began to feel a touch of doubt. "You don't need anything on paper in this country. They shook hands."

"That's not enough anymore. Old Man Thomas can't help you. He can't even help himself. He's overdue on some notes he owes us. We've got him tied up to where he can't buy smokin' tobacco, much less some nester yearlin's."

Hewey swallowed, then caught hold, trying to keep Fat from seeing his misgivings. "Too bad about the old man. But we'll sell them to somebody else."

"Who?"

"I don't know. Somebody."

"There ain't anybody this side of Midland'll buy your cattle, and there ain't anybody there who'll come this far and buy them from you. You'll have to drive them all the way to town." Fat began to smile, but the smile carried a touch of frost. "That feed you're so puffed up about . . . who you goin' to sell it to?"

"No problem there. Walter's been sellin' it to ranchers around here for years."

"You talked to any of them lately?"

A chill touched Hewey somewhere down below his belt buckle. "No."

Fat said, "Then I wouldn't count my chickens till you see them pop out of the shell." He flipped the reins and brought the buggy team around in a long circle, then set them into a trot on the way back toward town. The black dog followed him a long way before giving up and limping back, its affections unrequited.

Worry gnawed at Hewey's belly all the way to the house. He drank a quick cup of coffee and left his dinner untouched on the back of the wood stove while Eve complained about cooking for nothing. He staked the bronc, saddled Biscuit and rode out in a hurry.

Late in the afternoon he came to a ranch house not far back up from the Pecos River. He found the rancher milking a Jersey cow to feed a growing flock of youngsters. Hewey waved, tied Biscuit to a fence and entered the cowpen, watching his feet. He shook hands, getting his right hand wet with milk.

"Howdy, Willis. I noticed comin' in that your feed stack's almost fed up."

The rancher nodded, glancing unnecessarily in that direction. "About time for the new crop to start comin' off."

"That's what I come to talk to you about. We'll be cuttin' Walter's pretty soon. You'll be needin' about the same as last year, won't you?"

The rancher shook his head and looked away. "Matter of fact, Hewey, I won't. I already got my feed bought. Contracted, anyway."

Somehow Hewey had known it all the way over here, but it hit him in the stomach anyway. "Mind if I ask who sold it to you?"

"It was Fat Gervin. He come by and contracted to furnish me all I need, and to do it at a little under the Midland market."

"Under the market? But him and old C.C., they don't raise any feed; they're always buyin'. How can he sell cheaper than the market?"

"I don't know, but he done it. Times like these, Hewey, a man takes his savin's where he can find them. There ain't no loose money floatin' around, you know."

"I'm *beginnin'* to know." Hewey reached up for Biscuit's mane and the saddle horn. "You know anybody else upriver who might want some feed?"

"I understand that Fat pretty well made the rounds. I think he's sold just about everybody."

Hewey gritted his teeth. "Nice to see you, Willis. You take care of them kids now."

"Doin' the best I can. Seems like I been takin' too good a care of my wife."

Hewey rode away with his shoulders drawn in. He would visit some more ranches tomorrow, but he already sensed what the outcome would be. A dark and ugly suspicion came to him. Fat Gervin was doing this to box him in. Worse, he was probably figuring on the Calloway feed to meet some of his contract obligations, after he took over the place.

I'll burn it first, Hewey thought bitterly. He spurred Biscuit a lot harder than he intended to.

He didn't get in until after dark. He nibbled a little at the cold

218

leftovers and filled up on black coffee. Eve asked what was eating at him, but he gave her no answer.

Next day, keeping his mission from Eve, he visited a couple more ranches. As he had expected, Fat Gervin had been there a few days ahead of him. Hewey knew of a certainty now: they had a crop of feed almost made, and there wasn't a soul in the Upton City country to sell it to.

On Sunday morning while Eve sought salvation in church, and in taking the boys with her allowed the weeds a day of grace, Hewey was out on his daily rounds seeking after screwworms to kill. In the afternoon he pursued romance in his own uncertain fashion. He tied some work into it, however. He rode to the Lawdermilk place on one of the broncs he was breaking for Alvin. This served the double purpose of training and transportation. It was an efficiency of which Eve could approve.

The Lawdermilk menagerie was out in force, blissfully unaware of the sacredness of the Sabbath. The peafowl momentarily put Hewey in some jeopardy of a hard fall from the skittish bronc. But Hewey was prepared for the sight, if the bronc wasn't, and he held the little sorrel down to a couple of short crowhops. He had no intention of ruining the last dress-up shirt he owned.

Julio watched from the shed door, waving. He seldom got to town. He had to appreciate whatever small amusements chanced to pass his way.

Alvin stepped out onto the porch to investigate the commotion, then walked down the steps to meet Hewey. Coming out the yard gate and shutting it behind him, a precaution to protect Cora's flowers from four-footed invasions, he looked the bronc over with a discerning eye before turning his attention to Hewey. "The bronc looks better than you do."

Hewey's good white shirt only accentuated the sun-browned face, the wind-chapped lips. "Maybe he ain't been workin' as hard."

Alvin grunted. "You ought to take better care of yourself." He reached out to try to touch the bronc on the shoulder. It pulled back, eyes wide enough to show the whites. "I expect you're about through with a bunch of broncs."

219

"I'll be bringin' them home in a few days to swap you for some more."

Alvin frowned and tried again to touch the bronc. He managed it this time, though the sorrel was not wholly in favor. "It'd be a lot easier on you if you'd come over here and ride them. Be easier on Walter's grass, too."

"I got to be there and watch after things. Got to hunt screwworms every day. Got to keep them boys a-workin'."

"You sound more like a daddy than an uncle. They probably liked you better when you vas just Uncle Hewey."

"They'll like me a lot less if they lose the roof from over their heads."

Alvin's frown sank deeper. He studied Hewey as carefully as he had studied the bronc. "It don't fit on you, Hewey. You're tryin' to make yourself into somebody you're not."

Hewey's voice was pained. "You got any better ideas?"

Alvin had no answer for that.

Hewey said, "I don't reckon you need to buy any feed, do you, Alvin?"

"No. Matter of fact, my crop's comin' along so good I'm liable to have a little more than I need." He brightened. "Would you believe Fat Gervin came by here a few days ago and offered to buy any extra that I find I've got?"

"I'd believe it," Hewey said darkly.

Spring Renfro appeared on the porch. Her eyes met Hewey's and came alive with joy. Hewey's tired back straightened. A smile flirted with his leathery face, but it didn't quite come alive.

Alvin looked from one to the other, his brow still twisted. "I believe I'll go down to the barn and see what Julio is up to. Come down later if you've a mind to, Hewey." He waited for a response but received none. He shrugged and walked toward the corrals.

Hewey stepped up onto the porch, glanced over his shoulder to be sure Alvin wasn't watching, then opened his arms for Spring. She came to him smiling, saying nothing, needing to say nothing. They held each other in a long, warm silence. She brought him a measure of comfort he had badly needed.

"I've missed you," she said finally. "A week can be a long time."

"There's been a lot of work to do."

She stepped back to arm's length and looked him over carefully, critically. "You don't feel well, Hewey."

"How can you tell the way I feel?"

"It shows in your eyes, your face. You're drawn, Hewey. You're not eating enough. I don't think you're sleeping."

"I'm all right. Just got a lot on my mind right now, is all."

She ran her fingers gently through his hair. She said, "The gray seems to be showing a little more. Taking responsibility is one thing. But you're letting responsibility take *you,* and that is something else."

"I've worked hard a lot in my life. It's never hurt me."

"It's not the work; it's what goes on up there." She gently tapped his forehead with her finger. "I'm not sure you know how to handle it."

Defensively he said, "I've never had a job of work yet that I couldn't handle."

Holding hands, they walked to the porch swing and sat down close together. The touch of her body against his was both bliss and pain, bliss in that it felt so good, pain in that he wanted to do so much more and couldn't, or wouldn't.

Hewey heard the squeak of the wheel chair making its way slowly across the parlor floor, and the bump as it was stopped by the screen door. From the doorway came Old Lady Faversham's voice, raw-edged and cold. "It's just that Hewey Calloway again, botherin' our Spring. If I was her I'd tie a dead cat to him and run him off."

Spring looked at Hewey, her eyes sparkling with laughter.

Cora's voice came from within the house. "Come here, Mother. I want you to hold this yarn for me."

"Somebody ought to be out there watchin' him. That kind'll take advantage of a woman every time."

"Mother . . ."

"It's an awful thing to be a woman. We yield up so much and receive so little in return."

Cora's voice turned strident. "Mother, you come here!"

The chair squeaked again as the old lady reluctantly retreated deeper into the house.

"If they ever hang me," Hewey said ruefully, "I hope they send that old lady an invitation. It'll be a high point of her life."

"She's just worried about my welfare."

"That's for me to do."

"I'm not your responsibility yet. Right now I'm afraid you have more worries than you know what to do with."

He stared morosely toward the low blue mountains, the flat-topped desert mountains of the Trans-Pecos. "I've never had it like this before," he admitted. "I've worked hard on a-plenty of jobs, but I always knew I could walk off and leave it any time I taken the notion. That made it easy. This time I can't ride off. It's like I was chained to a post."

"Most men are chained to some kind of post. Women too."

"I've just started kind of late. I'm like an old dog tryin' to learn a new trick and fallin' back on my tail. I growl an awful lot and learn damn little."

"Have faith in yourself, Hewey." She picked up his rough hand and pressed it against her lips. She looked at him so directly and without reservation that he felt his face warming. He tried to think of something to say, but nothing came. Romance had been sadly neglected on his part.

She said, "With all you've had to do, I don't suppose you've had a chance to see about making a deal on the Barcroft place?"

He stared at his hands, his eyes troubled. "Spring, I been wonderin' how to tell you. We'd better not figure on that place for a while. It'll take everything I've got—everything I can get—to keep C.C. and Fat from takin' that place."

"I can help. It's hard to save much out of a schoolteacher's salary, but I've managed. I have a little money set aside. We could put it down on the Barcroft claim, just to hold it."

He looked at her in surprise. "Use your money? If we get married it's *my* place to do the payin', not yours. A man don't take a woman's money."

"That's old-fashioned. In a lot of the world a bride brings a dowry into the marriage."

"We're livin' in *this* part of the world. And here it's up to me."

He went home a little earlier than usual from his Sunday courting, for a dark mood had settled over him, and he feared it might be contagious. To his surprise he saw Walter sitting up in front of the house, his leg stretched out straight in front of him in the cast, a pair of crutches resting against his hip. They were homemade, Cotton's doing. Hewey went on to the barn and unsaddled, then came back to stand and gaze upon his brother.

Walter's face was pale from the long confinement. He had never been one to carry any excess flesh, and he was even thinner than usual now. But Hewey saw pleasure in his brother's eyes at being able to get outside and see the world without a ceiling over it.

Hewey tried to pretend a cheerfulness he could not feel. "I got some broncs that need ridin', if you feel up to it."

Walter smiled thinly. "Ask me again tomorrow."

"You sure it's safe for you to be gettin' out?"

"I been goin' crazy lyin' in there where I can't see anything. I never knew how pretty an old barn could be, or even a milkhouse, or several broncs staked out on a flat." He turned his head in the direction of the fields, though he could not see them from here. "How's the feed lookin', Hewey?"

Hewey hesitated. "Fine. It'll be ready to cut pretty soon now."

"You'll need to be goin' around to the ranchers and tellin' them. We've got to start pullin' the money together."

Hewey couldn't tell him the truth. "I'll do it, Walter, first chance I get."

Eve called them to supper. Hewey helped Walter get the crutches under his arms and pull to his good foot. Walter moved awkwardly. It would be some time yet before he could do much for himself. Hewey hung back, brooding, until Eve called him a second time. He sat down at the table but found the food tasteless.

Eve watched him worriedly. "Hewey, are things all right between you and Spring?"

"Sure. Sure, everything's fine." He pushed to his feet and slid his chair back. "If you-all will pardon me, I think I'll go outside and have me a smoke."

He sat down in the chair Walter had vacated. Down by the grove he saw several freight wagons, the teamsters unhitching. One of them, he could tell, was Blue Hannigan. Somehow Hewey welcomed the company. He couldn't talk to anyone in the family about his problem. Maybe he could talk about it to Hannigan. Sharing it with somebody might make it easier.

Presently Hannigan and a couple of other men started walking toward the windmill, leading their horses and mules. Hewey moved out to the mill and stood with his shoulder against the tower. Blue greeted him and stopped to study him a minute.

He said, "You look like you been run over by a gut wagon."

Hewey found a touch of dark humor in that and almost smiled. "You could say that, in a way. I been run over by Fat Gervin."

Hannigan watered his teams; that came ahead of pleasant conversation or food or anything else when a man's livelihood depended upon his animals. He said, "Come on down to the camp, Hewey, if you've a mind to. We got a pot of coffee started. I expect you've already had your supper."

Hewey gladly walked down to the grove with the muscular, begrimed teamster. He helped him to take the rest of the harness off and tie the mules in their places alongside the wagons, then tie the morrals of feed over their heads.

That done, Hannigan fetched a pair of cups, poured coffee, then sat down for a few minutes of comfort on the heavy wagon tongue. "Now then, Hewey, what's that fat son of a bitch done to you?"

Hewey squatted on his heels and gritted his teeth. In a way he hated to tell. He felt somehow belittled that he could ever be in the position where another man could take such an advantage of him. But he told Hannigan the whole thing.

Morosely he said, "I don't know whichaway to turn, Blue. We can do somethin' or other with the yearlin's. Midland's a long ways to have to drive a little bunch of cattle, but we can do it. We can ship them to the Fort Worth stockyards if we have to. But that feed, that's what's got into my craw. If we can't sell the feed we just won't have the money to pay off that note. We can't go haulin' feed all over the country to try to sell it. The freight would eat it up."

Blue Hannigan scowled. When he did that, his face somehow reminded Hewey of a storm boiling up, about to let loose thunder and fire. Hannigan seemed to withdraw into himself a little while, thinking. At last he said, "It finally makes sense, Hewey. I hadn't been able to figure out what he was up to, but now I see."

"See what?"

"Fat hired him an agent in Midland to go out visitin' farmers and try to tie up all the feed they're raisin'. I didn't understand it because him and C.C. never bought that much feed before, not for their own use. Fat's doin' it just to nail you up in a box, Hewey."

"He's done it."

"Not yet. Maybe you can crawl out before the lid is hammered shut." Hannigan got some coffee grounds in his mouth and spat them violently. "He's a crafty devil, but you *could* out-craft him."

"I don't see how."

"That agent is buyin' from anybody who'll sell to him. He'll buy from me if I tell him I can line him up some feed. He don't have to know where I got it. You and the boys, you get that feed cut soon as it's ready. I'll get a bunch of the mule skinners together, and their wagons, and we'll haul that stuff to Midland for you."

"That's a long haul, Blue. Time we pay the freight . . ."

"There ain't goin' to be no freight. Half the time we're empty on the trip to Midland anyway. Most of our haulin' is *out* from there, not *in*."

"I wouldn't ask it of you. Neither would Walter."

"You ain't askin'. I'm tellin'. All of us boys, we like Walter, and we owe him. You think everybody in the country lets us water our teams without payin' for it? Hell no, they don't. And if Fat Gervin gets control of this place, you can damn well bet he'll charge for water and grass both."

Hewey could see some logic in that, enough to ease his conscience.

Blue added, "This country ain't got so many good people in it that it can afford to lose a family like the Calloways. You're damn right we'll do it for you, and be tickled to get the chance." His eyes narrowed. "But we got to keep it quiet. We got to slip up on their blind side or they'll fly the nest."

"There won't nobody know but me and you and whoever you tell."

For a long time now a stifling, heavy weight had been building on Hewey's shoulders. Part of it fell away. The evening had just turned dark, but he could see daylight. "Blue Hannigan, if you was a woman I'd kiss you."

"If I was a woman, be damned if I'd let you."

Hewey couldn't afford to tell the family yet for fear the plan might somehow leak out. Besides, none of them knew of the block Fat had thrown in their way; Hewey had kept that to himself. In the days ahead he worked at tying up all the loose ends. In the course of riding, looking for screwworm cases, he started picking up the yearlings that were due for sale and hazing them to the milk-cow pasture.

He began trying to put the finishing touches on the current set of Lawdermilk broncs. Tommy was getting to be a problem there. He was too eager and too reckless.

"Stay out from behind that horse," Hewey yelled at him. "He'll kick you plumb into next Saturday."

Tommy *had* been too close, but he didn't recognize it. "Why don't you let me ride this one, Uncle Hewey? He's not so tough."

"You're too young to be ridin' broncs like this."

"I'm older than you was when *you* started. You've told me many a time. Spinner James is ridin' broncs already, and he's a year younger than I am."

"One broken leg in this family is enough."

But Hewey could tell by Tommy's actions that he had all the makings of a good cowboy. There wouldn't be any holding him back much longer. The boys were growing up and getting away from him while he stood there and watched them.

The day came when Hewey knew the feed was ready to cut. He took his string of broncs to Alvin Lawdermilk and pronounced them broken. He gladly accepted the pay which Alvin counted out for him, including a few dollars in extra bonus which Alvin said he felt was due for the speed and thoroughness of the job.

"And now, Alvin," Hewey said, "could I ask you for the borry of your row binder?"

Alvin's own feed was probably about ready to cut, but he didn't have a big note falling due at the bank. "You can have it on one condition. I've got a couple of green-broke work horses that sure do need the practice. Take them and you can take the binder."

"I won't charge you a red cent for the trainin'."

Cutting and bundling the feed was hot, dry, dusty work. The chaff got into Hewey's shirt despite his buttoned collar and sleeves, and it itched like a rough-wool coat on a sunburn. It was a type of work he would normally have ridden a hundred miles on a lame horse to avoid. But he gloried in this because it marked the end of his captivity, the payment of his debt. An added pleasure, like a side bet, was that he would be able to kick Fat Gervin in the butt with his own boot.

Hewey sang as he worked, a manifestation to the boys that their uncle had been kicked in the head by a bronc without their knowledge.

The black dog, lying at the turnrow and watching for rabbits to flush ahead of the binder, raised his head and turned to stare at something. He got to his feet and went trotting off, wagging his tail. Hewey's curious gaze moved past the dog and picked up an approaching buggy. He broke off singing "Bringing in the Sheaves" and groaned, "God Almighty damn!"

The gray horses and the buggy belonged to C. C. Tarpley and Fat Gervin. Fat was driving. Easing the binder team on up to the turnrow, Hewey assumed the second man would be C.C. But as he stepped down from the binder and wiped the gritty sweat from his face onto his sleeve and then onto a handkerchief, he noticed a dun horse tied behind the buggy. Hewey blinked his chaff-burned eyes and stared at the second man. He combed his memory, and suddenly his breath went short.

The marshal from New Prosperity!

Fat Gervin reined up and looked a moment at Hewey. He turned to his passenger. "Marshal, is that your man?"

The marshal held a pistol in his hand. It was pointed at Hewey. "That, sir, is sure as hell him." To Hewey he said stiffly, "Hugh Holloway, I arrest you in the name of the law."

The breeze was light, but it worked through Hewey's sweaty shirt. He felt a chill. "The name is Calloway." He stared into the muzzle of the pistol. It looked as big as a cannon in a courthouse yard.

The marshal said curtly, "You raise those hands, Holloway."

"If I turn a-loose of these lines, this green team is apt to take fright and run over all of us."

Cotton and Tommy watched wide-eyed. Hewey motioned for Cotton to come up and take the reins.

Fat said, "I'd watch that man closely, Marshal. He is a slippery character."

Hewey frowned. "Fat Gervin, I hope when you get home that

your old mother comes runnin' up to you on all fours and bites you on the leg."

Tommy trembled. "Uncle Hewey, what's this about? What does that man want with you?"

Hewey looked at Cotton, but he spoke to Tommy. "Your brother can tell you."

The marshal smiled coldly. "I had just about given up on you, Holloway. I wrote letters to sheriffs all over the country, and not a one of them answered me. But your kind always floats to the surface like a dead fish. You want to know how I caught up with you?"

Staring at that pistol and feeling that chill, Hewey didn't much give a damn. But the marshal told him anyway. "Last week our paper picked up an old item that had been printed in San Angelo. The name wasn't quite the same, but a little bird lit on my shoulder and whispered in my ear. So I came to Upton City. The sheriff here wasn't no help. He swore he'd never heard of no Holloway. Left me feelin' kind of low. But I went to the bank to get me some travelin' funds and happened to mention my trouble to Mr. Gervin. Now, he's a good law-abidin' citizen, Mr. Gervin is. He knew right away who I was after. So here I am, Hugh Holloway, and justice is fixin' to be done."

Hewey and the boys all glared at Fat Gervin. Fat said, "I've always tried to do my civic duty."

Hewey argued, "I never really done anything to you, Marshal, at least nothin' to justify you takin' all this trouble."

"You ignored an order from an officer of the law, and you attacked that officer in the carryin'-out of his legal duties. Let one man get away with such as that and you open the doors for all kinds of dangerous elements to come in and take over the country."

"I ain't no dangerous element."

"Any man who disrespects the power of the law is a dangerous element."

Hewey turned his head and surveyed the field. It wouldn't take long to finish the cutting. "I got a job of work to finish here. If you'll let me do that, I'll go along with you real peaceable."

As he expected, the marshal vigorously shook his head. "I been lookin' for you ever since last spring. I've finally got you, and you're goin' back with me right now."

Hewey looked at first one of the boys, then the other. "It's up to you two, then, to finish here. You know what you've got to do."

Cotton protested, "I don't know if we can do it without you, Uncle Hewey."

"You can, and you've got to, for your mama and daddy."

Cotton's lips were tight. Tears came to Tommy's eyes.

Hewey couldn't look at the boys anymore. His eyes burned, and not just from the chaff. He turned back to the marshal. "I need to go down to the house first and speak to my folks."

"And have them help you escape? No sir, you're comin' with me. We're leavin' from right here."

"My horse is down at the house too."

"You can take one of those out of harness."

"These don't belong to me; they belong to Alvin Lawdermilk."

The marshal clearly didn't believe him. "They'll do."

"I'll still need my saddle."

"You can ride bareback. By the time this trip is over with, you'll be more impressed with the majesty of the law." He fished a set of handcuffs out of his pocket. "Will you please put these on him, Mr. Gervin? I'll keep him covered so he won't try anything."

Gervin said, "The pleasure will all be mine."

Hewey agreed, "It damn sure will."

He had had a few minor run-ins with the authorities in his time, but never had steel cuffs been snapped shut around his wrists before. Their embrace was cold. He felt that chill again.

He was sorry the boys had to be here to watch this. He felt humiliated, demeaned. But he brought himself to look back at them. "It's up to you boys to keep on. Finish the job just like I was here."

Cotton said, "We'll do our best." But his doubt was painfully clear. Hewey wanted to hug the boys, but he couldn't, not with these cuffs on. His throat went tight again, and he turned away from them. He chose the horse he thought might be the easiest to ride, and he started unhitching him from the binder. The handcuffs made it difficult.

Cotton moved to help him. The marshal swung the pistol toward the youngster. "Boy, you stand back from him."

Cold fear struck Hewey. "Marshal, don't you point that gun at the kid." He stepped back away from the horse, away from Cotton. "If you got to point it at somebody, point it at me."

The marshal seemed to realize what he had done. He let the muzzle dip a moment, then brought it back to bear on Hewey.

Cotton swallowed hard. His face had paled. He said finally, "If it's any comfort to you, Uncle Hewey, I know now that you and Wes Wheeler were right."

"It *is* a comfort."

When Hewey had mounted the plow horse bareback, and Fat Gervin was satisfied that everything was proceeding according to his pleasure, he bid his good-byes to the marshal and turned the buggy around. He set the team of grays into a good trot and departed whistling. The black dog followed after him a way, wagging its tail, hating to see him go.

Hewey watched him, wondering if Fat knew anything about Blue Hannigan's wagons. He was glad they hadn't been here yet, for if Fat had seen them he might have been able to figure things out for himself.

The dog came back in time to bark at Hewey as he rode off in a northeasterly direction with the marshal, leaving the boys standing desolately to watch.

They rode across country awhile, Hewey's head down as he darkly pondered the misfortunes he had brought upon himself and others. The marshal talked incessantly, mostly about other desperate criminals he had managed to bring to justice. Try as they might, they had never been able to escape the long arm and longer memory of the law at New Prosperity. Listening to him, Hewey wondered why the state hadn't disbanded the Texas Rangers and saved itself a lot of money. The marshal of New Prosperity could have handled the whole job by himself.

They came eventually to a barbed-wire fence. Nowhere up or down as far as they could see along the length of it was there a gate. Hewey said, "This is Alvin Lawdermilk's. If we follow along a ways we'll find a drop-gap tied with wires instead of fastened with steeples."

The marshal contemplated him in dark suspicion. "We'll cross right here."

"Alvin's kind of narrow-minded about people messin' with his fences. We'd better find where he's made a place to cross."

Suddenly the pistol was back in the marshal's hand. "I am the law, and I can do what I goddamn please!"

Hewey swallowed. He shuddered, fearing the man might get overwrought and accidentally squeeze the trigger. There were no witnesses. He could tell any story he wanted to. "I sure wisht you'd point that thing off to the side a little."

"You pull the steeples out of that post."

"I've got no pliers."

"You've got a pocketknife, haven't you? Use that."

Hewey poked around and broke a blade out of his good Barlow that he had bought one time in Miles City, Montana. But he managed to worry the steeples out. The wires were fairly tight, but the posts were far enough apart that he was able to put his weight on the barbed wires and push them down to ground level with his foot. He led the plow horse across, then looked up expectantly at the marshal.

The marshal's dun must have had some bad experience with wire at one time or other. It rolled its eyes and made worried noises in its nose as the marshal tried to make it approach the fence. He made two tries, both unsuccessful. Each time he circled the horse out a little way and came back, never taking his eyes or the pistol off of Hewey.

The third time the horse shied a little, then nervously picked one forefoot up high and stepped across the wires that Hewey held stretched. He picked up the other forefoot and brought it over, trembling. For a moment he stood that way, half on one side, half on the other, fearful about bringing his hind feet across. The marshal cursed and spurred him, and for a moment he let the pistol point upward.

On impulse Hewey let go of the wires. They sprang up, the top one catching the dun horse just a little past mid-paunch. The horse squealed in fright and went straight up. The surprised marshal let the pistol fly and grabbed at the saddle horn with both hands. He bawled louder than the horse. The second jump brought the dun clear of the fence, and also clear of the marshal.

There was only one small clump of prickly pear within fifty feet, and the marshal slammed down on his back squarely in the center of it. He lay there rigid, the breath knocked out of him, his startled eyes staring straight up into the sun.

Hewey saw a badger hole dug beside a fence post. He picked up the fallen pistol, dropped it in and caved off the edge of the hole with his boot. The marshal lay groaning and rolling his eyes, seeing little or nothing, struggling for breath, impaled on the mushy green but hostile round pads of the prickly pear.

The dun had stopped pitching and stood looking back, trembling in the aftermath of panic. The saddle was half turned, resting on the horse's right side. Hewey mounted the plow horse and rode to the dun, talking softly. "Whoa, son. Ain't nothin' goin' to hurt you now. Whoa there." He caught the trailing reins, got down and lifted the saddle back into its proper position, then led the horse to the marshal.

By now the man had partially recovered his breath. He lay staring at Hewey in terror, sure Hewey was going to murder him in cold blood.

Henry looked the dun horse over carefully for cuts. He found none of any account. To the stricken marshal he said, "You're awful lucky. This horse ain't hurt a bit, hardly."

Not daring to move, the marshal groaned. "I think my back is broken. I've got pain in a thousand places."

The prickly pear had cushioned his fall. Hewey knew the pain was not caused by broken bones. But a broken back was much more dignified than a butt full of thorns. If the marshal preferred the importance of a catastrophic injury, who was Hewey to deprive him?

"You *do* look like you're in a bad way," he agreed. "If I was you I wouldn't move a muscle. I'll ride over to Lawdermilk's and send help."

For the first time the marshal realized Hewey wouldn't kill him. "You wouldn't leave me here?" he protested hoarsely.

"You might die if I don't get somebody here who knows what to do. Don't you worry; there's some good ladies over at that house who'll take care of you. And don't you worry about *me*, either. I'm goin' to finish up that job I was workin' on, and then I'll come back and turn myself over to you. That's a promise."

Losing his prisoner seemed a mild concern to the marshal at the moment. He groaned piteously.

Hewey said, "Till Alvin comes with a wagon, you'd better lay real still. Try to be comfortable."

He fished in the marshal's pocket for the handcuff key. It took some doing to fit the key with his teeth, and he had to hook it into a steeple in a fence post to turn it. But in a few minutes he had freed himself from the cold embrace of the cuffs and hooked them over the horn of the marshal's saddle. He tied the dun horse, pushed the wire down, led the plow horse back over it, then set out in an easy, swinging lope toward Alvin Lawdermilk's.

When he finally got back to the field he saw that the boys had finished the cutting. Blue Hannigan's freight wagons were there, the men starting to load the bundle-feed. The boys came running. Both threw their arms around him.

Cotton demanded, "Uncle Hewey, how did you get away?"

"I didn't. The marshal just decided to take himself a rest before we start all the way back to New Prosperity."

XI

Hewey and the boys worked with the freighters until dusk, loading the itchy, dusty feed until they were exhausted, and until they knew it was time to get home and do up the chores before dark. The teamsters camped where they were so they could resume loading the rest of the feed at daylight. By the time the sun was up, Hewey and the boys gathered the sale yearlings he had been putting into the milk-cow pasture. They tried to push them through the wire gate nearest the field. The cattle warily eyed the opening and rushed past it, refusing to go through.

Tommy suggested, "Maybe they realize they're leavin' home."

"They don't realize nothin'," Hewey replied. "They're just actin' like cattle." He rode up to the gate and pulled it shut, then casually dropped it to leave only a narrow opening. He rode Biscuit back to where the boys waited, holding the cattle in check. "Let's ride off a little, boys, and give them air."

They retreated fifty yards and watched. Presently a couple of the more curious yearlings worked their way cautiously to the gate, sniffing at it, looking around in suspicion. One of them lifted its tail and half ran, half pitched through the opening. The second did the same, and the others followed suit.

Hewey said, "All it takes to be a good cowboy is to be a little smarter than the cow-brute. Let them think they're sneakin' out and you can put them anyplace."

By the time the yearlings reached the field, the teamsters were finished loading the wagons. The cattle hungrily scattered through the fresh stubble, enjoying a luxury to which they would never be able to become accustomed in this part of the country. Tommy looked toward Hewey with concern about the cattle scattering. Hewey said, "Let them fill up. It's a long ways to Midland."

The feed was stacked high on the wagons. Hewey entertained some fears that it might be top heavy enough to tip over in a little visitation of bad luck, but he had to trust Hannigan's judgment. The big man had probably followed mules far enough to make five or six trips around the world if all his traveling could have been put together in one straight line. Hewey rode up to Blue and shook his hand.

"Blue, I wisht I could tell you how I appreciate this."

"And I wisht you'd learn when to shut up." Blue looked across the newly cut field at the scattered yearlings. "You're goin' to *follow* us with them cattle, ain't you? It's bad enough lookin' a set of mules in the rear."

"Every man to his own brand of whisky. We'll follow you."

Hannigan climbed up onto his wooden seat and uncoiled a long blacksnake whip. He circled it once over his head, then popped it behind him and again in front of him. The mules leaned into the collars and started Hannigan's pair of wagons into a slow, protesting movement. He hadn't touched any of them with the whip, but they knew from past experience that he could. He could not only lift the hair from any mule of his choice but could pick the spot where the snake would strike.

Not all the mules took up their fair share of the load immediately. Blue had all the vocabulary considered vital to a Texas mule skinner, augmented by extra verbiage learned along the Mexican border. That language, and a little judicious application of the whip, soon had every mule toting fair. In a few minutes the wagons were lined out in tandem pairs, Blue Hannigan in the lead.

Hewey and his nephews slowly and patiently coaxed the yearlings out of the stubble and back onto the kind of pastureland they were used to. They followed in the wake of the wagons, Hewey riding point awhile to set the pace.

More than once he turned in the saddle to look behind him. He half expected to see that marshal trailing him. But in all probability the lawman was not going to feel like sitting in a saddle—or anything else—for three or four days.

He dropped back with the boys. "When you've got grandchildren, you can tell them you made one of the last great trail drives north. You don't have to tell them you was followin' a shirttail set of spotted yearlin's and a string of freight wagons loaded with bundle-feed."

Tommy squared himself in the saddle, pleased by the concept. Cotton didn't seem overly impressed.

They watered the cattle at the windmill which bore Hewey's name. He climbed most of the way to the top, surveying their back trail and looking across country toward Alvin Lawdermilk's. He saw no one.

Even if the officer *did* show up and carry Hewey away now, it wouldn't ruin things for Walter and Eve. Blue Hannigan would handle the sale of the feed, and he would take it upon himself to look over the boys' shoulders to be sure they weren't cheated in selling the yearlings. From here on, if Cotton and Tommy had to, they could handle the situation without Hewey. He had met his responsibilities.

The thought started him humming to himself. He climbed down the wooden ladder and dropped the last long step to the ground, resolving to waste no more of his energy worrying about the marshal and the New Prosperity jail. Those were problems for another day. He glanced up once more at the mill tower. "Damn," he muttered, "but I wisht that thing was painted."

The trip took three days . . . three days in which Hewey knew once more the joy of being on the move, of riding free, of good camaraderie, of being without a heavy burden of worry and guilt. His old humor came back to him. For three days he regaled Tommy with outrageous stories of places he had been, great jackpots he had gotten into and out of, stories of the wide-open country of blessed memory when there were no barbed-wire fences and improved roads, no poverty farms checkerboarding the broad seas of prairie grass like smallpox scars on the face of a beautiful woman.

Tommy listened with enthusiasm if not with total belief. Sometimes Hewey wished the boy had been born earlier so he could have seen all these things for himself rather than have to share them vicariously with an uncle whose selective memory helped him recall the smiling times and pass over the dark as if they had never been.

Cotton listened with easy tolerance but without Tommy's occasional open awe.

Slowly, as Hewey watched these two boys, it came to him how different they truly were. Cotton talked of the future as a time of automobiles and great machines and fantastic inventions waiting to burst forth upon the world. Hewey shuddered. He tried, but he could picture no place in such a world for him. The wonders that made the future look golden to Cotton made it bleak and terrifying to Hewey.

Tommy showed no anxiety about those mysterious times which lay ahead; yet, he still had a lively interest in the times already gone. Hewey suspected that Tommy would probably make his life right here in this country of his youth. If Walter and Eve could weather the rough years and save what they had acquired, Tommy would be the one to carry it forward, to build on it and keep the Calloway name alive on this land. He had the adaptability, Hewey thought, to accommodate to the changes the Cottons would bring upon him, but he would always have roots deeply implanted in the traditions of the past. He would be one of those men blessed with the ability to save what was good of his heritage without slipping hopelessly behind the pace of his own times. In his way, Tommy would never grow so old that he would not somehow need his Uncle Hewey, even when Hewey was no more than a distant memory.

But Cotton had already outgrown him. Cotton needed and wanted little from what had gone by. His gaze was fixed on the future. To him the past was a ladder already climbed, to be left behind without regret, without nostalgia.

Sadness came over Hewey along with this gradual realization. Cotton already had all he would ever need from Hewey—a searching mind, a lively interest in things unseen. This, and the Calloway name, was all they really shared anymore. Hewey had his memories of a closeness that once had been; he would have to settle for that. He would have to let go of Cotton as Cotton had already let go of him. He felt a strong need to pull up beside Cotton and hug him once before he was gone forever.

But he did not do it, for Cotton would not understand. It was too late to say good-bye, for the boy was already gone. In his place was a man—a man for whom time started—not ended—with the year Aught Six.

Hewey swung the little herd away from the wagons as they approached Midland from the south. No one needed to know—until the feed was sold and the money in hand—that any connection existed between Hewey Calloway and Blue Hannigan. Blue waved as he started his wagons up the grade that led across the Texas & Pacific Railroad tracks, and into the town that looked like a forest of wooden-towered windmills.

Hewey hunted around for a likely looking patch of good green grass on which no other cattle seemed to have any immediate claim. He found one a little way east up the tracks and back far enough that a passing train would not throw the yearlings into a panic. They had never seen anything bigger than a freight wagon or heard anything, man or machine, with a voice louder than Blue Hannigan's. Hewey told the boys to stay and loose-herd the cattle, letting them graze while he went into town and scouted the market.

Midland was a moderately bustling railroad and cow town, a supply center not only for the outlying ranches but for a dozen or more small and speculative towns which lay back off of the railroad and which had only a tenuous claim on existence. Many of their names had been penciled onto maps for easy erasure in case they lost that claim. Some already had; more still would. This was a time of quick land promotions, quick disappointments, of boom today and bust tomorrow.

Hewey spotted a black automobile parked among a dozen farm wagons and knew Cotton would enjoy his stay here. Damn contraptions, seemed like a man ran into one of them everywhere he turned anymore. Next thing, people would want to ride to the outhouse in an automobile to save walking from the back door.

He visited two saloons and invested in two shots of whisky while he plied the denizens about the cattle market. For about a dollar's expenditure on liquor of uncertain quality he learned what he could logically expect to get for the yearlings. He then visited two local butcher shops and set up a time for the butchers to ride out and bid him for what they needed—not both at the same time, of course. He knew they would want only the fleshier of the cattle, usually heifers. For the rest he visited a cattle trader whose occupation it was to ride around the country picking up small numbers of cattle from farmers and little ranch operators, putting them together until he had a boxcar load or two. Then he shipped them to the Fort Worth market and hoped he could sell the whole lot for more money than he had invested in them. Usually he managed to do so, or he would long since have gone back to working for wages. Hewey set it up for him to come out to the herd after the butchers had finished and gone.

Thus it was that before the day was done he had split the little herd three ways and had the money in hand for all of it. As the trader and a kid helper started drifting the yearlings toward holding pens on the tracks, Hewey made sure the roll of greenbacks was safely stowed in the bottom of his deepest pocket.

"Boys," he said expansively to his nephews, "I'll set you both up to an ice cream."

As he expected, the sight of the automobile meant more to Cotton than all the ice cream in town. Hewey watched him, reading the wanting in his nephew's face. It was all Cotton could do to keep from lifting the hood and getting in where the motor was. It would be futile to try to make a farmer or a cowboy of Cotton. He knew how, but his heart was not in it; it never would be.

Tommy saw all he needed in two minutes, and he was ready for the ice cream. "If he doesn't come on, Uncle Hewey, we ought to go without him."

Hewey shook his head. "Let him be. Your brother knows what's important to him."

When Cotton finally did come along, he told them more than Hewey really cared to know about the automobile, who had built it, how it operated and what service could be expected of it.

Cotton said wistfully, "It'd be fun if that feller had a breakdown right here in the street. I'll bet I could fix it."

Hewey smiled. "I'm glad you don't have ambitions to be a doctor. You'd be wantin' me to fall down sick so you could poke at me with a pocketknife."

He found an ice-cream parlor and left the nephews there for safekeeping. He mounted Biscuit and rode to the Springer wagon-yard, which Blue Hannigan customarily frequented when he put in at Midland. Blue was turning his mules loose in a pen which Springer had assigned to him or which, more likely, Blue had simply claimed by being there first. Blue's wagons were empty. So were the wagons of the other freighters. Hewey grinned. It was a relief to see the wagons shed of their loads.

Blue forked hay into wooden racks while a swamper spread oats into the long open troughs beneath. He finally laid down the fork and walked to where Hewey leaned patiently against the fence.

"Any trouble?" Hewey asked.

Hannigan laughed. "They asked me where the feed come from. I just said, 'South of town.' They didn't ask how far south, and I didn't say. They acted real glad to get it." He reached into his pocket and brought forth a leather wallet. Inside was a sheaf of bills greener than a barnful of alfalfa hay. "They offered to pay with a bank draft, but I told them they was dealin' with a man who couldn't read nothin' but the numbers on a greenback."

Hewey riffled the bills and tried to add them in his head. He feared the first time that he had made an error. A recount showed he had more money than he could rightfully have expected from the ranchers who normally bought from Walter. "Blue, you sure you didn't get some of your own money mixed up in this?"

Blue shook his head emphatically. "I been known to make a mistake or two with a mule, but I never make a mistake with my money."

Fat Gervin was paying more for feed here at Midland than he had contracted to sell it for to the ranchers down south. *Damn,* Hewey thought, *but he's God-awful anxious to freeze us out.*

The other teamsters finished their feeding and began to gather round. Hewey's spirits soared as he stuck the roll into his pocket to keep company with that which he had received for the cattle. He said to the teamsters, "I—me and Walter, that is—we owe you-all somethin' for makin' that haul. I'd sure like to pay you."

Blue made an exaggerated gesture of putting one hand behind his ear, as if deaf. "I don't hear a word you say, Hewey."

Hewey's throat seemed to swell shut. None of these men had any intention of taking money. They had done it for friendship, a commodity beyond price. He cleared his throat but couldn't speak. He tried again. "I reckon I've eaten too much dust. A drink of good whisky might be just the cure. I'd be tickled to set you fellers up to a round."

Blue Hannigan grinned. "Funny how my hearin' has all of a sudden come back to me."

With all that new wealth in his pockets Hewey felt able to give the boys a dollar apiece to spend any way they saw fit. He turned them loose to seek their own entertainment. He figured if two boys couldn't have a night's fun on a dollar per head, they weren't trying very hard. The only requirement he made was that they show up at the wagonyard by sunup, because that was when he planned to start south. Eve would probably raise hell when she found out, but she couldn't keep the boys under her thumb forever.

As it turned out, both were in their bedrolls asleep long before Hewey got through drinking a pint or two with Blue and the other freighters at the wagonyard.

The last thing Blue said before Hewey left him was, "I've got a load of freight to take north off of the railroad. You wouldn't guess in a month what it is."

Hewey didn't try.

Blue said, "It's gasoline, to power them horseless carriages. Seems like just about every little town has got at least one or two of them stinkin' things anymore." He laughed. "Funny, ain't it? People say them glorified spit-cans is goin' to replace the horse, but without the horse or mule to haul gasoline to them, they can't run a lick. The more of them things they get, the more horses and mules this country is goin' to need. You ought to take up freightin', Hewey, while you can still get in on the ground floor. There ain't nothin' goin' to take the place of a good stout freight wagon."

Hewey and Cotton and Tommy set out south before good daylight. A trip that had taken three days with the wagons and the cattle could be done in one day by men a-horseback, moving in a good steady trot. Biscuit was by instinct a pacesetter, not a follower. The boys' horses had no choice but to keep up.

Hewey intended to reach Upton City while the bank was open because he itched to get this money out of his pockets and the note paid. He pushed hard. He sent the boys home when he was close enough and took out across country to short-cut the wagon road's meanderings. By midafternoon he rode into the lower end of Upton City's dirt street.

He didn't think much of it when barber Orville Mulkey waved at him and then set out following him up the street. But in a minute he looked back and saw half a dozen or more men walking along beside the barber. Somebody saw him coming and shouted into the Dutchman's saloon. Hewey saw five men come out, one of them Schneider. They stood watching as he rode by, then fell in with the procession. Pierson Phelps left his store and joined the parade.

Hewey looked back uncertainly, suddenly nervous.

Ahead of him, at the courthouse, big Sheriff Wes Wheeler walked down the steps and strode casually out to meet him, nodding a silent greeting. Hewey reined up, glanced back, then looked at the sheriff. "Wes, if I'm in trouble . . ."

Wheeler was not much given to smiling. He said, "If you are, Hewey, looks like you'll have a flock of reliable witnesses."

These men were friends, or at least acquaintances. He saw no hostility anywhere and knew no reason there should be, unless that New Prosperity marshal had been spreading lies about him. Nervously he wiped a sleeve across his mouth, waiting for somebody to say something. Nobody did. He tugged the reins gently and set Biscuit into a walk, crossing the street to the front of the little stone bank. The front door, set crossways on a blunted corner, was still open. He was in time. Hewey looked once more at the crowd who had followed him afoot. There had to be sixteen or eighteen of them now, not counting Wes Wheeler. Wes was big enough for two men, all by himself. Hewey licked dry lips and said uncertainly, "Howdy, fellers." All he got was grins and silence. He swung out of the saddle, wrapped the reins around a hitching post and stepped up into the bank.

His gaze fastened immediately upon Fat Gervin, sitting at a rolltop desk behind the stockade-like fence through which the sheep and the goats were customarily separated before they ever reached him for an audience.

The look in Fat's florid face was of sullen dismay.

"I come to see you, Fat," Hewey announced.

Fat said nothing. He only stared.

Hewey said, "You got a note here against my brother Walter. I come to settle up with you."

Fat still said nothing. A young man who had been hired out of a Fort Worth mercantile company as a bank clerk pulled a file drawer from a heavy oak cabinet and rummaged through the papers. He withdrew one and laid it in front of Fat. "This is the one, Mr. Gervin."

Fat flared, resenting his mixing in, then stared down at the paper. Hewey pulled the rolls of greenbacks out of his pocket and laid them on Fat's desk, flaunting them a little. He picked them up one at a time and counted out the bills. He knew to the penny what Walter owed. He had lain awake nights adding it up in his mind. When he finished counting the feed and cattle money, and that which he had earned from Alvin Lawdermilk, he said, "I got authority to draw on Walter's account for what else is due. You tally it up and write the draft, Fat."

Face a deep red, Gervin dipped a pen into an inkwell and wrote out a check. He turned it slowly and shoved it roughly toward Hewey. Hewey took the pen from Fat's stubby fingers, made a long flourish and signed his name.

"Now, I'll thank you for a receipt. In handwritin'."

A delighted clamor arose among the crowd, and several clapped their hands. Fat Gervin seemed to shrink, to draw inward, shutting all of them out.

A thin, bent-shouldered old man pushed through the festive

243

onlookers with some anxiety and a little profanity. C. C. Tarpley demanded, "What's goin' on here? We had a bank robbery?"

Hewey blew on the receipt, trying to rush the drying of the ink. "Same thing, C.C., only just the opposite. I've headed off a robbery *by* a bank. I paid off Walter's note."

C.C. stared at him in momentary disbelief until a look at Fat's sullen face disabused him of doubt. C.C.'s disappointment was keen and painful, but he made a gallant effort at covering it up. Nobody could accuse C. C. Tarpley of being a sore loser; well, not a *very* sore loser.

"That's fine, Hewey. To tell the truth, I never thought you could do it."

"I know. In fact, I remember a little pledge you made." He shifted his gaze to Fat, who remembered it very well also. Hewey said, "I intended to hold you to it, Fat, but I'm a generous feller at heart. I'll let you off because I don't want to take my britches down in front of a crowd like this."

The bystanders laughed. Somehow they all seemed to know about C.C.'s pledge.

C.C. regarded his son-in-law without any fondness. In his face was a look that said he wouldn't care if Hewey demanded full payment. He said, "I know what Fat done to you about your yearlin's and your feed. I would have to figure you found a buyer anyway for the cattle. But what in the hell did you do with all that feed?"

"I found buyers for that too."

"Who?"

Hewey let his grin break wide open, warm and bright. "You and Fat."

The old man's face reddened as realization soaked in. "For how much?"

Hewey told him.

C. C. Tarpley's anger built slowly, like water coming to a boil in a chuck-wagon coffeepot. Finally it would hold no longer. Making angry noises deep in his throat, he ripped off his dusty old felt hat. He began to beat Fat about the head and shoulders with it, while Fat cringed and tried to cover his face with his arms.

Hewey lost interest in banking affairs. He sought out Schneider.

"Dutch, I'm goin' to set up one round of drinks for this bunch. After that, I'm savin' my money."

Hewey had ambivalent feelings about the Lawdermilk place. Spring Renfro had been much on his mind, and he itched to see her. But she wouldn't be the only person waiting for him there. He dreaded facing that marshal from New Prosperity, whose prickly-pear wounds, if not yet healed, should at least have reached a point of toleration.

Somebody must have seen him coming, for when he rode up to the ranch house, Spring, the Lawdermilks, Old Lady Faversham and Julio all stood on the porch waiting for him. The old lady was on her cane. Spring ran down the steps to meet him at the gate. She was no longer shy about showing her feelings in front of people. She threw her arms around him. Hewey hadn't realized a small-built woman could be so strong. She kissed him and didn't seem to care whether Old Lady Faversham watched or not.

"Did everything go all right, Hewey?"

"Like a brand-new Ingersoll watch. You ought to've seen Fat Gervin's face when I paid him off."

"I wish I could have been there. Have you told Eve and Walter?"

"No." The joy left him. "I'll have to let you go tell them for me. I came to give myself up to that marshal. You-all get all the stickers out of him?"

She smiled. "That was a private matter between him and Alvin and Julio. I think they left a few where they thought they would do the most good."

"They won't do *me* any good. Where's he at?"

Alvin came down from the porch. His voice held a promise of laughter. "He's halfway back to New Prosperity, I imagine. He decided they needed him at home more than he needed you."

Hewey turned, not quite believing. "What did you do to him?"

Alvin held up his hands. He was the personification of purity and innocence. "Not a thing. Never laid a hand on him except to pull pear thorns. But I had Wes Wheeler come out and explain a few things to him about law in *our* part of the country. Like when he made you pull the steeples out of my fence. That was willful

245

destruction of private property. Then there was the matter of my plow horse that he made you ride. Horse theft, pure and simple. I had Wes explain to him how narrow-minded we are about such as that.

"Then I just happened to mention to him that if he would drop his charges against you, I'd try my best to talk Wes into tearin' up the charges I had sworn out against *him*. He got to actin' kind of homesick, all of a sudden."

If Preacher Averill had been there, Hewey would gladly have made a contribution to the church. He squeezed Alvin's hand so hard that the old horseman flinched. "Alvin, I'll owe you as long as I live."

Alvin shook his head. Wistfully he studied Hewey's face. "You done proud for yourself." He looked at Spring, then back to Hewey. "I liked the old Hewey an awful lot, and I hate to lose him. But I reckon I'll get used to the new Hewey bye and bye. He's a pretty good old boy himself."

Julio saddled Spring's paint horse for her so she could ride to Walter's and Eve's with Hewey. Hewey turned and waved at the family as he rode away. Alvin and Old Lady Faversham looked sad. But Cora was smiling, and so was Julio, a romantic to the end.

Spring suggested, "I don't suppose you'd want to make a little circle by the Barcroft place on the way?"

Hewey hunched a little, finding no joy in the thought.

"Tomorrow, maybe. Right now I'm anxious to turn this receipt over to Walter and Eve."

She gave him a worried glance but said nothing.

The sun was going down as they approached the Calloway house. Hewey could feel how tired Biscuit was; the steps were labored and slow, for it had been a long, long day. It was seldom that he ever pushed a horse so hard.

As at the Lawdermilk place, they had evidently been seen. Everyone stood in front of the house, waiting for them. Walter leaned on his crutches, his face expectant. Eve was trying to smile confidently, but Hewey had disappointed her many times before; the anxiety showed in her eyes.

Hewey stepped down from a grateful horse which was almost

trembling from fatigue. He turned to help Spring to the ground. He stood with his left arm around her while he fished in his shirt pocket for the signed receipt. He brought it out, extended it toward Eve and grinned broadly.

Hands shaking, she unfolded it, glanced at it, handed it to Walter and threw her arms around Hewey's neck. She hugged him as tightly as Spring had done at the Lawdermilks', but for much different reason. She stood back, her eyes brimming with tears. Her voice broke when she tried to speak. She got it under control.

"Hewey Calloway, there've been times I've said hard things to you in anger, and most of them were justified. But right now I take back every word. Every word."

Then the four of them were standing with their arms around each other. The two boys stood off to the side, watching, smiling, Tommy turning sheepishly to wipe his sleeve across his eyes.

Walter's voice cracked. "Hewey, I wisht I knew how . . ."

Hewey said, "You got a lot to thank them boys for. Without them, it wouldn't of got done."

Walter nodded. "The boys know how I feel . . . how me and Eve both feel." He crumpled the receipt. "We still got a hard row ahead of us, but we've taken the roughest of it. We're goin' to make it from here on."

"Damn right you'll make it."

Eve wiped her eyes and turned toward the door. "Let's get into the house. We'll have supper directly."

Hewey started toward the horses, but Eve caught his arm. "The boys can turn the horses loose. You come on in this house."

Hewey poured coffee for Spring and himself. Spring put sugar in hers, but Hewey liked his coffee the way he liked his whisky, straight. He stood at the window, looking out toward the barn.

Eve couldn't get through thanking him. She put her arms around him again. "Hewey Calloway, you just don't know . . ." She leaned her forehead against his shoulder. "If there's ever anything me and Walter can do for you, anything you ever need . . ."

Hewey shook his head. "You don't owe me a thing. I owed *you*, and I done what I could to pay. I don't want a thing." His gaze fell upon Cotton, pulling the saddle off of Biscuit. He watched thoughtfully. "I take it back, Eve. There *is* somethin'."

"Anything we've got, it's yours."

He looked at her. "You may not like the price."

"We'll pay it."

He pointed his chin at the window and looked back at the boy by the barn. "Let Cotton go."

Eve drew a sharp breath. "Hewey, I couldn't do that."

"You'll have to, sooner or later. Do it now, while he knows what he wants and has a real chance to go and get it. Eve, it's been six years since we came into the new century. We still belong to the old one, me and you and Walter. We always will. But there's a different road in front of Cotton. One day he'll pick up and follow it whether you let him go or not. Let him go now, with no hard feelin's to pain him when he looks back."

Eve turned to Walter. She began to sob. Hewey couldn't look at her; he kept gazing out the window.

He heard Walter say, "Hewey's right. Cotton's come to his time."

Eve fished in her apron pocket but didn't find what she was looking for. Spring gave her a handkerchief. Eve used it, then wadded it in her hands. "It's a scary world out yonder that you're askin' me to send him off into. I don't understand half of what I hear or read about it."

"Us three, we never will. We was born too soon. But Cotton'll make himself a place in it. We don't have to understand it; all we have to know is that he'll be all right."

Eve didn't answer. She hadn't made up her mind to it yet, but she would. Tomorrow . . . the next day . . . one day soon, she would. She turned to the stove, to busy her hands and perhaps thereby busy her mind on something else.

From behind, Spring put her arms around Hewey and laid her head against his back. She said softly, "Thank you, Hewey, for Cotton."

Eve said the blessing at the supper table, and it was such a long one Hewey was afraid the food would get cold; she had a lot to thank the Lord for, and he couldn't think of a thing she overlooked. The last little while the realization had begun to come upon him with some force that he hadn't eaten anything all day. It was an experience not unknown to a drifting man, but one to be avoided whenever possible. He was into his second helping of red *frijole* beans and cornbread when he heard a commotion outside. It sounded like a bunch of horses, running.

He pushed his chair back and went to the window.

"I'll be damned!" he exclaimed.

"You probably will be," Eve scolded, "usin' language like that. What's the matter out there?"

Hewey pointed his chin, smiling. "Look who's comin'." He walked quickly out into the yard and hurried toward the corral.

From the west, like phantoms out of the dusk, came a remuda of horses in a hard trot, heading for a gate someone had loped ahead and opened for them. Snort Yarnell swung back into the saddle and pulled off to one side to give them room. The horses raised a gray cloud of dust as they rushed through the opening. Hewey climbed over the fence and grasped the wooden gate, pushing it shut as Snort rode his blue roan in behind the string of young horses.

"I'll swun, Snort," Hewey exclaimed, "you're like a bad penny. Where'd you come from this time?"

"From the KCs. Like I told you, I went out there to pick up a string of horses to take back over onto the Concho. I wonder if Walter would mind me keepin' them in the corral here tonight?" He knew very well that Walter would let him; few people would turn away a stranger, much less an old friend.

"Unsaddle and come up to the house," Hewey said. "We're in the middle of supper. There's a-plenty."

Snort's gold teeth gleamed. "I been countin' on that."

The rewards of the day had been so great that even Eve had a nice welcome for Snort. Spring stood back away from him a little, eying him with reserve, even a touch of fear. Tommy kept wanting to bring things from the stove for Snort, and when Snort had more spread in front of him than he was likely to be able to eat, Tommy said, "I'll go out and feed your horses, Snort."

"Not too much, boy," Snort cautioned, pointing a fork at him. "These is wild ranch horses, and they're like wild ranchmen, used to doin' for theirselves. We don't want to be spoilin' them none."

The kitchen fell silent except for the clinking of Snort's utensils on his plate, and the loud slurping noise he made over his coffee. He could put away a fearsome amount of food when he set himself to it. But finally he pushed his chair away from the table and rocked back on its two hind legs. He belched. He glanced from Hewey to Spring. "This good lady got the knot tied on you yet, Hewey?"

Spring looked at the floor. Hewey said, "Not yet."

"Well, when are you-all goin' to commit the deed?"

Hewey rubbed his hands together, suddenly self-conscious. "I don't know. We ain't really talked about that."

"You in any great rush, Hewey?"

"Rush?"

"I was thinkin' if you-all wasn't in any real big hurry, you might like to go off on a little trip with me. Last bachelor trip, you might say."

Hewey's interest began to pick up. "Trip? Where to?"

"To Mexico. *Old* Mexico. I got a job lined up down there with an American outfit, soon's I get these horses delivered. They said if I found any more good cowboys that wanted a job, just to bring them along. Got a winter's work, at least. Maybe on into next year too."

Hewey's pulse began to pound at the thought of it. Mexico.

Snort leaned over the table, his voice eager. "It ain't just on that penny-ante border, Hewey. It's way down yonder, way down deep. Beautiful country. Not spoiled like this country's gettin' to be, but big and wild and wide open. It's like Texas was before they commenced puttin' fences across it and cuttin' it up for farmin'. It's like goin' back to when we was young. I think me and you ought to see that just one more time, while there's a little of it left."

Hewey was still rubbing his hands together. He felt a hand gently touch his arm. He saw Spring staring at him, her eyes pinched with pain.

Eve cleared her throat. "Mr. Yarnell, I believe Tommy is havin' some trouble down at the pens. I believe some of your horses are tryin' to get out."

Snort jumped to his feet and hurried out the door.

Eve said severely, "Hewey, don't you listen to him. It's the devil that's brought him here."

Defensively Hewey said, "I wasn't listenin'. I mean, I *was* listenin', but I wasn't really studyin' on goin'."

Spring reached up and put her fingers under his chin, turning him to face her. He saw tears in her eyes. Quietly she said, "You *would* like to go, wouldn't you?"

"You oughtn't to pay any attention to Snort Yarnell," Hewey said. "It's always a beautiful country if he's never been there. He's fiddlefooted, just like I used to be."

"Used to be?" She tried hard to smile, but she couldn't bring it out. "Hewey, I can see it in your eyes. I saw it at the Barcroft place. I saw it when Snort was by here the last time, but I tried to tell myself I was wrong. I tried to tell myself you'd changed. You *haven't* changed. You never will."

He wanted to say something to convince her she was wrong, but no words presented themselves. Nothing came, because he knew she was right. "Spring . . ."

She touched her fingers against his lips to stop him from trying to speak, to argue. "There was never anything false about you, Hewey. I loved you for being just what you were. You were happy, and I felt happy just being around you. But lately I've watched you trying very hard to be something else, some*body* else. You've been miserable, and I've hurt for you. If I marry you, you can't stay the same as you've always been. You'll have to change, for me. And when you change, you won't be Hewey anymore.

"Some things we just can't have, because if we try to hold them they die. There's no way I can have you without changing you. So go ahead, Hewey, go with Snort. I know it's what you really want to do, deep in your heart. Go on then . . . go on to Mexico."

Hewey took her hand and gripped it tightly in both of his own. "I do love you, Spring. You know that."

Nodding, she whispered, "I know. But I know that you love freedom even more."

"Spring, are you sure you won't regret this?"

"Certainly I'll regret it. I'll regret it a thousand times. But I'll always know I was right."

Eve protested, "Spring, you don't know what you're sayin'. Let him go down there and you'll never see him again. We may none of us ever see him again. Like as not he'll wind up dead someplace under an outlawed horse."

Tears welled up in Spring's eyes and spilled down her cheeks. "Alvin knew all along. He said Hewey is a free spirit, like an eagle. I can't bring myself to put an eagle in a cage."

At daylight Snort Yarnell opened the gate and strung the horses out eastward, into the pink glow that came just ahead of the sun. He shouted and slapped his coiled rope against his leg and put them into a long mile-eating trot. He looked back once for Hewey, then went ahead.

Hewey stood halfway between the house and the barn, leather reins in his hand, Biscuit waiting saddled and patient behind him. The family stood lined up to see him away. Spring Renfro waited alone, a little to one side.

Hewey extended his hand, and Walter leaned forward on his crutches to take it. "Walter, you're goin' to make it. You and Tommy, you'll build yourselves a place here better'n anything old C.C. ever had."

"It's always part yours, Hewey."

Hewey shook his head. "A piece of land is for those who'll root down on it. You know *me*." He moved to Eve. She couldn't talk. She put her arms around him and said, that way, all there was to say.

He moved down to Cotton. "Boy, you really think them automobiles are goin' to put us old cowboys out of business?"

Cotton swallowed, his voice thin. "In time, Uncle Hewey. In time."

Hewey gripped his nephew's shoulder. "Well, you go out there and give them all you've got. But just remember—me and old Biscuit, we ain't goin' to lay down easy."

Tears had cut a trail down Tommy's face. He put his arms around Hewey's neck and hugged hard. "You'll be back, won't you, Uncle Hewey? You ain't goin' to let some old bronc kill you?"

"Button, I ain't never been killed in my life."

He turned finally to Spring. He saw her through a haze, because his eyes were burning. He tried to speak to her, but his throat had swollen suddenly. He put his arms around her and pulled her against him, and he felt the warm strength of her arms against his shoulders. She said nothing either.

From the distance he heard Snort Yarnell holler at him. Reluctantly he let Spring go and stepped back. She lowered her head, trying to hide her eyes. Gently he put his fingers under her chin and raised her head a little. He winked at her, though doing so squeezed out a tear that tickled as it ran down his cheek. He gave her a half-smile and got one from her in return.

He turned quickly. The gal leg spur tinkled as he shoved his boot into the stirrup and swung up into the snakeskin-covered saddle. Biscuit was rested and rearing to go. Hewey touched him very lightly with the spurs, and Biscuit set out in a trot to catch the horses.

Hewey turned once, reined up and waved his hat. Then he rode on.

The sun broke over the prairie in a sudden red blaze. The family all pulled together, arms around each other, Spring standing to one side, still alone. They watched as Hewey seemed to ride into the fire, sitting straight-shouldered and proud on Biscuit's back. And finally he was gone, melted into the relentless glow of a new day.